Coroner's Dance

A Novel

Greg Phelps MD

Coroner's Dance

ISBN: Softcover 978-1-955581-99-8

Parson's Porch Books is an imprint of Parson's Porch & Company (PP&C) in Cleveland, Tennessee. PP&C is an innovative organization which raises money by publishing books of noted authors, representing all genres. Its face and voice is David Russell Tullock (dtullock@parsonsporch.com).

Parson's Porch & Company *turns books into bread & milk* by sharing its profits with the poor.

www.parsonsporch.com

Coroner's Dance

Publisher's Note

This is a work of fiction and any resemblance to any persons or institutions living or dead is incidental and unintended. Craven County was the original 1600's appellation for the whole northern half of South Carolina. to its' western border.

Other works by this author

Education of a Hospice Doctor

(Memoir-Nonfiction)

Author's Website

Gregphelpsmd.com

Prologue

Christmas Season 1991

Richard Harris, hospital administrator, smiled when the sound of sirens woke him before dawn. Their sound wafted through the slightly open bedroom window along with a hint of air carrying pre-Christmas chill. Harris listened intently for a moment- an ambulance, he decided, business for the hospital. He smiled again and turned back to his still-warm pillow. A few minutes later, another siren and then yet another established a cacophony of impending disaster. Richard Harris's smile began to dim as the ululations continued.

Harris still had a ghost of a smile, more of a grimace, when the hospital called. In the days before Christmas, many hospitals resemble high-tech ghost towns. Expensive ghost towns, as patients put off caring for all but the most life-threatening illnesses. Nurses and techs gather to chat idly under festive garlands and cards and small Christmas trees at the nurses' stations beam twinkling lights that illuminate otherwise darkened halls.

Like an Armani-suited grinch, at this time of year, Harris would prowl the halls of Merry Hopes Hospital and grit a smile to the nurses, while his CPA trained mind tallied salaries and benefits going to waste.

Revyval Hospital Management purchased Merry Hopes from Craven County two years ago. Harris's corporate instructions were simple: make a profit in three years or seek new employment.

He was knotting his tie, briefly strangling a cheerfully whistled tune, when the phone rang. The nurse was in tears and virtually unintelligible. Something about the emergency room being full. It must be even better than he thought. He snapped out a short response and hung up. As he walked out of his bedroom, he checked his tie in the mirror; he was smiling again. Correcting himself, he frowned and tried to look professional. "You're a hospital administrator," he reminded himself, "great tragedy, whatever it is."

The engine in his BMW coughed once in the cold and then settled down to an expensive purr. Harris wheeled the car out of the drive and onto the town bypass. He saw lights flashing up ahead. As he watched, an ambulance turned into the high school and headed for the gym. Harris's brow furrowed while he mentally accessed the emergency disaster plan that included the high school gym as a makeshift morgue, he thought. He slowed the car and peered down the school's drive to see another ambulance backing up to the gym. Harris felt the first clutch of unease. This was not your usual holiday crack up. What was going on here? Dead people would not help him. He wanted wounded, wounded that healed and were grateful, preferably after a protracted stay.

The speedometer was close to eighty as he turned on the final stretch to the hospital. Blue lights flashing, the sheriff's car arrowed onto the horizon behind him. Harris slowed and began to rehearse his speeding speech. He watched the rearview mirror in astonishment as the blue lights and siren dopplered by him without pause and then faded in the distance ahead. The sense of unease worsened.

The tires on his Beamer screeched as he rounded the entrance to the hospital drive and pointed towards the emergency room in the back of the hospital. He reflexively ducked and braked as a shattering roar burst up over the hospital. Several seconds passed before his eyes could make sense of the flashing bulk as a helicopter rose above the hospital. As he peered through the frosty windshield, the helicopter spun on its axis and hurtled north towards Charlotte.

"Shit," Harris muttered. Whatever it was, clearly some of them were already dead, while the ER was already exporting others to big city hospitals. This was not the way to make a Christmas bonus. He gunned his shining black car back to life and rounded the corner of the hospital ER ramp. One lonely ambulance sat unattended, doors akimbo. Harris slammed the car to a stop nose to nose with the ambulance and stormed inside.

The ER was a mess. Fran, the night nurse, sat on a gurney amid a clutter of bloody sheets, discarded instruments and papers. She was resolutely filling in paperwork. Pauses were punctuated by an occasional sniffle. The scent of char permeated the air. She looked up as Harris crashed open the door.

"Fran!" he exclaimed. "My God! What the hell happened? Where is everybody?" The sight of Fran shocked him. Fran was the night ER nurse of twenty years. Nothing upset her…ever.

She looked at him dully. He noted that her nose was red as a tear dropped off from-its tip. "It was a fire," she said, "in a church." She shook her head. Tears and mucus dripped from her nose. Methodically she pulled a tissue from a box and blew while Harris waited, a toe tapping furiously. "All those people trapped inside, " she continued. "The rescue squad is still out looking for bodies. There were only a few survivors. Dr. Wilder was one of them, though," she said, brightening slightly.

"Dr. Wilder?" Harris snapped. "What's he got to do with this?

Fran shook her head again, another small dribble. She reached for another hankie. The tissue muffled her reply.

"What?!" Harris asked.

"I'm not sure," she repeated. "But I think Dr. Wilder started the fire."

Chapter 1

Officer Sudie Feaster broke open her fortune cookie as she exited the tiny Chinese restaurant. The small strip of paper was blank. "Crap," she muttered. "Can't even get a fortune printed right." Merryville's newest police officer shoved the slip of paper deep into her uniform pocket.

In truth, the fortune was right… Dead right.

Sudie stepped briskly across the small-town square. A red brick Victorian courthouse loomed over the tiny concrete block building that served as the Merryville police station. Red dust from the unpaved parking lot swirled over her freshly shined black patent leather shoes as the hot early summer sun beat down on her upturned face. The orange slanting sunlight of late afternoon indicated the beginning of the second shift. The light that shone across Sudie's long thin face reflected her hill country forebears. Curly red hair framed a face punctuated by a short pug nose and a spattering of freckles that decorated the sharp cheekbones that elevated emerald eyes.

Her nose wrinkled as she reflected again on her bargain with the city: a four-year contract in exchange for training at the state police academy. Sudie's plans went well past the narrow roads of Merryville. Still, she accepted this price as one more cost of eventual, but inevitable glory. She had only three years and six months to go.

A thin hand shaded her face as she peered in vain around the parking lot for her partner, Jake Starnes. Her hand jerked up to smack her forehead as she remembered that she was supposed to pick him up at Glover's service station. She hurried to a dusty, aging patrol car and hastily pulled into the meager Merryville traffic.

Merryville was a mill town like many in the South Carolina upstate. It was not a town to nestle in the hills, but rather sprawled across them like strewn litter.

The people were, for the most part, like the town, poor and run down. As Sudie bounced over the uneven tracks that bisected downtown, ancient men, bent in posture, wheezed slowly up the sidewalks past even older brick storefronts. Most waved a languid hand of recognition to Merryville's most recognizable officer.

Here and there a false front of vinyl or extruded metal siding with bright plastic accents reflected the aspirations of some enterprising merchant. The plastic did not help. Periodically the town fathers attempted cosmetic surgery by transplanting shrubs and trees to hide the more bedraggled eyesores. Sudie noted that this year's crop of shrubs was already dying from lack of water. On a particularly tall hill east of town loomed the Merryville water tank. The ovoid tank was emblazoned with a brightly colored carnival merry-go-round. The cheerful carousel logo was that of the town's major employer, Merry Mills. It stood in marked contrast to the otherwise dusty reds and browns of the town and surrounding hills.

The mills and their accompanying villages sat paradoxically, outside the Merryville city limits. For almost one hundred years, the Merry Mill Corporation had held the town to lines the corporation had drawn, forbidding growth or annexation. In earlier years, the town had tried on several occasions to annex the mill and its properties to increase the town's meager tax base.

Gerald Merry, patriarch and founder of the mills, retaliated by temporarily shuttering the mills demanding, "I made these mills that make this town. Why should I be charged twice?" Production ceased and the mills laid off hundreds of workers, whose income was already barely above starvation levels. The city quickly relented. The ruling had stuck for years.

Recently, as the mill worker population retired and settled into their company-owned housing, things had begun to change. As honorable retirees, the mill hands began to perceive themselves as due a few services from the company: streetlights, better paved streets, ambulance service. A few timid letters to the editor in the town's weekly paper were quickly seized on by the larger regional press.

Sensing an impending public relations disaster, the mill abruptly closed the two oldest plants. They permitted workers to buy their lifetime abodes in the mill village. The prices were far higher than the appraised values for such antiquated structures but still less than any other available housing, including the ubiquitous trailers that dotted the hillsides.

With a show of largess, Merry Mills announced it was dropping its long-term opposition to city incorporation of two of the oldest mill villages. The company executives watched with private pleasure as the city rushed to annex the corporation's problems.

The inexpensive housing however, had begun to attract other less desirable elements. The mill villages began to experience a rising wave of drug-related crime, burglary and rape. With state mandated tax deductions for the elderly, the minimal value of the mill housing, and a spectacular increase in the demand for services, the city of Merryville found its long-sought deal, a bad one.

The city of Merryville's loss was Sudie Feaster's gain as the city was forced to expand its tiny police force by two officers. After a decade's long standoff, ostensibly attributed to low turnover in its ranks, the city was finally forced diversify its officers, Sudie was one beneficiary; Jake Starnes was the other.

Jake Starnes waited in front of Glover's station. He cracked his knuckles as he stood under the massive live oak that shaded the small service station. The hands moved with a certain grace. They were massive, callused, and black. He knew he told Sudie to pick him up at the car repair shop where most of the towns' African Americans got their work done. A few minutes later, his squinting gaze was rewarded as Sudie zoomed into the lot spraying dust. She jumped from the car stammering apologies to a bemused Jake. From the single bay of the run- down garage, Pink Glover, the mechanic, shook his head in amusement.

The contrast between Merryville's two newest officers couldn't have been greater. Jake was enormous. A former army MP, Jake was six foot eight and retained most of his former South Carolina State football player build. The formidable aspects though were slightly spoiled by a large pot belly, grizzled side bums and trademark half smile that Jake always wore. Jake was a friend to all he met. His personality had helped him considerably as Merryville's first (and only) black police officer. Jake languidly waved Sudie back to the car, and they headed off to patrol the gathering dusk.

The mill company store was a product of an earlier generation. It was a general store built by the mill for the mill villagers. For a long time, the store had accepted only company scripts allowing the mill owners to recycle their employee's wages profitably. The store still carried a mixed variety of basic groceries, garden goods, hunting and fishing supplies. The store even stocked farm implements for some of the workers who farmed during the summer and turned to the mills for winter employ. One of the few modern adaptations in this monument to a by-gone age was the security system. As a window in back crashed open, a small silent red light beneath the aging cash register flickered.

The evening's catch had been light so far. Two speeders and one drunken fight had used up most of the shift. The emergency room doctor was inserting the final stitches and pronouncing the inebriated loser of the fight fit for jail when a call came in from the dispatcher. Jake was flirting with the night nurse, while Sudie sat with the patient, hoping the doctor would take notice of her. Jake leaned in, dashing her hopes of upward social mobility with a curt jerk of his head. "Possible break-in at the mill village store, Quit mooning at the doctor. We're on company time." Jake winked at the doctor as Sudie's face flushed the color of her hair. A handcuff between the now snoring patient and stretcher ensured the patient would wait.

Arriving at the mill store, Jake levered his bulk out of the car and into the summer night air. Sudie swung open her door, but Jake waved her back. "Don't worry. I'll holler if I need you, but it's probably a cat or some such. Not worth TWO whole police officers' time."

Sudie settled back in the worn police cruiser's seat. Jake had been fair about letting her in on the action, such as it was in a small town. She'd wait this time. She watched as Jake pulled out his heavy flashlight and scanned the front of the aged brick store building crowned with the ubiquitous company carousel logo. With a sigh, he lumbered around the side of the brick building towards the back. A longish pause stretched into minutes. Just about the time Sudie was beginning to worry, she heard Jake's voice, somewhat muffled by the interposed building but containing a tone of recognition mixed with relief in it.

"Well, hey there," he called. "What the heck are you doing out here?" There was a murmured answer, an indistinct noise that might have been a grunt and then silence. Sudie waited a few minutes, then called out to Jake.

There was no answer.

They must have gone inside, she thought. Sudie got out of the car and extinguished the moonlight that was shining on her reddish curls as she covered them with the patrolman's cap. She walked around to the back of the store.

At the end of the grassy alley by the store sat a single dumpster. Beyond the dumpster: a small space of dirt, edged with an overgrown chain link fence which enclosed the back of the store. A single lamp pole with a bright greenish mercury vapor security light towered over the store's lot.

The store's back door hung crookedly ajar. A pane of glass from a window in the door lay shattered on the ground. Glare from the security lamp competed with moonlight to cast garish reflections in the shards of glass scattered on the ground. Darkened humps of vegetation and garbage lined the fence. Beyond the leaning wooden door hung quiet darkness.

Jake was nowhere in sight. It was suddenly very lonely.

Sudie reached for her holster and unsnapped her gun. The officers on the force disdained the standard issue police revolvers. Most affected .357 Magnums as a show of manliness. Sudie had, of course, tried to outdo them all by being the first to get .44 Magnum- the gun from the movie Dirty Harry.

They had almost laughed her out of the squad room until she proved she could handle the massive gun. The pistol was now a comforting weight in her hand. For a moment, 403 lives hung in the balance. Then, a wave of foolishness came over her. Clearly whoever Jake had met was someone he knew. If she came charging in with this cannon drawn, she'd never live down the already growing use of the nickname "Super Trooper." As she snapped the holster shut, a movement flickered in her peripheral vision.

Sudie turned. Stepping towards her, out of the glare of the light, an enormous figure loomed over her. The only detail she could make out between the dazzle and shadows, she could make out was the reflection glinting from a wickedly long hunting knife with the price tag still dangling. She recalled from a crazily detached part of her mind- it's only 39.95 in most stores…guts the largest fish and game like slicing butter. Frantically she tried to recall the police academy manual, the section she thought should have been entitled

HOW TO HANDLE A PSYCHO WITH A KNIFE, but the words wouldn't come. In a few seconds, they never would.

Chapter 2

As he passed his fortieth year, Dr. Chris Wilder began to understand that the Nobel Prize would probably never be his. In medical school he'd dreamed the high dreams of youth and thought he might find a cure for some dread disease.

Later, when he moved to Merryville, he occasionally daydreamed of receiving a Nobel Prize for service to humanity in a poverty-stricken place like Albert Schweitzer.

The child of factory workers from the Midwest, Chris was the first in his immediate family to attend college. He'd done well in school. Fueled by ambition and scholarships, he'd pressed on through medical school. In choosing a specialty to practice, idealism won out over financial considerations. Fresh from the University of Chicago Medical School, he selected a residency in the new field of Family Medicine at the Medical University of South Carolina. This was one of the first family practice residencies in the nation.

When he had first arrived at Merryville, people frequently asked him, "What made you come HERE of all places?" The implication clearly being-Gee, you had a bright future, but now you've thrown it away. The reasons were several. First, while in residency he'd married a local South Carolina girl who had no desire "to move up there with all that cold and all those Yankees." He had also found, on a largely unconscious plane, that his social standing had risen enough to make him uncomfortable about returning to within the proximity of his Midwest working-class family.

Chris found it much more appealing to come to a small South Carolina town and care for people who could act as surrogates for his parents and family while simultaneously enjoying the enhanced social standing his education gave him. Furthermore, according to state health statistics he'd reviewed, Merryville had a genuine need for physicians. With the arrogance of youth, Chris thought the older physicians would be pleased to see how "modern medicine" was really practiced. His plans hadn't quite worked out. The other doctors appeared to be holding their own with what they had. Moreover, they were less than receptive to any new ideas from the younger upstart competition. Chris also found that the patients' greatest threats were those of the rest of the civilized world: tobacco, alcohol, fried foods, fast cars and stupidity. As yet another year brought the "BIG FIVE O" closer, Dr. Wilder* realized in a blinding double whammy that neither of his two children was enthralled with the art and science of medicine as they'd seen it practiced close at hand. His vision of a Nobel for succeeding generations passed from view.

A good mid-life crisis is hard to have in a small town as the usual alternatives are getting a sports car, a mistress or a mustache. Rutted country roads ruled out a sports car, and he had grown a mustache years ago to compensate for a thinning of the mane topside. In a town small enough to include the doctors' homes on a newcomer's tour, privacy for the traditional good-old-fashioned affair never existed. From long experience, Dr. Wilder knew the only people who thought a liaison was a secret were the people having it.

It was about this time that the Craven County Coroner chose to leave office involuntarily. That the coroner had been a mortician was normal. That he happened to have the bad fortune to be discovered by a grieving family while working in the nude on a female cadaver was not. The scandal led to endless titillating gossip and an opening for the coroner's position. Looking for a little variety in life, Dr. Wilder decided to branch out into politics.

Like much of the South, South Carolina's coroner system is a holdover from the Middle Ages. It provides for investigation into deaths that occur outside normal, expected medical routine, suspected suicides, homicides, or accidental deaths. The usual candidates for office holder in most cases was the local undertaker. Undertakers are the most common candidates since they fulfill two necessities: no serious aversion to dead people and an ability to deal with grieving families. The only practical job prerequisite for the job was an ability to gather the needed majority vote.

Although he'd had no specialty training in the field of forensic pathology, having a "medical" professional seemed a major step up to the voters of Craven County. Dr. Wilder had handily won the Republican primary against a tool-and-die salesman with a hankering for gore. In this rural conservative Southern County, there was no Democratic challenger. The job was his.

The day following the election, a most insistent woman called Dr. Wilder's doctor's office. Her name was "Iris, just Iris" and she demanded in tones only a bureaucrat could enunciate that she must speak with "Coroner Wilder" immediately.   As Dr. Wilder emerged from the exam room, Marie the receptionist held the phone away from herself as if it carried a rare and highly infectious germ.

"Dr. Wilder?" asked Iris in officious terms, "This is the coroner's office. Where are you? Why haven't you reported it yet?" Wilder's mental image formed by the no nonsense voice implied was a woman, sixty plus, overweight, smoker, steel wool in a bun, one maybe two pens anchoring the arrangement.

"Dr. Wilder!" Iris's smoke-stained rasp cut through the mental image. "Dr. Wilder, you are now a law enforcement professional. I demand that you come down here immediately."

"I'm sorry…Miss…ah…Ms…"

"It's Iris, doc, just Iris, nobody calls me Ms. Maynard. I'm the secretary for Mr. Fraser, the county executive. There are only two secretaries for the county offices. The sheriff's secretary and I drew straws for the new coroner, and I got you." Iris's tone of voice strongly implied that she had clearly lost the draw.

Wilder's thoughts were interrupted by Marie's frantic gestures to the growing crowd in the waiting room, and as she waved, a tired looking mother entered the office followed by four small children all coughing and furtively wiping their noses on stained sleeves. Methodically, the mother began signing in children filling line after line.

Iris was still droning on in the receiver. "So, you'll need to come down immediately, Dr. Wilder. Oh, by the way, we'll have your badge ready by Friday and the sheriff will issue you your permit and side arm." Dr. Wilder was beginning to steam but the last words caught his attention. "Sidearm, Ms. Maynard? I am a doctor; I do not plan to need to shoot anyone. And I do not have time to come down immediately. I have an office full of sick patients, some of whom are waiting for me right now." Egged on by Marie's agitated gestures, his voice had acquired a particular edge.

Iris sounded only marginally contrite. "Alright doctor, I'll let you go for today, but you really do need to come by real soon." Her voice dropped a full octave into a Germanic snarl that would make Arnold Schwarzenegger proud, "I'll be back," she warned. Without further ado, she hung up. It took Wilder a few moments to realize the woman had a sense of humor.

Despite the inauspicious beginning, Iris became a part of Chris Wilder's life. Alternating from demanding to solicitous, it was Iris herself that eventually renamed herself the 'grandmother from hell,' to eventually just 'granny'

Dr. Wilder's first year in the coroner's office had held little excitement. Most deaths were either accidental or a natural result of old age. Often the neighbors would notice that the 'Old Widder Smith' ain't been seen watering her front porch plants the last couple days. Then, the sheriff, or occasionally the rescue squad, would go to check on her, would force their way in after long and loud knocking and find the 'Old Widder dead in the bed or the kitchen, Frequently, when prompted by the light touch of death, people would roam into the kitchen for one last snack, When officials arrived, there they'd be, sprawled out in the light of the open refrigerator door, dead. Sometimes some enterprising soul would circle the house peering in windows and call Chris Wilder directly. These calls always bothered him not so much from the inconvenient interruptions, but more that the caller had the cold bloodiness of assuming that the hapless person was that far beyond the need of any other assistance. However, he was forced to concede and go onsite; as far as he could remember, he'd never actually found a 'live one' after any of these calls.

There was of course, an occasional murder, but almost always the killer and victim had known each other, sometimes intimately as husband and wife and other times drinking buddies. Often as not, the police would find out about the murder when the perpetrator showed up on the station doorstep, filled with remorse about sticking a knife in his drinking buddy. On the rare occasion that called for a true forensic autopsy, Dr. Wilder followed the old coroner's protocol. He bundled the body in a leak-proof, smell-proof body bag and sent it to the hospital pathologist. If he anticipated a need for some serious medical sleuthing, he sent the body to the medical school in Charleston.

In the small town of Merryville, everyone knew Iris and what her calls meant. So eventually the unofficial code at Dr. Wilder's office. and home was, "Granny called." This particular night it wasn't Granny.

Chapter 3

Like most doctors, Dr. Wilder had mastered the fine art of waking and answering the phone on the first ring, so as not to wake the spouse or kids. His kids were now in various stages of boarding school, but the habit remained. Most of the time he or his wife Ashley could even be sufficiently roused to make sense of what the caller was saying from the beginning of the conversation. In the early pre-dawn hours of this early summer Saturday, this was not the case.

Harold Givens, the Merryville police chief, had started out with ambitions much like Sudie Feaster's, but somewhere along the way, the flame of his ambition began to flicker. After losing a particularly rancorous Democratic primary fight to the current incumbent sheriff, one Junior Charles, Harold Givens settled back and began to mark time on the Merryville police force. Eventually, he outlasted and outlived every other officer to take the title of chief. Not that any of the officers had ever died in the line of duty. That is, unless one counted Warren Rushing who had a heart attack chasing a teenage shoplifter. No, most officers simply moved on as they aged and found easier work as a security guard at the mill or a local bank.

*Chief Harold was principally a day person. The night dispatcher took close to twenty rings to wake him, and a few minutes thereafter to get him to understand that car 43 could not be raised on the radio. Actually, there were only four cars in the entire Merryville police department, but everyone thought it sounded bigger, and therefore better, to have the cars numbered 41 through 44.

 Probably out cooping, thought Chief Harold. Sleeping through a boring night shift was a time-honored tradition for small town cops. At this hour, as he pried himself out of bed, his only concession to rank and uniform regulations was the large brass badge with "Chief" on the base dangling heavily from the pocket of his pullover shirt. The emblem on the badge matched the door of an aging Crown Victoria, hunkered in his darkened drive.

Once in his car smelling of a thousand cigarette butts, Harold Givens settled comfortably into the worn upholstery. Reaching for the microphone, he called the dispatcher and asked for the last known position of car 43.

Car 43 remained where Sudie left it- in front of the company store with the engine still running. The mill village of faded, sagging clapboard houses stretched out beyond the store. Aged, rusting cars and pick-up trucks jostled with each other for space on the dark and narrow streets. From behind the company store, the very top of the security lamp could be seen casting dense shadows forward.

Chief Harold reached inside the idling car and killed the motor then pulled the keys from the ignition and. slid them in his pocket. Sudden silence. The chief paused for a moment letting his ears adjust. The only sounds: the ticking of the aging engine as it cooled and the distant whine of the mill's late shift.

Chief Harold flicked on the car's search lamp and slowly scanned the front and side of the aged brick building for any sign of the officers or their passage. He squinted carefully in the glare of the security lamp, trying to discern form from shadows. Finally, he slipped out his flashlight and began to follow its bright beam along the ground to the back of the building. Chief Harold paused to unsnap his regulation 38. point, the ominous silence shouted danger The fragments of glass no longer glistened. but instead, were splattered with brownish ooze. He knelt stiffly to get a closer look. The brown was joined by another, redder drop. While he stared stupefied at this drop of blood, then another fell next to it from somewhere up above and then another fell to create a grisly connect-the-dot game. He glanced up.

Chief Harold was not usually the sort of man to curse. In this case he could not anyway. The curse he had in mind ran into the sudden knot that formed in his throat. Momentary frozen terror gave way to the need for flight, and he leapt to his feet. The adrenaline-fueled leap carried him almost high enough to look straight into Sudie Feaster's bloated and staring face. As his heart slammed to a stop, all tone dropped from his body. Chief Harold collapsed bonelessly to the ground. His last sight was that of the bodies of Jake Starnes and Sudie Feaster hanging by their feet suspended from the single, slightly bent aluminum light pole. Like an oversized pendulum, they traced slow and lazy arcs back and forth.

A few drops of blood were still occasionally dripping onto Chief Harold's body when the back-up team wandered by to see where the party was. Enough time had passed that it never occurred to anyone to call the rescue squad. It was clear everyone was dead. They called Dr. Wilder direct.

As usual Chris Wilder answered the phone on the first ring. "Doctor Wilder here," he mumbled quietly in the pre-dawn hushed darkness.

His wife Ashley, long used to nocturnal calls, snored softly another moment only to be yanked awake by the voice that shrieked through the receiver: "DOCTOR WILDER, DOCTOR WILDER, COME QUICK, THEY'RE DEAD, THEY'RE ALL DEAD, OH JESUS! "

Chris Wilder sat up in the bed with a jerk! "Who's dead? Who is this?"

From the other side of the bed, Ashley grumbled, then her covers parted sharply as she jerked her head up to stare wide eyed at Chris. "What the hell?"

Chris waved her to silence with a frantic hand. "Who is this?" he demanded again. "Who's dead and where?"

The voice on the other end belonged to Buzz Rushing, son of the late Warren. Chris had learned the hard way, early on in Merryville, never to speak ill of a person, because the listener was undoubtedly related. Buzz was calling from the pay phone in front of the company store. He had already called the sheriff's department, the state troopers' office and, if there had been a swat team in Merryville, he probably would have called them too. This scene had more blood than Buzz had seen in his entire tenure on the Merryville police force. His term was two years longer than that of Sudie, who along with Jake was still swinging from the lamp pole when Chris Wilder arrived.

Chapter 4

"You told us never to touch nothin' at a crime scene with bodies," said Buzz for about the hundredth time. "Oh Jesus," he moaned in visceral despair, "why did it have to be the chief?"

The professional performances of all three now deceased officers had been gray and undistinguished. Considering their spectacular demise, however, soon all three would assume reputations of mythic proportion.

In the meantime, a series of bloody footprints ran from chief to light pole and back repeatedly. These footprints, along with one set of prints detouring to the dumpster that smelled suspiciously of vomit, belied Buzz Warren's contention that he had avoided disturbing the crime scene.

Chris looked in vain for Sheriff Charles. Relations between the sheriff and him had always been formal and restrained. Even though they had never differed, Chris's status as a physician, an insider in the knowledge of life and death, seemed to distance the two. Sheriff Charles however, generated calm and organization currently absent in the men here. His presence was sorely missed.

Ignoring the gathering crowd, Chris silently studied the victims as they continued to swing from the pole. Someone in the distance urged them to 'cut the bodies down' but Dr. Wilder held up a delaying hand as he peered closely at the bodies measuring and cataloging the violence in his mind. Each bore a deep laceration across the breadth of the neck. Blood spattered on the still clothed bodies. From each end of the deep slashes, dangled small trickles of clotted blood like persistent mucous. Feeling his gorge rise and thinking Buzz's trip to the dumpster wasn't such a bad idea after all, Chris Wilder backed away from the dangling bodies.

By now the entire Merryville police force, along with a smattering of sheriff's deputies, bustled around at a safe distance. The deputies helped contain the growing cluster of mill villagers huddled in bathrobes beyond. Everyone's faces dimly lit by the farthest reaches of the halos of flashing multicolored lights cast by various emergency vehicles. Chris wondered again why the sheriff was absent. Obviously, there would not be much left of the crime scene if someone didn't act soon. Chris sighed and then approached the little group of men. He assumed the crime scene chaos was a combination of the shock of seeing several of their own killed, including the Chief who would ordinarily be directing the activity

As a physician, he was accustomed to entering scenes of chaos and bringing order to them. He quickly drew the men's attention to the matters at hand. "I think it is unlikely that the killer first hung the victims up and then slit their throats," he began without preamble, "but before we can get them down, we need police photos. Does anyone here do that?" One hand shot up.

"Good, get your camera and get all the angles you can. Next, get some barriers up and tape off this area." In no time, rolls of yellow plastic tape emblazoned over and over with "Police Line-Do Not Cross" encircled the gory scene. Two otherwise unoccupied officers began marking off the area to keep the curious mill town villagers away.

Once the photos were finished, Chris returned to survey the gruesome scene one last time. Something was wrong with the picture, but he couldn't think what. Some officers loaded the Chief's body onto a waiting gurney and trundled it away. Then, Chris called three of the officers to aid him, in letting the bodies down. Jake Starnes was first. The rope was tightly knotted and after a brief but unsuccessful effort to untie it, each deputy grabbed a section while Chris cut the rope. The deputies did the best they could, but there was simply not enough room for each to get a good grip and so, before the bodies could be lowered all the way down, the blood-slickened rope slipped through their hands. The bodies landed in a tangle with a sickening thud punctuated by profanity from the deputies. Forewarned and much lighter, Sudie's body came down without incident.

An ambulance carried the bodies back to the hospital for examination by the pathologist. Given the evident injuries, it was unlikely a forensic pathologist would be needed to establish a cause of death.

Shaken and still slightly queasy, Chris Wilder returned home in the dawning light to shower, shave and prepare for the day's patients. A thought kept niggling at the back of his mind. He had seen something… but its significance eluded him. Like most thoughts pursued, this one dove deeper, dodging inquiry, into the black waters of his subconsciousness.

Chapter 5

Merry Hopes Memorial Hospital had its beginnings as the private home of Major Merry's eccentric sister Cornelia. She had followed her brother from Charleston to the town of Briceburg, as it was known then, some years after his initial successes in reviving the town's mills. Purchasing a large home on a palatial lot across the street from her brother's, she settled quickly into community life and improvement. Many people, knowing Gerald Merry's mean streak, looked on in surprise as Cornelia began several enterprises aimed at helping those worse off than herself.

She soon viewed the coercive economy of her brother's mill village with dismay. Looking past the surface generosity of providing housing, stores and even childcare, she saw the subtle but powerful dictates of control that were set to ensure that, without the mill, the village people had nothing.

There was, however, one benefit her brother had omitted: a hospital. Cornelia, ever socially concerned to the embarrassment of Major Merry, suggested it would be a demonstrable measure of largess to fill this gap.

"Hell," Major Merry expostulated. "If they're sick, I don't want to give them someplace to go get coddled! If I did that, pretty damn soon the whole mill would be down there wanting time off. Let them go somewhere else if they want to be sick. Make 'em work for it!" Cornelia briefly pondered on this assault on her compassion. Then, surreptitiously, she went to visit several of the town doctors and finally her lawyer.

Gerald Merry awoke a month later to the sound of hammering. Pulling up his curtains, he looked across the street to see workmen erecting a large sign- **Merry Hopes Hospital**. Gerald Merry did not waste time dressing but stormed across the long lawns in his robe. He hammered furiously on Cornelia's door. Before he was done venting his spleen on the heavy wooden door, it opened. The composed face behind the open door was not Cornelia's or her servant's but that of Dr. James McAbee.

"What the hell are you doing here?" Gerald Merry demanded. "Is my sister sick?" Dr. McAbee pursed his lips and looked at the red-faced Gerald Merry. "She told me you'd react to this," he began. Picking up an envelope on the hall table he handed it to Gerald. "She's not here, but she told me to expect you. and make sure that you read this." Gerald Merry snatched the note from

Dr. McAbee. It was short and sweet. Cornelia had left her house to the community for use as a hospital. She herself had decided to return to Charleston. In a postscript, she added that she hoped he enjoyed watching his poor mill workers 'laying around' across the street from his house. She had planned well, and all Gerald Merry's threats, bribes, and other machinations to retrieve the house were denied. In his seventy years of life, it was his only defeat.

As time went on, the sick outnumbered the rooms in the hospital. To accommodate increasing needs, village houses were moved up against the original house. The contemporary Merry Hopes Hospital grew out of this aggregation. A layer of brown stucco across the facade glued the conglomeration together. Only a bell tower on the roof gave visible evidence of the original house. A new brick several story wing, donated in memory of Gerald Merry, stuck out of the brown stucco. like an obscene gesture. The new wing housed the laboratories and pathology. Chris Wilder hurried down the corridor of the new wing oblivious to the usual hospital smells of alcohol, formalin, room freshener and urine.

Imposing "NO ADMITTANCE" and "BIOLOGICAL HAZARD" signs grimly festooned the door to the hospital morgue. The door was locked. Chris knocked. The whine of a small buzzsaw died with a whine and a meaty sounding plop. There was a rattle at the lock, and the door swung open.

Dr. Mubashir Sayaad, the hospital pathologist, had always reminded Dr. Wilder of Mr. Spock from Star Trek although he hardly shared the actor's saturnine physiognomy. Dr Sayaad was short and pudgy faced with a halo of silver hair. He looked like everyone's idea of a grandfather until he opened his mouth. Then, in dry and erudite terms, he could calmly dissect and discuss the most gruesome tragedies without a particle of emotion. His reserve transcended all displays of feeling, except occasional dry humor…very dry. Everyone, including the medical staff, called Dr. Sayaad "Doctor. "Some of it was that most people had difficulty pronouncing Mubashir correctly, part of it was that his aura of aloofness did not invite the informality of a nickname. Doctor Sayaad suited him just fine. Dr. Sayaad spoke with a clipped English accent that belied his Middle Eastern origins. His grave tones carried all the dispassionate facts from the computer screen that glowed behind him in his private office adjoining the morgue.

"Ah, Christopher, good. I was just finishing." The room behind him was jammed with gurneys, their cargo discreetly covered with sheets. "Standing room only I am afraid. We usually don't usually have so much business all at once. The results of these three are a bit of a surprise." Gesturing to one over laden gurney, Dr. Sayaad continued. "The chief died of a simple myocardial infarction. Most of his arteries weren't really that bad, except one big lesion in the left main coronary…the widow maker." He shrugged, "Of course when that goes, there's not much left. No trauma whatsoever."

"The surprise is in the other two. They both died from a single stab to the heart with a very narrow blade. It was a well-placed thrust, coming under the lower edge of the ribs and then up and into the heart. It appears the obvious laceration to the jugulars and carotids occurred shortly thereafter, to what end, I am not sure. Perhaps the murderer thought the blood and gore from the neck injuries would hide the smaller wound to the chest. It was really a kosher job. Oh, and by the way, there is no evidence of sexual foul play with the woman. The only other finding of note was a skull fracture on Mr. Starnes."

"Skull fracture?" asked Chris.

"Post-mortem I surmise to judge from the lack of bleeding."

Chris paused in momentary recall of the thud the body made when the rope slipped. A wince flickered on his face.

"I think I know how that happened," he said.

"So, I heard," replied Dr. Sayaad, dry as ever. He gestured to three gory buckets filled with various organs. "Still, I have more sections and microscope work to do, but I don't expect any more surprises." Dismissing Dr. Wilder with a negligent wave, Dr. Sayaad marched into his office and sat at a pristine desk. As Dr. Wilder watched, Dr. Sayaad fished a small key out of a skull shaped vase nearby and accessed his computer's memory. His face puckered and as peered at the screen; he began to type furiously. "I'll send you a full report when I'm finished."

Nodding to Dr. Sayaad, Chris stepped out of the morgue and turned back to the hall. He paused in a nearby room to wash his hands carefully, although he had touched nothing in the morgue. Suppressing a shiver, he strode up the hall to finish patient rounds before heading to the office.

As he circled Merryville on the town bypass, Chris drove by a series of pastures. Several of them showed signs of construction. Since the building of the mills at the turn of the century, the town of Merryville had not grown an iota. This stagnation had suited Major Merry fine. No growth meant no competition for workers willing to accept low paying jobs. Long years ago, one industry had contacted the Craven County Chamber of Commerce about building a new factory. Gerald Merry would not stand for any competition. With a combination of covert threats and a large public donation to the chamber coffers, he had induced the chamber to lose the request for site information. After repeatedly having their phone calls met with polite deferrals, the industry decided to locate in greener pastures. It had been years since then. Only recently had another company braved the wrath of the Merryville Corporation. Now a few industries drawn by the lure of the railway and a new interstate, not to mention Gerald Merry's eventual passing, were finally coming to town.

In other farm pastures, cows swatted flies with their tails. The day promised to be one of the first real scorchers of spring. Cows thought Chris. Kosher food. He knew pigs weren't kosher but could not remember why. Was it something about cloven hooves? There was something else though, things could be made kosher… who could he ask? He should have asked Dr. Sayaad what he meant when he was in the morgue. Jews were in short supply in mill towns like Merryville and there were only a few Catholics or Episcopalians like himself. Merryville citizens tended to run more to Baptist and other more fundamental religions.

Chris pulled up to the stoplight. The thought *kosher* hovered like a mayfly above the dark waters of a persistent, but urgent thought trapped beneath the surface. Chris looked across the intersection at a dilapidated pickup truck facing him. Even in the early morning heat, water dripped from its ancient air conditioner forming a small greenish puddle in the dust of the road. The light changed and the truck wheezed off. Chris stared at the little pool of fluid already drying on the road. *Kosher.*

Finally, from out of the puddle clarity exploded onto the screen of his conscious thought. To make meat kosher, you bleed it. The human body contains about twelve pints of blood. There should have been twenty-four pints on the ground behind the mill store. He had seen far less. The ground at the murder scene should have been swimming with blood. Shouldn't it?

Behind Chris a horn honked impatiently, jarring him from cascading, dizzying thought. He started in surprise. The horn then blared louder as Chris executed an abrupt U-turn back to the hospital.

Blood volume has a way of being poorly estimated. Most patients, confronted by blood, especially their own, tend to overestimate the amount. Many obstetrical patients believe they are "hemorrhaging" when merely passing a bloody mucous plug when starting into labor. He had learned long ago that efforts to quantify blood in terms of tablespoons or cups resulted in answers ranging towards buckets. As a result of these inadequacies, he'd moved towards a ruder means of measure. "Is there so much blood that it runs down your legs and fills up your shoes?" he'd ask. Only the rare responses that answered yes, got him into high gear.

Unlike their patients and because they are used to blood, physicians tend to underestimate losses that soak into bandages, or in this case, possibly the ground. Chris left the car engine running at the hospital while he ran into the lab and asked if they had any expired blood. The lab tech looked quizzically at him but rooted around in the refrigerator and found what he asked for. He turned the car around and headed out to the mill store.

A sheriff's deputy still guarded the site festooned with yellow police ribbon. A regional station's camera crew filmed the site from a distance. One reporter ambled towards Dr. Wilder in hopes of seeing if he could offer any information. With a miniscule nod to Dr. Wilder, the deputy guarding the site seemingly randomly intercepted the reporter just long enough for Dr. Wilder to get safely out of his range behind the yellow tape. The store manager was engaged in an angry dispute with the state crime lab people who had forbid him from opening. Nodding covert thanks to the deputy, Dr. Wilder walked around to the murder site.

The brownish red stain behind the store was pretty dry. A few flies buzzed in the way as Dr. Wilder measured the size of the stain and counted the footprints that marked Buzz Rushing's panicked forays. The stain still didn't seem like enough blood, but how much would the ground absorb? Returning briefly to his car, Chris retrieved the bag of expired whole blood he'd appropriated from the hospital. He selected a spot similar to but apart from stain. As the deputy looked on in astonishment, Dr. Wilder slit the blood bag and carefully poured out its contents of blood onto the ground. He observed how the blood spread out and then settled into the ground. The single bag provided a stain almost as large as the two bodies had left.

"Whatcha doin' doc?" The store manager leaned over Chris as he squatted, studying the small pool of blood. A massive friendly hand planted itself on Chris's shoulder, tipping him off balance. Chris started in surprise and toppled forward. He caught himself within an instant, but his hand plunged into the still damp bloody dust beneath him.

There was a momentary pause. The manager froze as Chris pulled his hand out of the bloody mire and stared accusingly from his hand to the manager. With a visible effort to keep his temper, Chris asked for the nearest sink. The manager followed him into the store, floating a verbal cloud of apologies Dr. Wilder scrubbed at his hands with vigor. The blood, of course, had been tested for AIDS and hepatitis. A new OSHA law, Blood Borne Pathogens mandated a lot of testing and restrictions related to blood and bodily fluids. Still, he inspected his hands for any cuts or abrasions that might allow an escaped to infect him. He knew he should have been wearing gloves, but like many doctors, he tended to be casual about blood.

The manager continued to hover behind him. Dr. Wilder turned to him and asked, "Have you noticed anything missing?"

The manager began to light a cigarette. He stopped with a guilty glance at Dr. Wilder. "Odd things" he said as he reluctantly pocketed the smoke. "A few tools, knives mostly. Fishing, hunting, even a set we sell for hog slaughtering." He paused. "Oh yes, a rope and pulley, which we found out back." Here he cocked his head towards the back, indicating where and how these were found. "Only other thing was a five-gallon wash basin."

Chris paused for a moment as he converted pints to quarts to gallons. Five gallons would have held all their blood. He thought. But why?

The dust in the store would have been adequate by itself to preserve fingerprints if the crime scene investigators had wanted prints. Unfortunately, half the mill village would have been implicated on prints alone since many still shopped there. He looked at his watch. Oh God, he'd forgotten all about the office! Patients would be waiting. Of course, he thought to himself as he hurried to his car, that's why they call them "patients." Still, he drove off at a speed that caused the still waiting deputy to shout at him to slow down.

Satellite dishes looking like upside-down mushrooms adorned the tops of a bevy of media vans clustered on the lawn next to a sign that stated in discreet letters: C. Wilder M.D. P.A., Family Medicine. Chris muttered a low oath as he caught sight of the bevy of news vans. It had been rare in this rural area, but the part Chris liked least about the coroner's job was dealing with a bloodthirsty press.

The reporters were in a foul mood as they caught sight of his car pulling around the building. They had missed their chance for a nine-a.m. feed. They were looking for a victim. As Chris headed for the back door, a posse of reporters rounded the building in full pursuit. Chris slipped inside and locked the door. After a bit of thumping and muffled curses, the press returned to the waiting room to mingle with the increasingly impatient patients.

Dr. Wilder knew better than to try to dodge the press. A coroner colleague in a neighboring county had tried to do so out of compassion for a grieving family. The dodge ended up slanted on a TV news show, looking like a cover up.

Chris had learned there was indeed truth to the old joke: You know it's going to be a BAD DAY when you find Sixty Minutes setting up in your waiting room. Pausing to collect his thoughts and jot a few notes, Chris Wilder strode out into the waiting room and led the pack of reporters outside and away from his patients.

He had long ago learned to avoid the sensationalism of a lay description of a murder. As a physician, he was at ease reverting to the clinical and unemotional descriptions that the press called Med Speak. Thus, he was able to describe the wounds and injuries without either prevarication or giving out grisly sound bites like "stabbed in the heart, throat slit" or "bled dry." The press, of course, tried to coax such words from his mouth, but he simply responded to their phrasing with a clinical affirmative.

"At this point," he concluded "in view of Chief Given's tragic death, I believe that the case has been handed over to Sheriff Charles who will be working with state law enforcement."

"They don't know a damn thing more than we do," muttered one reporter. With that, the impromptu press conference broke up. The case played big for several days, but without leads, a corruption scandal in a neighboring county, a revolt in Eastern Europe and an earthquake in Missouri finally pushed the case off the front page. News of the killings dwindled to a final disclaimer that police were still following up on any and all leads. Only an occasional nightmare of drizzling blood woke Chris for the next several months.

Chapter 6

Ashley Wilder, Dr. Wilder's wife, attacked good causes with the damnable energy and enthusiasm that can characterize recovering alcoholics and small children. Whenever she was questioned about her prodigious charitable and church work that kept her flying from one meeting to another event, her default answer was "I've already been through hell. I want to be damned sure I don't go again." Ashley had been vociferously sober for almost seven years.

Chris Wilder had met Ashley in Charleston the year he began his Family Practice Residency at the medical school. Ashley was a senior in English at the College of Charleston, an ancient and well-respected school just a few blocks down from the medical school. Ashley Barrineau was everything Chris aspired for in a wife. She was the only daughter of a family that was part of the ancient Charleston aristocracy known as the South of Broad crowd. Her family had owned a brick mansion on Tradd Street for almost three hundred years. She belonged.

Ashley, a tall willowy blonde of exceptional beauty had a loud and earthy sense of humor that occasionally defied her rarefied breeding. She also had a keen sense of social circumstances. To Chris, who came from a factory family up North, she filled his idealized vision of what a perfect contemporary Southern belle would be. (Ashley would have corroborated that notion)

It was a party for the medical school fraternity, off campus. Ashley had apparently made her mark as the life of the party as early as her sophomore year, according to a tale she was regaling a small group of admirers with. The story seemed to begin with submarine races at the waterfront Battery Park and ended with her in the harbor in formal wear.

The first night Chris saw her, she had arrived with her date, a cadet at the Citadel, the state military college. After Ashley drank him under the table, she'd needed a ride home. Chris, the shy and somewhat withdrawn "Yankee," was the closest image of a sober driver, and he was nominated. The two were a study in contrasts. Ashley, flamboyant and social, her laughter always stood out in a party. Despite herself, Ashley found herself attracted to this studious and thoughtful physician in training. and took it upon herself to keep in touch. The romance had been slow to blossom but blossom it did.

In married life, soon after her first pregnancy Chris noticed Ashley's drinking, reminiscent of her college years, resumed and began to accelerate. She resolutely quit drinking and smoking during her second pregnancy, but her willpower subsided after the birth. With a second baby clinging to her ankles, she quickly returned to evening cocktails. Chris assumed she was still in control and could quit if she needed. He was wrong. He didn't know she was struggling with a daily battle. Ashley fought long and hard. They had initially planned on four children. By the time the discussion came up about number three, Ashley had decided two was enough. Motherhood and sobriety did not go hand in hand.

Over the succeeding years, while Chris worked to build his practice in Merryville, Ashley slid down the long slow path from life of the party to lush. She was hospitalized twice. One hospitalization followed an accident on her teenage son's motorcycle during a party. Intoxicated, she had made it all the way around the neighborhood on a bet. Turning back into the driveway she waved gaily with both hands to the discomfited guests, only to topple over while plowing into the end of her own station wagon.
Chris tried to talk with her doctor, Charles Orr, about her drinking. Dr Orr was plainly uncomfortable with the discussion. "I'm sure she just had a little too much at the party," Dr. Orr counseled, "tell her to take it a little easier. Don't worry about her being an alcoholic, look at all the good work she does." Her discreet discharge summary from the hospital included only the diagnosis of a concussion and abrasions.

The accident scared her. In a private moment, Ashley realized she had gotten out of control. She resumed her role as model wife and mother for many months following that episode. Then the cycle began anew. First it was drinks before dinner, then before and after dinner and, soon drinks began with an eye opener in the morning and resumed in earnest after lunch. Months went by as Ashley slipped again into a boozy haze.

Chris returned to talk with Charles Orr, who only counseled patience. Chris wasn't sure he had any of it left. "Remember Chris, you know what they say, you've got to wait until she hits bottom and asks for help. You can't fix her. She must ask for help." Chris thought the advice seemed a little bizarre and knew that Ashley was far from asking for help. Fights and teary promises became more frequent. Finally, after one of Ashley's blackouts, Chris persuaded Dr. Orr to have Ashley admitted to a plush and discreet inpatient psychiatric hospital. Despite the care, the antidepressants, tranquilizers, and sedatives only seemed to make matters worse. Eventually, Dr. Orr advised

Chris to get Ashley to stop therapy. It had only loaded Ashley up with a good supply of reasons as to why she should drink.

Shortly after, Father Bob, Merryville's Episcopal priest, provided Ashley a way out of her private hell. The Episcopal Church is a premier attraction in the pantheon of entities that Ashley and old Charlestonians revere. It ranks right up there with old houses, ancestor worship, house parties, ocean fresh seafood and summers on Sullivan's Island. Ashley's only condition on marrying Chris had been that the service be held in one of the grand old Episcopal churches in Charleston's South of Broad district. They had been Episcopalian ever since, not that Ashley was a regular, her idea of good church attendance was Christmas Eve, Easter and maybe Ash Wednesday. She called herself a "faithful Chreaster." Nevertheless, in a small parish like Merryville, Father Bob dutifully counted the Wilder family as part of his flock and visited them periodically.

During one memorable evening visit, Ashley indecorously fell asleep in a drunken stupor. A mortified Chris had quickly ushered Father Bob out, mumbling excuses. Father Bob began to engage in subtle listening and discrete fact finding. Now that he was paying attention, he quickly found his suspicion corroborated that this drunken evening was not an isolated event. But how to help her?

Chris was a doctor. Surely if there was a potential medical solution to get her to quit, he'd have tried it. Still, Father Bob felt honor-bound to initiate a conversation with Ashley and to voice his suspicions and offer what help he could. It was not a fair match. Ashley had years of experience in denying the problem. All Father Bob got for his trouble was that Ashley announced she was getting tired of the Episcopal church and maybe the Wilders should consider the Presbyterians. Ashley did not insist that the Wilders attend Christmas Eve service that year. Father Bob noted their absence. Neither Ashley nor the priest mentioned their talk to Chris.

Several months later, Father Bob called Chris. "Chris, could we get together for lunch? It's about Ashley."

The tightening in Chris's gut was so automatic that he hardly noticed it. "Sure." he answered noncommittally. "What's she done now?"

"I'll tell you at lunch, but I think I may be offering a small ray of hope. Bye now." Father Bob rang off, leaving a puzzled Chris staring at the phone. What hope exists for the family of a drunk waiting for a bottom that never comes? he thought bitterly.

Georges was a restaurant typical of many small towns, a great social leveler. Everyone from the lawyers uptown to the occasional mill hand ate there. A faded green plastic sign surmounted glass doors under an aluminum awning that fronted on Main Street.

Inside, the decor ran mostly to aluminum and Formica. Towards the back, George, a massive red-faced man, presided over the cash register. Behind him, hung a chalk board with the day's specials. Menus were available in a dusty pile near the front door but to pick one up immediately marked one as an outsider.

George waved a cheery greeting as Chris entered. Neither Chris nor Father Bob picked up a menu or even consulted the chalkboard as they ordered. The waitress automatically brought iced tea when she came to get the order. With ordering finished, the preliminary chit chat quickly ran out. Father Bob cast an expansive arm over the back of the aluminum frame chair. He leaned back and fixed Chris with a speculative stare. He was about the same age as Chris. Dark thinning hair with streaks of gray, grazed the top of his clerical collar. The noisy hubbub of the restaurant gave them relative privacy.

"How many times have you tried to confront Ashley about her alcoholism?" he began without further preamble. The word "alcoholism" hung in the air for long seconds like a netted badminton birdie.

"You mean her drinking problem?" Chris answered. He ran a hand over his head and then a finger over his mustache as he stalled for a moment. Honesty won out. "Yeah, a couple dozen, maybe a hundred times. But, as you probably know, according to the experts, she's got to hit bottom and ask for help," he said with more than a trace of bitterness as he made 'hit bottom' in air quotes.

"I tried to challenge her too, a while back. Or didn't you think it odd that Ashley skipped Christmas Eve for the first time in twelve years? I'll bet Ashley never even mentioned our conversation."

"No, she didn't," Chris said flatly.

"That's the problem. Each of us tries in isolation to make Ashley see the light. She has years of experience in denial. None of us alone is her match. I 've just come back from a clergy conference where I learned about a technique called intervention, a way to 'raise the bottom.' Chris, do you hate Ashley's drinking enough to be willing to consider leaving her for it?"

Chris settled back in the chair; his eyes fixed on the ceiling as he spoke. "When Ashley and I fell in love," he began, "I couldn't believe my luck. She could have had anyone she wanted, and she chose me. Later, as the drinking got worse, I tried to focus on those good times. Occasionally I see a little flash of the old Ashley through the booze. I still love her, but I hate what she is becoming." He sighed and favored Father Bob with a sad smile. "It's ironic, isn't it? She needs me while she's ill, so I can't bring myself to leave, even though I hate to see her killing herself. If she were well, I could leave, but who'd want to quit then? She is funny, smart, still beautiful and good with people in a way that I can only aspire to be."

Bob was touched. He knew what he saw here was indeed true love, and he found himself wishing he could have met this other Ashley of years ago. "Chris, do you think you're ready to threaten to leave Ashley if she won't go into treatment? Are you willing to change the game and upend both your lives if she won't?"

Chris opened his mouth and then closed it again. He thought hard. He fixed Father Bob with a hard stare. "What do you have in mind? "

Father Bob found himself warming to the topic. "It works like this. As I mentioned, none of us by ourselves, individually is able breach this protective wall of bottles she's built around herself. Instead, we get everyone who loves and cares for Ashley together and we have a 'surprise party.' Collectively, as a group, we hold up a mirror of how we see her drinking, how it is hurting her and how it is hurting us. And Chris even though she is your wife, it's 'alcoholism', not just a drinking problem." He then proceeded to outline the technical aspects of the intervention.

At last, Father Bob sighed, tired by the force of his presentation. "It doesn't always work, but studies have shown it works better than any other approach, and at least it puts the problem out in the open instead of tiptoeing around it. In effect it 'raises' the bottom you've been waiting for."

Chris leaned forward on the edge of his chair, staring across the table at Father Bob. His expression was intense but unreadable.

"Goddamn," he said at last. "After all these years it would feel good to give it a try with a hope of success, wouldn't it? I feel better already knowing that someone else is in this with me."

The oath passed by Father Bob without comment. He found that he'd been holding his breath while waiting for Chris to answer. He exhaled with a gust of relief. They shared a grim smile and then turned to plotting the details.

Chris packed Ashley's things in preparation for the showdown. The car was gassed up and ready to go. There were to be no last-minute side trips or excuses to keep her from going to the rehab center the moment she conceded to go. Chris had one bad moment when Ashley wanted a dress to wear that he had packed. Knowing she had blackouts during which she could function, but of which she had no memory, Chris simply said, 'Don't you remember, you took that dress to the cleaners along with my plaid coat?" Ashley didn't dispute him.

The next day Chris, Father Bob, the two children and Ashley's best friend sat down and held up a mirror to a very ugly picture. As calmly as they could, they explained their individual perspective of what she had been doing as they saw it. One by one they showed how her alcoholic acts hurt Ashley, and how it hurt them. Each one then insisted that she enter treatment, or she would be cut off, never see them again, never to be a family again. All the way around the room it went as Ashley went slowly from defiance to tears of remorse. Finally, it was Chris's turn. He reviewed her behavior from the day they met until last night when she had briefly passed out drunk at dinner.

His gaze sought hers. "This is it," he said slowly and himself near tears "This is where it ends. Ashley, I love the person you were before this disease took you from us. Frustrated as I am, I love you still, but I swear to God that the kids and I will leave you if you do not go to inpatient rehab, if not for yourself, then for us. You decide what's more important, your husband and children or that emergency bottle of bourbon you're hiding in the toilet tank."

Ashley looked stricken. She scanned the circle around her. There was not a dry eye on any of the resolute faces that looked back at her expectantly. She saw that the threat was real. She was at once horrified and exhilarated that these people still cared so much.

"Tomorrow. I'll go tomorrow, I swear." She looked up expectantly. The tension in the room persisted. They'd been warned she'd say this.

"Today… now," they chorused back.

The fight was not in her. She simply nodded as tears dripped freely off her cheeks. Chris pulled out the waiting suitcase of packed-up clothes, Ashley was hustled to the car surrounded by Chris and family with Father Bob guarding the rear. Off she went.

It wasn't easy. Extensive detoxification was required and despite medication, she suffered withdrawal seizures. Later, she supplied a forgotten history of a febrile seizure as a child that may have rendered her more vulnerable to convulsions. As she sobered up and feelings returned. Beyond her overwhelming guilt, she felt rage. Anger at Chris for making her come here, at the family for letting her so low, and finally at herself for refusing to face the problem. It took Chris's repeated threats of divorce to get her to finish treatment. When treatment was nearing completion, she wasn't sure she was ready to leave. Her hesitancy was taken as a good sign. Ashley never touched a drink again. Now, seven years later, Ashely was a demon for church work, and the congregation knew if a job needed doing, Ashley was the first call. Her newest passion was American Sign Language; she had learned to interpret for a deaf member of the congregation. Now she had been badgering Father Bob and others to learn. Her only demonstrable progress was to teach the church members the words- "I love you" in sign. Pointing to oneself, crossing the wrists over the heart and then pointing at the recipient became a popular expression at the passing of the peace during the church service.

It was the custom at St. Andrew's Episcopal for a designated family to bring up the communion elements of bread and wine. This symbolized the offering of the whole church, and today Chris and Ashley stood in the back and gathered the elements. Chris was wearing two beepers under his coat. One for the practice, the other for his job as coroner. It was the coroner beeper that squawked in the church silence preceding communion that day. After three months of calm, was the serial killing nightmare was coming back.?

Chapter 7

Junior Charles was not what most people expected of a southern county sheriff. He had no uniform or trooper's hat, no Magnum .357 pistol hung from his belt. In fact, Junior Charles looked remarkably like the CPA he had been before running for Craven County Sheriff. He was tall and lean, almost gaunt, with a thick mane of salt and pepper hair that was his only source of vanity. Junior was a local boy made good, an oddity in Craven County who returned home again. Long ago, he had sought adventure by working for the FBI. After twenty years in Washington, D.C., where he had gone by his given name of Richard, nostalgia for warmer climes and a calmer, slower pace had set in. Like the prodigal son, Richard came home.

Richard Charles opened a private accounting firm in Merryville. Business was good, but after several years, accounting and the slower pace no longer held its appeal. When the current sheriff of Craven County was caught skimming bribes in a fashion too blatant for even Craven County voters, a replacement was sought. To reconnect with county voters, Richard resumed his childhood nickname of Junior to campaign against and win against the now late, police chief Harold Givens. Junior Charles stood at the mouth of a short dirt road that branched off an extension of Main Street. A forest of second growth timber which was swagged in kudzu that threatened to overwhelm the rutted track. Dr. wilder was called to this spot on an early Sunday morning in fall. The foliage was ablaze in a riot of cheerful fall colors that stood in marked contrast to the grim expression on Junior's face as he flagged Chris down. Several police cars were parked by the roadside, their lights rotating a syncopated cerulean rhythm. Junior led Dr. Wilder down the dirt road.

"She was found by some hunters," he began. "The method of execution was reminiscent of that of the two officers last spring." Leaves scuffled in the dry dirt of the road as they approached a clearing at the road's terminus. As they approached their destination, a sour decay insinuated itself into their nostrils. A small collection of deputies and emergency personnel clustered by, yet another police car and ambulance dominated a large part of the open area where the track ended. Junior led the way around the van towards the far side of the clearing.

A body, naked, hung head down from the branches of a large oak that towered over its neighbors. A light breeze caused the body to sway back and forth in a rhythm that reminded Dr. Wilder of Jake and Sudie. The coroner's dance he thought wryly. All the emergency personnel and deputies tried to appear nonchalant, but none appeared eager to be the first to approach the body.

"I thought they usually used virgins for this sort of thing," a deputy tried to crack.

Sheriff Charles shot the man a vile look, and the group fell silent. Dr. Wilder looked up in puzzlement as an errant gust pushed the body a quarter turn. Then it registered what the deputy meant. Hanging down close to her shoulder, by its umbilical cord, was a near-term baby. Both her neck and that of the baby were slit ear to ear. Dr. Wilder gulped once and looked reflexively at the ground under them: again, only a few tiny puddles and drops of blood stained the yellow and orange leaves below their heads. The bodies were pale almost to alabaster, except for the faces below the slashing wounds, which were the purplish color of settled blood. The first scattered frosts had come, so the flies were fewer than last summer's killing. Only a few maggots crawled on the severed surfaces of the bloated bodies.

Taking a deep breath, Dr. Wilder forced his scrutiny away from the body and inspected his surroundings. The clearing was perhaps one hundred feet across and had probably been a house site, now grown wild. A substantial stone circle occupied the far end of the clearing, a faint scent of char from a several days old bonfire competing with the sour smell of decay. Dr. Wilder stepped aside as the police photographer brushed past him. In a moment, the stuttering flash of the camera began to punctuate the shadows of the clearing.

Crossing behind the photographer, Dr. Wilder circled the bonfire. On the far side, he noticed some indentations in the bare earth as if a tripod had been set down. The camera flashing stopped. Dr. Wilder looked up at the ropes and mindful of the last episode lowering bodies he and deputies lowered the bodies very carefully until they came to rest on a blanket spread on the ground. Once the woman's body was in a more normal position on the earth, identification was painful and quick. Ironically, it was from Justin Wilkes, the deputy, who had made the crude comment about virgin sacrifice.

Justin helped man the line that lowered the bodies. As Dr. Wilder knelt beside the blanket to inspect the bodies, Justin wandered over to satisfy his own curiosity. "Say Doc…," he began. The casual salutation ended in a strangled gasp. Dr. Wilder looked inquiringly over his shoulder. Justin's eyes locked on the girl's face, his face a pale mirror of hers "Oh my god, oh my god, it's Janie!" With that he retched and collapsed on the ground.

Something about small town police officers and their stomachs, thought Dr. Wilder distractedly as he went to the officer's aid. Unable to get any meaningful information from Justin who lay moaning inchoately in the grass, Chris motioned to another deputy to cover the girl's body.

Dr. Wilder really needed some answers and Justin was not in a state to give him any. Dr. Wilder decided circumstances called for stronger measures. He then returned to his car and rummaged around for a plastic toolbox that doubled as his emergency kit. He dug out a ten milligram Valium. After a few quick medical questions answered only by shakes or nod of the deputy's head, he gave the Valium to the stunned and sobbing deputy. Justin swallowed the pill reflexively. After a few minutes, he sat slightly amid the leaves and vomit staring blankly towards the bodies as Chris supervised their loading into the ambulance for transfer to the hospital.

Justin became more coherent. In tranquilized monotone he explained that the woman was his cousin, Janie Johnson. A senior at Merryville High, she'd been running with the wrong crowd the last year or so. Getting pregnant was the final straw that led her family to turn her out on her own. She had not been seen for some time and it had been assumed by all that she had left town, which of course she had, in a manner of speaking. Again, the body was 'tagged and bagged' and sent to Dr. Sayaad.

"A fairly cut-and-dry job again," said Dr. Sayaad the following day, the pun unintended. The air conditioner labored in the background, not so much to cool the room but to keep the smell from getting any worse. The body stretched out on a metal dissecting table under Dr. Sayaad's examination light made the room seem even smaller. The angled surfaces of the table led to a gutter on the side, dispelling any illusion that the body was merely asleep. The numerous wriggling small white fleshy maggots added to the gruesome scene. Knives and saws hung on the wall in cool clinical counterpoint, while over the body hung a metallic bowl and scale for weighing organs. The walls and floor were tiled to ease cleaning. All of this made the sounds generated within particularly harsh. Dr. Sayaad used the blunt end of a bloody scalpel as a pointer. He casually brushed aside a few maggots in the open neck wound.

"Once again, notice the wound to the neck. and on this one too. From the shear pattern in the skin, I'd wager it's the same knife in all four cases. The maggots here in the wound would seem to indicate the bodies were hanging there for at least 36 hours."

Despite years of practice in medicine, Chris felt his stomach knot in rebellion as he forced himself to peer into the wounds as Dr. Sayaad talked. "From the bleeding around the abdominal incision, I would assume the infant was extracted and murdered before the mother The minimal amount of bruising on the mother is unusual. One would think that to vivisect a person in this way, one would almost have to use general anesthesia. But look…" and here he pointed to a place on the dead woman's abdomen that Chris really did not want to view. "The incisions could not be this smooth if she struggled. We will, of course, must do toxicologic screens to see if she was drugged or sedated. The preliminary screens are quick, the final toxicology can take longer. But I should have a preliminary answer for you soon."

The answer was not long in coming. The next morning the paging system called for Dr. Wilder the moment Chris entered the hospital. It often did that. For the hundredth time, he wondered if there was a special sensor in the hospital operator's station that somehow announced his comings and goings.

"She was drugged all right," Sayaad began without greeting. "Stoned out of her mind would be the colloquial term. Her urine tests show she was high on marijuana, cocaine AND her blood alcohol was three times legally intoxicated. She probably never felt a thing. pity," Dr. Sayaad concluded. "One ought to avoid all those drugs when one is pregnant. Bad for the baby." Chris bit back a reply to the effect that it apparently hadn't done the mother much good either.

This particularly gruesome murder and the renewed medica frenzy did much for reviving community terrors. Usually, open porch doors were slammed shut, streets cleared at dark, and people gossiped on street corners by day. For the next several days, Chris read his morning reports in laconic, composed medicalese to a crowd of whirring cameras on the front lawn of the courthouse, as Junior Charles stood beside him to be next in the hot seat. "Death by exsanguination through wounds to the neck and abdomen. Subject was intoxicated on a poly-drug regimen. Murder was perpetrated by person or persons unknown, for purposes unknown."

Chris found his medical practice to be an ideal place for overhearing clues and rumors in the community. Everyone had a theory or wisp of gossip.

According to Ginger, a high school senior in for a cheerleading physical, Janie, had a side worse than even the now repentant deputy Justin had suspected.

"She ran with the really bad crowd," Ginger confided as Chris checked the boxes indicating normal on the form. "Drugs were just the first part." Ginger rattled on as Chris silently shook his head wondering what his own children, away at boarding school might be doing.

On the other side of town, Junior Charles was remembering with a twinge of guilt the old saying: Be careful what you pray for, you might get your wish. Junior now had a total of five murders on his hands, Chief Givens now included among the murdered. This press conference became a savage grilling that was enough to make him wish for the good old dull days as a CPA. In front of a collection of microphones, lights and cameras, Junior and Dr. Wilder had faced an hour of hostile questions from the national press. Junior shook his head trying to clear his ears of the condescending tones of the correspondent from Los Angeles.

"Tell me sheriff, do you have ANY access to modern crime facilities?" Junior, afraid his temper would not outlast an answer, subtly signaled to Dr. Wilder to take the question. Dr. Wilder stepped to the makeshift podium. He resisted the urge to shade his eyes to peer out into the crowd. Rifling dim memories of long-ago medical school, he borrowed the even and pedantic tones of an ancient anatomy professor.

"The coroner's office, as well as the sheriff's office have been in close consultation with the state crime lab, our local pathologist and the forensic pathologist's office at the medical school. We are able to confirm by comparison of micro-photographs of the wounds that the same knife probably killed all four stabbing victims. The weapon was an exceptionally large knife such as one might use to slaughter livestock. The lab has also

confirmed by the pattern of lividity, that is settled blood, that Ms. Johnson was murdered in the upside-down position in which she was found. As to who or why, as coroner, I must defer to Sheriff Charles. With that Dr. Wilder stepped back and allowed the ravening cameras to have another go at Sheriff Charles. Dr. Wilder was glad his job was only to ascertain the cause of death, unlike Sheriff Charles who was expected to produce the perpetrators.

The next morning, with a night to brood on the press conference, Junior Charles was an even less happy man as he drove to Dr. Wilder's office. He planted huge hands crowned with knobby fingers on Chris's desk. Junior used his height to advantage as he loomed over the seated Chris. "Dammit doctor," he hissed. "Can't you find one clue, one small clue that might help me here? Surely your expertise, or at least some of the money we're paying Dr. Sayaad for all these damn autopsies ought to provide us something more than you're giving me!"

Dr. Wilder held out sheaves of reports. "I promise. I have called everyone. The state crime lab, forensic experts at the med school, you name it."

Junior slapped the air with an angry hand. "It's not enough. It's just not enough." Chris could see a hint of desperation about the man.

"I'll keep trying," he promised.

Junior snapped a curt nod.

Dr. Wilder and Sheriff Charles met more frequently over the next several days to share what little bits of information each was able to glean by rumor, interview, or lab data. Junior looked increasingly haggard as the weeks progressed without any new leads. If a few days went by, a worried Iris would call Dr. Wilder to report on how the Sheriff was faring. Chris could never tell if this was a political or medical report.

The following Saturday morning when Shelia Owens called, she sounded a little defensive. "Dr. Wilder," she began, "this is Shelia in the emergency room at the hospital. Our emergency room doctor for today has not yet arrived, and the patients are beginning to pile up. The night shift doctor had to leave. Since you're on backup and unassigned call, would you please come in and help out 'til he gets here?"

Dr. Wilder groaned. All the doctors in Merryville were responsible on a rotating basis for those patients who had no doctor. Sometimes the patients were new in town or passing through when illness struck. These were the rare ones. More often the patient was one of the regulars in town who simply declined to pay their doctors. Most of these were down-and- outers who made the rounds of the local physicians. To be on unassigned call meant that the doctor was the designated victim for whatever dirty jobs the hospital needed. doing that day.

None of the doctors in Craven County had Saturday or Sunday office hours. So, from 5:30 Friday evening until 9:00 Monday morning, the Merry Hopes Hospital ER was the only place to receive care. Often the weekend patients had been ill for days and had not the time, inclination, or funds to see a private doctor during the week. This meant that during the legitimate emergencies, crowds of people used the ER as a weekend free clinic. Dr. Wilder vividly remembered one man who had gotten him up at four am with a toothache he'd had for two weeks. When he asked the patient why he hadn't seen a dentist earlier, the patient looked surprised and said, "But the dentists won't see you if you won't pay them." At the time Dr. Wilder had looked up in sleepy surprise from the prescription he was writing. He spent the rest of the night thinking up brilliant, caustic replies.

Nowadays, the ER was staffed on nights and weekends by residents who moonlighted from their training programs to supplement their meager stipends. These doctors-in-training came to Merryville and other small-town hospitals from training programs all across upstate North and South Carolina. Occasionally one would not make their assigned shift. The unassigned physician of the day would then find themselves treating patients who had declined to pay to see him during the week.

Still, duty called, and Dr. Wilder was gritting his teeth while examining a screaming preschooler with a week-old rash, when the next patient arrived. She entered the ER, arms draped over two family members who struggled to support her. They said that she had seemed 'weak the last few days.' Shelia moved around the end of the nurse's desk to escort them to room number three. Something about the spineless loll of the girl's head as it thumped down on the pillow of the stretcher rang alarms in Shelia's mind. Rather than getting a history, Shelia decided to go straight to checking the patient's vital signs. She quickly jerked a blood pressure cuff out of its wall clip and took a reading,

or rather tried to. She pumped up the cuff to the expected level and listened, there was no thump, thump, thump in the stethoscope indicating blood pressure on the metal gauge she held in her other hand. Puzzled, she pumped the pressure in the cuff up a little higher for a second try. Her face furrowed as she listened intently without results.

Sometimes the fingers are a little more sensitive than the ears, so Shelia pumped the gauge up a third time resting her fingers lightly on the girl's wrist, as the needle swung down to the bottom of the gauge, she was rewarded with a light momentary rapid tickle of pulse that began at forty. Well under half of what it should be.

Women have a tone of alarm that is instantly recognizable. Mothers use it to warn children of snakes and speeding cars. Nurses use it too. "Doctor!" Shelia shrilled, "Doctor Wilder I need you in three, STAT!"

Dr. Wilder knew the tone and without the specifics, knew what it meant, but he still hesitated momentarily. He had only had to finish filling out the prescription for the child with the rash so that the family could go. Dr. Wilder knew if he stepped out of this room and into room three where Sheila waited, hours would pass before he came back. Shelia, knowing that he might stall, and apparently reading his mind, shouted "Now! Doctor."

Dr. Wilder grimaced an obviously insincere but apologetic smile, as he stepped out the door, "Excuse me. I'll try to come right back." This child with the rash then became the victim of an old French principle called triage. The triage concept divides emergency patients into those who will live and get better regardless, those for whom a vigorous effort will make the difference between life and death and finally those who will die no matter what. The child with the rash was in the first group, The new patient was probably in the second group but might yet qualify for category three.

Like many family physicians who work mainly with patients well enough to be seen in the office, Dr. Wilder hated dealing with desperately ill patients. But in small towns like this, often he was the only doctor available. He did his best to look calm and alert as he strode through the door asking, "What's up?" in an authoritative voice. On the inside however, his stomach knotted up as he looked at the limp and perspiring girl who lay gasping on the stretcher.

The tension on Shelia's face matched her voice as she hissed. "Doctor, I'm having trouble getting a blood pressure and I don't know why?" Dr. Wilder felt a momentary surge of irrational irritation. One part of his mind wanted to snap, "Well if you don't know, how the heck should I?" The problem, however, was that as the doctor, he was supposed to know or at least be able to quickly find the reason. His tension came from knowing that if he did not discern the cause and treat it quickly enough, the girl would become a permanent member of category three.

While a small part of his brain still yearned to panic, training and the cold rational mind asserted themselves in the statistical probability of various illnesses. Feelings quickly drowned in data. Algorithms of diagnosis, priorities, and treatment, drilled in by hours of study and practice began to bubble to the surface imposing order. Without notice, reference went from the person 'she' and 'her' to the impersonal 'the BP', 'the lungs' 'the patient.'… a problem to be solved. Orders tumbled out faster that Shelia could perform.

"I need an IV now; no, make it two…wide open. Call the lab. I'll need blood for a CBC, Chem six, type and cross for blood and a pregnancy test. Put the table in Trendelenburg to get blood to her head. We may need MAST trousers to squeeze what blood we can out of her legs to vital organs. We'll need a urine specimen too when we can get it."

The monkey of pressure had leaped from Shelia's back to Dr. Wilder. All she had to do now was follow instructions. Despite the welter of orders, Shelia simply nodded and leaned out the door. In a more composed and now commanding voice she yelled down the hall, "I need some help in here…"

Often, one of the most frustrating aspects of a crisis is that more people answer the call for help than can fit around the patient. A few cranks of the stretcher controls yielded a modest angulation of the patient's bed so that life-sustaining blood flowed from the feet into the more vital organs and brain. While Sheila tied a tourniquet to one arm to start the first IV, the lab tech arrived to obtain the blood samples. The girl strained for breath, rapid gulping gasps as if she'd been running for hours; oxygen tubing was quicky applied to her nose. The lab tech shook her doubtfully as she substituted an IV needle for her regular needle. After drawing the requested specimens, another nurse slipped in the second IV line. The specimens Dr. Wilder requested would provide information on the patient's most basic, but vital parameters, such blood concentration, infection measures, serum glucose and other chemistries and other clues as to what might ail the patient. Wilder's duties as a physician to this patient were twofold: to keep his patient alive long enough to get a diagnosis, then to treat the specific problem. As the nurse and techs bent to their tasks, Dr. Wilder pulled out his stethoscope and quickly listened first to the heart and then to each lung to make sure the most basic life functions persisted. Satisfied these were still adequately functioning, he gently but firmly pushed on the abdomen and looked for signs of injury.

Sheila reported that the blood pressure was up to a less threatening seventy five over fifty-five. The girl moaned as Chris's probing hands slid across her lower abdomen, a mental flag went up, but he continued his exam shifting his attention to her head. Quickly he pulled an examination light out of its wall niche. He peered at pupils and then the ears for signs of head injury. He found no clues.

The primary concern in a disaster like this is to keep from focusing too quickly on one problem or diagnosis and thereby miss the relevant facts that might point to another more pressing problem. The physician must remember during all the commotion to pause and widen his scope to consider what he might be missing. As the girl's pressure slowly rose, the remaining clothes were quickly and ruthlessly scissored off. Dr. Wilder began a second, more detailed, exam and noted a small amount of vaginal blood trickling out. About this time, the lab reported back that the patient had a hemoglobin of six, less than half the necessary amount of blood. Her pregnancy test was borderline. High pressure bags that looked like blood pressure cuffs were hastily wrapped around newly arrived bags of blood to force speed quickly force a lifesaving transfusion into the patient.

Dr. Wilder surmised that it was looking like a case of a ruptured ectopic pregnancy. This leading killer of young women occurs when a fertilized egg falls short of the uterus and begins to grow in the narrow confines of the fallopian tube which should deliver the egg to the womb proper. The pregnancy grows and pushes on this small tube that is not designed for the purpose. The tube cannot stand the strain and ruptures. Was this the problem? Dr. Wilder wanted to be sure. Usually, an ultrasound would confirm the diagnosis. This equipment was, of course, locked up in X- ray for the weekend. An alternative method would be to see if there was indeed blood leaking from the tube into the abdomen. Dr Wilder asked for a culdocentesis tray.

Culdocentesis involves poking a six-inch-long "spinal" needle through the far end of the vagina into the abdominal cavity to check for blood pooling where it shouldn't. Shelia obtained hasty permission from panicked relatives. The nurses held the girl's legs up and apart as Dr Wilder positioned himself, speculum in hand, between her legs.

As he parted the mouth of the vagina, he noticed a small blue image buried in the hairs of her labia. Pausing a second, he brushed the hairs back and stared. There he saw a small tattoo of a star. Dr. Wilder shrugged. Different strokes for different folks, he thought, as he slid in the speculum. A nurse shoved a tenaculum, an instrument that looks like pliers with sharp teeth, into his hand. He grabbed the cervix with the tenaculum and drew it up and out of the way. Next, he took a plastic syringe with the spinal needle mounted and slid it inward to a point just under the short of the end of the cervix. He knew this was going to hurt. Looking up at the nurses, he asked, "ready?" The nurses nodded grimly. He then jabbed the needle through the end of the vagina. The girl came to with a shriek and tried to slam her legs together. The nurses clung tighter to her legs keeping them apart, as Dr. Wilder pulled back on the syringe. A flood of black, cherry-colored blood flooded into the syringe. "Bingo!" he murmured, then louder "How are the vitals looking"

"Better. One-ten over seventy "called the nurse

"Call Dr. Smith or whoever is on call for his OB/GYN group and ask them to come attend to this ectopic pregnancy."

The mood in Room Three changed almost to festive as the nurse called the OR crew. The patient continued to improve every moment. When she snarled at a probing nurse, Dr. Wilder almost smiled. He knew she'd hold until surgery. Winning one always felt good, Dr. Wilder thought as he pushed himself off the stool and stood. Now that his adrenaline started to slow, he realized his shoulders and neck ached from the intense concentration. While the others talked and laughed, he felt drained. Shelia patted him on the shoulder. "Nice going," she said.

"Thanks."

Dr. Wilder went out to the ER waiting room and explained to the patients' distraught relatives what had happened. He asked if they had a personal physician, they wished him to notify. The family, still shocked by the news of the unsuspected pregnancy, merely shook their collective heads. Dr. Wilder found that he was not surprised the girl had not yet found a doctor for the pregnancy. Considering the poor education levels in some parts of Craven County, she may not have even known that she was pregnant. Even if she knew, it was typical of many girls to wait until they were far along in their pregnancy before seeking care, if they bothered at all.

Finally, Chris was able to return to the mother of the child with ringworm who was, even an hour later, still waiting. He wrote out the prescription and handed it to her."

'Sorry," he mumbled, not meeting her eyes. "Sometimes emergencies have to come first." She yanked the prescription out of his hand without a word and flounced out. Four or five small children caked with varying layers of dirt followed her out.

Dr. Wilder had just begun an interview with an embarrassed high school student wearing his football jersey complaining of "a drip or something," when the errant resident doctor finally appeared. Hearing the resident explaining his absence to the wrathful Sheila, Dr. Wilder stepped out of the patient room and eyed the red- faced junior doctor coolly as he proffered the chart. Dr. Wilder jerked his head towards the room where the student with the "drip" waited "Do you think you can handle this one, doctor?" he queried acerbically

The resident glanced at the chart thrust into his hands. His face reddened as he looked at the student's complaint and matched the diagnosis to Dr Wilder's. He nodded contritely, and Dr. Wilder headed for the door.

Pulling himself into his car at last, Chris gave vent to a fatigued explicative and jammed the key in the ignition. The car roared to life, but before he put the car in gear, he paused to pull a post-it note with pharmaceutical advertising on it out of the glove compartment. "JJ at CCHD" he scribbled under the name and logo of a famous laxative to remind him to check a hunch at the Craven County Health Department. He stuck the note on the comer of the rear-view mirror by several others meant for action Monday. Although

Ashley didn't drink, Chris certainly felt he could use one. He looked at his watch, not even noon yet. "Crap," he muttered.

<h1 style="text-align:center">Chapter 8</h1>

The following Monday, Chris wheeled his car into the doctor's parking lot at the hospital under sullen skies. As he looked around the lot, he felt slightly out of style. His gray Taurus wagon was a hold-over from the last few years of shuttling kids and their friends to various functions. High fashion transportation was not a high priority to the kinds of doctors who settled in small towns, often for the proximity of hunting, fishing, and gentleman farming. The doctors' lot was littered with a variety of pick-up trucks and jeeps along with a stray Mercedes.

Chris smiled remembering the time the ER had called in the orthopedic surgeon out of the tree from which he'd been hunting deer. He had hustled straight to the emergency room, pistol and hunting knife still strapped to his camouflage clothes, hunting rifle in hand. The poor blue-haired old lady with the fractured hip waiting for care took one look at him, turned to the nurse, and said, "Oh dear, I guess it's worse than I thought." Then, she fainted dead away.

Dr. Wilder hurried through rounds. Usually, he had only a few people in the hospital at any one time. Today there were more on his census from the weekend of "unassigned" calls. Among them: a mother and baby he delivered the night before, both doing well and a child with croup who'd arrived gasping for air during the night and was now in the next room in a misting plastic net. The child, Dr. Wilder saw, was sleeping quietly now. He could quickly see the child's breathing, an even up and down motion, so different from the stuttering struggle for air last night.

The mother of the "crouper" wanted to ask a lot of questions about the possibility of recurrent infection and whether the child should be seen by a specialist. Chris sat on the end of the unused patient bed by the crib and heard the mother out. He tried hard to reassure her that croup was a viral illness with essentially no significance beyond the acute course. Yet, ever mindful of the possibility of malpractice charges, he concluded by saying, "however, if you're not satisfied with the course that little Jimmy is taking, I certainly can arrange to send him to a tertiary care center in Columbia for further tests." Dr. Wilder never wanted to sit in court and have a mother explain to the jury how she'd known that little Jimmy was "bad sick and THAT dumb doctor (here his mind often supplied a mental picture of a theatrical gesture from the plaintiff to the defendant's bench) REFUSED to send MY baby (God rest his soul) to see the specialist that could have saved his life." To this type of patient, the grass was always greener at the bigger hospital.

Chris hurried up the hall nodding to Howard Blassingame, a GP from the old school. Chris noted that Howard's son Edward, a senior medical student, was in tow this morning with an armload of charts. Ed nodded a shy grin to Chris and ducked into a room at a bellow from his father.

The next patient, Artie Sykes, was a gift from the stint on unassigned call. Artie, an alcoholic with pneumonia, sat up in bed smoking a cigarette in violation of hospital policy. The oxygen mask pushed up on his forehead hissed uselessly at a lock of sodden hair. "Say doc," Artie rasped. "Ya gotta do something, I'm still coughing' and blowing' like a damn racehorse." To emphasize the point, he coughed until his face matched the deep blue of his hospital gown and then expectorated a massive clot of phlegm onto a hastily plucked tissue. He held the tissue out like a trophy for Chris's inspection. "Look at that will ya?" he wheezed. Chris sighed and looked at the tissue.

Artie was a regular. He rolled in every several months half dead. Sometimes he had pneumonia, sometimes DTs. Once, on a memorable winter weekend, he was brought in with hypothermia. Celebrating Christmas early with his buddies, he'd fallen asleep outside in a park. His body temperature was in the low eighties, far below, almost fatally below the expected 98.6. Chris had spent an anxious day by a re-warming tub in ICU watching Artie's heart crank out virtually all known possible and potentially fatal arrhythmias. Artie slept blissfully through the whole affair and never turned a hair. Smoking and alcohol cessation counseling rolled off Artie like the moisture from the oxygen mask rolled off his greasy hair.

Dr. Wilder took this offered opportunity to suggest that maybe Artie needed a specialist to take over his care. "Where ya thinking of sending me, doc?"

'Timbuktu' was the answer that rattled around Dr. Wilder's mind, but instead he tactfully suggested, "The big medical center in Charlotte, North Carolina"

"Jeezus," Sykes wheezed. "I ain't got time to go up to Charlotte. You just do the best you can to fix me up and quick as you can. I trust ya."

Dr. Wilder tried again. "Well, we really need to see about this alcohol dependence problem, Artie."

Artie snapped up an arresting hand to stop the conversation. "This stuff is gonna kill me. Doc, speak plain. I'm a drunk, you know it, I know it." Artie rummaged in the nightstand pulling out a dilapidated wallet. Digging around in it he extracted a grimy card and held it out for examination. To Dr. Wilder's surprise, it was a college alumni card. "Doc, I'm a college graduate, but covering up a plain diagnosis with fancy terms won't help me."

Sykes leveled a callused finger at his chest. "I gotta help me, and I don't think I'm worth the effort." Dr. Wilder looked at the card; it was a Wofford College alumni card. Wofford was a well thought of private school further up-state. His residency director, he recalled, was also an alumnus. Artie made shooing motions toward the door, clearly wanting the conversation to end.

As he headed down the hall, Chris suddenly thought he might be able to find Janie Johnson's Johnsons records from obstetrics Because the health department patients had no regular doctor, their ongoing care records were brought over to Merry Hopes Hospital from the health department and updated weekly. A large filing cabinet, somewhat battered, waited by the nurses' station for whatever doctors and nurses might need the records when the big day arrived.

The nurses sat enjoying a quiet morning in the tiny OB lounge, and they invited Dr. Wilder to join them for coffee. He took the proffered Styrofoam cup and chatted a few minutes with the nurses before he rose and went over to the file cabinet. The search was a brief one. A single file card lay in the folder. It simply stated, "Patient deceased, records returned to Craven County Health Department." Bad news travels fast, Chris thought. After a few moments of reflection, Chris decided to get the information from the source, the Craven County Health Department. He reflected, as he retraced his footsteps toward the car, that a face-to-face chat was usually best. Nurses often had insights they were willing to talk about but unwilling to commit to paper.

The Craven County Health Department was located not far from the mill villages that used it most. It was situated in a vintage brick schoolhouse that had last been refurbished last in the 1950s. It had the typical institutional antiseptic smell and faded green paint of most such institutions. Lines of indigent women of both races holding runny-nosed babies and surrounded by squalling toddlers did little to improve the buildings' overall depressive and neglected atmosphere.

In contrast, the nurses were some of the more ebullient souls he knew. They also had the best collection of crass jokes and tasteless but funny cartoons.

The public health nurses were nominally overseen by a district medical director. The DMD, as he was called, was an aging General Practitioner in semi-retirement. Furthermore, his district covered an area of five counties leaving the nurses often to their own resources and make do they did.

The job attracted and encouraged strong personalities. Brenda Knox, the head nurse at the health department was hazel-eyed, auburn-haired, and fierce. Her feelings towards the streams of downtrodden and often dirty mothers and children ran from affectionate toward the rabidly maternal. When it came to "Her" patients, she feared no doctor. Often bypassing the DMD, she would call any member of the local medical community to ask, beg, wheedle, or demand special attention for certain patients she thought needed it. She cheerfully pulled the records she wouldn't have rendered up without a subpoena to anyone but one of "her" doctors. She recalled Janie well. "Trouble," she said.

"She didn't come until well into her seventh month. She smelled of alcohol on that first visit. I wanted to get a blood alcohol along with her prenatal labs so I could confront her but the doctor on call wouldn't permit it. He said he was afraid of getting dragged into court if it could be proved that she did drink, and he hadn't tried to get her treated. We also tried to get her to identify the father, which would have made her eligible for Medicaid. She never actually told us who the father was. Instead, she kept spouting garbage like maybe the father was, and I quote 'the great lord of darkness': she was a bad character. I'm surprised her VD and AIDS screens were negative though.

"Are you seeing that much AIDS here?"

"Some," Brenda admitted. "HIV has a long reach. Also, it is pretty much standard in the health departments across the state now. Besides, poor rural counties like this one are VD heaven. A lot of the AIDs patients are gay young men coming back from big cities to die. But once home their families kick them out."

"The HIV tests are to inform and protect the doctors and staff caring for the patient I suppose? "

"No." Brenda countered, "We try to trace down sexual contacts. In fact, originally, the state forbade us from telling hospitals and doctors that patients were HIV positive. You should have seen the fur fly when the doctors working at the health department indigent clinics found out about that!" Brenda thought a moment then continued, "our nurse-midwife who examines the patients happens to be here today. She might be able to give you a little more information. Would you like to talk with her? She's in back having coffee."

Martha Reilly was all those things that well-bred Merryville residents detested. She was from New York, Catholic and extremely liberal. Dark haired, short, almost squat, she had once flirted with being a nun. Her trial vocation, however, had not worked out well. She had been utterly unable to keep silent for the periods required.

Even worse, when she couldn't keep silent, she said exactly what she thought regardless as to whether or whom it might upset. She had made her Merryville debut several years ago when she called a particularly pompous obstetrician to offer some information regarding a patient's possible high-risk status. That particular physician was suffering from a major 'M. Deity complex'. Certain she had nothing to add, he cut her off in mid-sentence.

"Thank you, my dear, "he had intoned in a patronizing voice he imagined sounded akin to Walter Cronkite's baritone. "I'm certain that I'm aware of all the relevant and IMPORTANT facts of the case. Goodbye."

Martha a feminist who detested being patronized, stared at the phone and gave vent to her feelings as she hung it up. "Asshole" she barked in her booming voice.

As fate would have it, at that particular moment, "Dr. Walter Cronkite" was writing a prescription for a waiting patient, his phone remained cradled on his shoulder as he finished. Both the doctor and the waiting patient heard Martha's closing comment. The insult might not have been so bad had the patient not laughed out loud.

Shocked at the insult from a "mere nurse" and humiliated in front of a patient, the enraged obstetrician vowed revenge. He made a major effort in the medical community to lobby to get Martha fired for insubordination. Probably the only thing that saved her was the fact that every doctor at Merry Hopes hospital not only agreed with her assessment but admired her courage for saying aloud what they'd all been thinking. Several months later, this physician decided to relocate to a place he was certain he would be more seriously valued.

Martha's utter frankness surfaced again as she recalled Janie at Dr. Wilder's prompting. "Oh yeah," she brightened as she recalled, "the druggie with the star by her tush."

"Star?" asked Chris, raising an eyebrow while struggling to suppress a smile at the phraseology that was so clearly vintage Martha.

"Yeah, she had a couple of tattoos. One on her shoulder that read 'born to lose' and something else. You could tell they were homemade, you know, a needle and stamp pad ink. The writing was fuzzier than a commercial job. Crooked too. I remember because I gave her a lecture about the risk of hepatitis and AIDS when using tattoo needles," Martha snorted. "You know the other way I could tell the star was homemade? It was upside down like she put her head between her legs and drew the star in that position, right below her labia. It was a tiny thing, small and dark blue. I thought it was a mole at first but then I realized you could see the individual spots of ink. You probably couldn't see it if you didn't do a pelvic exam on her. Doing it must have hurt like hell."

Martha threw her cup in the trash. "Oh well, back to digging in the salt mines I guess," she said to Dr. Wilder with a wink. As she reached the door, she turned back, "say, Chris, this star thing. I think it may be a fad or something. I've got a couple of girls here that have them. You never know what will strike these kids next.

Dr. Wilder was still mulling over that last comment as he walked back down the halls of the Craven County Health Department. The talk of mothers hushed in a rolling wave as he walked by. Real live doctors weren't seen that often by the kinds of patients who go to the health department. They were more accustomed to nurses and nurse practitioners. Chris climbed into the gray Taurus wagon and headed to the office. As usual, he was late.

Chapter 9

Having a nurse any length of time is kind of like having a second 'work' wife without the fringe benefits. Dr. Wilder's second wife, Mary Ann Reyes stood in the back hallway waiting for him as he came through the door. Medium framed and buxom, she had strawberry blonde hair streaked with white that she insisted came from professional frosting and not age. She had worked at the hospital as a staff nurse for several years. When his first nurse left after only a few years to pursue the joys of motherhood, Dr. Wilder thought first of the cheery banter and professional care Mary Ann had lavished on his hospitalized patients. He never advertised the position; he simply called and asked if she was interested. She'd been waiting for the call. Now, after ten years in his office, she dealt with Chris with the easy familiarity of long association. This had its benefits; she usually knew what he was going to need or do before he did. Often, he would ask for an instrument or piece of equipment only to have her standing there expectantly with the to-be requested item in her hands, usually with a smirk or arched eyebrow. Pelvic exams and other procedures were set up and executed often without a word of instruction. Assorted instruments and articles would whizz back and forth between them without interrupting the three- way banter intended to distract and relieve the patient's anxiety.

Only twice in recent memory had Mary Ann faltered. Craven County, along with much of the South Carolina upstate, had been settled by Scotch-Irish settlers. Consequently, an inordinate number of the local residents possessed a variety of shades of vibrant red hair. Chris and Mary Ann had been carrying on one of those trivial but diverting arguments that lasts through the day as to whether there were too many redheads in Craven County and what to do about it if there were.

The patient on the table at that moment was very blonde. Chris guided her feet into the stirrups for a pelvic exam as Mary Ann stood behind the patient to adjust her pillow. She pointed to the patient's head and mouthed the word "blonde" with a smug smile of victory. Chris flipped back the sheet as Mary Ann circled the table to assist. He pointed down, "but a natural redhead." Satisfied with his victory, he stuck out his hand for the speculum that should have been there but wasn't. Puzzled, he looked toward the instrument shelf that was Mary Ann's usual perch and saw nothing. A flicker of movement to the wrong side of him drew his gaze to the door where Mary Ann leaned, rocking in silent, helpless laughter.

The other time had been one of those particularly bad days when it seems like someone must have put out a "TWO FOR ONE SPECIAL" sign somewhere in front of the office. The rooms were packed, and both Mary Ann and Dr. Wilder were trying to do four things at once. Standard policy pretty much dictates that a nurse be in the room whenever a male physician examines the parts of female patients that require the removal of clothes. Chris had twice flipped the little buzzer to call Mary Ann. He knew she hated it. She said it made her feel like maid service, so he rarely buzzed. However, today he was particularly mindful of the string of appointments that were falling further and further behind while he stood wondering where she was. Finally, he reached across the patient to the buzzer knob and spun it from its discreet low setting to "loud" and pushed long and hard. Mary Ann entered unnoticed during the long loud buzz and with a wink to the patient, stood with her nose almost buried in Dr. Wilder's back, waiting. After another irritated pause, with an apologetic smile, Dr. Wilder shrugged at the patient and said "The nurse must be tied up. I'll go see what's keeping her". He turned abruptly and plowed into the waiting Shelia with a startled shout of surprise knocking them both to the floor. It took a good five minutes before the patient stopped laughing enough that the exam could proceed. The patient was still chortling as Mary Ann, preparing to leave, paused by the door and curtsied.

"Your Majesty," she said to the chastened Dr. Wilder and flounced out of the room.

This morning, Mary Ann stood in the back hall of the office, Chris's coffee cup on a low table beside her (two Sweet' N Lows, no cream) and a sheaf of messages in her hands. Late as usual, he barreled through the door. The chart racks on the exam rooms bulged with the records of the patients waiting within. The crusty face of a small African American child peered out one door, which he quickly slammed as he saw Dr. Wilder enter. Mary Ann shoved the coffee cup into his waiting hand and expertly deflected him from the waiting hallway into his office.

"Messages first," she ordered. "First, the hospital called to remind you of a Pharmacy and Therapeutics committee at lunch today and a Medical Records and Utilization Review Committee meeting this evening. They were both most insistent. You apparently forgot the last couple of meetings."

"I didn't forget," Dr. Wilder replied petulantly. "I didn't feel like going. All they do is argue about which new antibiotics they should trim to save money, and then they always end up getting all of them anyway. It's a waste of time."

"They must have figured that, because they said if you 'forget' again, your hospital privileges are in jeopardy."

"Whoopee," Chris grunted noncommittally.

"Next, Joyce Smith called and wanted a refill on her blood pressure medications. She was just here last month, and her pressure was okay then."

"Yeah, she's been good for the last year, give her three months' worth."

". . . And Melissa Bagley wants an antibiotic for a cold her three-month old has. . ." Mary Ann leaned back from the expected blast which came. Wilder had made well known his feelings about the uselessness of antibiotics for viral illnesses such as colds,

"No, damn it. The baby needs to be…"

"…seen and evaluated. I told her, but she said to ask anyway." Her frosted hair brushed a white sweater as she shrugged. "Okay, that's the lot for now.

Rising to his feet, Dr. Wilder gestured impatiently to the hallway of waiting patients, "Is it as bad as it looks?"

"Worse."

The first several patients were straightforward-- a backache, a simple ear infection and a cold. Chris always wondered why people go to the doctor for colds. There was no cure but time. Over the counter medications worked almost as well as prescription drugs which is to say, not much. With or without any medication the viral course and severity were little changed. Early on, he had tried to point this out, but patients clearly believed they'd been cheated if they left without a prescription in hand. This patient was a little different. He didn't even want an antibiotic if it wasn't needed, he just wanted to get his cough checked out. Chris gave him a non- narcotic cough medicine, reassured him that he would remain among the living, and the patient went happily out the door.

The next patient, James Sanderson, was a pudgy forty- five-year-old executive from one of the local industries. He was there because he didn't "feel right." On Dr. Wilder's careful questioning, Mr. Sanderson spun a tale of diminishing exercise capacity and constant fatigue. Until recently, as he repeatedly volunteered, his health had been perfect. This was the first time he'd seen a doctor since having a company physical fifteen years ago.

Red warning flags began to semaphore in Dr. Wilder's mind. One of the unspoken rules in training is that a man who hasn't seen a doctor in "years" probably should have. People like this, even without a complaint of chest pain, were usually a heart attack waiting to happen.

Dr. Wilder gradually teased out a series of risk factors, a family history of heart disease, and a smoker. Exercise? 'Are you kidding?' Probabilities doubled and trebled. Finally, Dr. Wilder pushed back from the counter. He gestured to Sanderson's shirt, "OK, let me listen." The physical exam revealed little, as did a cardiogram.

Dr. Wilder had Mary Ann tell Mr. Sanderson to dress and come to Chris's office. Mary Ann frowned at this. She knew that Dr. Wilder only took patients into the clutter of his office to deliver bad news in private. Sanderson was buttoning a sports coat that stretched across his girth as Chris closed the door behind him. Sanderson emerged a few minutes later, chastened, and clutching a slip for an exercise test scheduled for the morning. "Do I need a specialist?" he'd asked anxiously.

"If you flunk the test, THEN you need a specialist."

The next patient was one of Chris's delights, Annie Johnson, a peppery retired schoolteacher. Annie had first gone to the doctor, ANY doctor when she hit 65. Annie reasoned that if the state of South Carolina thought she was so worn out she had to retire, then there must be something wrong. Chris's first meeting with Annie ten years ago had been a memorable one.

Annie had been sitting in the exam room, white hair pulled up in a bun. A rumpled white sweater hung over her exam gown. A cane lay across her lap ready for quick use, although for what Chris wasn't sure. Annie was engrossed in a novel and didn't even notice Chris's entry until he cleared his throat loudly. Steely eyes peered over the rims of half-moon reading glasses and fixed Chris with the same glare that had terrorized generations of Craven County eighth graders. The book went down as the tip of the cane came up to waggle in his face.

"I certainly hope you're better than the last doctor," Annie began ominously. "When I retired, and went for a physical, my first. THAT doctor spent two minutes looking at me and twenty telling me how stupid I was not to come to him earlier. Wrote me four prescriptions. I never took them, and HE died of a stroke the next month. I haven't been to a doctor since, and I am still here!"

With a few placating words to convince her that he was harmless, Dr. Wilder managed to get a medical history and an exam. He found only borderline high blood pressure. He decided to monitor her pressure for a few visits. Over aggressive treatment of mild hypertension in the elderly can often lead to side effects worse than the disease such as dizziness that leads to a hip fracturing fall. Only partially tongue-in-cheek, he assured Mrs. Johnson that she was in good health and to continue to try to avoid doctors and 'their poisons.' He had made a friend for life. Now Annie, a little more bent over, cane still at her side but unused, was a regular visitor.

Her reasoning was that as long as she came here, she was safe from "those other doctors" who might try to poison her.

Annie waved her cane in greeting as Dr. Wilder entered the small exam room. Most of the visit was social in nature. Like many of the rural elderly, Annie had few friends left and little social contact. Coming to the doctor was a rare opportunity to visit. Dr. Wilder knew this, and despite the time pressures, let her make the most of it. They exchanged information about family friends and neighbors. Annie was a little less animated than usual but didn't volunteer as to why. At length, the conversation wore down to enlarging gaps of silence. Dr. Wilder could have steered the visit to a close but continued to feel there was unstated business. To buy time, he undertook a brief exam, a ceremonial laying on of hands.

To Annie's raised eyebrow, he explained, "Sometimes I have to justify my existence to Medicare. Annie endured his prodding in silence. Finished, Annie tugged her coat on with Dr. Wilder's assistance. Reaching the door, she turned and impulsively hugged him as he reached for the door. Her face was clouded with tears.

"Dr. Wilder, that girl that was murdered, Janie Johnson, was my grandniece. She was in some bad company, but it wasn't just dopeheads that killed her. She told me she was involved with the devil himself. The day before she disappeared, she told me she'd found God and was going to straighten her life out. Now, she's dead." Annie laid an entreating hand on Chris's "You've got to put a stop to it. The devil's spawn is loose in Craven County." Nonplussed, he stopped short and watched as Annie shuffled down the remainder of the hall and around the comer out of sight.

Dr. Wilder paused in the hallway a moment surveying the line of exam rooms with colored flags indicating patient order and what each patient might need based on the color of the flag. Mary Ann popped out of his office instead of an exam room and gestured him in. Inside was a familiar face, Brenda Knox, the director of the health department for the second time today. He was wary of Brenda though because she was always approaching the local doctors with new projects. But the projects and task forces she proposed were always well thought out and for the better health of the community. Dr. Wilder always had trouble saying no. He thought he's gotten away clean this morning.

"Hey doc! I shoulda caught you at the health department" she greeted him, "I just need a couple minutes of your time." She made an exaggerated begging gesture. "Please, I really, really, need your help."

Dr. Wilder produced a smile that ended in a grimace. "What now?"

Brenda grinned conspiratorially, "Don't be like that, we're on the same side here. Anyway, I need your help. I know you're super busy, but this is right up your alley."

Dr. Wilder cocked a skeptical eyebrow and motioned for her to continue.

"Hospice, it's the new thing, "she said brightly.

"Hospice?" Dr. Wilder says. "I've heard that Congress passed a Medicare benefit for that a few years ago. But isn't it just like giving dying patients morphine and putting them out of their misery?"

Dr. Wilder thought he could almost hear Brenda's sarcastic eye roll. "Unnngh," she groaned. "Not you too. No, hospice is about quality of life for people near the end of life. It is intended to be for six months prior to death. Hospice provides care not just for the patient's fatal disease but also the patient and the family. It is not just nurses, but chaplains and social workers and medical equipment and medications all in the family home, all designed to give the patients nearing the end the best care when there is no cure. I figured this would be right up your alley: bio/psycho/social/spiritual care. Yes, sometimes we use morphine, but I promise we don't kill people. Or at least we wouldn't," she amended "except…"

"Except…"

"We have all the staff, people and parts we need except one. We need a medical director. It is only part-time. You'll have a friend there; your church's Father Bob has even agreed to get some extra training and be our part time chaplain. Please! It's only maybe an hour or so a week to attend an interdisciplinary group as required by Medicare."

"But why me?" Dr. Wilder asked almost plaintively.

"Well first you're already the coroner and work with the deceased and I've heard so many families tell me how kind you've been. The other reason is, quite honestly, that even though I know how busy you are, I've tried every other doctor in town. They all refused." Her face took on new urgency as she pleaded, "Please Obi Wan, you're my last hope. My budget will buy you some books and some training, but you really are my last hope to help people in this town find some peace near the end of life."

Despite himself, Dr. Wilder was intrigued. He had seen patients die moaning uncomfortably, one even screaming in the hospital and there thought to be a better way. "Okay," he conceded, "Let's try it for a few months and see how it goes. How long until you are ready to start operations. Brenda grinned, "I have a patient with lung cancer named McKeever Lange. I told him if I was lucky, we could take him this afternoon." Brenda levered herself out of the chair with a conspirators' grin. "I knew I could count on you. Thanks Doc. I'll send over the paperwork." She nodded to Mary Ann on the way out.

Chris leaned back, chagrinned. He knew he'd been played but as he thought about it, he found he didn't really mind. As he stood and stepped back out into the hallway Mary Ann's head popped out of the lab and appraised his face. "Thanks Doc," she said, I knew you'd do it. McKeever is a cousin of mine." Mary Ann nodded to one final flagged door. "One more, doc. Here for the 'voodoo' treatment." Making an effort to pull his head back to the flow of patient care, Dr. Wilder reached for the chart and glanced at the heading and groaned inside. The patient was there for hypnosis to quit smoking. The AMA had recognized hypnosis as a reputable and effective modality in 1957. Dr. Wilder had received a novel introduction to the field of psychosomatic medicine as a family practice resident years ago followed by several medical education courses. Word of his interest had leaked out and even now, years later, word of mouth continued to bring him patients. Today's patient was an unwelcome surprise. Mary Ann shook her head in commiseration. "Good luck on this one," she commiserated. "If you can fix her, I will nominate you for 'Most Likely to Raise the Dead and other Miracles." Wilder glanced down at the chart name as he rounded the door. It was Iris Maynard.

Iris waggled a pack of cigarettes at him. "I think I'm ready to quit at last. She punctuated the comment by a fit of soggy coughing that ended a few moments later in a series of fitful wheezes. Wilder was struck by how his initial mental picture from her first phone call was so on target, down to the matching pencil and pen that protruded from Iris's hair.

After providing Iris with a few words of history and explanation, Dr. Wilder dimmed the lights and launched into the practiced monotone of his hypnotic induction. Within a few minutes, Iris's eyes fluttered and drifted down. He began to discuss the taste of cigarettes, unfavorably comparing them to a pile of flaming tires. Just then someone hammered on the door.

All the office staff knew never to interrupt him when he was performing hypnosis. Iris's eyes flew open as she licked her lips and grimaced at the remembered taste and smell of burning rubber. "Are we done already?" she asked thickly.

Dr. Wilder shook his head in annoyance and yanked open the door. Harsh light flooded in as he stepped through the doorway. Mary Ann stood outside looking grim. "Sheriff Charles called, there's been a fire at the Jaycee hut near the Number Three Mill."

Chris blinked and spread his arms angrily. "Do I look like a fireman to you? You interrupted me to tell me there was a fire? I'm not even a Jaycee anymore." He turned back angrily to the exam room door.

Peeved, Shelia waited until he turned the knob. "Sheriff Charles called because he couldn't find 'Granny.'" she volunteered, "There was a body in the hut." Mary Ann turned back to the door. "Hi Iris," she called as she stalked away.

Chapter 10

Major Gerald Merry was a bastard in both senses of the word. He was tall, auburn haired and corpulent and his face was a chronic choleric red. He had grown up the illegitimate son of a well-to-do farming family from the Carolina Low Country be adopted by a local farm hand.

Young Gerald's ancestry was never openly acknowledged. Still, his coloring so strongly reflected that of the farm's owner as to make his parentage an open secret. Largess, fronting for guilt on the part of his unacknowledged father, ensured basic needs and an adequate education. What Gerald Merry lusted for, however, was recognition, and he would do anything for it. With the early death of his natural father, he changed his name to his father's—Merry. His adoptive family objected of course, but Gerald then set out to top anything his natural family had ever done.

Fresh out of college, he served in the Spanish American War as a lieutenant. By the time World War I rolled around, he had made his way up to Major.

World War I changed Gerald Merry in a way that the Spanish American War hadn't. It fed the latent cruel streak that began in childhood because of the taunts he endured. Many men came back from the war gassed and broken, but Major Merry came back highly decorated from heroic and savage combat. He should have been made colonel or even general, based on his exploits, but his volcanic temper and sadistic personality served to undermine his overriding ambition. His search for a task worthy of him brought him to Briceville, South Carolina.

Back in the early 1900s, the town had tried to enter the cotton mill market. A group of investors raised money to start the Briceville Mill Company. The mill was built, and mill hands hired. It promptly went bankrupt. Over the next decade, various entrepreneurs tried to restart the mill with notable lack of success. The mill acquired a reputation as an unlucky bottomless money pit. When the mill was closed again in the post—war slump, a group of distant investors unfamiliar with the building's unlucky reputation hired the brash and arrogant Gerald Merry to run it

Gerald Merry MADE the mill work. Ruthless was his byword. He slashed wages to subsistence level. He built the first of the mill villages so that control of the worker might be extended not only through the workplace but to home and hearth too. A goon squad of enforcers and mill supervisors made sure malcontents and agitators did not last long. The word 'union' was only whispered and only briefly. The system was brutal; the system, however, worked at Briceville Mills. The mill posted profits for the first time in history.

Too late, the investors learned they'd brought a shark into a gentile pond of investors. One at a time, Gerald Merry quickly forced his sponsors out and seized full ownership in the company. His first change in the new company was the name: Merry Mills Incorporated. The town name changed soon thereafter. The town's people, happy to have a functioning industrial plant, learned to turn a blind eye to the mill villages and the rumors that came out of them.

The building that most recently housed the Jaycees had always occupied a special place in the Merry family consciousness. The building began its life as a union organizing hall. During the Depression, all across the South, wages sank lower and Gerald Merry led the plunge, squeezing his employees ever harder trying to remain profitable at all costs. Other mill owners and employers soon followed. The United Textile Workers of America led a union organizing drive in the South trying to counter what became known as the "Squeeze." Violence quickly ensued. In nearby Honea Path, South Carolina, at Chiquola Mills, strike breaking goons slaughtered seven mill workers in a hail of anti-union bullets.

Merry Mills was of course a prime target for the union organizers. The UTW hall was built on one of the very few pieces of land near the mill village not owned by the Merry Family. Gerald Merry vowed not to let it stand there long.

The Fourth of July 1934 was the night of the town picnic. Merryville tried to break from the tensions that had been growing in the summer heat like the swelling melons in the mill hands' yards. Normally, the Merryville Fire Department sent a truck to the fairgrounds outside town and kept the others in reserve for possible fireworks related fires. This particular fourth, Major Merry invited all the firemen and their trucks. In fact, he insisted they come. In a town like Merryville such a strong invitation was not to be ignored. That evening as the crowd oohed and aahed at the company fireworks display, a company supervisor walked over and waited near Gerald Merry. Merry motioned him over. The supervisor bent to Merry's ear and whispered a few words. Merry's blood red face creased with a seldom seen smile. He nodded in acknowledgment and then turned back to the show.

The blaze at the union hall was particularly tragic because both of the union men assigned guard the building were found dead inside, "presumably trying to extinguish the fire." The coroner, a supervisor at Major Merry's newest mill, ruled the deaths accidental.

 In a blaze of rhetoric, the union rebuilt the building on the same brick supports of the first building. The deaths and fire, however, took something vital out of the mill community. The town quickly settled into an anti-union attitude; it seemed safer. With no small satisfaction, Gerald Merry quietly bought the building.

Gerald never lost the cruel and ruthless streak that made him a success. His children, particularly his sons, were something of a disappointment, being interested primarily in spending his hard-earned money. Gerald Merry grieved that he had been unable to spend the necessary time raising his children to see the world as he viewed it. He promised himself to do better with the next generation.

When grandchildren came along, Grandpa Merry often told them about the cruel and rough world and shared tales of his exploits from his war days. When he felt his message of ruthlessness was not getting through, he took stronger measures that had long lasting effects.

The sun shone through cotton-like clouds one spring day at a family reunion. Gerald suggested his children and their spouses take the afternoon off together. Granddaddy Merry would keep the grands. To start the afternoon off with something fun, he produced a large floppy eared bunny. His children were delighted at this mellowing of their patriarchal terror. His children and in-laws left their collection of children eagerly petting the rabbit. The children had a wonderful day playing with that docile, lop-eared bunny, and grandpa enjoyed it with them. When Gerald suggested a tour of 'Granddaddy's mills' to see where cloth came from, he carried the bunny along. Grandad explained how the mill worked and showed them the spinning and weaving rooms. The children covered their ears in the deafening clash of the machines. The bunny squealed in pain from the noise, but no one noticed.

Back at the house, Grandad explained how discipline and law and order were needed to keep the mill hands in line. As he explained to the children he sat and stroked the bunny. Almost finished, he admonished them that sometimes it was necessary to seem cruel to ensure the system worked and everyone was fed. "Sacrifices," he continued "are often necessary. In the war, I often had to send men to their deaths in order that the rest might fight on." The children began to drowse through this oft—repeated sermon. Suddenly, with one fluid yank, he wrenched off the sleeping bunny's head. In one of Gerald's hands the bunny's eye remained open in shock. In Gerald's other hand, the body twitched furiously, spraying the children with its still warm blood.

There was a moment of shocked silence as his bloody hands held the still twitching body of their new pet. Then screams erupted as the children scattered. One grandson remained glued to the ground in catatonic terror.

"Like I learned in the Big War," Gerald continued in conversational tones, "sometimes the sacrifice must be in blood." Gerald stood and carried the body of the rabbit to the kitchen. Dinner that night was roast rabbit. Grandpa made sure that the grand kids ate their part and was satisfied with his demonstration. Gerald had successfully imparted his vision of the world, and the Merry family place in it. The union men who died in the Jaycee hut would have understood the lesson too. Now, many years later there was another body in the hut.

Chapter 11

Chris fondly recalled his time after he had first moved to Merryville and joined the Jaycees. The high point of each year was dressing up as the mad doctor in the Jaycees annual Halloween haunted house. The "mad doctor's office" was the grand finale of the tour as Dr. Wilder covered in stage blood, gibbered, and shouted, brandishing a chainsaw while his "victim" writhed on a table in the lab in pretend agony.

All those fun memories evaporated, as he pulled the Taurus wagon up to the ashy remains of the Jaycee hut. Only the original brick pylons of the clapboard building remained. A few charred beams projected from the ashes like so many tombstones set off-kilter by the heat. As Dr. Wilder paused in his car a moment, he could see that the intense heat had turned the leaves of the nearby trees to a shriveled brown.

Johnny Riggs, the fire chief, knelt with one of the sheriff's deputies beside him upon scorched boards that remained of the building. He waved at Dr. Wilder as dust and ash kicked up by the tires settled around the Taurus.

The smell of gasoline burned wood and flesh assailed Chris's nostrils as he stepped out of the car. Johnny smiled apologetically, freckles bunching up on his aged face. "I 'm afraid we didn't leave you much to go on, just bones and teeth mainly. We found them at the far end of the building where the pulpit used to be, before the Jaycees moved in."

"Pulpit?" asked Dr. Wilder,

"Yeah, the hut used to be a Baptist church and before that was a union hall."

"I didn't think there were any unions in Craven County."

"Not now, Merrys and them run 'em all off." Johnny ambled around the brick pylons to the far end of the building. "Once we realized what we had, we tried not to disturb the body. Most of it's been cooked down to just the bones. They're in there, mixed in the dust.

Dr. Wilder looked down into a thick clump of ashes where Johnny gestured. His mind took a moment to sort the ashes into the suggestion of a figure within. Without Dr. Wilder's knowledge of human anatomy, most people would not have been able to identify the blackened stick projecting from the debris as a thigh bone. Dr. Wilder shot a questioning glance at Johnny. Johnny shrugged, "First thing we found was a skull."

Dr. Wilder scanned the men assembled at the site. Brow furrowed; he turned back to Chief Riggs. "Where is Sheriff Charles?"

"Come and gone to get more help." Johnny dug his hands in his back pockets. "Madder than hell too. He takes all this stuff personal." The fire chief stared off at a nonexistent cloud beyond Dr. Wilder's right shoulder. "He said he was going to call the state crime lab to look at the body. 'Get some experts,' he said." Dr. Wilder's shoulders settled a little; Junior Charles was trying to go around him. Well, he hoped the state people had better luck than he'd had so far!

Junior Charles returned shortly thereafter. His expression was locked down tight. He stood avoiding Dr. Wilder's gaze, compulsively snapping, and unsnapping the leather cover of his walkie-talkie. With a shrug, Dr. Wilder bent to study the body one last time, careful not to come too close. Straightening back up, Chris nodded to Chief Riggs and returned to the office to finish the last few patients. When he returned an hour later, the state mobile crime lab was set up and literally sifting through the ashes.

By late evening, under floodlights, the technicians assembled a dark, reasonably intact skeleton on a blue tarp as Dr. Wilder looked on. The skull and jawbone were secured, and dental patterns were noted to send inquiries to the local dentists. A good many of the ribs were burned down on the ends. Some of the spinous processes on the spine were similarly charred. As the team dug deeper in the ashes, they had to exercise more caution as the ash heap was still smoldering. One of the forensic experts held up a piece of bone from the sifter.

"Doesn't look like this guy burned to death after all."

Chris came and looked at the piece. It was a vertebra. One of over two dozen from the spine. By its size and configuration, it was from the upper neck. A clean cut had removed the lower third of the bone.

"From the looks of it, doc I'd say…"

"…he was beheaded." finished Chris.

"It's kind of interesting," continued the lab man. "If you look at the cleavage marks, you can see the blow was struck from the front." He tilted his head back in thought, subconsciously echoing the presumed angulation at time of impact "You know, it's really hard to deliver a blow to the front of the neck: the victim usually lowers his chin and deflects part of it. I wonder how whoever did it, managed." The sifting continued for a while longer as Junior and Chris held a strained conference to the side. A brief stream of profanity from the sifter interrupted their discussion.

"Damn it, Sheriff. It ain't bad enough we got the fire department guys messing up what little bit of evidence we got but your guys go around dropping your badges into the ashes. The man handling the sifter gingerly held up a five-pointed star with a pair of tongs, as he shook off some clinging ash. "Sucker is still hot too. At first, I burned my fingers on it."

Junior crossed the space to the sifter in three long strides. Oblivious to the heat, he snatched the star from the tongs. Fortunately for the sheriff, once free from the insulating bed of ashes, the star quickly cooled. He only bobbled it once or twice before being able to get a firm grip on it. He turned it over and around as Chris looked over his shoulder.

"It's not one of ours," he concluded. "It's not even a law enforcement badge. It's a necklace of some sort. See the two eyes drilled and welded at the rim?" Dr. Wilder noticed another detail that the sheriff's eyes didn't think to look for. The eyes were welded in such a way that the star would be hanging upside down from the wearer's neck. An unpleasant rumble twisted through Chris's innards. Just what exactly was going on here?

Chapter 12

Captain Donald Ferris woke up on the last day of his life a happy man. He was moving up again. He had passed his final flight supervision in the copilot's seat. Today he would accomplish his dream-to pilot a 747. Until recently, the airlines had long denied people with even the slightest visual impairment the opportunity to fly for them. Donald had grown up worshiping the jets that flew over his house from what was now Douglas International Airport. He was a gawky teenager with glasses, who made and played with model airplanes. Other kids called him a geek, but Donald didn't care. All he wanted to do was fly.

Two days after his high school graduation, on his eighteenth birthday, he joined the Air Force. Only after he'd already signed up did he learn the terrible truth. His request for pilot's training came back marked "Application denied. Recruit lacks adequate uncorrected visual capacity for requested assignment." Twenty years later, Don still counted that day as his darkest. Still, he reasoned, if he couldn't fly aircraft, at least he could be around them, so he trained as an avionics technician.

The years flew by as Don learned all there was to know about aircraft and their maintenance and flight. But he hadn't forgotten his secret ambition. Outside of working hours, he labored towards earning a private license. Eventually he left the Air Force for lucrative maintenance work with Universal Skyways based in Charlotte. In the private world, flying is a rich man's hobby, but Don had not a single other thing draining his finances. Aside from a single bedroom apartment not far from the airport he had no other major cash expenditures. Because of its proximity to the airport, the apartment complex where he stayed was heavily populated with stewardesses. Even they did not deflect Don from his only true love.

In the late 1980s, the airlines changed. Many of their pilots, holdovers from the Vietnam era, began to retire. At the same time, deregulation increased the number of competing airlines. Faced with a shortage of pilots, the airlines began to look for ways to increase the pool of possible applicants. One way was to drop some requirements, including the strict requirement that all pilots have perfect 20/20 vision without correction. This was the moment Donald Ferris had spent his life waiting for, and he seized it.

He started with the smaller conventional airplanes, commuters, from Charlotte to smaller cities and towns all over the two Carolinas. Next, he went on to small jets and then slowly, he leapfrogged to larger jets, until he became the navigator on a large plane. Strikes by pilots and airline workers helped accelerate Donald's climb. Shrinking wages did not deter him. All he wanted to do was fly. Today, Donald would finally realize the fruits of a lifetime ambition. Today for the first time he would captain a 747.

Thirty miles south, another pilot was also preparing for a flight. Grady Hawkins was the pilot for the Merry Mills Industries corporate jet. Call it vanity, sense of history, or simply inertia, but the Merry Mills corporate headquarters, despite its now global reach, remained in Merryville proper. Major Merry's original home, across the street from Cornelia's hospital, was the ceremonial greeting place for visitors to the corporate headquarters. Behind his restored home on what had been his gentlemen's estate, a complex of modern office buildings over-saw the day to day running of the Merry Mills industry. Because many of the financial and creative people employed by Merry Mills were based in either New York or Los Angeles, necessity dictated the company ferry them to Merryville for conferences.

Periodically, someone interesting would come along on these rides such as a minor royalty doing a series of designs, a movie celebrity, or a rock star coming out with her own brand of jeans. Grady Hawkins took them all in stride. The Merryville airport, eager to keep the Merry Mills Company happy, had recently extended the runway to handle the new company jet. The airport authorities had not yet been able to get the tanks installed for the jet fuel required by taking a jet. Refueling required a brief hop to Douglas International to refuel to take today's celebrity, a punk rock artist and his collection back to New York. Grady Hawkins was sitting in the plane working through his preflight checklist. Grady looked like everyone's idea of a pilot. . . gone to seed. He still affected the aviator glasses and leather flying jacket, but the buttons strained to restrain a growing paunch that was nonexistent when Grady flew in Vietnam. Dark hair, grown long on the side, was combed over a balding pate. Grady Hawkin's mind was not wholly on his checklist. He had other problems as well.

His difficulties began with a simple invitation to a party. He was several times divorced because of the many separations inherent to a pilot's life. Social life in Merryville for a single man was 'dullsville'. He tried to spend most of his time in Charlotte. However, one of the private pilots at the field (Grady still thought of the small airport as a field) had invited him to a party. Grady had not been aware that Merry Mills had a "swinging side" to it. Usually when he was in town for the night, he noted that the sidewalks rolled themselves up around nine p.m. Oh, there were a few country bars that stayed open until late, but the kind of rednecks that hung out in them didn't appeal to Grady's sense of aesthetics. The first party had turned out to be a wild affair with heavy traffic to the bedrooms. Grady particularly enjoyed that part. After one repeat invitation, he had a standing invitation. By the fourth party, Grady was a regular. One of the girls asked if he'd like to go to another place where they could really have some fun. A blindfold was required for admittance.

'Voodoo heaven' is what Grady first thought when he entered the darkened room decorated like a devil's mass. The party began with a formal invocation explaining that it was the master's wish that people come together to enjoy spirits and each other. A "cup of the blood of the brotherhood" was passed to all present. The wine, slightly salty tasting, was shared by all. Not even Grady Hawkins' jaded imagination could have called up the caliber of the orgy that followed.

Grady found the rituals akin to circles within circles, what began as a party slowly, over time, revealed itself to be a coven of Satan worshippers. The final announcement was virtually anticlimactic. By then, Grady counted these orgies as part of his regular life. As an eyewitness to some of the bloodiest parts of Vietnam, neither God nor country inhibited him. As long as the party rolled, Grady didn't much care who the patron saint was. When they told him the cup of the blood of the brotherhood was blood mixed with wine, he hadn't been too shocked. Grady reasoned "Doctors draw blood from patients every day. They probably get it from some medical supply house like anything else. Grady had seen a catalog from one of these places. Everything, including human skulls, was available, so why not blood? A small voice deep inside him asked occasionally. "Are you sure?" Grady partied harder at times like that so as to obliterate unpleasant thoughts

Grady was at a small private airport outside New York City to ferry down a famed punk rocker who was working on an erotic set of sheet and cover designs. The set was to be marketed under a different trade name through men's fashion magazines. The artist had climbed aboard early. The artist was Grady's only passenger on this flight.

Bored with the passenger area, he came up to sit with Grady and view the sights. His long hair arranged in sharp spikes, neon orange clothes; his fey manners and New York accent began to grate on Grady's nerves. After a brief look around, he began to whine about everything from how unappreciative the Merry Mills Corporation was towards his work to the deplorable condition of the New York art world. After a few clipped words from the tower, Grady spooled down the runway and launched into the air.

With each new complaint Grady inched the air speed up a little more. Grady loved to fly, but this trip set a new Merryville record for brevity.
Having driven the company limo to the guest house and safely deposited his charge, Grady retrieved his own car and went to the small duplex he kept on a side street in Merryville proper. Grady showered to relieve himself of the smell of the artist's cologne, and then dialed the number he'd been given by his contact. The coven still did not let him know them by their full names. Ever since the original set of parties, he'd been taken blindfolded to all the meetings.

His regular girl Betty, along with others, was in the Toyota sedan that picked him up this evening. Several vaguely familiar faces looked out from within. He lifted his chin for the inevitable blindfolding, but Betty shook her head and kissed him. "Not tonight, lover. Tonight, we have something special in mind."

They had made no effort to drive around to disorient him but drove straight for the bypass and then around to a dirt road. Once in the dark, they bounced down the rutted track to a small clapboard hall. A sign in the headlights identified this place as the JAYCEE HUT of Merryville. Only dim starlight showed outside the hut. The doorway was marked only by a faint blood red light shining out of a crack between door and threshold.

Betty and the others paused a moment outside the door. Another car pulled in and disgorged more passengers. Betty nuzzled suggestively in his ear and whispered, "Tonight's your special night, your initiation." A low noise inside grew to a cross between a chant and a collective moan. The doorway opened and Grady was swept inside with the others around him.

Grady paused inside the door and blinked in the dim light. The air reeked of clouds of incense that drifted about within. The hut's walls had been scrawled with various arcane and satanic graffiti. Upside down stars, and symbolic goats' heads competed with elaborate 666s in multi—hued fluorescent spray paint. All of the coven members were naked and shiny with oil. Betty eagerly helped Grady disrobe and anointed him with oil as he stared around in surprise. Toward the far end of the hall was a large altar with a large bucket at one side and behind it on a higher platform a cauldron. The cauldron flamed from something burning within which was casting the dim scarlet light that illuminated the hall.

Grady scarcely had time to take all this in before Betty guided him over to a large floor mat and pushed him down. She then slithered down beside him, handing him a drink which he thirstily swilled. The chanting stopped, and from the back door a huge figure emerged, stooping to clear the door frame. Shaggy skins enveloped a massive figure topped with a mask set with deer antlers. Clearly a costume of some sort Grady thought., as the figure stepped aside. A man and a woman followed in its wake coming up to the altar. Like the others, these two were both naked. The girl wore a thick laurel of flowers and leaves in her hair. Her step was light and provocative. Her partner, by contrast, shambled along as if drugged.

"Tonight, brethren," boomed the figure in a voice so deep and so loud that Grady wondered if it was electronically enhanced. "We add another member to the brotherhood of blood through the ritual joining with the Earthmother." Grady watched with interest as the man was helped up onto the altar. Now that his eyesight had adapted, Grady could see the altar top was padded. The chanting, slow and hypnotic, resumed and soon Grady joined. The scent of incense became heavier and more pervasive. An air of expectancy infused the trance which to his mild surprise, Grady felt overcoming him.

The girl, Grady noted, had not yet joined the man on the altar. Instead, she circled the altar teasing its occupant. First, she offered a stroking hand, then a brush of a naked breast and lastly a tongue tickle on the groin. Soon the man on the altar responded. The light of the cauldron behind offered a profile view which offered ample evidence of the man's growing interest. Grady too, found himself aroused also. At last, the girl mounted the altar and its dweller, sitting astride his manhood. The tempo of the chanting increased toward the inevitable climax.

When the blow struck, Grady was getting so distracted by Betty's similar ministrations beside him that he almost missed it. He knew the climax was coming: the chanting was painfully loud and frenetic. Suddenly both bodies arched back. The man, his head over the end of the altar, and the girl, bent back almost double. A glint of silver from the darkness behind was all Grady saw as the massive blade swept down, clearing the girl's arching chest and severing the head of the man beneath her. A gush of blood ejaculated from the neck into the basin below and slowly ebbed to a pulsating trickle as Grady watched in shocked horror. The body twitched fitfully a few times and shifted as the girl casually dismounted and moved round the altar.

A shrill ululating scream that mirrored Grady' s thoughts rose in the crowd behind him. It broke into a loud whoop of joy from the crowd. In a collective rush, the celebrants charged both the altar and the bloody basin. Grady watched in horror as the first of the crowd reached the still steaming basin and dipped their eager hands in the steaming bucket and then tasted its contents. The first arrivers were then shouldered aside by the rest of the jostling crowd. Grady's stomach gave a warning jolt. He needed no further urging and bolted for the door to be sick outside.

He was almost finished when Betty arrived at his side in a panic. "You must come back inside," she pleaded. "We must finish, or they'll know you are missing and that something is wrong. Grady spit repeatedly on the ground trying to exorcize the foul taste from his mouth as he dumbly shook his head. "You must," she repeated urgently. "They punish people who don't join in. You will never be allowed to return please, for me, come back inside

He straightened and took a few deep breaths. By shifting his attention from the carnage inside to Betty's obvious charms, Grady managed to calm his stomach enough so that he could be led in to consummate the activities. When the inevitable cup was passed to him, he faked a sip and passed it on trying not to wince. Fear of not being allowed to return wasn't what drove him, but rather a concern for survival. If the poor geek on the altar was being honored, he didn't want to guess what being punished was like.

Later he joined the group in sloshing gasoline on the building to destroy the evidence. One question nagged him. "What about this guy?" he asked Betty, "who was he? Where did he come from? Won't he be missed?"

"Oh no," Betty commented as she threw a mass of curly black hair casually over her shoulder, her earlier terror for him forgotten. "He's just a homeless drifter- a nobody."

"How do you know?" Grady persisted.

She dug playfully at his ribs. Her answer chilled him. "He was in the hospital where I work. I helped pick him out."

The next morning, Grady finished his pre-flight check off and his morbid reverie of last night's events about the same time. He had no doubts of his course of action. As far as he was concerned, this flight was a one-way trip out of insanity. His resignation would be effective on his return to New York. He took an early dawn side trip by the corporate offices to leave his resignation on the corporate president's desk. The artist was safely ensconced in the back with the cabin door securely locked this time. After today he didn't EVER plan to return to Merryville or South Carolina. He was right. He never would… alive.

Ignorant of his plight and with the artist in the back cabin, Grady taxied down to the end of the runway for the hop to Charlotte for fuel. Putting power to the engines he thundered down the tarmac and into the air with the usual thrill as he lifted off and headed up and north towards Douglas International Airport.

Chapter 13

Grady reveled in the faint scent of fuel and ozone permeating the cabin. These smells and others had always reminded him of his beloved planes, but today they seemed even more intense. Even the pull of gravity against the seat fascinated him. The awesome true blue of the azure sky and the incredible symmetry of the complex woven patterns of the cirrus clouds pulled his gaze outside. His mind skipped and jumped, evermore fascinated by the unfolding sensations. Unchecked, the auto pilot flew northwards.

Meanwhile, Captain Donald Ferris had completed his own pre-flight checklist for his maiden flight to Miami. He was loaded down with tourists motivated by the first hard frost to seek warmer climates. Donald took great pleasure in welcoming the passengers as their captain. The 747 lifted off and began to climb.

The Merryville Gulfstream had ceased to climb at only a few thousand feet, when Grady took his hands off the steering yoke to brace himself against the frontward looking canopy. His face was set with awe at the sky. It seemed as if the very air was ablaze in a mystic light. In a small corner of his mind a tiny, confused voice desperately asked what was happening to him. In just a few minutes he saw an even more inspiring sight: Captain Ferris's long coveted 747. The questioning voice became still. To Grady's dazed and assaulted senses, the huge airship reminded him of an angel with outstretched wings.

Grady blinked and shook his head. He looked again. Yes, it was. It didn't just look like an angel; it was an angel. His angel of the sky. Blonde hair wafted around silvery flowing garments. Wings fluttered angelically behind. The angel looked at him and offered a smile indicating a long and hearty welcome. Her arms extended and beckoned to him. "Come," she whispered.

Training that had become muscle memory took control as Grady grasped the wheel and turned a barrel roll of joy and headed up towards those waiting arms. In the distance, unnoticed, came a shriek of protest from the doomed artist in back. His beloved awaited as he streaked towards the 747.

On board the 747, Donald's first warning was a notice from the air traffic controller that an unidentified aircraft had appeared "out of nowhere" and was currently engaged in a collision course. The tower called out a new direction and elevation. Captain Ferris abruptly jinked left and dropped altitude. The Gulfstream flashed by, only a few dozen feet off the port. Anticollision alarms screamed in the cockpit to match the screams from behind the cockpit door as the 747 lost altitude and shuddered in the turbulence of the near miss and then stabilized.

The usual laconic verbiage of in-flight communication eluded Donald. "Who was that jerkoff?" he demanded of air traffic control. "I want his ass!"

"Roger that flight 224. We concur," came the clipped tones of the air traffic controller. There was a momentary pause and then the radio crackled again. "Flight 224, we regret to inform you the rogue is coming around again."

His killer had planned well. In a way, it wasn't really a fair contest. Grady had flown combat in Vietnam. He had flown fighters. His Gulfstream was far more maneuverable than the lumbering 747. By contrast, combat tactics or even evading the suicidal was hardly a subject covered at Donald's flight school. Grady wasn't sure why his angel had dodged him. Perhaps she felt his flying skills were not worthy. Maybe she was teasing him. Whatever the reason, Grady Hawkins vowed to merge his wings with hers in a mating like that of eagles. This time his drugged fogged senses stayed alert for the last-minute dodge left, and he followed the left with ease. His angel wouldn't miss him this time. Donald meant it only to be a feint. He dragged the protesting craft in a hard left turn and then as the Gulfstream closed, he jerked it right again.

The Gulfstream screamed in from below the right wing where the passengers had a ringside seat to the view of the onrushing plane. Don faintly heard their collective crescendo, ending in a shout of alarm as the rogue plane ate up the gap. The feint helped a little. The Gulfstream struck only a glancing blow to the fuselage, tearing off a cargo door and gutting part of the underside. Sheets of metal pulled back in screaming protest. Two rows of passenger seats cantilevered into the sudden gap. The seats momentarily rested there as the final bolts strained. Two passengers who had failed to secure their seatbelts whipped out of the cabin and into the void below.

The bolts of the first row gave way, and it tumbled back, a mixture of shouts and metallic crash, into the second row. The doomed passengers' screams dopplering away as the two rows of passengers tumbled out into oblivion. The 747 lumbered on. Like an angry and wounded beast, the metal skin of the craft shrieked as it continued to slowly tear.

Grady's Gulfstream continued south and upwards in an uncontrolled trajectory. Pieces of his plane shredded off until the remains exploded. The majority of the plane managed to remain airborne until it crossed into Craven County, South Carolina.

Back in the 747, Donald was amazed to find himself still alive and in the air after the collision. Perhaps there was still hope. He paused to run a tongue over dry lips. "Charlotte Air traffic, we have an in-flight emergency. Request immediate runway clearance. You may wish to roll the emergency trucks," he added unnecessarily. Slowly, slowly, Donald inched the crippled and torn aircraft around to the north and back to Charlotte and safety.

Had he been able to keep his original altitude a little longer, Donald might have made it back. The battered fuselage combined with rising thermals from the fields below caused the plane to buck and shudder. The plane groaned and creaked with each fresh insult. Finally, as the 747 passed over a large freshly plowed field prepared for winter wheat, the extra heat generated from the brown earth threw up a particularly energetic thermal current. The big craft bent over the upward thrust of hot air like a boxer over a jab to the solar plexus. The bend turned into a fold. The wings lost their lift as they shredded from the plane.

No, not my fault I did everything right, were the last thoughts that went through Donald Ferris's mind as the ground rushed up to meet him. As coincidence would have it, he had managed to get back inside the North Carolina state line. The autopsies and deaths would be followed up in North Carolina. In South Carolina, Chris Wilder would have only two autopsies to do.

Chapter 14

The medical staff at Merry Hopes Hospital numbered close to twenty doctors. More than half of these were GPs and their successors, the family physicians. The other half of the staff included a variety of specialists such as Dr. Sayaad the pathologist, internists, surgeons, and urologists. Many of the doctors commuted in several half days a week from larger cities such as Charlotte, Greenville, or Columbia to offer their specialty in the smaller town. Dr. James McAbee, Jr., like his father, was a general practitioner of the old school. He had never thought much of all these new specialists and their new procedures that came to steal his patients and his income. He remembered the good old days when there were just a few GPs like his dad in Cornelia Merry's old home. They'd done surgery, comforted the dying and delivered babies. There wasn't much point in referring a patient elsewhere because not that much more that could be done even in larger cities. Also, in the good old days the patients also never thought about suing a doctor.

Dr. McAbee felt the recent changes that had been occurring in medicine were almost as bad as those changes that had occurred in his other passion, baseball. In his personal litany of events, both fields began to deteriorate about the same time, in the late seventies, when Dr. Chris Wilder had come to Merryville and the designated hitter rule first took effect.

Dr. Wilder had not appreciated the effort required to be privileged to do exercise stress tests at Merry Hopes Hospital. For years, cardiologists and internists had zealously guarded the privilege for themselves. At the hospital where Chris trained, only the cardiologists and their fellows were allowed to do exercise tests without supervision. But Dr. Wilder had spent a month at another hospital learning as a resident. In the late seventies and early eighties, this general restriction of stress tests began to loosen as invasive cardiology came into its own and exercise testing became merely a way to screen for candidates who might need the more invasive (and lucrative) cardiac catheterization. While the sensitivity and specificity of exercise testing improved with added refinements such as injecting Thallium dye during the procedure or ultrasound, the hot competition for rights to do the procedure began to fade.

When Chris first arrived in Craven County, it was unheard of for a family practitioner to ask for such privileges. In fact, no one was actually doing the test at the hospital. The board of trustees of the hospital met to discuss this newcomer's unusual request. Like most hospital boards, this one included a member of the medical staff. Dr. James McAbee was none too thrilled to have this new doctor bringing in ideas that might cost him patients. Still some caution was advised. While not taken with the idea of competition from a new front, McAbee conceded that he was also going to have to live with this doctor. In a very small medical community, it wouldn't do to make enemies. Best to get someone else to do the dirty work to make this request go away. and Dr. McAbee knew just who.: Dr Horace Johnson.

The Life cereal commercials had not yet aired at that time, with their 'Mikey hates hate everything' but Dr. McAbee would have recognized Mikey in the form of Dr. Horace Johnson. Dr. Johnson was one of the oldest and most venerable members of the medical staff. Dr. Johnson didn't like anything new…ever. He was also the only member of the small medical staff who was board certified in internal medicine, and he was proud of the fact. His father had, in fact, trained with Sir William Osler, the modern-day founder of internal medicine, and Dr. Johnson had grown up with Sir William as a family friend. Dr Johnson was imperious, perfect and sure. He, Dr. McAbee concluded, would be the perfect person to put an end to this stress test foolishness.

The meeting wound on for some time with the board evenly divided on what to do. Finally, one member of the board, a farmer who ran a large dairy operation and who was a patient of Dr. McAbee, turned to him and asked, "say Jim, you're awfully quiet, and you're a doctor. What do you think we ought to do?"

Dr. McAbee, like many doctors, detested being addressed by his first name by anyone not holding at least a doctorate. This was not the time to show pique, however. Now was the time for well-played humility. "Golly, John," he started, "I am not really sure about this new-fangled stuff. I think we ought to get an expert's opinion. You know Dr. Johnson is a board-certified internist, and this should really be his bailiwick. Why don't we ask him? He's the expert. I mean, I'm all for new medicine as long as it's safe for the hospital and the patients. Why don't we let Dr Johnson decide?"

There's the pitch, he thought, a fast ball with a curve to the left and…

"That's an excellent idea," said the farmer board member, to a chorus of agreement.

…a hit and out of the park, and out of my hair, concluded Dr. McAbee to himself with satisfaction.

"Dr. McAbee, would you be so kind as to explain the board's predicament to Dr. Johnson and ask him to look into the matter for us? We'll abide by whatever he recommends."

Dr. McAbee did his best to look humble. "Gentlemen, I think this is a wise choice, and I will plead the new doctor's case with Dr. Johnson."

Cornelia Merry's upstairs parlor had been converted to the doctors' lounge in the Merry Hope Memorial Hospital. This is where Dr. McAbee found Dr. Johnson ponderously dictating a history and physical. The secretaries who took dictation for the hospital hated Dr. Johnson. His work-ups took hours to type and often ran many pages.

Such was the case this morning while Dr. McAbee waited for the old man who was so occupied with a lengthy dictation that he had yet to acknowledge McAbee's presence. Dr. McAbee had time to finish skimming the Journal of the AMA and consume two cups of coffee by the time Dr. Johnson ponderously finished his highly detailed dictation, failing to hang up the Dictaphone immediately. Thus the harried transcriptionist duly typed ". . . and so it appears that virtually all this patient's symptoms could be traced back to long-standing laxative abuse and massive obfuscatory constipation. . . and how are you this morning Dr. McAbee?' before she realized that the tale of one woman and her bowels had finished.

Dr. Johnson was a dignified formal member of the old school. He addressed everyone, including his peers and more surprisingly, his patients, even regardless of their race or social status, by their titles and surnames. McAbee tried to play the role of confidant to Dr. Johnson. "Horace," he confided, "I'm concerned about that new boy, Wilder. He's asked the board of trustees for permission to perform exercise stress tests at the hospital, and they just don't know how to respond."

"I told them you're probably our best expert, what with being boarded in internal medicine. We're concerned about the boy's qualifications and of course concerned most of all for the safety of the patients. We were wondering what you thought and felt about the matter."

Dr. Horace Johnson was about as excited at being addressed by his first name by Dr. McAbee as Dr. McAbee was at having his first name used 'by some hick farmer' as he'd groused later. This indiscretion of informality and this alone gave Dr. Johnson pause. He knew where McAbee stood on losing patients and would not give him the satisfaction of an immediate reply after the implied slur of his informality.

"Let me study on it for a little while… Jim," he answered, the dig going right over James McAbee's head. "This family practice specialty stuff is new to me. I want to give the new Dr. Wilder a fair hearing." Nonplussed at the lack of what he assumed would be a quick and visceral negative reply, McAbee nevertheless left secure in assuming that the issue would never be in doubt.

The next Saturday afternoon, Dr. Johnson took the opportunity of a slow patient day to drive out to the old house Chris was attempting to restore. Two puppies tussled on the ground near a sandbox where a toddler was happily pouring sand into his diaper. Chris was attempting to replace a windowsill that had rotted out. Carpentry was not his strong point.

Dr. Johnson paused during a muttered stream of profanity before slamming the door of his ancient Cadillac to announce his arrival. Chris looked up in surprise at the formal figure of Dr. Johnson, even on Saturday dressed in a three-piece suit and watch chain. "Good morning, Dr. Johnson. You caught me by surprise." Chris came forward, extending his hand, looked at it, and thought the better of it. "Excuse the mess; would you like to come inside? "

"That would be most pleasant, Dr. Wilder, I haven't been in this home since the last occupant, a patient of mine, died several years ago."

"Call me Chris, please. Halstead, Osler, get away from there." He grinned apologetically and scooped up the two puppies in mid-charge toward the fresh leather of Dr. Johnson's shoes. He held open the screen door for Dr. Johnson, and, as he cleared the door, he tossed the two puppies back in the yard. He paused a moment and glanced at the baby still inefficiently shoveling sand into the diaper and shook his head.

"Ashley, we have company, and the baby is still outside and kind of sandy. Since I'm coming in, you might want to tend to him." Ashley paused long enough in the kitchen, wiping her soapy hands to shake Dr. Johnson's hand and plowed through the screen door. Within seconds, Ashley's muffled anguished cry was blotted out by the baby's wails, as Ashley saw the sand filled the diaper.

Dr. Johnson smiled. "Interesting names for your dogs.," he ventured.

"Yeah, " answered Chris. "The greats of medicine and surgery. Medicine kind of runs in the family. My great uncle studied under Osler, and my wife's grandfather was starting Johns Hopkins the year William Halstead died. But neither of my parents were in medicine so I'm kind of picking up the tradition again."

"Indeed, said Dr Johnson. "Yet you find yourself in family practice and neither the specialty of medicine nor surgery. "

"I think family medicine is what medicine should be," said Chris, somewhat defensively. "Not a lot of high technology whiz-bang at the sacrifice of people caring for people. I think if Osler had it to do over again, he too would do family practice."

Dr Johnson raised an amused eyebrow. "Do tell. "

Chris was warming to his subject, "Osler believed in the interaction of the patient, his environment and psyche. After all it was Osler who said, 'It is more important to know what patient has the disease has than what disease the patient has.' As it is now, we have a doctor for every part and a part for every doctor."

Dr. Johnson was impressed, despite himself. "But why family practice?" he asked. "And why," he gestured outward to the impoverished community, "here of all places?"

"What better place to be than where the need is?" Chris shot back. "It's kind of like the exchange between Emerson and Thoreau when Thoreau was jailed for not paying taxes that might support slavery. Emerson said, 'David what are you doing IN there?' and Thoreau answered, 'Ralph, what are you doing OUT there?'"

"Interesting," said Dr. Johnson, "tell me, to change the subject, I understand you're asking the hospital to buy a treadmill so that you can do exercise testing. I've always used the Master's two-step approach myself and done just fine. What good will all your fine gimmicks do you here?"

Chris was suddenly wary. He furrowed his eyebrows. "I guess the treadmill is a refinement of the other. An exercise test allows you to road test the engine. But with a treadmill, one can standardize the quantity and duration of exercise for later comparison. Also, the EKG monitor can be watched for life threatening arrhythmias and EKGs can be gotten at regular intervals. You can not only screen for heart disease, but also, by comparing standardized tests, see if medication is helping the patient beyond the placebo effect.

Furthermore, you can continuously monitor the patient and compare heart rate and blood pressure once an adequate test is completed. Additionally, thallium dye and/or ultrasound can further refine the results. We learned how to do them in our residency."

"Bravo, most impressive!" Dr. Horace Johnson's wintery face creased in an uncharacteristic smile. "Dr. Wilder, when the machine comes in, I certainly hope you'll help familiarize me with its workings."

Chris looked up, surprised. "Well sure, Dr. Johnson. I'd be honored."

Dr. Johnson aged face creased a rare smile, "Call me Horace."

Chapter 15

The building of the Interstate was bringing change to the counties along its path. Metropolitan Charlotte was growing out into the rural communities and bringing change with it. One of the changes was an influx of new industry along its path. One of the new executives, Dr. Wilder's patient Ross Sanderson, a pudgy mid-fifties smoker whom he'd seen yesterday at the office, was now trudging along on the treadmill, while Dr. Wilder monitored the controls. The set-up had changed over the years since he had first taught Dr. Johnson how to use the equipment. This model was computerized so one could preselect the speeds and elevations and could check blood pressures and EKGs at set intervals. Chris's main job was to push the on/off button and shout encouragement to the patient and be available in case something went wrong.

The machine droned on stage I, then II and then through the remainder of stage III. Dr. Wilder looked up at the monitor, a skip showed on the monitor. The tracing continued along and then a jerk in the rhythm, an extra beat called a PVC showed. Chris leaned forward to study the monitor. An isolated PVC didn't mean that much but there was another. In a few moments, the PVCs started raining down every fourth beat. The beats in between them began to shift and slur in a recognizable pattern that showed Mr. Sanderson's heart had worked beyond the capacity of his diseased arteries to provide him oxygen.

Dr. Wilder's finger jabbed at the "stop belt" and 'print EKG' buttons for immediate readings. The EKG tech eyebrow's rose as she glanced at the monitor.

"All right, Mr. Sanderson," Chris said smoothly, "I think we got you going fast enough for today. Any chest pain or shortness of breath?"

Despite obviously gasping for air, Sanderson shook his head in vigorous denial. Sanderson dried off and put back on his shirt while surreptitiously rubbing his chest. Dr. Wilder invited him to sit beside the desk while he

carefully explained the problem, showed Sanderson the skips and segmental changes that suggested poor cardiac circulation, and reviewed statistics. He then went on to discuss the next steps including cardiac catheterization in Columbia or Charlotte and possible treatments.

Sanderson looked shocked and started to shake his head in denial. Interrupting, Dr. Wilder began a recitation of what the EKG techs called *Dr. Wilder's patented story of the stubborn young father who wouldn't listen leaving bereft young children'* story. He then told Sanderson he wanted to make an appointment with a cardiologist for a cardiac catheterization as soon as possible. A chastened Sanderson agreed.

Chris dialed the cardiology group from memory. They agreed to see Mr. Sanderson the next day. Dr. Wilder and Mr. Sanderson were walking through the ER together when the news came over the radio of the plane crash in Charlotte. Sanderson pulled his cigarettes out of his pocket and tossed them in the trash as he headed for the door shaking his head. It would be the next day before the Gulfstream was found and Iris would call. He'd remember bitterly that he'd offered a silent thanks at the time that the crash was not in his jurisdiction

In view of how crazy things got at this point, it is not odd that procedure was not strictly followed. Ordinarily the FAA would have taken complete responsibility for the investigation, including postmortem examinations. But in the wake of one of the worst mid-air collisions in US history involving two separate planes falling into two different states and legal jurisdictions, it was no surprise, in retrospect, that Dr. Wilder was called. After all, the majority of the victims, over 300 people, fell in North Carolina at the junction of three counties. Only two landed in Craven County, South Carolina. It was, in fact, not until the next day that the South Carolina victims were found.

Shortly before the discrepancy in plane parts and victims was noted, a distressed farmer in northern Craven County called about a UFO crashing in a distant cow pasture. Two cows had been killed. The rest of the herd spooked. It took until after dark to round them up, and until the next morning to determine what had happened. The farmer first called the county extension office to see if UFOs were known to carry any germs hazardous to livestock. While he waited for the county agent to arrive, he noticed a hole in his cow shed roof and went to look inside. There he found the garishly clad body of the pop artist from New York. The appearance of the body and the clothes the artist affected did little to change the farmer's opinion as to the otherworldly origin of the craft; nevertheless, he called the coroner's office directly.

The Merryville Rotary club met on the 2nd Wednesday of the month. Each member was responsible for providing a speaker. When Chris Wilder had his tum, he usually did not bring in a speaker, but preferred to give a talk of his own on some topic he thought important to the community. He had been planning to address the critical issue of unwed and teen-age motherhood. Considering the recent murder and fire at the Jaycee hut, he decided a change in topic was in order. Dr. Wilder instead opted for a more appropriate discussion on the role of coroner and of scientific evaluation of evidence. From a politician's point of view, of course, this topic was also damage control. It provided an excellent opportunity to say, without saying, that his job was to identify victims, their cause of death and to rule on the nature of the death, be it natural, accidental, homicide or suicide. Actually, finding the perpetrators Dr. Wilder noted was a job for county and state law enforcement.

A few hastily grabbed stock slides made up in grisly detail for Chris's lack of time for preparation. The inevitable question-and-answer period at the end gave him a chance to sniff for theories and rumors on the murders, the arson and the plane crashes floating in the community without commenting directly on the cases at hand.

Rumors ran the gamut from drug smuggling to single psychopathic killing to satanic cults. As the spirited discussion wound down into repetition of previously stated ideas, Chris's coroner's beeper chimed softly, while still on the podium, he muted the instrument and took an unfamiliar number down. The number was followed by Iris's special code, "911" That meant an emergency.

A voice in the back jokingly called, "Looks like someone bagged him another one."

 The last thing Chris wanted to do was to run out of a crowded Rotary meeting to the speculation of all. A small white lie was in order. He smiled and shook his head. "No, sorry, this one's medical. I think we've got a

mamma about to hatch." With that he smiled, waved and went to the phone to see what was up. The county offices couldn't really be blamed for simply passing on the farmer's request for the coroner without requesting further explanation. After all, he did relay the message: 'A UFO crashed in his pasture with dead cows and aliens.' The county office simply figured that Dr. Wilder's other medical skills, particularly those related to psychiatric committal, might be useful. Thus, it was that Chris drove to the farm, beating the extension agent who stopped to pick up some requested soil samples along the way.

The mailbox by a dirt drive almost covered in bushes said Dan McKeown. The mailbox's namesake stood beside it shifting anxiously from one boot shod foot to another. The brown of the foot gear tended to hide the color, if not the odor, of dairy herd by-products.

Dr. Wilder's Taurus was the third car Dan had frantically waved down while waiting for the county agent. The others had driven hastily off when Dan began explaining about his alien invasion. Dan led Chris quickly to the barn. As Chris approached the bucolic structure, he too noted a large man-shaped hole in the roof. Inside was the artist. Ironically, he had passed through the roof and landed, nearly intact, on a large mound of hay awaiting pitching into the cattle bins. Chris was once again struck by how well the human body can stand up to incredible punishment. Blank, wide-open and staring eyes bulged from a bluish face that attested to hypoxia. The glued spikes of red and greenish hair still jutted up from the scalp. A shard of roofing board projected out of the body which was clothed in a silver jumpsuit. Other than the single board and a few flash burns, the body looked relatively unharmed.

"Fricking' Martians," muttered McKeown as he shuffled out of the barn. "If it ain't them, it's Mexicans or Russians, it's always somebody trying to get your stuff." Dr. Wilder later spent some time explaining about the 'aliens' to an irate Junior Charles why he had not been called first.

The FAA, meanwhile, was up to its elbows in the first crash. A clerk taking Chris's message assumed the call was a misplaced reference to the first crash. After several hours with no response, Chris and the Sheriff's deputies carefully photographed the scene and took the bodies to the morgue. Grady's body was found essentially intact, floating in an irrigation pond, his leather flying jacket acting as a balloon holding the body up. Dr. Wilder supervised the drawing of blood and urine samples for toxicology and drug screening and left the matter to Dr. Sayaad, who promptly re-bagged the bodies and shuffled them off to the medical school.

Ironically, the steering column had been in Grady's hand all the way down to the pond. There it was finally released and sank to the bottom washing off the drug that had been carefully applied. No one associated the cow's occasional strange behavior for the next few weeks with the wheel that was eventually recovered by divers. The routine toxicology screens failed to find a reason for Hawkins's behavior. Suicide was Dr. Wilder's best guess. Thus, it was that nobody associated the mid-air collision with the strange events that were taking place in Craven County.

Chapter 16

The Merryville Country Club, like so many other things in Merryville, was owned by the Merry Mills corporation. When recruiting executives after World War II, the company found it difficult to entice executives to come to a rural place that offered none of the amenities like tennis, swimming pools or golf. The corporation first inveigled the city to build tennis courts on city property. The city had heard that tennis courts were usually clay, so they simply brought in a bulldozer and scraped off the requisite-sized square. Next, they took the volleyball net the church leagues used and cut down the poles and sank them in concrete. The mill executives were not amused at the muddy mess that ensued. Only the mill families were happy to use the "children's" volleyball court.

The company got desperate as the post-war expansion took off. Lacking in managerial staff, supervisors and other needed staff Merry Mills, Inc. finally took the bull by the horns, bought the land, and built a nine-hole course, pool, two paved tennis courts, and club house. Chris entered the club house the following weekend ready for a stiff drink.

Chris was an anomaly among doctors. He didn't play golf. He didn't even like golf. Ashley, an avid golfer, had been horrified to learn that she had married a non-golfer. "But I thought ALL doctors played golf," she'd grumped on learning the news. It was for Ashley and for maintaining and advancing his social standing in what passed for the upper class in Merryville that Chris eventually, reluctantly, joined the Merryville Country Club. He eventually found it a helpful place to meet and have a drink

The club house was a fifties vintage cinderblock building that eventually had been brick veneered and wood paneled inside. The floor tiles were chipped from the constant wear of golfer's spikes. One small patch of carpet in a comer under two easy chairs marked a disastrous effort at trying to carpet the place.

As Chris walked in for a drink, the usual Friday evening after-golf group was gathered near the fireplace. Father Bob, sans collar, waved Chris over. "Come join us. He smiled in congenial welcome waving to the drinks around the table, "You know what they say about Episcopalians. Where four are gathered, a *fifth* can be found."

Chris smiled at the long-standing joke and nodded to the bartender who set out to make the usual bourbon and Coke. He settled in among the little group as the waiter brought the drinks. The group today consisted of Chuckie Peterson, John Gaskins, the Orr brothers, and Father Bob. All of them were members of St. Andrews church.

The Orr brothers were Charles and Ladson. Charles was another family practitioner and the Wilder family doctor. Ladson was an attorney in town. Oddly enough, Chris was much closer friends with Ladson than Charles. Chuckie Peterson did a little bit of everything--insurance, real estate, apartment managing. John Gaskins owned one of the two pharmacies in town. Chuckie Peterson looked up as Chris sat down.

"That's the source of our trouble!" he exclaimed. "Like I was saying. I can't sell houses in a town where people are getting slashed, chopped, smashed, and crashed. Jeez, in the mill villages you can't even give houses away. Those houses aren't worth much in good times. Lately, I've had two families who've had me trying to sell their homes just up and leave 'em sitting there." Chuckie took a long drag on his cigarette. I had five more calls today alone to put houses up for sale in the villages. The place looks like a "FOR SALE" sign farm.

Ladson looked sympathetically at Chris. Of all the people there, he probably knew best how much pressure Chris was under. "Any luck so far?"

Chris shook his head. "No witnesses, no motive, nobody's talking, and everybody is scared. And then these plane crashes. At least nobody cut up the pilot except himself. God, I'm just glad the big plane made it over the state line. But oh my God, what a disaster! He picked despairingly at the lining of the chair's arm. "You wouldn't believe how mad the FAA people were about me retrieving those bodies. Hell, they didn't even show up until midafternoon. What was I supposed to do, let 'em lay there and rot?"

Father Bob let Chris rant on a little farther. He had once been castigated by a little old lady in the congregation for attending these Friday sessions. But, as he'd told this judgmental parishioner, "I'm the shepherd. I'll have to go where the sheep are if I'm to help them."

"OK Chris, you've dumped on yourself long enough," he admonished. "You're doing your job; you've called in expert help and no one is getting anywhere any faster than you. Furthermore, if you keep wallowing in self-pity you *are* going to miss something you shouldn't."

Chris looked up, "Like what?

"Dinner." Bob answered. Sometimes the sheep need to be fed as well as watered, he thought. "Come on. I gotta go too. I'll see you to the car."

As they walked out in the cool evening air, Chris turned to Father Bob. "You're a priest," he said, "Maybe you can help me."

Bob raised an eyebrow, adopting a mock-pious mien, he placed his hand on Chris's head and murmured "Bless you, my son." In a louder voice he asked, "There, did it help?"

Chris at least smiled. "No, different kind of help: information."

"Information?"

"Yeah, on cults, and Satan worship, exorcism, and things like that. "

"Oh, "Father Bob replied with a raised eyebrow, "Kind of like 'know thine enemy' and stuff like that? "

Chris nodded. A look of dead seriousness stopped Father Bob in mid-stride.

"Our Catholic brethren are usually a little more up on this than I am. St. John's, however, is priest-less at the moment. Episcopal priests are forbidden to attempt things like exorcism. I certainly wouldn't want to try. What did you have in mind?" he asked.

Chris shook his head, "I don't need an exorcism, I just know. something bad is going on in these murders. They have a ritual feel to them. I hadn't made a big deal of it to the press, but I cannot account for the lost blood in four of the murders. What we found at the sites was not enough to fill even one of the bodies we found. Someone has drained them and carted the blood away, and I don't know why or where. At least that damn plane crash didn't have anything to do with the rest of it, thank God. "

Chris shivered involuntarily.

Father Bob noticed. Suddenly he felt very cold himself.

They finished the walk to the cars in silence. Bob stood watching, hands deep in his pockets against the cold, as Chris fumbled for the keys to his car.

As Chris opened the door of the Taurus, a thought struck Father Bob, and he ambled back over to the car. "Say, Chris, demons, cults and devils are not really my thing, but there is a member of the ministerial association who is interested in this stuff. He is convinced that this cult stuff is Satan's revival in the world. He's sure the trend is coming from California. He collects information on all this."

"He wanted to give a talk on it to the ministerial association, but his warmup was so gory we begged off. He might be able to give you some help. Father Bob took a card out of his wallet and wrote down a name and number. "Reverend John Mosley is his name. He's out of town until next week but would probably be thrilled to talk to you. I'd be a little general about why and what you want to know though if you catch my drift. Otherwise, your inquiries might end up in next week's sermon."

Chris thanked Father Bob. The two separated into the chilly fall air and each drove home to the warmth of house and spouse.

Chapter 17

When Chris and Ashley bought the old Victorian house on Chesterville Street, it was a mess. Chris and Ashley sorted out an interminable number of boxes. The days were still hot, and the house was not yet air conditioned. Open windows provided no comforting breeze. Tempers were short as the arguments over where to put what flared into increasingly louder snaps of temper. The neighborhood was filled with gargantuan, somewhat run down, Victorian homes of Merryville's largely departed gentry. Chris and Ashley received a bit of a shock, when one holdout from that era, a Mrs. Lewis from down the street, had wandered in two days after they moved in and asked for him by name.

She tottered into the living room clutter and exclaimed, "Well, you must be Dr. Wilder and Mrs. Wilder. I knocked at the back door, but you probably couldn't hear me, so I just came in. I wanted to introduce myself and be your first patient in Merryville. I'm Dolly Lewis." As she extended her hand, Chris reached up to shake it. At the last second, she turned it over and continued. "I think my arthritis is flaring up a little. See where my wrist is swelling."

Chris and Ashley shared a look. He stood and carefully examined Mrs. Lewis's wrist. He asked a few questions as to allergies and major medical problems and then dug through a few boxes for a prescription pad without luck. Finally, Mrs. Lewis offered the number of a local pharmacy, and Chris dialed the number. After a few minutes to work through the introductions, Chris asked the pharmacist to give Mrs. Lewis a prescription for a mild arthritis medicine. He then encouraged her to come into his new office in the next few weeks so he could make up a chart on her and see how the medicine was helping. Mrs. Lewis tottered around the house recounting various social functions that had occurred in each room. Her memory extended through over seventy years. Eventually she turned to Chris and Ashley, and said "Well, I guess I've troubled you enough. I just think it is so nice that as we old folks die off, your younger people are buying up our houses and filling them with children. I just hope you last longer than the Smiths down the street," she mumbled half to herself.

"Excuse me?" prompted Chris.

"Bob and Emily Smith, a couple doors further up the street." Mrs. Lewis's face was crossed with a look of momentary confusion. "Oh, I guess that was before your time. They're gone now." She cleared her throat. "The Smith's bought the old Parson's manse that was up the street. They were going to restore it in the grand old way and make what they said would be an elegant bed and breakfast. Only they had never taken time to learn about each other. They fought like cats and dogs through the whole renovation. If he wanted red, she wanted green. If he wanted to modernize inside, she wanted bric-a-brac. The day they finished the house they split up," Dolly sighed. "The house broke them up but kept them together until it was done. In the end, they both left town and the house burned soon after. The city bulldozed the site. Such a dreadful scandal."

Dolly paused and re-seated her glasses firmly on the end of her nose. "You know, it's funny," she said with a penetrating look over her trifocals which she pushed down her nose. "People fighting over sticks and boards and plaster when there's so much love needed in the world. I regret the time I wasted arguing with my late husband more than anything else." Dolly looked around the walls at memories only she seemed to see. "I so often think that he and others are watching us, loving us and waiting for us up there while thinking how the little things we fight about here on this earth are so stupid."

Dolly's voice faded almost to a whisper. Suddenly it strengthened again, "But then I'm just a crazy old lady…" she finished and shuffled out the way she came. After being a loyal patient of Chris's for about several years she died peacefully in her sleep. But "Dolly's watching" became a by- word for peace in the inevitable marital squabbles. It held them together through working on the house, Ashley's alcoholism and then some.

Their house was a Queen Anne monster with six bedrooms, three baths and a total of fifteen rooms. Ashley saw it when they toured Merryville as a possible practice location while Chris was finishing his residency. She had fallen in love with the neighborhood and the house. Both reminded her a little of Charleston. As the house had been vacant for several years, it sold for a song. It was in an older neighborhood, and few doctors lived anywhere nearby. Most had moved to a newer neighborhood close to the golf course. So many, in fact, that Quail Run was usually called Pill Hill.

The house proved to be Chris's nightmare. Before they moved in, they had a local contractor come by to give the Wilders an estimate. The contractor looked it over, shook his head and declined the job. "Cheaper to tear it down and start over," he opined.

Ashley was not dissuaded and convinced Chris to attempt the work saying, 'After all, you're a doctor. Isn't plumbing like urology, electricity like the nervous system and orthopedics like carpentry?" It took one bone shaking shock and he gave up on electricity the first week, a month later on the plumbing and finally after a year and a trip to the emergency room for a saw cut, he threw in the towel on the carpentry. They hired out each job to a small contractor as they progressed room by room, piecemeal.

While they had delegated much of the work out, Chris and Ashley continued to paint together. They still fought when they did it. The house almost ruined their marriage, but "Dolly's watching" got them through the rough spots.

Their marriage was again in trouble but this time the problem was Chris's increasing obsession with the series of murders. One evening Ashley met Chris at the door. She decided that the best defense was a good offense. "So," she asked in a conversational tone. "What will it be this evening? Shall we chat like normal married people and maybe even engage in a little hanky-panky? Or would you rather go up to your study for yet another night of obsessing over police reports and autopsies. If so, please remember to emerge occasionally even if only to snap at your loving spouse. I swear with the headaches you're giving me; I see more of Dr. Charles Orr than I do you. I think he's more interested in seeing me than you are. Of course, our insurance does pay him." She brightened mockingly. "Say, I wonder if I can buy husband insurance. If the first one bums out, I get another free!"

Chris's responding glare set the stage for a sullen dinner together, storm clouds rumbling around the kitchen. Medical marriages are always fraught with tension as conflict arises over time pressures, patient demands and family needs. One long-ago physician called medicine his mistress and was not far wrong. Chris now had a wife, a mistress and a murderer all competing for his attention.

As is so often the case, the fight later that evening broke out when he decided to make amends. After dinner, Ashley stalked off into the living room to her usual perch on the couch by the phone. Chris finished loading the dishwasher, started it and wandered out of the kitchen. Usually this is when he would head for the study. This evening he looked guiltily into the living room that Ashley had ornately decorated in high Victorian style. Ashley had already turned to the phone for companionship in the face of Chris's increasing withdrawal. Now she was engaged in an animated conversation. Chris always envied Ashley for her ability to form so many deep and lasting friendships when he counted so few people as truly his friends.

Chris came into the living room and sat down on the red Victorian style medallion couch next to Ashley and put his arm around her shoulder. Ashley glared at him a moment for the intrusion and then deliberately shrugged his arm off. And turned aside

Guilt flushed to anger, and Chris rigidly rose to leave. Ashley covered the phone with her hand and hissed, "That's it, you bastard, you ignore me for days and then come make a token effort when I 'm trying to talk to someone who really listens to me and cares about what happened to me today! Just run on back upstairs and sit with your bodies and bones, you ghoul! "

Not even in medical school or even during his internship had Chris felt the pressure that had been building on him these few months. Now the lid blew with unreasoning white-hot fury, Chris's hand slashed out and snatched the receiver out of Ashley's hand and slammed it down. Chris never knew who he hung up on that night, but the fight was just beginning. Like most doctors he took the high road, a variation of the theme "how dare you ask for my time when sick people need me?"

"I'm trying to help solve a murder here!" he barked, "No, not just a murder, but lots of murders. I'm under more pressure than you can ever dream about at your garden club meetings. You feel left out? I feel left out! I could use some support here too. My God, I feel this is killing me, but I can't let go with so much at stake." He paused, slightly surprised at his uncharacteristic loss of control. If he thought the pause would bring a placating response, he was wrong. Ashley immediately hacked back in the momentary silence.

"I'm trying to raise two kids who have decided that their father is a homicidal maniac in his own right. I just thank God they are both away at school now, so they don't see the towering wreck their father has become." The fight was developing into one of the most emotionally violent experiences they'd had since Ashley's alcohol intervention years ago.

"JEEZUS CHRIST I…" Chris began

Just then the phone jarred them both with its intrusive electronic demands. In what was a tribute to the habits of a long-standing medical marriage, Ashley answered the phone in a voice that betrayed none of the tension that sizzled between them.

"Dr. Wilder's residence. May I help you?" She listened for a moment. Then, without another word, stiffly shoved the phone at the silently raging Chris.

He snatched it with a glare, "Dr. Wilder here."

A worried young mother wanted her sick infant evaluated. Ordinarily, this was done after hours in the emergency room by the ER doctors. Virtually every doctor in town had an answering machine with essentially the same message: "The office is closed. If you have an emergency, please go to the hospital emergency room. Should you require admission, the ER staff will contact your local physician." The ER doctors, of course, hated this system as it added markedly to their workload

When Dr. Wilder first arrived in town, he had tried to answer every call and every request for after-hours care. This sort of total effort lasted almost as long as the exercise in do-it-yourself plumbing. He found that it was not physically possible to care non-stop for people twenty-four hours a day. The final incident that drove Dr. Wilder to quit was the patient who succinctly put it one night, "I've been so sick these last few weeks; I just couldn't get out of bed to come see the doctor 'til tonight and I couldn't sleep."

Talking however with this particular concerned mom, he learned that she'd already been to the ER the night before. She wanted "HER" doctor to check little Billy out since he was no better. On a moment's reflection, Chris was glad to have an opportunity to leave the fight with Ashley, which he was beginning to lose anyway. There are not many better ways to escape the doctor-versus-wife fight than to have to ride off into the sunset to stomp out disease and suffering. Neither of them had mentioned "Dolly watching."

At the emergency room, Dr. Wilder examined the baby with care. In addition to reviewing last night's X-rays and ER chart, he examined those places that served as likely hiding spots for infection, such as the ears and throat. He also looked at the baby as a whole. He watched the baby's level of energy, inquired about his appetite and feeding. Billy's mommy, like many, had overstated Billy's illness to secure Dr Wilder's promise to come.

He looked at his watch. Seeing the child had taken only a few minutes, not enough time for Ashley to have calmed down yet. Chris decided to go check on a few of his hospital patients.

Dr. Horace Johnson was back in the hospital again. Now pushing towards the century mark, his long-standing robust health had finally begun to wear down in the last year. A series of respiratory infections finally led to the chest X-ray Dr. Horace Johnson would have ordered immediately on anyone but himself. The film told it all in an ominous irregular lesion in the left lung. Still as he wandered down the darkened hallways, Chris reflected that the radiation had shrunk the cancer a good bit, buying some time. This hospitalization was for a simple case of pneumonia. Nonetheless, Dr. Johnson had insisted on a do-not-resuscitate or 'NO CODE' order.

"Just in case," Horace had insisted, "I have what we both know is a terminal disease and I don't have long. I want to go without a lot of fuss or being hooked up to some wheezing blow bag while relatives who haven't seen me in years standby tearfully wondering what this care is costing them in inheritance." A large purple dot pasted on the front of the chart reminded the staff of the NO CODE order.

In contrast to the baleful message the dot gave, Dr. Johnson sat in a chair in his room fully dressed, looking much younger and robust than his age, only a deep and extended cough suggested his illness. He glanced up at the door and seeing Dr. Wilder's gaunt profile, carefully marked his place in a large medical text and set it aside. Despite an absurdly late retirement when his diagnosis was made, Horace Johnson still saw himself first and foremost as a doctor.

He followed Dr. Wilder's gaze toward the title of the book. "For years I moaned about all the reading I had to do for medicine. Now I finally have the time for something else, and I find that all that appeals to me is this literature. I thought I did it for work." Horace glanced at Chris's face in the half-dark of the room. Receptive eyes, trained by the years, missed little.

"Who dragged your cat through the mud, boy?" he asked. Chris smiled in spite of himself. Only Horace would refer to Dr. Wilder as a boy. Chris mumbled a disclaimer of standard doctor fare: late nights and overwork. Horace gazed at him with still sharp blue eyes multiplied in his trifocals. "Bullshit!"

Chris's head snapped up in surprise. In close to twenty years, he'd never once heard Dr. Johnson use any word stronger than 'nuts.' "You heard me," Horace muttered as a passing nurse poked her head in to see what was up. "Now give." Perhaps the surprise of Horace's profanity loosened his tongue or the stress of the fight earlier, but Chris unburdened himself.

"I feel so inadequate, " he mumbled in frustration. "Some doctors specialize in this coroner's work as forensic pathologists. They know all the tests and equipment. I keep wondering what procedure or test I've missed. Sheriff Charles is convinced that I'm to blame since I continue to fail to find the case-solving clue. I'm just not equipped for all this." he concluded miserably.

Horace Johnson looked at Chris fondly. "What does Iris Maynard say?" he asked. Chris looked up in surprise. Johnson continued. "You know for years, Iris was the brains, often the only brains, in the coroner's office. She also used to be my patient for decades until you got her to quit smoking with that hypnosis mumbo-jumbo." Horace leaned back in the bed expansively hooking his arms akimbo behind his neck. He smiled at Chris's attempts to demure before continuing. "Iris has been at the courthouse for over forty years. She's seen county executives, sheriffs and coroners come and go. She also knows most of the coroners and medical examiners in this state and the Southeast. She tells me you're the best she's ever seen in this hick town. If Iris says your 'okay', you're okay. And one more thing. Remember: You're new here."

Dr. Wilder opened his mouth to object. Dr. Johnson rode over him. "Chris, you'll be new here until the day you die here. These people have been here for generations. Heck, they look at the Merry family as *arrivistes*. Your children won't even be natives, though they'll be close."

"Iris's family has been here for generations. She grew up here, went to school here and married here. She knows details about this place that no patients would tell you in their darkest moment." Johnson leaned forward with renewed intensity. "The woman has a wealth of knowledge; spend some time with her. Now, as for what I think. Who else here in this little county is better equipped than you? It's not the tests or procedures. You have Sayaad for that don't you?"

Chris nodded.

"No," Dr. Johnson continued. "You have exactly the right instruments for this investigation. They're the same for any good family doctor. Not machines, or scopes or scanners. Your instruments are your ears, your eyes, your hands and especially your finely trained brain to look for patterns, meaning and connections amidst all this unrelated information. My God has medicine gotten away from all this?"

Dr Johnson nodded his head reassuringly, "You'll do okay, boy. You have the humility to ask for help when you need it, the energy to keep looking and the sense to know when you're on to something. If this psychopath can be caught, you'll catch him. Don't worry about Junior Charles."

Chris nodded his thanks. "I'll see you in the morning," he said huskily, emotion coloring his voice.

Horace shook his head ever so slightly. "Maybe, maybe not." Dr. Wilder turned back in surprise. Horace offered a depreciating smile. "Just one of those funny cold feelings hinting at mortality approaching. When you get my age, the wall at the end of the tunnel begins to loom in front of you. You ever heard that phrase, 'somebody steppin' on your grave?' Chilly feeling." Horace read the concern on Chris's face, as he stepped back towards Dr. Johnson who made a shooing motion saying, "Then again probably nothing, probably just a draft."

Chris looked hard at him. Experience told him that people who talked of impending death often were accurate prophets.

Horace appeared embarrassed and waved his hand again dismissively. "Forget it."

"Are you hurting or short of breath?" Chris asked. Dr. Johnson shook his head. He began to protest in earnest as Chris bent to examine him.

"It's just a goddamn draft," he muttered. He pulled a blanket around him effectively, blocking Chris's attempts to poke and prod. "I'll see you in the morning, okay?"

Chris nodded dubiously. He felt put off.

Ignoring the fact that he was still dressed, Horace reached up and turned off the lights and snuggled down in the chair. Only his shrouded form showed in the dim hospital night light. "Good night, Dr. Wilder," he said pointedly.

Dr. Wilder shrugged, scooped up the chart and headed back up the hall. After looking in on a few more patients, he sat at the nurses' station thinking hard. Finally, he decided to order just a few tests on Horace whether he wanted them or not. He grabbed the chart and set off down the hall to tell him.

"Dr. Johnson, Horace?" Dr. Wilder snapped on the light. The book was sprawled on the floor, pages bent. The blanket was an untidy heap on the floor. Eyes stared up, unseeing at the ceiling. He took in the scene at a glance. Quickly, he slid Horace from the chair to the floor for CPR. He blew two quick breaths. He'd need help. His hand jabbed towards the bedside nurse call button. His eyes landed on the chart he'd hastily dropped and its large purple DNR dot.

He paused for a moment. "Fuck!" he gasped halfway between a sob and a curse, "Fuck, fuck, fuck!" Then he slowly pulled out his stethoscope and listened intently. His shoulders dropped as his ears confirmed what his heart already knew. He pulled the blanket over the resting form. Stethoscope still dangling from his hand like a hangman's rope, he walked slowly up the twilight-colored hall.

The night was freezing as Chris dejectedly wheeled the Taurus towards home. The frigid dark seemed to Chris an ideal place for his depressed ruminations. Chris dimly recalled a bible verse 'let not the sun go down on your anger.' Father Bob had once preached one of his better sermons on this passage. Chris Wilder tried hard to live by that proverb. Tonight, he was simply too drained to try to finish the fight and break the news of Horace Johnson's death as well. Still, he did not want Ashley to read about it in the morning's paper. After some reflection, he wrote a note. It said: *"I am sorry about last night.*

I hope we can talk at length tonight and try to make some changes. I also have some sad but not unexpected news; Horace Johnson passed away last night. We'll all miss him."

Love, Chris"

The note looked inadequate, and it was. He could think of nothing else brilliant that came to mind in his exhaustion that would restore him to Ashley's good graces or bring the dead back to life. He left the note on the kitchen table, mounted the steps, and entered his study. He sprawled on the couch fully clothed and after a turn or two, grief and exhaustion took him.

Chapter 18

The next day was appropriately rainy, and Chris's shoes were muddy before he reached the car. The note in the kitchen was gone, so was Ashley. There was no reply. Chris's mood was echoed in the thunder that rattled in the mist. After sloshing through the gravel of their drive, he flopped down on the red velour seat of the Taurus wagon. He turned the car around and headed through the early morning gloom. On the way to the hospital, he remembered his conversation with Horace about Iris. He roused from his almost catatonic usual morning route to the hospital and veered off towards the courthouse.

Iris had said she was a morning person. "I like to come in early and get my 'real work' before the phones start ringing and the coffee gossip starts. When you're old and single, that coffee pot *is* your social life. That's why I keep it on my desk."

Wisps of mist and rain crept past the Victorian courthouse as Wilder drove up and parked. Red brick rose to heights of terra cotta pilasters. The courthouse began life as an opera house before the turn of the century. Opera failed in Merryville and now the upper windows of the building's former balconies with the seats removed, looked in on floors of boxes of mildewing records. From inside, the begrimed windows looked out on the town square like eyes clouded by cataracts.

Iris was pouring fresh water into a large coffee pot in a clearing on the corner of a cluttered desk. She looked up as a brightly polished brass bell tinkled as Dr. Wilder opened the door. A greening copper watering can stood guard by a tropical forest that crept up twelve-foot walls and threatened to take over the floor.

"Iris," Chris began. "One of these days, this tropical kudzu is going to eat you up and spit out the bones. We'll never find your body!"

Iris laughed a basso rasp. "Just look for the brown spot in all the green and dig there." She fixed Wilder with a speculative eye. "So, doc, what brings you out so early. Has good health broken out in Merryville to threaten that lavish lifestyle of yours?"

Wilder fixed her with a sad smile and told her of the death of her friend and physician. After a trip to the ladies' room and several hankies later Dr. Wilder told Iris of Dr. Horace Johnson's admiration for her insight.

"So, you see," he concluded, "I'm stuck. I'll take any suggestions you might offer. Horace said you've seen more in this county than anyone he knows. If you have any hints or suggestions, tell me, call me, tell me where the bodies are buried or how to avoid the land mines."

The brass bell tinkled again. Iris bustled forward to assist a farmer looking for the county assessor's office. Task finished; she turned back to Dr. Wilder. "Doc, I'd love to tell you who did it."

"So would I," Wilder muttered.

Iris skirted the desk and picked up the watering can.

"Doc, I can think of two things right now that are worth you knowing about. One about the job, one about the town."

Wilder raised a querying eyebrow. She paused and looked down while watering a huge fiscus. "First, the town. The Merrys own almost everything. What they don't own, they influence."

"Are you saying…"

"What I'm saying," Iris cut in, "is that it doesn't pay to piss off the Merrys and their relations- unless you're another Merry." Here she gave Dr. Wilder a crooked smile before continuing, "The other is about the job. Everything is connected to something else. You keep telling me you're a family doctor and that you look at the illness in the context, a network of family, occupation, social and psychological relations. Don't spend too much time looking at items in isolation. Junior Charles talks about the chain of evidence-connections. You instead look at individual clues like each might be the Holy Grail. They're not, they're road signs. I've watched you in the coroner's office pouring over reports and bits of bone. Don't look so much at the signs, look at the road that connects them.

The bell tinkled again and then again. Iris set down the can and turned towards the door. Out of the side of her mouth she concluded, "Doc, get out of the lab and the office and out into the world. That's where this nutcase is wandering around right now." She gave him a nudge towards the door. "That's where you'll find him."

Stopping by his hospital mailbox, he found a manila envelope with his name on it with a return address of the medical university in Charleston. Inside was a brief report of the forensic examination of the bones taken from the late Jaycee Hut. The report read:

John Doe case file #?

Craven County

Retrieved is a nearly intact skeleton from a fire occurring in the Jaycee Hut of Merryville, S.C. Missing five phalanx bone from the hands along with a carpal and three metatarsal bones. Examination of skeletal structure shows the victim to have been a white male of 30 (+/- years). Evaluation of dental structures reveals poor dentition with several remaining teeth exhibit large caries with bone resorption. Only one filling is intact, and it has marked cracking consistent with advanced age of the filling.

Oh well, thought Chris, so much for tracing this guy by his dental records. Now what? No fingerprints, no dental records, no picture, nothing. The report continued,

Examination of the individual bones reveals a cleavage of the C-6 vertebra. Grooving of the bone indicates the blow was struck from the anterior position. An old fracture of the left ankle is noted.

There are also more recent fractures of ribs 7,8 and 9 on the left that appear about four to six weeks old. Estimated height of the patient is 5'11" weight, 200 lbs.

There was a much longer report attached enumerating weights of a few mostly burnt organs and pathology but the report on the ribs, at least, was a little something he could pursue. Although there was no definitive care other than pain management for rib fractures, the pain was usually sufficient to cause rib fracture patients to seek medical attention. Although the media would publish information on the particular injuries, Dr. Wilder found it more helpful to informally call doctors in the area and talk doctor-to-doctor. Often the personal touch spurred memories that otherwise went unexamined.

Dr. Wilder would send out a note for the doctors at Craven County Memorial asking if they'd had any male patients of this description in the last month or so with fractured ribs. Dr. Wilder would also make a point of calling all local the radiologists who read X-rays for a living. If an X-ray was taken of this patient, and with the malpractice situation the way it was, Chris thought it likely that a radiologist had looked at the film. One of the many radiologists would have the diagnosis on their computer billing services. Dr. Wilder could ask them to provide him a list of all the male patients who had rib fractures in the last two months. In the five-county area surrounding Craven County, each hospital had only one or two radiologists; his research would progress quickly. Across the border in growing Charlotte, North Carolina, almost a dozen hospitals, the work would go a little slower.

Chris placed the file back in the folder and wrote "rads" on the cover as a reminder, placed it back on the shelf and went on down the hall. He had come in early to make rounds because he had another hospital committee meeting. Hospitals were fertile breeding grounds for committees. The Joint Commission on Accreditation of Health Care Organizations mandated many of them. In larger hospitals, many doctors served on only one or occasionally or no committees. In small and rural hospitals, doctors might serve on as many as five or six, chairing two or three. Chris was lucky; he was on only four committees. He did, however, serve as chairman of three. Still, he counted himself lucky. He'd almost been elected Chief of the Medical Staff for a second time. Today, he would preside over the Medical Records and Utilization Review Committee.

Today's meeting was not much different than most meetings: in other words, stultifying boring. Dr. Wilder desultorily worked his way down the provided agenda. For most hospital committees, the doctors were nominally in charge, but it was the staff that actually knew what was supposed to transpire. Dr. Wilder called on staff members in rotation by the agenda.

First and most important from a billing perspective was the list of physicians behind in records. The medical records director reviewed the accounts of which doctors were completing and signing the hospital records in a timely fashion and those who were late and how many records were outstanding.

Several doctors would get form letters from Dr. Wilder to bring their charting up to current. Several other doctors, including Dr. Wilder would get reminders about signing orders called in during the night. Lastly, a few more docs whose charting was unacceptably tardy, would be getting a form letter that their admitting privileges were under threat. Next, under the watchful eye of Mr. Harris, the hospital administrator, Erin Roddy the Utilization coordinator rose and expounded on rates on excessive usage of hospital days and length of stays. All this data was duly transcribed to show evaluators from the Joint Commission that Merry Hopes Hospital was dedicated to high quality care and more importantly was qualified to receive Medicare payments.

The nursing home director then rose to complain about what Dr. Wilder imagined was the hundredth time that physicians were not making timely visits to the patients. The state of South Carolina and Medicare mandated visits every thirty days. Many doctors came once a month, often on the thirty-first day, if even then. This left the nursing home in chronic non-compliance. Chris gestured a little impatiently to move the discussion along as this story was told each month.

Next, the committee reviewed letters from oversight companies. These insurance company watchdogs ensured patients were not kept overlong in the hospital.

"The recurring joys of managed care," Administrator Harris muttered. Heads nodded up and down the table.

Strangely, the private insurance companies hardly ever complained about a stay that was too short. For Medicare, hospitals were paid by diagnosis, not length of stay. Medicare watchdogs, by contrast, didn't care how long the patients stayed, their concern was that the patient does not go home until they were in perfect condition. Thus, the committee reviewed the complaints about inappropriate care leveled by these watchdogs. Usually, the committee sided with the doctors.

The meeting finally wound down to the final item on the agenda: special reports and communications. Usually there were none. Chris read this item aloud, pro forma, as he pushed his chair back from the conference table. Time to press on into rounds. It was the look on Harris's face and an eye roll to the waiting lab tech that warned Chris to sit back down.

Jimmy Stinson, the head lab tech, waved his hand apologetically. "Excuse me sir, Dr. Sayaad asked me to bring up one matter." Dr. Wilder nodded for Jimmy to proceed.

"It's Dr. Orr, sir. He's on a testing binge again."

Chris sighed. Dr. Orr was noted for developing peculiar interests in a particular test. Once he'd read an article about a resurgence of syphilis. He'd then ordered syphilis tests on the next years' worth of patients. Another time, he'd gotten a whim to check daily blood sugars on everyone in the hospital.

One patient awaiting a nursing home bed had a blood sugar test every day for two straight months. They'd all been normal. "What now?" Chris asked.

"It's AIDS/HIV testing again, sir. "

Chris sighed. "What do you mean AIDS testing? I thought we got him to stop ordering those indiscriminate tests a year or so ago.

"Yes sir," Jimmy continued. "We have, of course, had a very few cases. Most people come from Charlotte, to get tested so that their results won't be known in their home state. Dr. Orr, however, has come up with a new wrinkle by devising a 'Blood Borne Pathogens panel' reflecting the new OSHA regulation about HIV, hepatitis B and C and the 'Universal Precautions' we're supposed to be implementing. Many of our less-educated patients come in asking to get their blood tested for diseases or as it is often called 'bad blood.' Chris nodded in recognition. Another reflection of patients' faith in blood tests.

"This panel is a variation on the OSHA regulations," Jimmy continued. "It's hepatitis A, B and C, syphilis, and HIV. He seems to be testing people almost at random. A lot of the blood comes from his office marked Jane Doe or some such. Some of it is from patients in our hospital. He's testing people with no known risk factors or contacts. He's testing people who aren't scheduled for surgery. It is getting hard to justify all these tests to insurers." Jimmy regretfully shook his head. "I doubt that any of these patients are getting the recommended posttest counseling."

Dr. Wilder sighed. He could feel Mr. Harris's gaze on him. There would be no getting around an unpleasant conversation with Dr. Orr. Still, Dr. Orr wasn't directly hurting anyone except financially but there was, of course, the problem of anonymous testing. South Carolina law required that all HIV positive tests be reported to the state. Jane Doe was not a reportable name. He'd have to discuss both the problems with Dr. Orr eventually, but he first had one avenue he wanted to pursue that could also help him procrastinate the confrontation.

"Jimmy, could you get me a list for the last six months of all the people Dr. Orr has tested? I 'd like to look at it." That should buy me a week or so, thought Dr. Wilder. Like most doctors, he was much better at healing than confronting, particularly one's peer. Not to mention the fact that Ashley and the kids were Orr's patients. He heard Harris mutter in frustration.

Dr. Orr wasn't that bright as doctors went, thought Dr. Wilder, but he sure looked the part. Very tall and athletic, Orr had a physique of a man half his sixty years. He kept trim from regular tennis and golf. His head was topped by a mane of silvery hair that gave him an air of elderly distinction. Although he was only eleven years older than Chris, he treated both the kids and Ashley with fatherly affection.

It wasn't long before word came, via the hospital grapevine, that Dr. Chris Wilder had asked for a list of people on whom Dr. Orr had ordered his Blood Borne Pathogens tests. Dr. Orr was only mildly annoyed.

Chapter 19

Ashley Wilder was proud of her role as a doctor's wife. As a product of the old Charleston gentry, she never thought to plan her own independent career. She had always planned to marry a doctor or lawyer as her mother had. Her mother had done both, in a time and society when divorce 'was not done.' Ashley had hoped to remain in Charleston or its environs, but several factors had conspired to push the acorn farther from the tree. First, of course, was her mother's divorce and remarriage. This little bit of scandal and the ensuing snubs from the insular Charleston society made her think twice about living in such a tightly knit world.

Then, there was the problem of her mother's alcoholism. Ashley's mother, Victoria, like Ashley, began college as the life of the party. As Victoria aged, the alcohol problem slowly worsened. Ashley's first introduction to her mother's alcoholism began with the minor scandal that erupted when Victoria had shown up at Ashley's graduation from a private girls' school roaring drunk and very loud before vomiting profusely on the headmistress. Very shortly after, Ashley's father divorced Victoria. This subsequent fall in Victoria's social stature, as well as finances, prevented Ashley from escaping to a private college such as Agnes Scott, Hollins, or Furman.

Instead, Ashley attended the ancient, newly public, and therefore much cheaper, College of Charleston as a day student. Subsequently she met the newly minted Doctor Chris Wilder as he began his residency.

Chris's Yankee heritage was not necessarily a detriment to Ashley. Her initial line of reasoning was that he could take her up north and away from Charleston for a fresh start. Although the idea of living surrounded by Yankees held little appeal. It was not until later that Ashley discovered that Chris Wilder was fleeing his personal issues with his parents up north. Meanwhile, Victoria continued the long slow slide of an alcoholic. Victoria's looks as well as her luck held for a while though, and she managed to snare an older lawyer. For a time, her drinking moderated, but eventually it began again to increase. Towards the end of Chris's family practice residency, Victoria's alcoholism had become hell for Ashley.

Ashley was an only child, so she had no one to share the load with except Chris. Ashley was too much the dutiful child to let her mother suffer the consequences of repeated intoxication. She spent large amounts of time rescuing her mother when the neighbors called to say she'd passed out drunk in the yard or had wrecked her car and was in jail for drunk driving. Amazingly, Victoria beat the rap time after time. She'd show up in magistrate's court or traffic court, dressed to the nines, clean and sober, and plead that her allergy medicine had reacted with "one little martini."

By the time Chris was ready to look for a practice site, the last place Ashley wanted to live was Charleston. Any place, even Merryville, seemed like heaven to her. Two weeks after Chris and Ashley moved to Merryville, Victoria missed the rotating bridge approaching Sullivan's Island. Ordinarily this would simply have resulted in getting bogged down in the ubiquitous pluff mud near the bridge, but Victoria was late to a beach party and was pushing 90 on the narrow run up to the bridge when she left the road. Airborne off the rise to the bridge, she demolished an ancient wooden guardrail and plowed into the channel. She drowned in the intercoastal waterway before the astonished bridge keeper could climb down and help her. Victoria's demise was almost a relief to Chris. Ashley, however, was stripped of the opportunity to 'save her mother.'

Soon however, Chris was forced to deal with Victoria's ghost. Ashley swore she would never become an alcoholic like her mother, but the stress and guilt of her mother's death soon pushed her into the escalating spiral that would lead to her own alcohol intervention years later.

Since stopping drinking, Ashley had become a new woman. She had not realized what hell her life had been until suddenly and miraculously the drinking stopped. Ashley, however, had one problem: she regarded herself as cured. She had faithfully attended Alcoholics Anonymous for two years following her hospitalization. Since then, her attendance became increasingly less frequent. She never much liked the meetings with their smoke-filled rooms. Many of the people were, in Ashley's opinion, much worse off than she.

Over a year had passed since Ashley had been to a meeting. In AA there is a saying: "Once pickled, always a pickle and never a cucumber again." Ashley never intended to take another drink, but she was beginning to think like a cucumber again.

The pressure on Ashley was beginning to build. When Chris felt pressured, he withdrew into himself. Ashley was the opposite. She needed to share her pain and frustration. Chris's coping method of building walls made Ashley's problems worse. She responded by building bridges to others. She also began to visit Dr. Orr for counseling.

Ashley had always enjoyed his fatherly care. Chris had always been frustrated that she would have Chris look at the children at night when they were ill, and then take them the next morning to Dr. Orr. When he asked her why she didn't just trust him, her response always infuriated him. "Well, I just wanted to make sure they'd make it through the night before I took them to their real doctor." While Chris understood that the doctor who cares for himself (and by extension his family) has a fool for a patient, he didn't see the problem with his treating colds and other minor matters. He never understood that as her peer, he could never give the same comfort the tall silver-haired Dr. Orr provided.

As Chris became increasingly obsessed with the killings, Ashley turned to Dr. Orr. who followed her concerns with interest. Along with many in the community, he too was interested in each new development in the bizarre serial murders. Ashley's increasingly frequent visits were, out of professional courtesy, never billed. Dr. Orr found Ashley a unique pipeline to the inside story. As the case progressed, Ashley's anxiety levels began to rise. Earlier Dr Orr had offered to give Ashley something mild to help her sleep. He knew Chris would disapprove, so he urged Ashley to keep the frequency of her visits and the use of medication to herself. Today, Ashley had come in with the latest chapter in her life story, which included the fight of two days ago, Dr. Johnson's death and Chris's newest determination that the rib fractures might lead to a clue to the Jaycee Hut murder victim.

The fight had brought much of what was wrong with the Wilder's marriage close to the surface. In Charles Orr's opinion, Ashley lived in secret terror that Chris would divorce her as her father had left her mother. If Ashley acknowledged her fear of abandonment to Chris, he might leave her.

Sitting across the massive mahogany desk from Ashley in his private office, it became obvious to Dr. Orr that Ashley could not believe her luck that Chris had not left her in the throes of her alcoholism. In her treatment, she had learned that while most wives hang on to an alcoholic husband, most husbands leave an alcoholic wife. Aside from her love for Chris, she also more calculatingly considered her status as a physicians' wife, a prize she was not willing to give up. "If only I could have kept my goddamn temper under control, this fight wouldn't have happened," she sobbed.

Doctors know there is an art to steering and controlling a doctor/patient conversation. Studies have shown that the average doctor interrupts a patient only seventeen seconds into the recitation of complaints. At this point, they begin steering the conversation to its quickest outcome. Although Dr. Orr was a master of such conversational guidance, for the moment, this time he simply listened to Ashley and let her talk and cry. He knew the therapeutic value of tears and consolation and despite an increasing back-up of patients, he let her recite the events without interference. He did, however, manage to make sure he'd gotten all the information he could without appearing nosy. Finally, he made a suggestion:

"I know that Chris doesn't approve of tranquilizers or nerve pills as such, but let me put you on something mild, so you won't be so stressed. It might help you tame your temper. You'll be able to deal with your husband and maybe even be able to give him some strength and support. I'll limit the prescription to run just until all this stress settles down. This way, I can help you both. It'll be our secret. It probably wouldn't be a bad idea to see if Father Bob couldn't do a little counseling with you. You know he has a little more time to work with you both, and perhaps Chris won't be embarrassed about talking about his problems with a peer."

Ashley nodded while she thought Dr. Orr's suggestion over. "Okay," she said. "I'll do it for Chris. I'm not ready to give up on him yet." Dr Orr smiled and wrote out a prescription.

"Chris has told me often that you offer him immense help and comfort and what pride he takes in his marriage to you. I think once this whole crazy affair blows over things will get back to normal." He tapped the completed prescription on the desk as he rose, "Remember…our secret," and he handed her the prescription. Dr Orr was aware of the therapeutic value of touch, and he cheerfully submitted as Ashley gave him a firm hug on the way to the door. "You'll see, life will sort its way out and it will eventually get better."

Outside, Janice, Dr. Orr's nurse waited, an armload of charts jiggling in her arms. She hated Ashley's lengthening visits. These long sessions threw their whole schedule in the toilet. Dr Orr turned to her as Ashley disappeared down the crowded corridor. "Is it as bad as it looks?" he asked.

Janice's answer was the same as office nurses everywhere, "Worse."

It was early evening before Dr. Orr finally won the race with his schedule and eased the last patient out the door. He walked back to his office and grunted softly as he lowered himself down in the large leather chair behind the desk. He slipped off an elegant leather shoe and massaged his foot while he peered around the office in satisfaction. The office, in a building that fronted the square of downtown Merryville, was richly decorated, even for a physician. Dr. Orr had had it specially decorated to his tastes. He didn't rent the building; he owned it. In fact, he owned the whole block. He was a very wealthy man.

Chapter 20

Dr. Orr's grandfather, Gerald Merry had three children: Gerald Jr., John, and Alicia. Gerald Sr. had proudly thought of Merry Mills passing Merry Mills to Gerald Jr. with John loyally assisting his older brother. Alicia, as a daughter, didn't really figure into his plans. Finally, the long-expected transition of the corporation passed to Gerald Jr. just as the elder Merry hoped. Gerald junior had a much larger passion for booze and women than the company, passions his brother John shared and encouraged. They began an indulgent spending spree.

Only sister Alicia resisted. She was easily outvoted. The resulting spending spree almost destroyed the Merry Mills Company and the family almost lost control of the company. Only death saved the company.

On Christmas Eve, the two brothers took a quick run to the liquor store to ensure an adequate weekend supply. They never made it to the all-night storefront. Their late-night excursions to the bootleggers were a common enough event that no one worried over their absence that night. Early Christmas morning, the police found their late model Ford wrapped around a scarred brown Merryville telephone pole. The remains were so badly pulverized as to preclude even a determination as to who was driving.

After a very brief period of insincere mourning, Alicia began the long quest to restore the family company. Her lifetime goal became to retrieve the squandered patrimony and rebuild her daddy's company. Her quest assumed a holy nature that Alicia imparted to her sons, Ladson and Charles. Alicia had long survived her husband, Dr. Charles Orr Sr. a dedicated physician who worked himself into an early grave. While a majority of the stock eluded them, the family had finally succeeded in re-asserting control of the company. Although not widely recognized in the community, executive staffing and control of the directors took place in a limited family setting. Charles Jr and Ladson alternated as chairman of the board and president of Merry Mills. A chief operating officer ran the company. Alicia contented herself as corporate secretary. Interestingly, the secretary could still occasionally outvote both president and chairman of the board.

Dr. Orr had only dim intimations of Chris Wilder's low opinion of him. He was, in fact, a knowledgeable physician. Through continuing education, he had kept up with medicine, and he was a charter member of the American Academy of Family Practice. He had managed the challenge of board certification without the residency training which had not been available when he had graduated from his one-year internship. Five times he'd passed the every seven-year test required by the Academy of Family Practice for his board certification.

He had also found time for other areas of interest. Since Ashley's near resurrection following her treatment for alcoholism, he had become quite interested in addictions. He attended classes and seminars on the subject and had even been one of the first to be certified by the American Society of Addiction Medicine. He also served as consultant to the hospital's small alcohol detoxification unit. He knew of Chris's concerns about sedatives, but he was confident in his clinical treatment plan. Ashley meanwhile returned home in a much better frame of mind. The pills were already helping.

Dr. Wilder's training path had been somewhat different as he began the internship and residency that would bring him to Ashley. In Detroit, 'A Monday Car,' is a term of derision. It implies that the workers are somehow impaired or ineffective at their task. Most often, they come back after the weekend too drunk or hungover, to do a decent job. The medical version of a Monday Car is a July intern. A July intern, fresh from medical school, is a collection of random medical facts wrapped with insecurities. July is not a good time to be in a teaching hospital.

In the fall preceding medical school graduation, twenty years earlier, Chris Wilder and other medical students fanned out to interview at teaching programs in their chosen specialties. At the time, internal medicine and surgery were the most popular. In later years, the preferred specialties became those that were more lucrative but less involved with the total patient--- radiology and ophthalmology and sub-specialties like gastroenterology and cardiology. Family practice was a new specialty in which few medical students could see much future or prestige. Chris found that there were not many family practice residency training programs to choose from. He had to travel far and wide to interview at the few family practice programs available. Then with interviews complete, he came home and waited for the Match.

The Match is one of the great crap shoots of all time. Each year, thousands of medical students and training programs list their preferences. A computer then matches residents and available spaces based on the priorities of each side. Both sides are honor bound to respect the results. In July, Chris Wilder, along with all the other newly minted MD's, began his training according to the dictates of fate, odds, and computer algorithms. In his case, it was the off to a residency in Charleston, South Carolina. It was during his first month there, Chris Wilder acquired his fascination with hypnosis and psychosomatic medicine.

The first month or so of an internship is probably the most stressful time for the physician-to-be. Medicine is both an art and a science. Medical school focuses heavily on the scientific and virtually ignores the softer, interpersonal artistic side. Four years of training- two years of basic science and two years of clinical exposure--grueling as they are, can never prepare a newly minted doctor for the responsibility for another human being's life. This stew of stress and new responsibilities and sleep deprivation combine to produce a very punchy group of junior doctors. In August of his intern year, Chris got his unique initiation into the Art of medicine. In addition to seeing patients in the hospital, family practice residents receive training in office care of patients. With each year, the amount of office exposure increases. During the internship year, first year residents see only a few patients one afternoon a week. Chris Wilder had seen his two patients at the family practice center that Wednesday. His work had been reviewed by the attending faculty physician, and he was at loose ends sitting at the nurses' station trying to remain awake while reading a massive textbook on internal medicine.

Benjamin Robinson, a new third (and final year) year resident was enjoying being at the top of the heap again. He was chuckling as he walked through the nurses' station wearing a black academic robe and sunglasses. A scrub suit, the official attire of experienced residents, peeked out below the billowing gown. Several syringes and some IV tubing competed for space in his arms with the large book he was carrying. Chris's look of obvious curiosity was a beacon waving Ben in. "Ever been to an exorcism, kid?" he asked congenially. Chris shook his head and debated whether lack of sleep was interfering with his hearing. Robinson repeated the question.

Chris peered at the spine of the massive book Ben carried. It was, as he suspected, a Bible.

"Are you interested in seeing psychosomatic medicine at its finest?"

Chris nodded perking up; he was hooked. "Sure, I'm just sitting here rereading Harrison's textbook of medicine. What are you really doing?" he asked as he took the Bible that had been precariously perched on top of Ben's armload of medical equipment.

"Like I said, kid, kind of an exorcism. Ben led the way down the hallway containing the resident's exam rooms. The hallway was lined with cheery posters promoting good health habits. At the end of the hall, he entered the last room, which typical of residents' exam rooms, was a cramped space with an exam table, a small desk and two chairs, one for the patient and one for the doctor. The walls were a uniform drab lime green. A blanket hung over the window darkening the room which suggested that this was not Ben's first equipment-gathering excursion. Amid the clutter, a metal IV stand competed for space in the tiny room. Incongruously there was also a huge brass candlestick with a towering unlit paschal candle. A large and somewhat gory plaster crucifix hung on the wall. The healthy habits poster which the crucifix supplanted was on its side in the corner. A tape recorder and cassette rested on the tiny desk.

Chris laid down the Bible and peered through the gloom to see the title of the tape-a recording of Gregorian chants. "You're serious?" he shook his head doubtfully.

Like many residencies, the examining rooms were equipped with cameras so faculty could monitor the residents' care of the patients. and their patient interactions. Chris wondered how the faculty would feel about this effort and glanced up at the camera. A purple lectern pall with an embroidered gold cross, presumably borrowed from a church, hung tidily over the camera.

Chris had heard of residents trying new and untested therapies on their own. Occasionally these experimental, unapproved forays ended residents' medical careers before they even got started. Nervously, he glanced at the door and began to back towards it. Ben saw his glance and understood the panic, but he needed Chris to help, so he pushed himself out of his seat, extending a restraining arm.

"Whoa, whoa, here wait a minute," he urged. "It's not really an exorcism. It just needs to look like one while we carry out the therapeutic treatment prescribed for the patient. He gestured to the syringes and IV tubing. "Let me explain. You're not from around here, are you?" he drawled

Chris shook his head, unwilling to so much as open his mouth before he could get away.

"We have a sub-culture here", Ben began, "of Sea Island African Americans with their own heritage, traditions, beliefs and even speech. Have you heard Gullah spoken yet?

Chris nodded. He'd been walking down a hall in the hospital when a black man came up to him and asked Chris a rapid fire, completely incomprehensible question. From the upward inflection ending the sentence, Chris could tell that what he'd asked was a question, but none of the words made any sense to Chris. The man tried twice more, then threw up his hands and went on down the hall. Chris assumed the man was simply drunk until he saw a patient in the emergency room the next day who spoke the same incomprehensible language. There a nurse had seen his look of utter confusion. To Chris's surprise, the nurse walked over and replied with the same accent. A conversation ensued with the nurse providing translation. Later, Chris found out that this patois of African American and highly accented English called Gullah to be common in Charleston.

Ben continued. "These people have their own belief system about medical care. In addition to what we think of as normal medical care, these Gullah speakers have a whole alternative care system called root medicine."

"Root medicine?" Chris asked sarcastically with all the superiority only a first year resident could muster. "You mean like voodoo and all that stuff? They should see a real doctor!"

"They do," Ben responded, "when all else fails. Haven't you seen any patients with a homemade wire bracelet around their left ankle or a penny drilled and hung around the neck?

"Well sure, you mean that's root medicine? That's just superstition. Don't they know you can't cure disease with mumbo jumbo?

Dr Ben Robinson sighed, "That's it. You have all the answers. Science will lead the way, right?"

Chris felt argumentative at this point, "Sure, eventually. We may not have all the answers yet, but science is surely the key to them."

Ben sighed and appeared to be counting. "Have you ever read the book <u>Porgy</u> by DuBose Heyward?"

"You mean like the musical Porgy and Bess?"

Ben sighed again. "Yes, the book was made into a musical. But before that it showed the plight of black citizens including a cripple named Porgy right here in Charleston. To them, the medical school, *this* medical school was a horror and site of experimentation to be avoided in all but extremis. Coming here for this patient is an act of desperation. So don't sneer that he tried what he knew in desperation to avoid us."

Ben rolled his eyes and looked at his watch. "All right, have it your way. We're going to see if our 'mambo jumbo' can help. Come on, I have a patient coming in for you. Think of it as a clinical exercise."

Ben led the way to another exam room. A bulky chart hung in the rack by the door. Ben grabbed the chart as Chris reached for it and said "No, no, Doctor, first see the patient. Go in and introduce yourself and examine the patient. I've got some stuff to set up. Take your time."

The better part of an hour passed before Chris returned to the darkened room. Ben had turned the lights on and was reading the Bible.

"Well, what's your opinion doctor? Your *scientific* opinion that is."

Chris furrowed his brow and focused on organizing his thoughts to follow the standard protocol for presenting patients to senior staff. The recitation begins with an introduction to the patient by age, sex and ethnicity, and progresses through the current complaint, past medical history, allergies, habits, physical exam and then finally ends with relevant studies and lab work. He began, "The patient is a 55-year-old negro male. His current complaint is that of a rising…"

"Ascending," corrected Dr Robinson. "Never use two syllables where three or four can be gainfully employed, a basic rule of 'med speak'."

"…ascending weakness and loss of sensation in the lower extremities that have progressed over two months. His past medical history is pretty much unremarkable. He had the usual childhood. . . "

Ben Robinson quickly interrupted. If he hadn't, the recitation might have gone longer than the exam itself. "Whoa, I don't want his life story. Just give me the pertinent positives and negatives and propose a diagnosis"

Chris pondered a moment. "He has diminished sensation in his legs from mid-thigh down. Reflexes appear intact, but the strength of his feet, ankles and knees is diminished.

"Off-hand I think he might have a demyelinating disease of some sort. Cord tumor or multiple sclerosis would be other possibilities. I guess."

"Whoa again. I don't need an expostulation on all the possible differential diagnoses here doc. Bottom line, is there something physically wrong with the patient?"

Chris nodded. "I guess a neurology consult would be in order."

Ben reached into the large folder of the patient's chart, "Done and it confirms what you've said so far."

"How about X-rays of the spine?"

"Done and normal."

"How about a metabolic screen or psychiatric consult?"

"Done, done, and done. Quote the psych resident… 'The guy's not crazy.'" Ben Robinson fixed Chris with a wicked grin. "Did you ask the guy if he'd had any precipitating illness or injury?"

"Of course."

"And…?"

"He says there was no initiating injury or illness but that someone put a curse on him. The *root* as you called it."

Ben Robinson's tone was pure triumph, "Right! A root doctor put a curse on him so that he would die, and I quote, 'from the ground up.'"

Chris shook his head, "Coincidence. You can't talk a man into a neurologic lesion. "

Ben smiled, "Will you believe it if I cure his neurologic lesion with my 'exorcism?'"

Chris agreed, all thoughts of expulsion gone. This was for science.

Ben pulled out three cards and handed Chris three numbered syringes. "When I say the words on these cards, give these corresponding medications as numbered. Don't worry, none of them are harmful, but I want to wait until afterwards to explain. I'm going to start an IV for patient safety. They usually expect something medical like that, it's part of the show. The tubing will drape down behind the desk where you can reach an access port. Since you don't want to risk getting tossed out your first month here, you can sit on the floor and give the meds from behind the desk. He will never see you.

With that, Ben lit the candle and doused the lights.

Chris huddled behind the desk clutching the syringes. He could hear Ben usher in the patient. The lights flared again for a few moments as Ben started an IV. A link of tubing soon dropped down beside Chris.

"Mr. Jones, lifting a root is a serious business," Ben intoned. "This IV is in case your heart acts up during the procedure. Now let us pray." There was a brief opening prayer to bless the effort. Chris heard the pages of the Bible ruffle as Ben looked for the passage about casting out demons. Ben then read a lengthy passage in a droning monotone. Chris felt himself becoming drowsy in the confined space. Then he heard Ben call out from one of his cue cards, "May the peace of the Lord guide and protect all of us here." As cued, Chris picked up the first syringe and shot it into the tubing while Mr. Jones intoned "amen."

Ben read another passage and asked for peace again. You do feel more peaceful now, don't you, Mr. Jones?" A murmured assent could be heard as if from a distance. More scripture readings followed, and finally there was a pause. Chris risked a peek over the desk in time to see Ben rest his hands on Mr. Jones' shoulders, "And now evil spirits, I command you to leave this person and return to the fiery pit from whence you came."

This was another cue. Chris lifted the second syringe and shot in the contents. A few moments later, Mr. Jones suddenly erupted from the chair. He shouted. "Oh God! I feel hot! I feel like I'm on fire."

Ben's voice was soothing now, "Relax Mr. Jones. Take three deep breaths. When the evil spirits leave, you usually feel a little bit of the fire of them passing out of your body. It should pass soon."

Mr. Jones' ragged breathing soon slowed. "Yeah, yeah…it's goin' now."

"Now Mr. Jones, I believe we're just about through. Within the next day, you'll receive a sign that the spirit has passed out of you."

Chris started. That was the third cue. He shot the last syringe just in time, for Ben was beginning to take down the IV bottle. Ben continued in his soothing voice, "I want you to come back the day after tomorrow and let's see how you're doing. Let us have one final prayer."

Finally, Ben turned on the lights, blew out the candle and escorted Mr. Jones to the door. Chris quickly peeked down the hall to see that Mr. Jones' gait was already better. Ben closed the door. Chris erupted, eyes wide, "What the hell did you give him?" Chris demanded.

"No, no, doctor," Ben corrected. "What did you give him?"

Chris's mouth opened and shut, unhinged.

Ben laughed. "Okay, Okay, a low blow. Don't panic, I wouldn't let you hurt him. The first one as you may have guessed was a little diluted Valium for calming. The second was some nicotinic acid. It causes a flushed hot feeling."

"What was the last one and what was it for?" Chris asked. "I hardly had time to give it and he was gone."

"Oh yeah," Ben laughed. "Methylene blue, the color that symbolizes the devil in root medicine It's a harmless dye. The next couple times he urinates, he'll be pissing out the devil. Sometimes you've got to meet the patient where his beliefs and practices are. If you liked this, I'll start teaching you hypnosis. It's the same thing. Mr. Jones returned after two days as directed, a happy and well man, saying he'd seen the devil go down the toilet. Chris never forgot the lesson. What the mind thinks, and spirit feels can profoundly impact how the body's health.

<h1 style="text-align:center">Chapter 21</h1>

In a small town, medical advice, and not necessarily just physician's expertise, is highly valued. It had long been the custom to call a pharmacist "Doctor." While medical doctors are often considered unapproachable outside the office (and sometimes in the office), their office nurses are also frequently asked for medical advice on a variety of matters.

Interestingly, some people even believe that medical knowledge might be transmitted sexually. Thus, doctors' spouses are also approached in supermarkets for advice. Chris Wilder occasionally wondered why people still came to him for hypnosis when there had been no publicity about it for years. He hardly ever mentioned it himself, but word still traveled around somehow. Elizabeth MacPherson was a nurse at the hospital who played in Mary Ann's weekend golf foursome. Lately Elizabeth had been complaining that she thought she smoked too much and was having trouble sleeping. Mary Ann volunteered that Dr. Wilder still occasionally did hypnosis and suggested she should try it. As Dr. Wilder's office nurse, Mary Ann had always been very impressed with this unique skill of his. As it had helped her immensely.

Shortly after Chris began his practice, Mary Ann, the office nurse, was incapacitated with a migraine. Chris called Ashley and asked her to come to the office and fill in for Mary Ann. Although Ashley was not a nurse, she was a living female body. The female part was important as a witness to assure that no hankie-pankie occurred during examinations. With some extra work on his part, Chris could make do with Ashley's substituting for the day. After several repetitions of Mary Ann's debilitating migraines. Chris was frantic. He liked Mary Ann as an office nurse but had to have reliable help. He tried numerous medications without success as well as a referral to a neurologist in Columbia. He finally offered to hypnotize her as a last-ditch unspoken alternative to having to let her go.

The session, and those thereafter went well. Mary Ann was cured. It had been years since Ashley had been forced to come to the office to assist. Ashley was a believer and so, for that matter, was Mary Ann. Unbeknownst to Chris, these two women closest to him were the source of many of these requests for hypnosis.

Chris remembered Elizabeth well from the hospital. An attractive, red-haired nurse, she was single and had a widely known reputation for serious partying. Today she looked a little drawn and tired.

"What's the matter?" Chris asked, "Wild night?"

"No, I'm not sleeping well, and I think I 'm smoking too much. I was hoping you could hypnotize me and get me to quit."

Chris thought her story sounded like a problem involving stress or possibly masked depression. However, the careful history and pointed questions about psychiatric problems he always asked in these cases told him nothing. After a brief instruction about hypnosis and explaining as to what it could and couldn't do, Chris pulled a quarter out of his pocket and started to hand it to Elizabeth.

"What's the matter, Dr Wilder? Did you lose your swinging pocket watch?"

"That's old hat. All you need is something to concentrate on while I talk." He extended his hand toward her again. He handed her the shiny silver coin. "Now sit here and hold this quarter up at arm's length, up a little, towards the ceiling so the light reflects on it. That's it."

Elizabeth turned in the chair. "Is this for real? Aren't you going to have me lie down and turn the lights down?"

"Not necessary, but I'll dim them a little to make you feel like you're getting your money's worth." Dr. Wilder asserted with a smile. "The current approach to hypnosis no longer relies on the black cape and the intense stare, the swinging watch. Frankly, all that stuff is just a distraction. Now, concentrate on that quarter and hold it tightly. Notice as you breathe slowly in and out that the quarter feels heavier and heavier. Hold it tighter and tighter. Eventually, the quarter will become so heavy that it will fall from your fingers and onto the floor. The ringing noise you hear as the quarter hits the floor will be your cue to lay your hand in your lap. You will drop into a very relaxed and comfortable state."

As Chris talked, his voice dropped into a slow, low monotone. His rhythm matched her breathing. Slowly, Elizabeth's countenance assumed a glassy stare. As he droned on, the quarter inched out of her tightly clenched fingers and fell to the floor with a metallic ping. Elizabeth's hand dropped like a stone to her lap. Chris paused for a moment. Elizabeth was evidently a very good subject. He reached out, took her arm, lifted it up about six inches above her lap, held it there a moment then let go.

The arm hung -unmoving, unheeded. Even better.

Elizabeth demonstrated catalepsy, a loss of volitional muscle control. Chris leaned forward and asked, "Elizabeth, can you hear me?" and was rewarded with a slow nod. "Elizabeth, in front of you, just in front of your knees, you will see a blackboard. On it, please write three reasons to quit smoking. This ploy was a bit of a gamble for Chris. What Elizabeth did at this point depended on her depth of trance. She might merely imagine a blackboard, or she might truly see a blackboard in front of her, or she might see and do nothing at all.

Elizabeth opened her eyes and stared forward. Her brow wrinkled a moment. She then reached out into a spot six inches above her left knee, picked up a non-existent piece of chalk and began to write in a plane above her knees. When she finished, she set the 'chalk' down and settled back in her chair. Elizabeth was obviously a somnambulistic subject: one who was essentially asleep and yet could still function in a state similar to sleepwalking.

Chris paused for a moment and then continued, "Now without waking or rousing, read to me what you wrote."

Elizabeth took a moment to find her voice, her eyes scanned a spot where 'blackboard' stood, and then in a low tone she read: "smoking makes me cough and gag. It makes me smell bad. It causes my body to age and wrinkle before its time."

"That's right," Chris responded. Then he proceeded to weave her response into a long story-like form of images and ideas. "Picture, if you will, a cloud in the distance. That cloud is all the smoke from all the cigarettes you've ever smoked. Only notice as the cloud moves a little closer, it smells like incredibly stale smoke of burning tires." Here Elizabeth's nose wrinkled in distaste. "Now Elizabeth, we've all seen ads, how smoking supposedly makes you more glamorous. Right?"

Elizabeth nodded slowly.

"Now Elizabeth, you're standing on a cruise ship deck, your clothes are every bit glamorous as any cigarette ad in any magazine. You're young and as beautiful as you've ever been."

Elizabeth smiled.

"Now, you see the cloud getting closer, the smell gets worse, thicker. It's almost hard to breathe because of all the smoke. Elizabeth gagged and then began to softly cough.

Chris continued inexorably on. "Now, as last the cloud of smoke swirls by you and moves on, you take a deep breath of relief. But as you turn you see your reflection in a window. It is awful Elizabeth. The smoke has left you looking wrinkled and old. The thin, wasted woman peering back at you looks twenty years older than you. You raise a hand to your mouth in shock and watch her do the same. Then you see. The clothes, those glamorous clothes are stained, brown and nasty."

Elizabeth gasped, as Chris droned on. He took grim satisfaction in these details. He had seen too many people die from smoking. This hypnotic communication and his suggestions were rich in visual appeal, subtle metaphor, and engaging the other senses, and designed to appeal to her subconscious mind. The subconscious seems to generally respond more to feelings and images than to verbal logic.

He finally took pity on Elizabeth and opened with a relaxing description of a pleasant beach scene. After he wound down on this effort. Chris decided to throw one last bucket of water on Elizabeth's fire for smoking.

The New Age concept of the "child within" had always slightly irked Dr. Wilder, but he thought it might be an effective image. Chris occasionally used this metaphor as an attempt to refocus nurturing feelings towards oneself. As a closing, Dr. Wilder began to give generalized comments about children and babies before bringing the focus to Elizabeth's case. The child within concept is an attempt to redirect nurturing feelings towards oneself. Chris began to talk about children and babies in general in preparation to addressing Elizabeth's specific case. He began to spin out an image of a cute, swaddled baby cooing at its' loving mother when he was interrupted by a low, strangled moan from Elizabeth: it rapidly grew in volume.

Chris paused in shocked surprise and looked at Elizabeth. She was rigid, staring straight ahead and shaking violently. Chris wondered if Elizabeth was possibly having a seizure of some sort when she abruptly threw her hands over her eyes and screamed. "No, no! Not the baby too! Please! Not the baby!"

Chris was momentarily stunned. Mary Ann's head popped into the darkened room in concern. Chris frantically waved her out. The screams continued. Chris tried to think. This image, whatever it was, would be difficult to override, but he had to try.

"Elizabeth! Elizabeth," he called low and urgent. Elizabeth stared, sobbed, and moaned at some personal horror only she could see. "Elizabeth, you're watching a bad movie but it's not real. Come back to the beach. Look out over the ocean and see the waves lapping up at your feet Relax, take a deep breath, focus on my voice, and relax.

Elizabeth inhaled deeply and settled slightly into the chair and the look of terror began to fade as Dr. Wilder kept talking and pulling her back to the beach image.

"That's it, Elizabeth. Take another deep breath, smell the salt air, relax, and drift." Elizabeth settled back into the chair a bit more. A single tear still glistened midway down her cheek.

Chris sat back, shaken. "What the hell was that?"

He knew that occasionally hypnosis unlocked emotional issues buried in the subconscious of which patients were unaware. That was why a good hypnotist questioned patients about psychological issues. Clearly, she would need psychiatric referral, but for what?

"Elizabeth?"

Elizabeth stirred.

"Elizabeth, I want you to come back from the beach to this room. I want you to stay calm and relaxed and watch a movie with me. It's not a very well made movie, but will you watch it with me?"

Elizabeth nodded.

"This movie is on a video tape. We can speed it up, slow it down or reverse it. We can turn it off if we need to, but I think you should watch it and tell me what you see."

Elizabeth nodded again.

"The tape is about a baby and what happens to it. Now it's just a movie, and it's not real. You know that don't you?"

Another nod.

"Now the tape is starting. Tell me what you see."

Elizabeth's gaze focused on a spot just above the exam table. She cleared her throat and began softly "I see a clearing. It's dark. People are gathered in a circle around a woman hanging by her feet. She's pregnant. A fire burns off to the side. Behind it the sacred three-legged cauldron burns."

A cold shock of recognition swept over Chris. Sick with dread and foreboding, he slowly instructed, "Now Elizabeth, remember, this is just a movie and not real. Oftentimes, people in movies look like people we know. Watch as the camera zooms in on the person hanging from the rope. Describe her to me."

Elizabeth wet her lips and stared intently at the spot where she saw the tape playing, "She's late teens, long hair and pregnant. She looks a lot like Janie Johnson."

Chris sat back. The room seemed colder by the minute. He knew he should stop Elizabeth's recitation here and now. Call a psychiatrist, or the police or both, but he proceeded in queasy anticipation. "It sounds like a horror movie, Elizabeth. You know it's amazing what special effects can do. It can even make people look like they've been hurt or even killed with no serious damage to the actor or actress. We're restarting the tape. Tell me what happens next."

"He comes out. He is tall and majestic, cloaked in fur and topped with horns. He pulls out the sacred knife and begins to cut." The scene was too much even for Chris.

"Stop. Who is he? What does he look like?"

Elizabeth sounded a little querulous at being interrupted as she was watching her movie. "Satan's priest, of course!"

Chris's voice asked with pent-up emotion, "Who is he?"

"Who does he look like?"

"He wears a mask with horns. None of us in the circle know his name."

"Why is he doing this to her?"

"Janie tried to leave the circle. Once in, none may leave or even speak of the circle to outsiders. To leave is death."

"So, now she's gone?" Chris murmured.

"Oh, no. Her body is gone, but her blood lives on in the circle, carried in the cauldron of life."

Chris didn't know what to make of recitation. He felt so close to getting an answer, and yet the string to the clue was so fragile. It was hard to process his roiling thoughts. He tried a new tack." Who else is there? Do you see any, uh, actors who look like anyone you know?" Elizabeth's unease was beginning to show. Chris knew he shouldn't push further, but he felt he had to. Anything to break open this case.

Elizabeth shook her head violently. "No! I recognize no one. To speak of the circle is death!"

"What of the others?" Chris hissed. "Who was the man in the Jaycee hut?" Elizabeth shook her head harder. Tears began anew. "Did you know any of the others? Please, we've got to find a way to try to save more babies!"

Elizabeth's gaze at the TV wavered. Her trance was lightening. She shook her head again. "No, I knew none of the others except, of course, Grady. He was not fully in the circle yet." She relaxed at this and settled back into the chair.

"Grady?" Chris asked.

"Oh yes. Grady Hawkins, the pilot. He was not yet a member of the circle. He was found wanting at his initiation.

"How?" Elizabeth's trance began to lighten again.

She began to fidget as he pushed harder. Chris asked a different question. "Elizabeth, do you have a tattoo of an upside-down star?"

Elizabeth moaned.

"What does the star mean?"

Elizabeth moaned again, louder. Tears began to drip off her cheeks. Abruptly her eyes flew open. Her demeanor and expression changed to surprise. She straightened back up in the chair.

"Oh my!" she exclaimed. "I'm sorry, I must have drifted off. How'd I do? Can you help me with my smoking?" It took Chris a moment to shift from the person who was narrating a murder to one who wanted to quit smoking. Elizabeth obviously had no recall of the events of the last hour. Absently, she brushed her cheek. Her fingers came away wet.

She gazed uncomprehendingly at the moisture on her fingertips. "Was I crying?"

Chris hedged. "You recalled a memory of childhood while we were discussing when you started smoking. It was a little sad, but it's okay now. Yes, I think I might be able to help you, but let's give my hypnotic suggestions a few days and then meet again to see how you're doing. Dr. Wilder handed the chart to Elizabeth with the bill. It had no notes. He couldn't think of what to write just now. He certainly didn't wish to write down in front of a now-awake Elizabeth, what had transpired.

The remainder of the afternoon passed in a blur. Chris tried to reason out the ethics and legality of what he'd done. At length, he called Ladson Orr, his friend and more importantly, his lawyer. After the pleasantries, Chris asked if he could speak to Ladson in person, in private, immediately. They agreed to meet at the Merryville golf club in one hour.

Patients done for the day, Chris walked down to his office and tried to think what he would do next. Mary Ann quickly supplied the answer. She hurried down the hall with a look of urgency. "Hospice called about McKeever Lange," she began without preamble. "His wife wants you to make another house call right away. They think he's really close." Dr. Wilder sighed from one death reported to another death pending. He could tuck the house call in on the way.

Chapter 22

The lounge at the golf club was lightly populated when Chris arrived. Ladson was already seated in a distant corner, a drink in hand. He waved to Chris as he walked in and held up his glass. "Hurry up, you're one behind already." The bartender nodded to Chris as he passed.

"What's up?" Ladson asked with curiosity written on his face. "You sounded like you'd seen a ghost when you called."

"Maybe I did." Dr. Wilder proceeded to tell the entire story of the afternoon session carefully leaving out Elizabeth's name.

"Jesus," Ladson breathed. "I have never heard a story like that before. Are you sure she was on the up and up? Maybe she just wanted a little, I don't know, vicarious participation? Can people really do those things you say she did in hypnosis? I mean like narrate a murder and then wake up and forget? That seems a little far-fetched."

Chris nodded. "Yeah, by everything I know about hypnosis she was in a deep somnambulistic trance and showed no recall of the events when she awoke."

Ladson leaned back thoughtfully in the booth. Chris was struck again by the contrast between Ladson and his brother. They shared roughly the same height and build and only five years apart, but Charles affected a leonine dignity that made him appear older than his age. Ladson's lazy grace as he sprawled in the chair bespoke a more youthful athlete.

"You've brought up more legal problems in that little story than I can shake a stick at. The first, of course, is the Fifth Amendment: the freedom not to incriminate yourself."

"Incriminate?"

"Sure, this unnamed person is at least a material witness if not an accessory to murder for starters. Even worse, she confessed when she was not competent to refuse. We also have breach of the doctor-patient relationship which, while it has no legal standing in South Carolina, is at least, a serious issue. Finally, once a witness has been hypnotized, her testimony might be impeached in court as an unreliable witness." Ladson took a long pull at his drink and stared moodily into the glass's contents. "Damn what a mess. Did you glean any other information out of recitation, besides discovering that she was there?"

Chris paused his own drink untouched on the table, "she said that this circle had gotten rid of the pilot Grady who flew for the Merry company. I don't know how but that ties him, and by extension, all those people on the 747 to this case too."

"With what evidence?" erupted Ladson. Several of the other patrons in the club lounge and the bartender turned to look in their direction. Lowering his voice, Ladson hissed, "That pilot was incompetent and had resigned. The letter was on Charles' desk. Charles and I were getting ready to fire him as it was. He must have been suicidal when he hit that plane. You told me yourself that the tox screens were all negative. So how did they kill him? It was a classic locked box mystery. The pilot was locked in his cabin, the artist was in the back, the plane was off the ground, and no one could reach him. The investigation found nothing wrong with the plane. Pilot error is what they said. What other explanation is there? Come on Chris, think like a lawyer for a few minutes. If you go out and tell anyone that you've obtained a confession by this…this hypnosis, this magic, you'll be a laughingstock."

Chris opened his mouth to object.

Ladson held up a hand. "Chris, I'm your lawyer as well as your friend. What you've told me is protected by a legal lawyer-client relationship. Keep working on the case, but this little confession doesn't help you at all, and if you go around alluding to it and asking questions in public, it could hurt you a lot. All her confession shows you is that something is going on. I guess you could say you've been given a hint as to where to dig." They finished their drinks in silence. Chris decided not to mention that Elizabeth had a return appointment next week. He would not cancel it.

As the next week passed, Chris's home life continued to spiral down and as Ladson had made it clear he was not to discuss this case with anyone, not discussing anything was not improving his home life any. He and Ashley had made another effort to improve relations but, under the ongoing pressure and secrecy, these efforts soon died a natural death. Their relationship regressed to near constant stony silence. Ashley continued to visit Dr. Orr. "Any news of late?" asked Dr. Orr at the most recent session.

Ashley looked up sadly, "No we don't speak much anymore. Chris has quit talking about the cases. I've encouraged him to ventilate, but in the last couple of days he's clammed up almost completely." Tears began to leak from Ashley's eyes.

Dr. Orr reached for the box of hankies he kept for these increasingly common occasions.

Ashley accepted the proffered tissue without even glancing at it. "The pills helped for a while, but they don't seem to do as much anymore. Isn't there anything stronger? I've got to be able to control myself if I'm to help break down this barrier that's growing up between us."

Dr. Orr thoughtfully considered her comment. "You know, Ashley, alcoholics sometimes build up a higher tolerance to sedative type medications. It maybe we haven't been giving you enough of this medicine to help you get things under control. Tell you what, take two pills three times a day instead of one. But remember no more." Ashley nodded gratefully.

Dr. Orr considered again. "You know you may be getting depressed as well. God knows, you've got reason; a lot of medical marriages don't survive just the practice demands, let alone all that of the coroner's office. Let's add an antidepressant at night and see if that doesn't help some as well."

Ashley smiled gratefully through her tears. "I'd wondered about that too. Thanks, I think this will help." She stood and hugged him. "What would I do without you?" She offered him a subdued half-smile and turned towards the door. Dr. Orr settled down lightly in his office chair and looked thoughtfully at the closing door. He wondered what it was that Chris wasn't telling Ashley.

Another week passed before the lab came up with a list of the patients Dr. Orr had tested for AIDS and other blood borne diseases. There were over 100 names. Chris scanned the list with interest. The names Jane Doe and John Doe were heavily represented, but so were other names he recognized, plus some names that appeared genuine, but he couldn't place. With rounds still to make, Dr. Wilder slid the list into his box at the hospital.

Rounds took longer than usual. Fall and Winter bring flu and pneumonia. The millworker population, most of them smokers, were hit hard, as usual. Chris did what he could to minimize the expected seasonal morbidity. He urged his smoking patients to quit and aggressively pushed flu and pneumonia vaccinations, but still the people rolled in coughing, gasping, unable to breathe and reeking of tobacco. Often during an intense flu epidemic, the patients jammed the ER and lined the halls of the hospital on portable oxygen tanks. There'd be so many patients that the hospital could accommodate them all. Periodically the hospital overhead pager would call one doctor or another including Dr. Wilder to the phone to answer calls from more sick patients.

Dr. Wilder was cynically certain that Mr. Harris, the administrator, was thrilled with all the extra business. The overhead pager went off again as Chris exited yet another patient's room. He went to take the call. "A Dr. Wilder, I'm trying to get a hold of Dr. Chris Wilder" the basso African American voice boomed in his ear.

"This is Dr. Wilder; can I help you?"

"No, but I can help you. This is Reverend James Mosley. My good friend and colleague Father Bob, tells me you're looking for someone interested in the workings of our common enemy." Chris paused for a moment while the wheels spun. Reverend Mosely? Oh crap, the minister interested in satanic cults. Chris had completely forgotten to call him.

"Yes sir, I am quite interested in talking with you. When could we meet?" The two took a few minutes of comparing busy schedules to find a mutually acceptable time.

As he hung up the phone, the pager sounded his name again.

This time it called him to the emergency room "Stat."

He hurried down the hall. The scene that greeted him as he rounded the comer in the ER. was chaos. A clearly early teenage mother held a limp baby and shouted shrilly for help while resisting a nurse who tried to pry the baby out of her hands. A security guard tried to hold back a small mob of friends and family members. Everyone was screaming.

Dr. Wilder ran to the mother. He leaned in close to her, eyeball to eyeball, his face blocking her field of vision. When he had her attention, he whispered, forcing her to strain to listen. "I'm the doctor. Let me help your child." It worked, alone among the shouting, his soft voice was heard. She handed him the child and collapsed in a heap. A crowd of family members quickly engulfed her. Dr. Wilder hurried into the disaster room with the child. It was a baby, maybe a year old. The nurse stepped deftly around the milling family and followed him in.

A speedy exam showed that the child was breathing, a pulse throbbed under Dr. Wilder's probing finger. However, the baby was mottled, cool and probably in shock. Starting IV's on a small child with veins collapsed from shock is every physician's nightmare. Wilder had recently attended a pediatric advanced life support course to learn how to better his skills in this area. During the course, the teachers had shown a technique for starting an IV by forcing a needle into the young bone of the lower leg. Doctors including Dr. Wilder had practiced on turkey legs purchased from the local supermarket.

Dr. Wilder made a brief futile effort to put an IV in the arm without luck. He grabbed the child's leg. It did feel like a turkey leg at that, he thought. "Josey," he barked at the nurse. "Gimme a number twenty-two spinal needle."

"Let me find a spinal tray," Josey answered.

"No time, just give me the needle and hurry." She slapped an enormous six inch-long needle into his hand. Chris paused for a moment to jerk a red jumper off the child's legs. He felt for the bony prominences which could serve as his guides regarding where to place the needle in the marrow. After prepping the area with disinfectant, he broke the seal on the needle case. Gloving, then grasping the needle firmly, he shoved it into the leg. The sharp point of the needle quickly met the resisting bone and ground to a stop. He slowly escalated the force and twisted, until with a jerk, it slid in. The child cried out once and went back to his rasping labored breathing.

Chris quickly figured an IV flow rate for baseline and additional fluid requirements were needed to bring the child out of shock. The IV then started a rapid drip. He then turned the infant on its side. While Josey held it, he took another long needle and performed a spinal tap. The baby hardly stirred as the long needle entered the skin and sought out the narrow canal where

meningitis germs grow. Chris took two stabs at the tiny back before he was rewarded with a slow ooze of pussy fluid which he quickly collected in sterile tubes for culture. Additional tests showed the baby's electrolytes were abnormal. Dr. Wilder puzzled a little at this, meningitis could but usually did do that.

With the spinal fluid in hand, he ordered appropriate antibiotics to be given 'as stat as you can run them in.' He knew that the bacteria in such infections could double in number in just under a half an hour and that minutes could indeed make the difference. The pharmacist had heard the commotion and guessed correctly what Dr. Wilder would order.

Chris felt himself relax a little as he watched the last of the medicine funnel through the IV. He went out to talk to the very young mother who was only slightly calmer. She was clearly still on the edge of hysteria, but Chris's hurried explanation that the child was still alive and getting medicine did much to calm her. Chris asked what had been going on with the child. The response sickened him. The baby had been ill for several days and feverish, not eating or drinking.

Elderly relatives had told the teenage mother that the child was probably constipated and needed an enema. This mother had dutifully performed multiple enemas for over twenty-four hours while the child worsened. This morning, the child had a short seizure. The mother called her family. After a long family conference, they decided to bring the child to the hospital.

Dr. Wilder struggled to control his anger. He knew that these people had not known any better that poor education and poverty had done its work of locking in a cycle that repeated itself. The woman who identified herself as the grandmother did not look much over thirty. This teen mother didn't have the education or experience to care for a baby. Dr. Wilder asked the family to sign the permission form for an IV stick and spinal tap he'd already done. The self-designated patriarch, a great grandfather, insisted on signing the forms. He did so with an X.

An infant as small as this patient would do better in a pediatric or neonatal intensive care unit. Dr. Wilder explained to the distraught mother that the baby needed to go to a large city hospital for more intensive care. A tertiary level hospital would provide the needed specialists and support staff. The family readily agreed. Chris planned with the teaching hospital in Charlotte to accept the baby despite a lack of insurance. Transferring patients without insurance was occasionally a problem, and Chris had even once had a baby die while he pleaded with a series of large city hospitals to accept the child in transfer. The Emergency Medical and Treatment Act passed a few years earlier was supposed to stop that but hospitals still found ways around accepting indigent patients at times

Chris returned to the baby. With some fluid, the baby looked better, less mottled. It began crying, which Chris regarded as a good sign. Still, for safety's sake, the best option would be if he accompanied the baby to Charlotte. While he waited for the transporting ambulance to arrive, he saw another patient in the emergency room complaining of increasing nervousness. Chris almost asked, sardonically, if the patient had a tattoo of an upside-down star on her backside. The thought of the star brought him up with a guilty start. Elizabeth's return appointment was scheduled for this afternoon. Dr. Wilder knew he must wash his hands of the matter. He felt his judgment was so clouded now by the inherent conflicts, that he could no longer see the patient's interest as his primary concern. He knew when this level of emotional involvement arose, it was time to step away. He would send Elizabeth to a psychiatrist and let the psychiatrist, who wasn't so intensely involved, deal with the problem.

The ambulance backed up to the door, and the EMTs loaded the baby and secured it for the run to Charlotte. Chris hated these high-speed runs but was always happier when patients this sick were in the most professionally skilled hands he could find. His pager sounded once more. He stood by the step of the ambulance bumper and debated. He could honestly say he'd been out of the hospital and let the relief doctor cover him. However, as usual, the guilt of leaving unfinished business won out, and he answered the phone.

"Is this Doctor Wilder? The guy who's the coroner?"

"Yes," answered Chris with a frisson of foreboding. It sounded like another direct call.

"This is J. C. McLeod, the superintendent at Merry Hills Apartments out on Highway 9. I got a young lady who appears to have committed suicide. She's dead. Cold and dead. Chris pulled out a piece of paper to get the address.

"Can you tell how she died?" he asked. Please not another throat slit, he prayed.

"Slashed her, uh. . . wrists in the tub." came the answer. Despite the tragedy of it, Chris felt himself relax a little. J.C continued, "Yeah, in fact you might know her. She's a nurse at the hospital. Her name's uh . . . Elizabeth, yeah, Elizabeth MacPherson." Chris sat down hard on the step of the waiting ambulance.

"Dr. Wilder. Yo, Dr. Wilder?" The EMT waved a hand in front of Chris's stunned face. "We're ready to go now." Chris looked stupidly at the phone and then at the EMT.

For a moment, he sat paralyzed by indecision.

He leaned into the ambulance doorway and was rewarded with a lusty infant squall from inside the ambulance. Guilt for Elizabeth's suicide overcame obligation to the living.

"Get a paramedic to ride with you," he mumbled lamely to the surprised EMT. "I've got another emergency." With that, he strode out of the ER ramp to his car and drove off.

Chapter 23

The Merry Hill Apartments were built with an FHA grant to help provide decent affordable rental housing in Merryville. Prior to their construction, potential residents were hard pressed to come try living in the town because it lacked affordable rentals. One clause in the grant that helped developers build the complex was that it designated a percentage of the units be subsidized for disadvantaged housing. Thus, this complex was one of the few truly integrated places in Merryville: A little African American boy pushed his power scooter round and round the waiting deputy's car as Dr. Wilder arrived. J.C. McLeod hovered a few feet away.

The deputy waited by the door stone faced. Without a word, he escorted Dr. Wilder through the small apartment towards the back. The bedroom was decorated in modern oak furniture. A poster of the TransAmerica building and the San Francisco skyline decorated one wall. The deputy led the way through the bedroom into the small but functional white bathroom.

Elizabeth lay in a small tub filled with blood-stained water. Bloody handprints marked the sides of the tub and a bloody blotch or two could be seen on the walls of the enclosure. Elizabeth's eyes stared sightlessly at the upside-down star drawn in her own blood on the wall above the shower knobs as if she'd been contemplating the sign as her life's blood flowed out. Dr. Wilder looked at the scene for a few moments and felt the walls closing in on him. He brushed through the bedroom and past the silent deputy and out into the hall. One detached part of his mind noticed that the deputy's stomach seemed to be getting stronger. This deputy seemed more angry than nauseous. This deputy had merely glared at the scene and Dr. Wilder.

Dr. Wilder started to settle down to wait for the state crime lab photographer and experts. He knew he should at least check in with the office, but he simply felt too emotionally drained to face Mary Ann and the day's patients. After a few minutes staring at his hands, Dr. Wilder looked back up at the deputy. "Any evidence of a suicide note anywhere?"

The deputy's glare slid into an expression of downright hostility. "I was wondering when you'd get around to asking about that." The deputy gestured to a desk in the comer.

Elizabeth McPherson's hobby turned out to be writing. A shelf above the desk held numerous how-to-write books. A computer with a word processing program pulled up its screen still glowing. Numerous sheets of printed texts lay scattered on the desk and a table beyond. Dr. Wilder jiggled the mouse and the screen lit up. He bent down to read what was on the screen. It was Elizabeth's farewell message. It began "My Darling Chris...

Chris straightened up with a jolt. He turned and looked at the deputy who still glared at him and then bent back down to the screen.

"My darling Chris,

After what we shared in your darkened office, my life can never be the same. As now I remember the words, memories and more that we shared, the pain is as fresh now as it was when I realized that you are a married man and forever denied me. It's better this way. Love and Goodbye,

Betty.

Chris looked over at the printer, an old one with punched hole tractor feed. There was paper in the tractor feed, but no message had been printed. The tractor feed was disengaged. He looked around the desk for a moment but was sure to touch nothing. He then called the hostile deputy over. There was no point in trying to explain the note. "Watch carefully what I do and touch." Dr. Wilder instructed. He then shifted the printer to "tractor feed" and advanced a sheet into the printer. Next, he turned his attention to the keyboard and pressed *Print screen* The note quickly poured out through the printer. Chris looked in vain for any sign of computer diskettes.

The crime lab people soon arrived. Chris showed them the bathroom and body. They tsked-tsked softly, but quickly and efficiently took scrapings of each blood smear. The body was removed from the tub. Out of morbid curiosity and under the increasingly hostile glare of the deputy, Dr. Wilder, rolled the body over and spread the legs-there it was, a small blue star, upside down. He nodded to the team with the gurney, as they spread a plastic body bag on the floor. Elizabeth was sealed up for one last trip to the hospital and Dr. Sayaad.

The crime lab people dusted the bathroom for prints and looked around the apartment for other places to dust. Chris motioned them to the word processor.

"You'll find my prints on these two keys, and the printer. The deputy will verify what I touched, and I'll give you a sample of my prints. I want the rest of the keyboard dusted."

Finished at last, Chris exited the apartment with a sigh of relief. Sheriff Junior Charles pulled up in front of him. From Junior's frosty demeanor, Chris deduced that the deputy had briefed him. "Could you explain to me exactly what your relationship with the deceased was?" Junior began. Chris motioned to Junior to follow him back into the privacy in the back of the apartment. He doubted Junior Charles would believe even an abbreviated version of his story. He was right.

Dr. Sayaad balked for a few moments when Chris insisted on a full postmortem exam. "Really Christopher, I'm sorry about the circumstances and all, but after looking at the body in the morgue, it really seems a pretty cut and dried suicide, and I am really backed up."

"Please, Dr. Sayaad, as a favor. She was in my office, and it was darkened, but it was for hypnosis. I must dot every i and cross every t to avoid any more suspicion; there is something funny about her suicide note. Now I've got Sheriff Charles after me too."

With a single curt nod of his balding head Dr. Sayaad reluctantly assented, "It will take time, a lot of *my time*, but all right."

On his way out of the hospital, Chris stopped to pick up his mail. He retrieved the list of Dr. Orr's Blood borne/HIV tests and found another envelope, with a brief glance as to the contents of the second, he saw another list of names. Chris shoved them all into one envelope and pushed it into his pocket. He reluctantly dragged himself off to what was left of his office hours.

Across town, another doctor was seeing a different patient. Ashley Wilder had added a new symptom to her armamentarium of complaints. She now complained of worsening headaches. Dr. Orr examined her extensively and could find nothing physically wrong. Ashley insisted her nerves were okay, but now she was getting headaches. Dr. Orr arranged for a CAT scan to be done the following week.

As he folded the up the chart, Ashley grimaced. "Dr. Orr…Charles, do you think you could give me something for the pain?" Charles Orr raised an eyebrow. "Something mild, not too strong. I just must have something for the headaches, I can't function."

Charles sighed, "Ashley, I'm a little reluctant to give you much more in the way of narcotics. Remember the tranquilizers and antidepressants?"

Ashley returned his gaze with pleading eyes. Dr. Orr with obvious reluctance pulled out his prescription pad and began to scribble. "These are quite mild, but don't take too many, too often. Ashley reached for the script, but he withheld it a moment. "And we can't keep giving you these for any great length of time."

Ashley nodded, gratefully hugged him, and whispered, "Thank you" in his ear. Dr. Orr settled lightly into his office chair with a grunt of annoyance as she left.

Dr. Wilder made it through the remainder of the day in a trance of his own. He stopped by the golf club on his way home. The lounge was almost deserted as Chris sat in a corner and began to medicate his own problems in a way that Ashley would have understood.

About halfway through his drink, Chris became aware of a growing discomfort on his right hip. He reached around and pulled out the bulky envelope to find the radiologists' lists of all the rib film patients in the last three months. Between sips of his drink, he went down the list of reports crossing off names of females and men whose ages were incompatible with that of the body from the Jaycee hut.

When he finished the first two sheets and the drink, he summarized the remaining four names on one page. He signaled the bartender and pulled out the next sheet, a long one, and began to check off more people. He passed several Jane Does and hit on another familiar name. Then he realized he was working on Dr. Orr's HIV/blood borne list that he had jammed in the same envelope. He mentally cursed himself and shoved the list aside.

As he waited for the next drink, he paused. One name had appeared on both lists. What was it Iris said? "Look at the intersections, the road that connects?" Hastily, Chris pulled up the shortened list of rib fractures and patients tested for blood borne diseases.

This time, a name jumped out at him: Jack Stoner. Chris quickly flipped back to the radiology list. The report was from Merry Hopes Memorial. He'd asked all the doctors on staff about rib fracture patients. Suddenly his request seemed to validate his suspicions. Had this Mr. Stoner been hospitalized for injuries related to a fall and then gotten his blood drawn for Dr. Orr's list?

Dr. Wilder suddenly felt considerably more sober than he had a few minutes before. He surveyed the two glasses on the table and waved off the bartender coming with a third. He looked at his watch. It was getting late. He'd pull the hospital record on this Stoner fellow in the morning and see what the chart showed. Maybe there was a link after all. As he headed home, he realized he felt better than he had in a long time. When he got home, he found that Ashley too seemed to be feeling better too. They made love for the first time in months.

The following morning, Chris wheeled the Taurus wagon into the doctors' parking lot. Frost crunched underfoot as he got out and blinked in the winter sunlight. He first stopped in pathology to check on Elizabeth's post-mortem exam. Dr. Sayaad, true to his word, was far behind and had not yet begun the exam. "Soon," he promised. He'd get to it as soon as possible. There wasn't pressure for a funeral because no family had come to claim the body.

Chris knew that burial customs in the South usually dictated that the deceased be interred within three days. This cultural requirement took some getting used to because in his home state up north, funerals might be up to a week or longer after a death.

Chris also asked for a few other tests to be run on the saved specimens of Grady Hawkins and then he headed down the hall to medical records. The room was a confusion of piles of charts stacked here and there. Gleaming screens of computer word processors punctuated the clutter.

Chris stepped over a small tilting mound of charts labeled 1989 to be filed and sought out the head medical record tech, Janice Tate. He asked for any and all records on a Jack Stoner. ASAP. Janice brushed a strand of graying hair off her face with a harried gesture.

"It may take a while to find it in all this." She gestured vaguely to the piles of charts. "Could I leave them in your box? What's it for, anyway?"

Chris was only partially fibbing when he replied, "It's a quality assurance check." Janice knew all about the vagaries and sudden twists in accreditation proceedings and simply nodded.

Chris headed down the hall to see his other patients, the ones who were still breathing. When he finished rounds, Chris headed out of the hospital with a small sense of anticipated freedom. Today was his half-day off. He cruised through the ER to make sure there were no impending emergencies. An EMT sharing coffee with the nurses told Chris that the baby from yesterday had made the trip to Charlotte uneventfully and seemed to be a little better.

Chris would cover his light office load and then he planned to meet with Reverend Mosley and plumb the good pastor's brains for any new insights. Then, if he was lucky, he thought, he might go home and try to spend some time with Ashley.

Chapter 24

The directions Reverend Mosley had given Chris led him out a long winding, graveled country road to an ancient clapboard church. A simple board sign in need of painting proclaimed it to be the Living Tree of Zion African Presbyterian Church. Given the remoteness of the location, the church was quite large; its facade was flanked with two square wooden towers all painted white. The church was set on a hillside with a long set of steps going up to the front door. A flat earthen expanse marked the parking area. Just beyond the parking area was a smaller building that had once been a shed or small barn and from this small building a chimney extended topped by a plume of wood smoke. A small sign nailed to the front of the building labeled it the Pastor's Office.

A very tall, heavy-set African American man came out the door in obvious response to the Taurus's rattle of arrival on the church's gravel drive. Reverend Mosley was dressed plainly in a sports coat, no tie or clerical collar to denote his status. He offered Chris a firm, almost bone-crushing handshake, as he introduced himself and invited Chris into the warmth of his office. The office smelled faintly of the wood stove within. A threadbare carpet lined the floor. An old desk, several pieces of wooden furniture including a rocking chair and a heavily laden bookcase filled out the room. An ancient wooden chair on wheels was pulled up to the desk. A well-used wooden toolbox in the corner gave evidence that Reverend Mosley was caretaker of the building as well as of the congregants. Jesus with a flock of sheep hung over the desk as the room's only adornment.

Chris took a seat in the rocking chair next to the desk. It let out a disconcerting creak as he settled into it, but the seat held. The minister skipped any further formalities.

He spun his ancient desk chair towards Chris, his hands rested at ease in his lap. He stared into Chris's face. "How may I help you, brother?"

Chris felt an instantaneous bond of trust growing; nevertheless, he paused a moment. Now that he was here, where did he begin? After several false starts, he finally and simply began at the beginning. He poured the entire story out, from the murders of the police officers through to Elizabeth MacPherson's death. There was something in the minister's hound dog jowls and unblinking eyes that caused Chris's natural reserve to fade slowly like frost in a Southern morning.

He unloaded his suspicions, his fears, his worries, and his beliefs. Finishing, he glanced at his watch surprised to see that an hour had passed. During the entire time, Reverend Mosley interrupted only twice to ask for clarification. When Chris finished, he felt purged, relieved to unburden all he knew.

He was also surprised at himself, for he had immediately trusted and told details to this stranger that he'd told to no one else. He concluded with the reason why he'd come.

"I don't know much about satanic cults. I don't know what they believe or how they operate. I thought if you could shed some light on their beliefs and practices, I might be able to get a jump on them, predict their next move or know where to look for the next clue. It is a slim hope, but I'm getting desperate."

The large man leaned back in his chair, steepled his fingers and contemplated the ceiling for several minutes.

"Are you a Christian, Dr. Wilder?"

"I'm Episcopalian."

Reverend Mosley sighed. "No, I am not talking about petty denominational labels. I'm asking if you believe. Believe in Christ the risen lord. Christ sacrificed for our sins. I'm asking if you believe that God in Christ is the ultimate force for good on this planet?"

Chris paused. He hadn't come here for true confessions or soul searching. On the other hand, the question seemed important to Reverend Mosley, so he took his time before he answered. Like many, Chris was comfortable with relegating his religion to relaxed Sunday morning services. The rest of the time it seemed a little impractical. But still... "Yes, I believe," he answered at length.

"Good, I was afraid you might try to qualify or minimize your belief. That will never do for what we face. Do you have any tokens of the enemy?"

Chris rummaged around in his pockets and dug out the fire-scarred star from the Jaycee hut. Reverend Mosley accepted it gingerly. He turned it over in his hands several times as he looked at it.

"A pentacle. This will prove an excellent spot to begin teaching. Chris leaned forward as huge work-marred hands delicately traced the design on the medallion with callused fingers. "Part of the reason I ask if you're a Christian is that if you know Christianity, then by looking for the opposite, you shall understand the opponent. This medallion demonstrates that principle of opposites."

He held the star point up. "The star is one of the more potent symbols of Christianity. Think of the star of Bethlehem, or the star of Epiphany. Think of the implications of the light of the world shining in the dark night of our existence." He rotated the star to point down as the welded grommets suggested it had been worn. "Think of the reverse."

"This is the way with satanic rites," Reverend Mosley continued, "the answer to the question 'what are satanic' rites? is that there are no satanic rites, merely perversions of Christian rights for evil purposes. Instead of the symbolic sacrifice of Jesus Christ, we see real sacrifice of real, even human blood."

The most common satanic rite is the Black Mass, a perverse version of the communion practiced in the Catholic communion, and it similar to your Episcopal rite. When I was in seminary many years ago, I was required to attend a variety of other church's ceremonies to become familiar with other forms of worship. One of the satanists' hallmarks is the perversion of the natural or accepted order. They create a cruel and sickly twisting of that which we consider good, normal, even holy."

Chris thought for a moment. "What of the tattooed stars on the women?"

That is most likely a badge of initiation, even ownership as a mark of the bride of Satan," Reverend Mosley ventured. "My guess would be that anyone wearing it has had ritual sex with Satan or his designate here on earth. The tattoo would mark the woman as his own."

The discussion continued for over an hour before it slowly wound down. Reverend Mosley finally concluded with some advice. "Remember, Dr. Wilder, these people are hidden and scared of the light; they hide from the public and our naïve eyes. A member could be anyone. The deceiver delights in lies and falsehood. Also remember that these people appear to be incredibly violent, sadistically so."

"You, on the other hand, are a lamp shining in dark places. Be very careful. Anyone can hide the evil within themself, even friends you've known for a long time. Question the motives and the intent of anyone who asks you for help or gives guidance. We are small players in an ancient and deadly war. I sense much blood has been shed, even here, about which we do not yet know."

The aging pastor slowly and painfully pulled himself to his feet and stretched. Chris followed. Daylight was fading outside a dusty window.

Chris felt surrounded by a chill of dread. He shivered involuntarily. Reverend Mosley looked at him carefully. "Perhaps someone even now is thinking of you. You've heard the phrase, 'someone walking on your grave?' Before you leave, would you like to see my church? That way, I can send you off on a positive note."

Chris had never been in a primarily African American church before, so he assented quickly. They climbed the slightly rickety steps to the front door. The pastor twisted the handle and shoved open the doors.

Ancient dark wood pews lined up beside a center aisle to a large altar bedecked with candle sticks. A massive lectern stood to the side with an enormous and ancient leather-bound bible atop it. A flow of ribbons streamed off it that could be used to mark passages. The particular churchy scent of candle wax and lemon polish perfumed the air. The church smelled dignified.

A lower stage which rose between the floor and altar area was arrayed with electronics, microphones and speakers. A threadbare carpet lined this section. Mosley grinned "I do a lot of pacing when I'm preaching." Above the altar and stages hung a massive cross with a life size plaster statue of the crucified Christ. A series of cables and pulleys attached the cross to the wall.

Chris looked in askance at the pulleys and cables. Reverend Mosely smiled and shrugged. "We don't like our savior getting dusty."

Chris inhaled deeply savoring the interior. "A lot of history here," he murmured.

"History!" snorted the minister. "Slaves helped build the first part of this church, Heck, we had the county's first Martin Luther King celebration here. We had a cross burned in the yard while we were all in here. Freedom Riders, Civil Rights, you name it, this church was part of it. To quote William Faulkner, 'the past isn't dead, it isn't even past.' It's like those you seek, the fight goes on and on, just in different forms. Come here, I'll show you a special feature of the church. Never shown it to a white man before. 'Course we never had a white man in here before, either."

As the surprise of this revelation registered with Chris, Reverend Mosley led him up the old wooden steps to the altar. He carefully removed the matching candlesticks and shoved hard on the large altar piece. It creaked and then tipped back. An opening in the floor appeared under the base of the altar. An escape tunnel burrowed into the hill behind the church. Chris looked in surprise at the grinning preacher. "Sometimes it helped to have another way out of the church."

Chris walked towards the back of the church; he noticed large brackets on either side of the double doors leading out. A large sturdy board leaned on a back wall. "Was this to bar the door in time of trouble?"

The pastor laughed. "No, sometimes we run a little short of cash at collection time. Then we bar the door and pass the plate until we can meet our expenses. An old custom in the church and even now the building needs a lot of work!" With the last word, he reached out a meaty hand and jerked a surprised Dr. Wilder back.

"Sorry, brother. Like I said, the building needs a lot of work. We've got termite damage there in the corner with a lot of dry rot. You step over there and you'd probably go right through. We're a poor people and a poor church. We struggle along as best we can. The congregation doesn't even pay me. I work as a teacher at the vocational school. Today's is a teacher's holiday, and here I am."

Guiding Chris, Reverend Mosley opened the door of the church and led the way back down the steps. He saw Chris in his car. They chatted a few more minutes and Chris got in the car and switched on the engine. Mosley motioned for him to roll down the window. To Chris's surprise and chagrin, the minister reached out and placed his hand in benediction on Chris's head. With the other he reached upwards and closed his eyes.

"Oh God," he intoned in his baritone voice, "Out of whom comes every good and perfect thing. Protect this, thy servant Christopher, in his battle against the minions of darkness. Guide his path and give him a faithful and discerning heart to do your will. Protect him in his struggles with our mutual adversary. Amen." As he finished the benediction, his calloused thumb traced a cross on Chris's forehead. "Go in peace, brother."

Chris nodded silently and backed out of the driveway. He'd learned a lot this day. Until now, this whole affair had been an intricate puzzle to assemble, a large mystery to solve. He had thought of it only as a case of an individual or group of people committing murder. Reverend Mosley recast the story in broader terms: the struggle between good and evil. He had also put in concrete perspective what had been only an abstract concept: that someone might not appreciate his investigation and might try to harm him or his family.

The chill of impending disaster loomed ever closer.

Chapter 25

The next several days seemed to just crawl along. Chris pestered Dr. Sayaad to expedite the slides and the analysis on Elizabeth, but the always unflappable pathologist proceeded at his normal slow and deliberate speed. "Christopher, I must be sure there are no errors and nothing to criticize. In these cases, above all, we must be most meticulous and careful. Be calm, it's not you they're after, after all." Chris looked up sharply at this. It was probable that Sayaad hadn't heard about the shouting session that he and Junior Charles had had in front of an astonished Iris Maynard. No, Dr. Sayaad had turned back to fiddle with something on his workbench, evidently dismissing Chris and his problems from his mind. Chris could do little, but seethe. After all, Junior had started it.

Finally, one afternoon several days later he received the call for which he'd been waiting. Dr. Sayaad sounded strangely subdued as Chris answered the phone. "We need to talk at your earliest convenience, Christopher."

"Tell me! What did you find??" Chris almost begged.

"I'd rather not discuss it over the phone. When you come to the hospital for evening rounds, I'll be waiting. But hurry, the opera in Charlotte begins tonight. The rest of the afternoon dragged on forever with winter's first crop of colds, rashes, and runny noses. Finally, Mary Ann shooed the last patient out the door. Chris finished his notes at his desk and faced a moment of trepidation.

What if Elizabeth truly had been so unraveled from her session with Chris that she had taken her life? Could he face the possibility that his meddling had caused her death? The thought haunted him as he backed out of the office parking lot and headed into the dusk toward town.

The road that connected Chris's office and town also ran out to the new interstate. Chris noted that the road was getting dirtier each day since the county began work to widen it. Construction had begun, but the road was still two lanes with muddy channels on either side that promised two more.

His mind was still on the anticipated results at the lab and not much on the road. Thus, at first, he missed the van that came from behind the logging truck. The van swung into the oncoming lane blocking both lanes of traffic. Unseen, the two vehicles slipped out of sight in a small valley in the road. It was the angry blare of the logging truck's horn that snapped Chris back to the here and now. He looked up to see a wall of headlights glaring in his face.

Dr. Wilder tried frantically to brake, to give one of them a chance to slide over. His suddenly sweaty hands clawed at the wheel as he jerked the aging Taurus wagon off the road and into the dark beyond. The car shuddered from a blast of wind as the two trucks flashed by, horns wailing into the twilight.

The car bucked and slid as it hit the muddy trail of the anticipated extra lane. Then, despite Chris's panicked efforts, it spun round and round and finally stopped with a thud, tail first in a bank of mud. Chris sat listening to the sudden silence and shuddered. His heart fluttered frantically in his ears. Shaken, Chris climbed out of the car and watched both sets of taillights vanish over the next hill with no flash of brake lights

 He knew he was lucky. Until a few weeks ago, the sides of this road had been heavily wooded, and he would have undoubtedly wrapped the car around a tree. Suppressing an adrenalin jitter, he slogged back through the mud to the car. The Taurus sat askew in axle-deep mud. Without trying to spin the wheels even once, he could tell he was hopelessly bogged down. Lights from a farmhouse twinkled in the distance. He walked toward them to call a tow truck. Dr. Sayaad was, of course, gone by the time Chris finally made it to the hospital that night.

Ever since Ashley had recovered from her alcoholism, Chris had stopped bringing home any liquor. Until recently, what little drinking he'd done had been outside the home. Tonight, though, he stopped by a small package store and bought a fifth of bourbon. He planned to smuggle it into the upstairs study. He needed a drink, and he was too nervous after his close call to consider going to the golf club.

The phone rang as he entered the door. Perfect diversion, he thought, as he waved at Ashley and rounded the corner of the steps. Chris could hear Ashley's murmured greetings to the caller as he bounded up the steps. He felt a little guilty bringing liquor into the house, but Ashley had been sober a long time now, and he really did need a drink.

From downstairs, the timbre of Ashley's voice suddenly escalated in a near shout of fear. "What? What did you say? Who is this?" He covered the bottle with his coat and tossed it on the couch. Chris bounded back down the stairs and around the comer. Ashley stood transfixed, gaping at the receiver tears erupting from her eyes. A man's voice was shouting. Chris leaped forward and snatched the receiver out of her unresisting hand.

"Who is this?" he snarled. "Who is this? What did you say to my wife?"

The only answer was the buzz of a disconnected line. Chris turned back to Ashley. Anger and shock played across both faces. "What did he say?"

Ashley folded onto the couch like a tire suddenly going flat and began to cry. "He said you better watch your step or they ... they'll cut you," she sobbed, "he said you better quit looking into things that don't concern you or they'll kill you a slice at a time. . . that they'll start by cutting off your balls and w-w-w-work their way up to your throat. Oh Chris, for the love of God, what is going on?"

Chris spent a long-time comforting Ashley. All thoughts of the drink were long gone. At last, she calmed enough that he could leave her and make a call. He dialed Dr. Sayaad's home number, but there was no answer. This was not a surprise. Dr. Sayaad had long been a bachelor and firmly regarded his time away from the hospital as his own.

Chris hung the phone up in exasperation. Dr. Sayaad's cultural proclivities were well known. Autopsy reports were daily fare for Dr. Sayaad. He still didn't understand how vital this one was to Dr. Wilder. In the end, Chris and Ashley sat and watched some television while he kept peering at the phone next to him daring it to ring.

Among the properties and possessions that the Merry family owned that few people realized, were the county liquor stores. Dr. Orr had made a specific request to all his stores to notify him if Ashley Wilder bought any liquor. He had been expecting that Ashley might relapse under the stress of the murders and Chris's part of the investigation. So far, she hadn't- though he'd been interested to hear that Chris had been in last night to purchase a fifth himself.

Dr. Orr had been keeping a careful count of the amount of medication he'd been prescribing for Ashley Wilder. She should be running out today.

Sure enough, Ashley barreled through the office doors as soon as the staff unlocked them. "I had the most terrible experience last night," she began. "Now I have the worst possible headache yet!" Dr. Orr listened patiently as Ashley told him of the disturbing phone call. When she finished, she looked expectantly at him. He settled back in his chair.

"You know Ashley, I 've been quite worried about both of you. You may not know it, but Chris has begun to drink a good bit more of late. I can tell the strain you've been under, But I had no idea it was this bad. I know since your recovery that Chris has avoided buying alcohol or bringing it home. That was why I was surprised when I was driving by the Food Lion Plaza last night and saw Chris buying something at Fetter's liquor store. I knew matters must be getting worse. I've not known him to bring liquor home since you got, uh . . . well."

Ashley was indeed surprised. In the back of her mind, a small bit of the old cucumber-Ashley filed this fact away.

She didn't know how quickly she'd use it. "Now about my medicine," she resumed.

"I'm sorry," Ashley," Dr. Orr interrupted. "I think matters are getting out of hand with your medicine. It was only supposed to be a brief prescription and has gone on far longer than I imagined. I don't think in good conscience I can give you any more medication for your headaches. Perhaps we should send you to Two Rivers Mental Health clinic for counseling. Despite his kindly tone, both knew that this was an insult. Generally, only those patients too ill or destitute to seek private care would consider the local county mental health and addictions clinic.

Ashley was taken aback. She paused, then resumed in wintery tones, "I'll have to consider that for a while, Charles. I have a hard time seeing the wife of one of your peers going into the mental health clinic and mingling with the kind of people Chris tells me frequent that facility. Now, if you'd just renew my tranquilizers, I'll go home and think this over."

Dr. Orr's face appeared the sincere picture of sorrow. "I'm sorry, Ashley. I don't think refilling those would be wise, either. I think it's time you and Chris face your problems without chemical assistance."

Ashley opened her mouth and then closed it. She had never been treated so rudely by Dr. Orr. She flushed deep red as tears welled up in her eyes. She jerked out of the chair as if on strings and stalked out of the office. Her hands shook visibly as she reached for the door. Not until the door closed did Charles allow himself a small smile of victory. Dr. Wilder would have his hands full for at least the next few days, and then it wouldn't matter anymore.

Dr. Wilder was having problems of his own as he talked with the harried lab secretary. "What do you mean you don't know where Dr. Sayaad is? How can he just disappear?"

The lab tech rolled her eyes at yet another concern in a series of problems this morning. "Sir, all I know is that his housekeeper called and said he was sick. That he would be out today and maybe a few more days. That's all I know."

"Are you sure?" Dr. Wilder snapped.

The lab tech was taken by surprise. "Why should I lie about it? Doctors do get sick, you know. Now sir, if you don't mind, I'm way behind, and I have a line of other doctors on me for results on tests I haven't done yet."

Dr. Wilder backed down. Perhaps he was getting a little too paranoid. Nevertheless, he decided to ride out to Sayaad's house at lunch to check up on him. Obviously, his greater concern was getting the results on Elizabeth and Sayaad was the key.

The office was the usual madhouse. Mary Ann greeted him at the door with his coffee in her hand and the comment, "I hope you've got your track shoes on today, because it's a pile of sickies. Yea verily, winter flu season hath begun."

Chris muttered in annoyance as he started up the hall to patient number one. Chris quickly discovered the god of patient schedules was unhappy. Every patient seemed a stumbling block to the next.

The first patient was a fourteen-year girl with a stomach virus. She'd been vomiting almost a week. No blood, usually first thing in the morning. Dr. Wilder's antenna perked up. Any diarrhea? No. Fever? No. Pain? Chris scrawled his notes in the chart as he snuck an oblique look at the profile of the child. She was awfully busty for fourteen. Chris asked about her last menstrual period. Her hesitation as the girl thought provided an even stronger hint. The girl's mother leaned forward more attentive now.

"I think it was last week," she decided. The mother settled back into her chair. Chris doubted her answer. As he performed a brief physical, he pondered his dilemma. He decided to result to a minor subterfuge.

"It's possible you have a low-grade bladder infection because I don't see much on the rest of the exam. Let's check a urine specimen." At Dr. Wilder's direction, the girl rose and headed down the hall to the bathroom. Chris stepped into the lab adjacent to the bathroom, where he caught Mary Ann's eye. He said out loud. "Let's check a urine on this girl," as he pointed to the pregnancy kits. Mary Ann knew the game well. She nodded and winked.

"Yes sir."

While the test was cooking, Chris headed into the next room. There a young mother complained that her two-year-old child wasn't using his left arm and cried when she moved it. Chris undressed the toddler and looked him over carefully. Several bruises on the back and upper arm caught his eye. The guilty looks, the bruises, Wilder mentally groaned in anticipation of the ensuing tears, denials, and recriminations about what he suspected would be child abuse. He went to find Mary Ann to order a "kiddiegram" X-ray to look for fractures that would signify abuse.

Stepping back out of the room, Mary Ann had a grim look on her face as she caught his eye and nodded, giving the thumbs up sign on the pregnancy test. He passed on his next request and squared his shoulders and stepped into the room to deliver the news to teen and mother. There were stony looks and head shakes of negation as the mother grimly gripped her child's arm, yanked her up and marched her down the hall and out of the office before Dr. Wilder could propose any additional treatment plans or referrals.

The next patient complained of a heavy, squeezing chest pain that made him nauseated and mildly short of breath. He thought it was probably indigestion. A quick cardiogram revealed the typical up-swinging lines of a heart attack.

Dr. Wilder went up to the front office and told the girls to call for an ambulance and to arrange with the hospital for admission for the heart patient. Dr. Wilder then picked up on the extra line and dialed the hospital dictation system and he dictated a brief admit note on the hospital call in line that connected directly with transcription. Meanwhile Mary Ann started an IV, pulled nitroglycerin out of an emergency kit and fed the patient an aspirin to chew. Because the dictation might take a day or so to be transcribed, he then wrote an even briefer admit note and then a set of orders.

Back with the child, A glance at the X-ray confirmed Dr. Wilder's suspicions and soon the mother of the abused boy was now talking in his office with the hastily summoned county social worker. Meanwhile Dr. Wilder's fingers beat a rapid tattoo of frustration. He knew he was falling farther and farther behind. There was not much left of the lunch hour when he was finally able to pry himself free to go to check on Dr. Sayaad.

The pathologist lived out in the Pill Hill section of Merryville in an elegant Tudor style home. A lifetime bachelor, he pursed his hobbies of classical music, opera, and literature with a passion. Chris had been to his house only a few times, usually for Christmas parties. No one answered his knock even when he pounded on the door. He walked around back and peered in the carport. The Mercedes was there. Chris approached the back door. It wasn't locked. Chris felt a surge of guilt, but concern for his colleague overrode his concerns about trespass. He went inside. He touched nothing.

A quick walk through the house showed that nothing was disturbed, and that Dr. Sayaad was as tidy at home as in the lab. Chris had barely walked out the

back door when a curious neighbor came round the corner, "Oh hello, Dr. Wilder," recognition in her voice. "Are you looking for Dr Sayaad? '

"Yes, I am," he replied. "His housekeeper called and said he was sick. I came to check on him."

The neighbor looked puzzled, "Dr. Sayaad's never had a housekeeper or a maid. He says he's neater than the pickiest maid."

Chris made a show of shrugging his shoulders and wandered back to his car in front. "If you happen to see him," he called from the car, "please ask him to call me. It's very important." Chris was beginning to doubt he would ever get the call

Arriving back at the office, Chris called Junior Charles to report that Dr. Sayaad might be missing and then he shared what he thought were potential reasons for his disappearance. He also mentioned the threatening call Ashley got the night before. Sheriff Charles' tone as he perfunctorily responded, coupled with the mess with Elizabeth MacPherson, suggested that his credibility with Junior had shrunk to an all-time low.

Chris declined to volunteer that he'd been in Dr. Sayaad' s house but asked Junior to check out the house and garage.

The sheriff decided at length to humor Chris and agreed to send a deputy around to Sayaad's home. As he agreed to this small request, he warned Chris that Dr. Sayaad would have to be missing for several days before a missing person report could be filed.

"I can't go filing missing person reports on everyone who decides to take a few days off without personally notifying you doctor," he sniffed.

The testy response was not quite what Chris might have hoped for, but it mollified him that at least he had made the report. He shouldered on his white coat, slung his stethoscope around his neck and headed out into the hall. The awaiting pile of charts promised this afternoon would offer no respite from this morning's load. Mary Ann walked briskly past him, as he adjusted the coat, "Atta boy," she encouraged, "you're saddled up. Now move 'em out." Chris wondered whatever happened to the good old days when doctors were men and nurses were scared.

Chapter 26

While Chris struggled through what he thought was a bad day at the office, Ashley was at home having the real thing. Dr. Orr had laid the trap well. Alcoholics have a natural, some say even genetic, predisposition for addictive substances, be they alcohol, tranquilizers, or other mood-altering substances. There is also a certain amount of cross-over addiction. Ashley's quiescent alcoholic tendencies were back up to a fever pitch with the combination of tranquilizers, antidepressants, and narcotics. Every nerve in Ashley's body was a jangle with need.

Had she looked up the medications in the Physicians' Desk Reference, it would have warned her that after prolonged use of her meds, habituation and even withdrawal seizures were possible. Combining medications multiplied the risks. Abruptly stopping them was highly discouraged. To Ashley, each passing minute seemed like hours. Small noises like the ringing of the phone seemed to catapult her from the couch where she took refuge. Ashley curled up in a tremulous ball and wondered what had happened to her. Why had Charles Orr suddenly turned on her like that? Quitting drinking wasn't even this bad!

The thought of quitting drinking rang a bell. She tried hard to think, to remember what Charles had said about Fetter's liquor store, what had Dr. Orr said about Chris a bottle? Last night he'd come in and gone straight to his study then the phone rang…It took only a few minutes for a pro like Ashley to check all the spots in a room that could hide a liquor bottle. She pulled it out of a desk drawer with a squeal of triumph. One last waning voice in the back of her head gave her a few seconds' pause. Why had Dr. Orr given her all those medicines? Then the carefully crafted demand of her body drowned that tiny voice out, and she drank deeply.

Despite the quick approach of winter's night, this day seemed like one of the longest in Chris Wilder's life. Ordinarily, this close to Christmas, the office and hospital patient populations thinned considerably. People had other things to spend their money on this season. Thinking about the bruised boy from this afternoon, I guess child abusers don't get holidays, he reflected glumly as he pulled in the driveway.

He hoped that the evening with Ashley would go well. He'd noticed in recent weeks that homelife seemed to finally be getting a little better. Ashley had been more relaxed and cheerful and even supportive. These last few days reminded him of the good old days before Ashley's final plunge into full blown alcoholism, back when Ashley was fun, the life of the party. Even last night ended well, when Chris's comforting hugs enkindled a renewed passion that left them both breathless and spent. A faint warning voice asked what might have caused change, but he quickly smothered it.

The house was unusually dark when he pulled in. At first, he thought that Ashley must be out visiting friends late. Then, as he rounded the corner of the driveway, he saw Ashley's BMW parked in its usual spot. He entered the unlocked back door and walked into a darkened kitchen. Reverend Mosley's admonition about his own personal safety suddenly flared to life. The house was much too quiet and dark to be normal. Chris paused, listening hard…nothing. Ordinarily he would have called out to Ashley, but the minister's words rang in his ear in accompaniment to the accelerating drum of his pulse. Instead, he sidled quietly into their nearby bedroom.

To Chris, he thought it incongruous for a physician to own a pistol, Ashley however had put her foot down years ago, and insisted that she have one in their room for security on those many nights he spent in the hospital with sick patients. At this moment, he was silently grateful for Ashley's demand. He pulled the pistol out of the drawer, checked the safety, and glided carefully, quietly room through darkened room, on the first floor. There was not a sign of Ashley.

He felt particularly vulnerable as he headed up the darkened staircase, muffling his steps as best he could. As he climbed, the thought occurred to him that it might be best to call the police. Then he chided himself. How long would it take the police to quit laughing that he called the cops because the house was dark? He could picture Junior's face now. That image pushed him along. He began easing through the darkened doorways upstairs.

His study was the final room. The door was closed. As he pushed open the door, he recognized his wife's unmoving form on the couch in the moonlight.

Without another thought, he flipped on the lights and shouted, "Ashley!" as he rushed to her.

Ashley opened her bourbon-fogged eyes and beheld Chris rushing towards her, pistol in hand, she screamed.

It is difficult to relate the welter of conflicting events that happened with near simultaneity. Chris saw the almost empty bourbon bottle cradled in Ashley's lap and recognized it as his own. Guilt and anger wrestled with relief that Ashley was still alive. Ashley was both guilt-ridden and terrified to see Chris towering over her, the forgotten pistol dangling from his hand. The bourbon, however, had only briefly postponed the inevitable. Fueled by the surge of adrenaline and the withdrawal of the heavy tranquilizer and narcotic load, Ashley looked up at Chris to explain.

"It, I... uh. . . I. .. uh…" she started. The words slurred into a gargle of vowels. Her eyes widened as she tried again to make sense. The eyes peered up at the ceiling a moment, and then rolled back the rest of the way into her head until only white sclera showed. Suddenly her arms jerked straight out in a rigid posture as her back arched. She appeared frozen that way for a moment, and then began to convulse, her whole-body flapping and writhing.

Chris stared in horror, shocked into momentary immobility by the sudden change of events. In the next moment, the physician in him overrode the husband. He pulled her back onto the couch and turned her on her side, so she would not inhale any vomitus. He stretched to the desk for the cordless phone rural Merryville phone company did not yet have 911 but he called EMS from memory.

By the time the emergency medical technicians reached the upstairs room with their stretcher, the seizure had passed. Ashley lay essentially inert, blowing flecks of bloody foam from flaccid lips.

As they arrived at the hospital emergency room, another seizure caught Ashley, and she flailed helplessly at the sides of the stretcher and restraining straps. The EMTs paused until the seizure passed, then quickly unloaded her from the ambulance and wheeled her into the emergency room. The ER doctor was awaiting them. As they situated her on the hospital stretcher, yet another seizure began. This one was the worst yet, and she was unable to spare the strength even to draw a breath. Ashley began to turn blue from the exertion and lack of oxygen. She tugged and jerked against the assembled staff trying to hold her down on the narrow bed. The two burly EMTs held down an arm as a nurse jabbed in an IV needle. The ER doctor nodded to the other nurse holding a syringe of diazepam, the treatment of choice for these unremitting seizures called status epilepticus. "Flush the whole thing in," he called. The nurse nodded grimly as she struggled to keep up with the still flailing arm. At the head of the bed, the ER doctor stood waiting with an endotracheal tube. When the drug reached the brain, there was an excellent chance Ashley would stop breathing. In view of her worsening color, it was essential that ventilation be started as soon as possible.

Soon the thrust and jerk subsided. An ambu breathing mask was slapped on her dusky face squeezing hard as oxygen began to force its way into her. Air squeaked and hissed around the edges of the mask as her stiff and spasming lungs resisted. The ER doctor, an unfamiliar face to Chris, skillfully slipped the long blade of the laryngoscope into her throat. Lifting the handle, the landmark vocal cords popped into the searching doctor's view, and he slid the tube into her windpipe. He jerked the mask off the ambu bag and applied the bag directly to the tube projecting from Ashley's throat. Squeezing the bag, he pushed air into Ashley's oxygen-starved lungs. Immediately, the purplish color began to fade into a pinkening blush. He watched as the ER doctor checked both lungs for air movement and, satisfied, began to secure the tube. From his position by the ER doctor, Chris realized he too was holding his own breath, and let it out with a whoosh.

The emergency room staff procured a room in the ICU and respiratory techs set up a ventilator. Dr. Orr bustled in as the techs finished setting the equipment parameters.

"My God, Chris, what happened?"

Chris relayed what he knew so far.

Dr. Orr shook his head sorrowfully. He knew now was the time for a little skillful truth-telling to complete the lie. "Must have been the headache pills I gave her. They were quite mild, but I never dreamed she'd relapse and mix them with alcohol. "He put his arm on Chris's shoulder as he escorted him out the door and then turned to examine Ashley.

A few minutes later, he emerged with the chart. "Her blood alcohol was well over legally intoxicated. Her exam is pretty unremarkable now, but she's still really out of it. She still isn't breathing well on her own yet. We'll arrange some tests, including a CT of her head tomorrow just to be sure we aren't missing a tumor or stroke hiding somewhere. We'll load her with Dilantin over the next several hours but keep her on Valium so she won't fight the respirator until we can try to wean her off."

Dr. Orr looked Chris in the eyes, compassion written on his face. "Chris, your place is here with your wife for now. I want you to stay with her. She's been through some rough times with all these murders. I've been doing some counseling with her. Just fatherly advice, you know. She asked for more nerve pills, but I told her no. What she needs most is you."

Chris opened his mouth. "No, no," continued Dr. Orr, "I'll cover your patients this week until we can get Ashley back into treatment. You need to stay here and be the husband you seem to have been neglecting to be of late. Stung, Dr. Wilder watched in silence as Dr. Orr swept out of the room. Chris felt a little relieved, guilty, and yet resentful at the implications of the last comments. But he realized there was probably more truth than he wished to acknowledge. Chris turned back to Ashley, pulled up a chair and clutched her limp hand and listened to the hypnotic hiss and wheeze of the respirator. After a while, he felt tears run down his cheeks. Finally, he slept.

The following morning, he awakened, still sitting in the chair, sunlight streaming into the room. Stiffness pinched his back and shoulder as he pulled himself up from the bedside and brought a wince to his face. Chris dragged himself to his feet as Dr. Orr swept into the room. Extracting a flashlight from his breast pocket, Orr pulled back one of Ashley's eyelids to check her pupillary reflexes. The eyes drifted a moment and then focused on his face. Recognition, and a terrified expression, suddenly animated her face. Ashley began to thrash around in the bed and fight the protective wrist restraints. The alarm from the ventilator began to whoop as she fought the machine. Dr. Orr straightened with a jolt. "My goodness," he exclaimed, "I thought all the stuff we gave her last night would be enough. I think she's hallucinating. Quick! Nurse, hand me that Valium, ten milligrams, stat." The medicine was taped to the headboard for such an emergency.

The valium was quickly pushed into the IV tubing and the frenzied struggle in the bed soon retreated to the steady wheeze of the ventilator.

Dr. Orr turned apologetically to Chris. "It's worse than I thought. We'll have to keep her sedated at least another 24 hours before trying to taper her meds."

He spent a few minutes reviewing the chart and wrote a series of orders. With a salute to Chris, he strode out the door.

Chris had barely settled back into his chair when a clerk from the insurance office peeked in the door. "Excuse me? Dr. Wilder? I don't mean to bother you. We know everything was a little wild last night, but I was wondering if you could give me your insurance card, so we can get Mrs. Wilder's insurance forms straightened out- please sir?" Dr. Wilder reached in his wallet and rummaged around for a few seconds, no card. Chris felt a new pang of regret.

"I'm sorry," he explained. "My wife usually keeps up with this stuff." He rose wearily to his feet. "I'll go home and get the cards for you."

"Oh, no," the clerk exclaimed. "Just bring them in next time."

Chris stood in a moment of indecision looking at Ashley now resting unaware. "No, I need a break here. I'll be back with them in a bit." He wandered out into the hall and down towards the doctor's parking lot.

He stopped in to check his mailbox to see if there were any notes or messages from Dr. Sayaad. There weren't, but there was an unfamiliar chart tucked in among the clutter. Chris pulled it out and stared dully at it. Jack Stoner, it said, the patient with the HIV tests and broken ribs. Happy for almost any diversion, Chris sat down to review the chart. According to the chart, Dr. Orr had had the patient in weeks ago with a simple pneumonia, common to young people, called mycoplasma. Stoner had an unusually severe case. The rib fractures were mentioned in the progress notes. Chris gave a measure of grudging respect to the fact that Orr also noted a detailed history that documented the patient's heterosexual history and lack of drug use. Chris knew that many doctors tend to avoid prying into such personal questions, yet this made the testing even more confusing. There was no plausible reason to test Stoner for HIV, yet Dr. Orr had. More important, why hadn't Charles Orr mentioned the patient after Chris's inquiry? The nurses' notes gave vital statistics that closely matched those of the skeleton. Despite the need for more checking, Chris suspected Stoner was his John Doe victim. Chris tossed the chart into the large "to be filed" pile, thanked the women in medical records and went home.

Chapter 27

The back door to Dr. Wilder's big Victorian house was still unlocked. Nothing was amiss. People often failed to lock their back doors in small Southern towns. The joke ran, "we lock the front door to show we aren't home but leave that back door open in case somebody needs something." Lately, however, Chris and Ashley had been much more conscientious about locking the doors. But in the ambulance frenzy it was again unlocked.

Passing through the kitchen, he remembered the insurance card request. He took a few minutes to find Ashley's purse. Her wallet lay on top of the pile of clutter that seemed to find its way into every woman's purse. At the office, Dr. Wilder often despaired when women patients began to look for a note, list or lost prescription in a purse only to emerge a few minutes still mumbling, "It must be in here somewhere."

He would never forget the patient, an ancient farmer's wife, long widowed, mostly blind, who had upset a nest of cockroaches living in her purse. They had swarmed out of the pocketbook and up her arm while she, oblivious to the disturbance, continued to root for the missing list of complaints.

Chris shook his head and fished the hospitalization card out of Ashley's wallet. He then put the wallet back in the purse and tossed the leather purse on the desk. It landed with a rattle familiar to doctors everywhere, that of a collection of pill bottles.

Chris walked back to the desk and picked up the purse and shook it. It rattled again. Feeling slightly guilty, he upended it on the counter. A dozen empty pill bottles spilled out and rolled helter-skelter across the counter. Stunned, Chris assembled and inspected them. They were all for narcotics and tranquilizers and other controlled substances. The doctor's name on all the bottles was that of Charles Orr. He recalled what Charles had said about Ashley asking for tranquilizers. Had she fallen so far that she had been forging prescriptions? Or was something else afoot?

On the slow, and now disillusioned, drive back to the hospital Chris remembered with a guilty start to check by medical records to see if Dr. Sayaad had dictated a summary of Elizabeth McPherson's postmortem. On arrival he first went to the ICU unit to see Ashley. As he entered the darkened room, a missing noise nagged at Chris as he opened the door wider. Then it hit him, there was no sound from the ventilator.   In a sudden panic, he flipped on the lights. The ventilator tubing hung like limp branches near the bedside. Ashley's bed was empty.

Chris exploded from the room, sprinting towards the nurses' station. A nurse heard the running feet and stuck her head out from the station's cubicle. Seeing Chris and his expression, she quickly stood up. "Dr. Wilder, it's all right. Mrs. Wilder's okay. They've taken her for the CT scan. Respiratory therapy is with her, bagging her. It's okay."

Chris stopped, nodded, and released a hiss of expelled relief. For a minute he didn't trust himself to talk. Then with a deep breath he gathered his composure around him like a lab coat of professionalism. "Thank you, when did she go to X-ray?"

"Just a few minutes ago, sir."

Chris turned and walked up the hall to the X-ray department.

The CAT Scan Unit was housed in a small brick building outside the hospital. The hospital, like many rural hospitals, had been serviced for years by a mobile scanner that came in a truck. A huge semi would back up to a garage door like opening specially made for it. Often the patients being scanned were unaware that they'd been outside the hospital at all. Recently, a permanent scanner which was an indication of the tremendous and growing need for this expensive and sophisticated technology had been installed at the hospital. The new unit was housed in a small building set off a few feet from the hospital proper.

Chris walked down the covered walkway to the little building. A technician looked up from the control panel and nodded to him as he entered. Ashley lay on the scanner table, head poked into the massive doughnut-shaped ring of the C. T. unit. A respiratory therapist wearing a protective lead apron could be seen in profile patiently squeezing the bag that was attached to Ashley's endotracheal tube.

Chris could bear to watch the sight only a few moments before lowering his gaze to the screen that showed the emerging images accumulating. So far, they looked normal, but the scan was just beginning.

Chris nodded to the tech and stepped out, relieved slightly now that he had seen Ashley with his own eyes. Restless, he wandered back into the hospital. He remembered he was going to check with the transcribers about Dr. Sayaad's dictation and went on to medical records. The clerk in medical records was not much help.

"I'm sorry," Janice Tate said. "Dr. Sayaad is always so fussy about everything being done perfectly. After the first year of my repeatedly retyping his reports for him, he gave up and started typing his own." She shrugged apologetically,

"That's when he bought the computer in his office, for word processing. We were so impressed with what his computer could do; we got the hospital to get similar units for us. By then, he had already decided he liked doing his own reports." Dr. Sayaad kept his office unlocked so reports and slides could be left on his desk after hours for later review. Chris let himself in and turned on the lights. Unlike most labs and pathology offices, Dr. Sayaad displayed his usual pristine tidiness. Only a small heap of slips and slides growing in his absence marred the clean symmetry of the office. None of the usual notes, cartoons or gag gifts adorned the walls. No plants or fish sat on the credenza behind his desk. The only decoration on the desk was a vase shaped to suggest a human skull. The computer sat on the credenza behind the desk. Chris fished in the skull's jaw for the key to turn it on. He slipped it into the computer and switched it on. He next turned for the small, hooded box of diskettes to begin searching the files. The box was gone from its usual shelf on the wall. A quick search of the tidy office showed no sign of it.

Chris looked back at the computer. It had a hard drive to store information in the unit. Perhaps the report was there. The unit was much like his own, and he had little trouble arriving at the program for stored files in the word processing section. He punched up the directory command only to be met with a challenge.

"Password" the screen blinked.

Chris blinked back. Password?

Chris tried several combinations to guess the password: Dr. Sayaad' s names singly and in combination, forward and backwards. his street, profession, and many others. To each the screen simply flashed "Error, please try again."

Chris spent an hour at this game. Leaving for a few minutes, he went to check on Ashley. She had returned to her room. Norm Smith, the radiologist, said the scan looked normal, yet Ashley remained responsive only to the most painful of stimuli. As much as Chris hated to play doctor for a loved one, he asked for her chart and carefully reviewed it. Dr. Orr seemed to know what he was doing. He had written a complex schedule for diminishing amounts of sedation. The schedule extended into the next day. Blood gasses and all the other lab work looked quite normal.

Slightly heartened, Chris returned to the pathologist's office. He kept a list of all the permutations he tried for access and now he reviewed them. The list was quite long and dealt mostly with personal data. Perhaps he should try some of Dr. Sayaad's interests, but the screen didn't budge for Bach, Beethoven, or Brahms. It flickered for Mozart, but this turned out to be a power surge in the system.

The more the screen denied him, the more desperately Chris tried to get in. He spun the chair as he surveyed the room for inspiration. His eyes fell on the skull. He tried skull and death. After all, Dr. Sayaad always seemed a trifle morbid. Next, he tried a poetic angle. "Death be not proud." There was a Latin saying, Dr. Sayaad of which was particularly fond. Chris sat as if entranced, in front of the flickering screen thinking futilely of forgotten high school Latin. As he contemplated the screen he was interrupted by a tapping on the door. Janice from medical records tapped again. "Dr Wilder?" she called. Chris rotated the chair towards the door.

"Yes?"

"Excuse me, she said, as she stepped into the office with a cassette tape in hand. "The girls in the lab said they thought they saw you in here." A flicker on the screen to his latest effort drew his gaze. The records tech oblivious to his distraction, continued. "You see, this cassette… it most unusual Dr. Sayaad never uses the transcription system, particularly the outside phone-in transcription line. I mean he only works inside the building." Chris's head snapped up. "This is not even a record; it seems to be a letter or message. It's addressed to you. My assistant brought it to me as soon as she realized it might be personal."

Galvanized, Chris jerked from the chair and took the tape from her. "A message? Where can I play it?" he demanded.

Janice led him back to medical records.

In the cramped record room, transcriptionists stared intently at computer screens as they hammered away at keyboards, transcribing the hospital records doctors had dictated. Janice gestured to a young blond girl. She took off her headset. "Gayle, store what you have and let Dr. Wilder use your station for a few minutes." Gayle reached forward, tapped a few keys, and stood up with a smile at Chris.

Janice reached over to the tape player and popped out the tape Gayle had been working from and slid the one in her hand into the machine. Pulling at a cord that ran under the desk, Janice pulled out a foot pedal.

"Large pedal in the middle plays the tape, Smaller one on the left rewinds; on the right is fast forward."

Chris thanked her and settled the headphones on his head. Eyeing the foot pedal, he pushed the large pad in the center. Sayaad's voice sprang to life.

"This is a personal message for Dr. Wilder. If I am not in the building, please deliver it to him as soon as possible. If I am in the hospital, please return this tape to me immediately. It contains a personal message." Dr. Wilder smiled. Dr. Sayaad knew his accent was so recognizable it never even occurred to him to say who he was.

"Christopher, I shall assume that you are listening to this and by implication, my foolish fears were not so foolish. I'm sorry I missed you this evening. I waited for you as long as I could, but I needed to make the opening curtain of Aida touring in Charlotte. I had to leave a little early because of all the mud and construction on the road."

Without noticing, Chris nodded ruefully to himself.

"On my way home, I noticed I was being followed. I normally shouldn't have noticed, but I've been having trouble with a warning light on the dashboard and stopped twice. One car behind me, twice pulled off without passing me. I decided to stop here at a gas station and call you. I tried to leave a message on your answering machine, but it seems you're not on call tonight."

"At any rate, I left a copy of the MacPherson autopsy in your box at the hospital. It appears the girl was murdered after all. Just in case, the report is stolen from your box, a possibility that hadn't occurred to me until I got to wondering why I was being followed, the report is on both the disks on the shelf and the hard drive. The password is '**memento mori,**' Latin for 'Remember, you must die.'"

Chris lifted his foot and sighed. How he wished he'd had this tape a few hours ago. The other bothersome concern was that the disks had clearly been on the pathologist's desk when Doctor Sayaad left the message. But they were absent now. He pressed back down on the pedal.

"The other bit of information I wanted to be sure you got is in regard to the additional drug screening you suggested on Grady Hawkins. Your hunch was correct. His specimen showed enough LSD in his system to render him unable to fly a plane intelligently. I must confess some chagrin because the routine tox screens will not pick up LSD. This is because we look for such tiny amounts and there is no reliable confirming test. Therefore, the federal government does not mandate it"

Sayaad's voice paused so long, Chris almost thought he was finished when the clipped accent resumed. "Assuming it was an intentional poisoning, I spent a good deal of time wondering how it got in Mr. Hawkins's system. It would have to be about the time he arrived at the plane. However, the autopsy showed he ate and drank nothing. So, I am at a bit of a loss."

"Be careful, Chris. The fact I am unable to retrieve this tape you're listening to implies that these people are killers unburdened by the usual codes of civilized conduct."

Clutching the tape, Dr. Wilder returned to Dr. Sayaad's office and the still-waiting computer. Memento mori, he typed. The directory blossomed before his eyes. Elizabeth MacPherson's name was the most recent addition. Chris quickly pulled up the report and skimmed it.

 Most of the report was essentially dry facts recording the weight and disposition of the organs and tissues and the injuries involved. Chris slowed to scan these more closely:

Bruising is noted on the left occiput near the base of the skull. The bruise covers an area of two by three centimeters. A small hairline fracture of the skull is noted at the sight of impact. Minimal swelling or hematoma formation is noted, indicating death took place very shortly thereafter. The next section was even more revealing.

Careful examination of the wrists indicates all of the flexor tendons in both wrists are severed down to the incisions in the radius and ulna. Chris skimmed the remaining report down to the heading: *Conclusions:*

Deceased is a thirty-one-year-old female in excellent health. She suffered a blow of sufficient force to her left occiput with a subdural hematoma of sufficient size to induce unconsciousness. Both of her wrists were slit in identical fashion instead of the usual variation in handedness.

Additionally, the severing of the flexor tendons would perforce negate the capacity to hold a knife to slit the other wrist.

Death was by exsanguination.

The next page had what appeared to be a personal note intended to be clipped to the report.

Christopher, it is almost certain this young lady was murdered. Most wrist slashers cannot place even one cut this deep, let alone two. This is, of course, assuming the patient was conscious to do it in the first place. Placement of the fracture on the skull implies the blow was most probably struck by a left-handed or ambidextrous person.

Sincerely,

Mobashir

Chris sat staring at the screen. He was glad he was right-handed. Janice Tate appeared in the doorway.

"Can I have the tape back now?" she asked as she extended her hand. Righthanded Chris thought. Great, now I 'm going to be spending all my time looking at people's handedness.

Janice stood, hand still out, peering at him. "Dr. Wilder, Mr. Harris, insists that we recycle our tapes. It is good for the bottom line, he says." Janice's tone hinted she doubted Mr. Harris's conclusion.

Chris reached out with the tape to give it to Janice when his hand jerked to a stop. He certainly didn't want to give it back to the medical records people and put them at risk.

"Let me hang on to it awhile Jan. Mr. Harris will have to wait for this one. It's got some personal medical notes I need." Clearly, for someone, the information on this tape was worth killing. But who? Chris pondered a moment. Who knew Elizabeth MacPherson had come to see him? The office staff members were the only ones who came to mind. He even considered Reverend Mosely's admonition, but he'd trust all his staff with his life. Chris hadn't discussed it with anyone else; after all, Ladson had told him not to discuss…Chris snapped up with a jolt. He might just need to have a talk with Ladson Orr!

Chapter 28

Dr. Wilder returned to the house and went upstairs to his study where the EMT's had evacuated Ashley. It took a few minutes of checking in nooks and crannies to find where he had tucked away the pistol before the EMT's arrived on that frantic night. He found it jammed under a couch cushion. As he pulled it out, he winced thinking of what could have happened if someone had sat down on it. He was just not a 'gun person' as he'd told Iris Maynard, as he clicked the safety on the pistol. But here he was getting it out for a second time in as many days after many years where it had never been touched. What was his life becoming?

Chris purchased the .45 automatic pistol at Ashley's insistence years ago when their neighborhood of stately older homes was plagued by a rare rash of burglaries. As a newly minted physician, Chris felt some qualms about owning an instrument for killing. Almost immediately after they bought the pistol, Ashley heard a noise outside. Chris tucked the pistol in his belt and went outside to look around. The gun was a comforting weight against his abdomen.

"I told you that the pistol would come in handy," Ashley noted with a hint of 'I told you so' as Chris stepped out the back door. A brief search quickly revealed the family cat, having escaped the confines of the house, was digging in the trash.

"Madame," Chris announced as he entered, holding the cat by the scruff of the neck. "I have faced danger and conquered."

Ashley was chortling softly as he entered. She glanced at him, only to double over with giddy laughter. "Chris," she howled, "the only thing in danger now, is your manhood." Chris looked down at the cocked pistol stuck down the front of his pants. Now that he looked hard, the angle of the barrel did indeed present a risk to a treasured part of his anatomy. Gingerly, he slid his hand down, taking care to avoid the trigger as he eased the cocked pistol out of its threatening perch, while Ashley doubled up in helpless laughter.

"It's not that funny," he pouted, masculine pride wounded.

"Yes, it is," she chortled as she held up the clip of bullets he'd forgotten to insert.

The next week, Chris got serious about the weapon. He bought a holster and signed up for lessons in shooting. Rural areas may lack many amenities, but Chris found that opportunities for target practice wasn't one of them. Several gun clubs in Craven County were happy to show that Yankee doctor how to shoot.

Once he had achieved proficiency, he asked Ashley to let him give her lessons. She had been strangely reluctant to shoot. It had taken several missed opportunities before Chris finally got her out to the pistol range. He began with a pedantic lecture on the parts of the gun. He held it out to Ashley as he demonstrated the working of the various parts.

Ashley grabbed the pistol from him in mid-lecture. Ramming a clip in, she dropped into a double-handed shooter's stance and emptied the clip. Metal casings rained down around them as Chris looked in surprise at the target. Nine small holes decorated the smallest circle.

Ashley handed him back the pistol. "Sorry," she said, suppressing a grin. "I was going to try to be ladylike and let you teach me, but the lecture was getting to be too much. My mother said it wasn't ladylike to know how to shoot. My daddy taught me on the sly." She giggled, "We're going to have to work on you Chris. You look so out of place here trying to out-macho these country rednecks while wearing a blazer and talking so northern."

The pistol stayed in the drawer from then until last night. Now for the second time, Chris was contemplating its use. He checked the clip and slid the holstered pistol in the small of his back; immediately he felt guilty. What if the police were to stop and search him? That would indeed make Sheriff Charles' day. Carrying a concealed weapon was a felony. He thought about calling the city police. What would he say? "I think my lawyer is trying to kill me?" No, he needed proof. Physical evidence, something to tie the information together.

Ladson Orr's law office was on the second floor of another of Merryville's Victorian brick buildings. It was across the street from the courthouse. Many other lawyers' offices were congregated in the same block. Chris felt certain everyone watched him as he entered and climbed the rickety stairs to Ladson's office. He and Ladson were close in age. Ladson had always been much more approachable than the rest of his family. Chris felt like he was doing something dirty by carrying a pistol with him to talk to one of his closest friends. The secretary knew Chris well, because she was on the phone, she waved from the phone call she was taking and pointed to Ladson's office door. As he reached the door, the secretary called to him. Chris turned around. She had her hand over the phone. "Dr. Wilder, I just wanted you to know how sorry we are to hear about Ashley. I'm sure Ladson's brother can get her through this."

Bad news travels fast in a small town. Chris nodded his thanks. He knocked as he shoved on the heavy wooden door. Ladson was inside, putter in hand, lining up a shot. Golf trophies lined the paneled, high-ceilinged office. Chris always felt a small pang of envy in this office. It seemed to reinforce his resentment of those born to wealth. The office seemed to say to the escaped factory in him: "We've got it made and you never will, and it's been that way for generations."

Ladson made the putt and straightened to shake Chris's hand. "Chris, I'm so sorry," he said for openers. "My brother told me about Ashley. Is there anything I can do to help? Coffee? Something stronger?"

"Coffee's good."

He motioned Chris to the leather couch on the side of the office. As Chris sat, the hidden pistol dug at not only his back but also his conscience. Chris accepted the proffered coffee and stared into it for a moment. He began slowly, "Ladson, I'm here on another matter. You remember the girl I told you about. The one I hypnotized?"

Ladson nodded.

"She was murdered, Ladson. Dr. Sayaad confirmed it."

Ladson stared at him. The implications of a murder danced across his face. "Who... who was it and when did this happen?" he asked. "Was this last night?"

Chris thought Ladson's expression was good for at least an Emmy, maybe even an Oscar. He sure _looks_ surprised, Chris thought. "No," Chris said out loud. "No, it was the Elizabeth MacPherson suicide. I have an autopsy report that says she couldn't have done it to herself."

"Jesus," Ladson exploded. "Who all knows this?"

Careful now, thought Chris. "I've told the sheriff and the chief of police." he lied. "But I've asked them to keep it close to the vest for the moment."

The shock was gone from Ladson's eyes, replaced by a calculating look. "This puts you in sort of a bad light, doesn't it, Chris? The girl leaves a suicide note addressed to you implying hanky-panky and then turns up murdered?"

It was Chris's turn to be surprised. "How'd you know she left a note?"

Ladson smiled. "It's the major courthouse gossip. There is one deputy on the sheriff's patrol who thinks you did it. Three say you couldn't; they think you have better taste. Don't worry, I know you're not dumb enough to leave a note implicating yourself at the scene of a crime."

Chris felt himself damned with faint praise. My turn, he thought. "Now I have a question. After we talked about the hypnosis case, did you tell anyone else about it?"

Ladson was affronted. "I never discuss my client's cases with outsiders! That would be a breach of professional ethics."

Somehow, Chris was not reassured by this claim of ethics especially considering he'd brought a pistol to protect himself.

"So, you haven't spoken to _anyone_ about this? "

Ladson looked thoughtful for a moment, "Well, I did ask my brother if a hypnotized patient could do and say what you said she did. But I didn't tell him her name -just that she was a nurse at the hospital. In fact, you never told me her name. So, I couldn't have gotten her implicated. I needed a medical opinion. This hypnosis stuff sounds like a lot of hocus-pocus to me."

Chris was angry now. "What if there is only one nurse at the hospital involved? That might make her identifiable."

Ladson paced the large office angrily. His agitation stood in marked contrast to the rows of musty law books behind him. "This is absurd! Are you implying my brother would be involved in something like a bloody scheme, that. . . that my brother, a doctor, would murder someone?"

Chris was not actually sure about the murder part, but he had many questions. "No, but he might have told someone or said something to point the finger at her. Look at it from my side. No one on my staff knows anything about what happened except that she was in my office. I discussed it with only you.

Hell, I didn't even talk it over with my wife. When you told me to clam up, I did! Now the girl turns up murdered, and the suicide note implicates me."

Ladson whirled around to face Chris. "There's another side to this, Chris. You have no idea who she told. Maybe she confessed to this witch's group herself. At any rate, I think the simplest approach is the direct one which is to ask my brother in person. He should be home now for lunch. We'll get the answer from the horse's mouth, damn it." Ladson flung open the heavy office door. "We're going to my brother's for lunch," he told the surprised secretary on the other side. "I'll be back soon."

Charles Orr's house was one of the old Merry homeplaces located about three miles out of town on rolling farmland. The white clapboard Greek Revival home, just short of plantation size, sat atop a low hill, brick wings running off the sides in back. The house looked down over pastures filled with cattle. The back of the house opened onto a wooded landscape.

Ladson parked in a car-sized pergola next to the side door. He bounded up the steps and knocked. There was no answer. "Sometimes he takes a nap during his lunch hour," Ladson remarked as he pulled out a key. "He may not have heard us." Ladson unlocked the door and held it for Chris. The two entered the parlor. "Wait here."

A brief trip to the master bedroom failed to turn up. Dr. Orr. Ladson excused himself to call the office and see if anyone there knew of his brother's whereabouts. "We'll find out where he is and go settle this thing," he promised. Chris took the opportunity to answer nature's call and stepped into the bathroom. As he relieved himself, he looked around the unusually large lavatory. A few magazines in a basket near the sink gave evidence of the older man's double curse-prostate enlargement and constipation.

Chris turned to wash his hands. He looked at the window. The screen was loose. Almost anyone could slide it out and break in, he thought. He turned back to the sink and washed his hands. To dry his hands, he pulled a towel off a nearby shelf over the toilet. There was a clunk behind the toilet. as something fell behind it. Chris peered curiously into the crevice between the towels and the wall. His eyes widened. Maybe there was a reason why Ladson hadn't led Chris through the rest of the house. A hammering on the bathroom door interrupted him as he reached into the crevice for a better look.

"Hurry up" Ladson called, "Have you taken root in there?" Chris stopped torn, the sound of the water faucet running covered the small squeak of the window lock as Chris flicked it open. With a last glance to judge the size of the opening, he flushed and yanked open the door.

When Chris emerged from the bathroom, Ladson was in the hall. His tone carried a tone of accusation, "The reason my brother isn't here is because he's over at your office on his afternoon off seeing your patients, so you could be with your sick wife. The remainder remained unsaid. Chris visibly reddened in embarrassment. Ladson's tone relented a smidgeon. "Come on, I'll take you back to town. I've got to go to the office to finish some work. I'll come by and check on you and Ashley later this afternoon." The atmosphere in the car on the ride back was almost as chilly as the air outside. All the way to town, Chris's silence was enforced by guilt over the trust he'd betrayed. What was worse was that he knew in his heart of hearts that despite all, he would make use of this opportunity. Despite the blast of the car's heater, he shivered. He realized with a start that Christmas was only four days away.

Chris returned briefly to the hospital. Ashley was still heavily sedated, but the respirator was no longer attached. Tara, one of the regular ICU nurses, shyly admitted that the anesthesiologist who'd been monitoring Ashley's care had insisted the machine was no longer necessary. "Dr. Orr wanted to get your second opinion to support him," Tara continued. "He was quite miffed you were not here to back him up. I just thought I ought to warn you." Another few bricks of guilt joined the heavy load Chris carried on his back beside the pistol still under his sport coat. The nurse continued. "Dr. Orr is afraid both you and Ashley are pushing too hard, too much stress. He said and I quote, 'I don't want them sharing adjoining slabs in Dr. Sayaad's morgue.'"

Chris smiled tightly at that. "I'll be careful. I promised I 'd make a house call on a friend's mother, will you cover for me if Dr. Orr calls? I don't want to get in any more trouble. I promise I'll be back in just twenty to thirty minutes." Tara was wary, but she'd been a friend and patient of Chris's for years. When he wheedled a little more, she finally, grudgingly agreed to cover for him.

The Taurus wagon sped down the two-lane blacktop near Charles' house. Chris noticed another new subdivision going up had stalled.. There was little construction work going on at present. Despite being in the path of growth emanating from Charlotte to points west and south, the series of murders had killed demand for housing in the area.

Chris slowed as he reached Charles's home and then pulled on past it. A few hundred yards further on, the woods came down around the pasture to border the blacktop. Chris turned up a dirt rut used mostly by hunters and continued into the forest until he estimated he was parallel with the house. Leaving the car in the cover of several large still green cypress trees, he hopped out and threaded his way through the trees toward the unlocked bathroom window. When he reached the tree line, he looked again to be sure he saw no cars. Charles's wife had divorced him several years earlier, and Chris's only real concern was a late-arriving maid. Both brothers had difficulty hanging on to their wives, he reflected.

Feeling foolish and guilty, but nonetheless determined, Chris sprinted across the pasture past several mildly curious cows and into the backyard proper. He paused to look around again. Then again. He found himself struggling to find the will to go to the window and open it. His conscience screamed: Civilized people do not search other people's homes. Orr is a doctor and a colleague. How will I face him when I find nothing here? Chris silenced the voice. Someone had threatened him and his wife. Someone was killing his patients. The need-to-know overrode all other reasoning. Pausing a moment to listen

for unexpected guests, he pulled up the unlocked bathroom window and let himself in. He returned to the cupboard of towels by the sink.

His interrupted glance had brought him to a single word on the towel filled crevice: SATAN. Taking care to note the arrangement of the towels so he could replace them properly later, Chris reached into the crevice between towels and toilet. His probing hand quickly encountered a heavy book. He carefully drew it out. The cover: *COVENS AND CULTS: THE INSIDE STORY OF WITCHCRAFT AND THE WORSHIP OF SATAN*. The book was a psychological treatise on forbidden magic. A folded-over page marked a spot midway through the book. With a growing sense of excitement, Chris thumbed the book to reach the marked spot. It marked a chapter heading entitled: PSYCHIATRIC IMPLICATIONS OF TATTOOS AND OTHER MARKINGS. The accompanying photo was a photo of a woman's privates with an upside-down star.

Chris felt a moment's dizziness as his head thudded painfully. He thumbed quickly through the rest of the book. There were no other markings or even a name in the overleaf. Was it a clue, or was Orr simply intrigued by the same star that Dr. Wilder was as coroner? So tantalizingly close, but it wasn't enough. He needed a smoking gun, an undeniable link, to justify calling Junior Charles, and to absolve himself for breaking and entering. He carefully replaced the book, replaced the towels, and headed out into the remainder of the house. Chris made a quick search of the more public rooms of the house, pausing only to flip through notes on the desk. He highly doubted that a man like Dr. Orr would leave clues to a murder in such public rooms.

He moved quickly to the back rooms in the brick wings. These, for the most part, proved to be guest rooms although several rooms were simply storage. Chris flipped back sheets from piles of old furniture. The clouds of dust he stirred made Chris believe no one had been back here in years.

He tried the upstairs next, pausing to look out over the fields to the road for any cars. Nothing there.

He looked at the attic. He still had the attic and basement to go, and with each passing second, the little scared voice of his conscience gained strength. Up or down? At a deep and unconscious level, Chris decided if there was evil afoot, it would likely be down in the bowels of the basement. Without knowing why, he headed down the stairs. Evidently this whole exercise was based on feelings and intuition, not reasoned logic.

Like the Jaycee hut, like so many structures in Craven County, the old Merry Home was built on the foundations of an even older farmhouse. The walls of the basement under the original house were lined with mortared stones and the floor was packed dirt. Pillars of crumbling brick thrust up here and there from the dirt to support the floor above. Two tiny cellar windows lightened the gloom. It smelled of must and age, and it hummed. Chris took one last look out the window for approaching cars and descended the ancient wooden stairs.

As his eyes adjusted to the gloom, Chris saw nothing unusual in the basement. A massive and ancient freezer chest hunkered in a corner, the source of the hum, Chris thought, as he descended the steps. He walked over to the freezer and rested a hand on it. There was no tell-tale vibration; the plug was out. Thinking of hidden bodies, Chris lifted the lid. It was empty. Chris turned around and surveyed the length of the basement. At the far end where one of the wings had been added above, the stone walls gave way to a concrete floored, cinder block hallway. Chris crossed the basement and started down the hallway. It was lined with doors. As he passed one door, the hum suddenly crescendoed. Chris stopped and tried the door. Locked.

If you live alone in a locked house, why would you lock a closet? he wondered. The answer was obvious. To keep people like me out. He was determined now not to leave without something, some evidence, some hint one way or the other. Conviction struck him that his smoking gun was behind this door. Chris pulled out his keys. On the ring was a small pocketknife with a screwdriver inscribed with the slogan of a popular anti-hypertensive agent. It had been given to him by a drug rep a few years ago.

Chris used the screwdriver end to pry back a little of the molding and then pulled out his wallet and extracted a gold credit card to spring the lock. He'd seen this credit card trick done on television and in movies. He wondered if it really worked. It did. The door swung open, and Chris switched on the lights. He could tell at a glance that he'd found what he'd come for.

Chapter 29

Against the wall hunkered a smaller version of Dr. Sayaad's blood bank, a chrome and stainless-steel refrigeration storage unit. Glass doors showed the unit was largely full of carefully stacked blood storage bags Each was labeled with a name, date of acquisition and the results of blood borne relevant testing--notably AIDS. A temperature gauge in the shape of a wheel hung to the side of the massive cabinet. There, pens marked the temperature over hour and week-long periods on a circular graph. Chris opened the unit and pulled out the closest bag of blood and glanced at the slip. He froze. It said: *Sayaad, M., acquired 12/19. Hold for HIV results.*

Chris placed the bag back on the shelf. Several more bags held the same notation. He reached further back and pulled yet another bag. This one said "MacPherson, E.

On the other side of the cabinet were dozens of tubes of blood. A neatly typed label proclaimed these as "potential donors." Chris pulled several of these out and turned them over. He recognized the names on several, including one marked "Wilder, A." He slammed the labeled tube back in the holder. Unnoticed, the tiny slow-moving pen of the temperature gauge inched up on the paper as the misty cold air continued to gush out while he rifled through the various bags.

Only a small freezer in the corner was left to be checked. The little voice of caution, suppressed by horror and fascination, was almost silent now. He needed more. Chris pulled open the large freezer lid. As he expected, it was full of neatly stacked frozen bags of blood. Chris reached far down into the back. His fingers quickly numbed as he separated one of the lower bags from the others. Carefully he pulled it out, shifting the bag to his other hand. He tucked his chilled fingers under his arm to warm them. After a moment, he brushed off the icy rime and scanned the label: *Feaster, S*

A bump and voice overhead jerked him back to reality.

Chris flung the bag back into the freezer and softly, but quickly, lowered the lid. Turning back to the open door, he almost tripped over a collection of knives and axes in a large gunny sack. A distant part of his mind cataloged their presence as probably the murder weapons. A more immediate and emotive part screamed for him to hide. Chris flipped off the lights, wincing at the audible snap and eased the door closed behind him.

Quickly, he hurried up the remainder of the short corridor frantically trying the knobs. They were all locked. The voices stopped in a part of the upper house that Chris tagged the kitchen. "Wanna beer"? called one voice.

"Sure," came the reply. "You get 'em while I go get the tools and the evening's libations." Neither voice sounded familiar. Chris was in a near panic. Hide! screamed the voice in his head. But where? He listened as the footsteps traversed the house towards the stairs. His eyes fell on the unused freezer.

Chris sprinted across the expanse of the old basement. He had to beat the footsteps to the freezer. Once someone started down those steps and rounded the corner, there would be no more time to hide in the abandoned box. There was no other place to go. He reached the freezer and jerked up the lid and began to climb inside. A shaft of bright light shone down the stairs as the upstairs door opened. Chris hastily pulled down the lid. It almost clicked shut, before at the least second, he remembered not to lock himself in the freezer. He jerked out his abused credit card and slid it over the locking slot. The lid closed as footsteps crunched in the dirt at the bottom of the stairs.

Chris watched through the miniscule slot the card afforded, as the middle part of a non-descript man swept by. Chris could only see from about mid-chest to upper thigh. A red lumberjack shirt stretched across the middle was visible. Wilder's heart hammered in his chest, and he was sure his ragged breathing would bring the man back to wonder why a freezer gasped at him. Footsteps proceeded in an unhurried fashion across the basement and a whistle started up as keys jingled. The snap of the light switch. Several minutes passed. Chris could faintly hear a repetitive thunk in the distance. It sounded like someone was emptying the freezer. Metal rattled as the sack of tools was hefted. The jingle/rattle quickly grew louder.

Hurry up, Chris silently begged. The sack of tools appeared in the hall along with a plastic trash bag filled with bags of blood. Both bags slithered to the ground as the man stepped out to close and lock the door. A hand dipped in a pocket as the other hand reached for the door. Both stopped. There was a muttered curse. Redshirt stepped back into the room.

"Crap! James, can you hear me?"

The voice upstairs answered in the distance. "Yeah, what? Are you comin'? The beer's getting warm."

Redshirt answered, "I think you better come down here. I think we got trouble." There was a clatter of footsteps followed by the heavy thumping of feet coming down the stairs. A blue work shirt crossed Chris's field of vision.

Blueshirt crossed the concrete floor. "What's up? Doc ain't been in here today, has he?"

"No, he's been filling in for that other doc. The one whose wife is in the hospital."

"Oh yeah, I heard about that. Boy, I'll bet that guy would crap stove wood if he knew his wife was going to be our next donor."

"Shut up. Look at the temperature gauge. See the bump here. Someone's been in this refrigerator today, and I don't think it's one of our circle."

The two studied the gauge. "Damn, the sucker's still coming up. Whoever it was, was just here in the last hour."

"Should we call an emergency? See if the Doc wants to cancel the meeting tonight?"

Redshirt again hefted the bag of tools. "Naw, Doc will take care of it if he wants to. Whoever it was is probably running like crazy. After all, who's gonna take up against our Doc in this town?" Redshirt and Blueshirt laughed as they clumped by and up the stairs.

At the top of the stairs, they split up. Their voices wafted down to the freezer, "I'll take the stuff on to the church, and you stay here and keep an eye out for a while in case they're still around or come back. There's a shotgun in the study behind the curtain. It's loaded. "The shaft of light down the stairs winked out as the door closed.

Chris paused in the freezer, stunned as he contemplated the conversation he'd just heard.

After another minute, Chris cautiously lifted the lid of the freezer. He retrieved his now useless credit card, gouged where the lock mechanism had tried to catch hold. As he climbed out of the freezer, his body groaned as it plainly told him he was getting too old to be playing James Bond.

He had to get to a phone and get Ashley protected, and he had to do it quickly. But how to get out of this basement with an armed guard overhead? Thinking about James Bond reminded him that he, too, was armed. He pulled out the pistol. Any thoughts of feeling silly or guilty had completely dissipated. Chris Wilder meant to protect his wife if he had to kill to do it. He chambered a round and flipped off the safety.

Stealthily, he climbed the stairs and peeked through a gap in the door frame. No sign of Redshirt. Chris figured that he had the advantage of the element of surprise because he doubted, the men thought he was still here if they had they would have combed the house and quite possibly found him. He slid silently into the kitchen and carefully made his way to the nearest opening to the outside. The door was locked with a deadbolt requiring a key. The ticking of a grandfather clock in a distant room was the only noise he could hear. Where the hell was Redshirt? Outside patrolling or upstairs checking rooms or on the roof waiting for a target to appear?

Chris slid through the house on tiptoe first to the front and then the side doors. All were locked. He'd have to go out the way he came in. He worked his way back to the bathroom without seeing Redshirt. During the entire trip, his heart pounded in anticipation of a shotgun blast from an unseen quarter. It appeared Redshirt was not in the house. Hastily he tucked the pistol in his belt and entered the bathroom. He crossed to the window. Unlocking it, he quickly began to climb out. Suddenly he remembered he hadn't locked the window on the way in.

Redshirt waited until Chris was straddling the windowsill, one leg in and one leg out, body trying to clear the screen. Then he yanked back the shower curtain while lowering his shotgun into firing position, he shouted, "Freeze, sucker!"

The shout saved Chris's life. He had recognized his peril but, frozen for a moment, he could not decide which way to go. The scream so jarred him that he lost his balance and fell out through the opening. As Redshirt fired, the window above Chris exploded in a loud geyser of glass and he fell in a curtain of shards. Chris had no conscious recall of using the pistol. He was not giving

Redshirt a chance to come to the window and aim again. He simply jerked the gun out and fired in a diagonal swipe through the walls into the bathroom, emptying the clip in the process. His aim was not improved by his stress. Bullets pierced the aging pine walls as easily as they would the open window. His ringing ears dimly recorded a muffled thump inside.

After a moment of stunned inaction, he hazarded a peek through a convenient bullet hole and was rewarded with a close-up view of Redshirt slumped around the toilet, his knees in a puddle of blood. Redshirt's eyes were wide, surprised by death. They looked back at Chris accusingly through the bullet hole. It didn't even occur to Chris to go back in and use the phone inside. If he had, the outcome might have been different.

Instead, he just picked up and ran for the woods. The trip to the car was a jumble of conflicting thoughts focused primarily on the struggle between a doctor deliberately killing someone and his sheer exultation at still being alive. A quotation from Winston Churchill rang through his mind as he sprinted past astonished cattle. "There are few things so stimulating as being unsuccessfully shot at." Pausing at his car, his questing hand noted a pulse that hammered in his neck. "Jesus!"

Flinging himself in the driver's seat, Chris turned the car around and blew down the rutted dirt road like a missile. Swerving to dodge a logging truck, he shot out onto the paved road. On the outskirts of town on Gaffney Street was a short rundown strip mall consisting of a liquor store, beauty shop, video rental store, and convenience mart It also had a phone. Chris pulled in and screeched to a stop. He uttered a low groan. An elderly lady was holding an animated conversation on the phone. Chris paused for just a moment or two. Finally, with a courage born of desperation, he pulled the lady out of the phone booth. In the face of her sputtered protests, he snapped, "Medical Emergency" and hung the phone up. Quickly he punched in a number. "ICU" the voice answered.

"This is Dr. Wilder. Is my wife all right?"

"Well. She's still heavily sedated but other than that she seems fine." Chris sagged against the phone booth in relief.

"Thank God. Listen, nurse, I just heard a rumor that I take very seriously. Someone might try to harm my wife. I want you to call security and have a guard placed by her room. No one is to bother her. Do you hear me? Absolutely no one." Surprise and fear sounded in the nurse's voice.

"Yes doctor, I'll call security immediately."

Chris hung up with a sigh of relief. He made it; she was safe. It didn't occur to the nurse, however, that such an instruction might include the patient's physician.

Doctor Orr ambled down the hospital hall after finishing at Chris Wilder's office. It had been an interesting day. He had learned a lot about the workings of the younger doctor's office. He was particularly interested in seeing how Chris's office computer worked. Dr. Orr had read long and hard about computers but had not yet had a chance to see what they could do. The office staff, delighted to have Dr. Orr for the day, had spent the day's slow moments demonstrating its high-tech possibilities. On his way home, Dr. Orr decided to check on Ashley. He stopped short, in front of the security officer sitting patiently in front of her room.

"What's up, Henry?" he asked.

The security guard stood shrugged in confusion. "Dr. Wilder called a little while ago and said he thought someone might try to kill his wife."

Dr. Orr's face furrowed in concern. "That sounds serious, Henry. We ought to get a Sheriff's deputy to come out here and guard her. After all, they can carry firearms." Henry, who was not allowed to carry a pistol, nodded at hearing Dr. Orr's wisdom. "Tell you what, Henry, I've got to check on Mrs. Wilder. I'll keep the door open, and you go up to the nurse's station and call the sheriff. Tell him I said to make the call. I'll watch Mrs. Wilder. If there's any trouble, believe me, I'll holler."

Henry turned and headed down the hall.

Dr. Orr hummed a low tune under his breath as he quietly entered the room. Out of his bag he drew a large vial and aspirated the contents into a syringe. He looked at Ashley's IV bottle. It was about half empty. He walked to the shelf by the bed where the next bottle sat in preparation for use and injected the contents into the waiting bottle. He had returned the vial and syringe to his bag and was listening to the sleeping Ashley's lungs when Henry returned. As he nodded to Henry, fingers on his lips to avoid waking Ashley, Dr. Orr heard his name on the overhead page. He went up to the phone and answered. He listened to an excited voice on the other end. "I believe we have the matter under control for the moment," he answered. "Just proceed with taking the medicine as I directed. I think the patient will be ready for the operation on time." The party on the other end hung up.

Chris had only one quarter to make the first call. The pay phone's previous occupant now hammered on the booth's door. With Ashley safe, Dr. Wilder headed to the hospital to call the sheriff's office. He had no sooner pulled into the doctors' parking lots when he saw Ladson's red convertible flying down the hospital drive in the gathering twilight. Ladson jumped out. "Jesus Christ, thank God you're here!" he exclaimed. "I think there may be some truth to all this stuff you've been talking about. I've had my ear to the ground this afternoon. Called some old clients on the sketchier side. The word around town is that something horrible is going on. There is talk about making human sacrifices and devil worshiping tonight. Rumor has it that it might involves that large black church outside of town, the Living Tree African Presbyterian Church. Charles is mixed up in this somehow too. We've got to hurry before someone gets hurt!"

 Chris nodded, relieved to be believed. "I know. I was just about to call the sheriff."

Ladson gestured to the passenger door. "I've already called the sheriff's office. They sounded skeptical, but said they'd send someone. We've got to hurry before someone gets hurt! Chris hopped in the car, and they roared out of the lot. Chris didn't have time to notice that Dr. Orr's pick-up truck was in the doctors' parking lot.

Dr. Orr stopped at the ICU nurses' station and beckoned to the nurse. His leonine features were grave as he ran a hand over his silver hair and leaned his tall frame over the counter.

"I'm a little concerned about Dr. Wilder, his mental state and these wild accusations he made about someone threatening to hurt his wife."

The Helen the nurse nodded emphatically in agreement.

"We'll leave the guard there tonight to humor him. I know he's been checking Ashley's chart, and that's okay, but don't let him change my orders without checking with me. You know what they say about doctors treating their own families." Dr. Orr looked down to the nurse, concern written on his face. "I think Dr. Wilder is a little overwrought. Let's try to help him get over all this, okay?" Dr Orr turned as if to leave, then turned back. "Oh, nurse," he called. "I'll be away for the next several hours. If you have any questions, call Dr. MacAbee. He's listening out for me."

The nurse watched him go thinking, what a lucky man Dr. Wilder was to have Dr. Orr caring for his wife.

As Chris and Ladson headed out into the countryside, Ladson attempted to explain what he'd heard that afternoon. "It was the damnedest thing I ever heard," exclaimed Ladson. "I got this client, a strictly second-rate thief, who is always in trouble for something. I ask him if he's heard anything about suicides or a devil's cult. He looks really scared. Says the word is out that that girl, Elizabeth, was murdered for blabbing. Says he's not going to be next." Ladson shook his head. "I tried to get a little more out of him. "Who's in charge' I asked him. Guy gets schitzy. 'Why don't you ask your brother?' he says. I ask him what he means, but he just takes off running. And me his lawyer for Chrissake!"

The heater was making the inside of the car warm, and the windows were beginning to steam up. Ladson appeared not to notice. Christmas decorations on the houses they passed looked like garish flares of fire. "So, I called Charles and asked what the hell was going on. He got cold on me. Me, his brother! Says, I shouldn't be asking questions if I don't really want to know the answers. I say we need to talk, and I mean now. You know what he tells me? He says, and I quote, 'Not yet.' I mean it's like he's a different person. I wondered if maybe he's had a nervous breakdown or something."

By now the windows of the car were almost completely clouded. The car became a cocoon, a tightening nest of warmth amid the rushing winter's wind.

The cocoon that Chris and Ladson were riding in was a tightening nest of warmth in the midst of the darkened rushing of the winter's night wind.

"Christ, I can't see a thing." Ladson said as he smeared a small circle on the windshield to peer through. "So anyway, I'm starting to really sweat now. Charles has always been the soul of the distinguished doctor, and I can't comprehend this mysterious behavior. I'm thinking if he's really decompensating, maybe he'll tell me where he is so I can come get him. That's when I know he's really lost it. I ask him where he is going, and he tells me to come to this church they plan to burn. Then he says he hopes I'll come and join them, like it's a goddamn wienie roast or something."

Ladson slowed the car a fraction. The familiar peeling sign of the Living Tree African Presbyterian Church appeared in the glare of the headlights. Ladson drove past. Chris started to stop him. "There's the…hey!"

Ladson gave him a sharp look as they headed down the hill. "What do you want to do Chris? Walk up and knock on the front door? 'Scuse me, I think you have someone who's murdered a couple of my patients. Would you mind putting this straight jacket on? These people have done something to my brother, brainwashed him or something. I think we both agree that they're killers, so let's drive on by and hide the car and wait for the cops to get here. I mainly want to be sure to stop any bloodshed and make sure that my brother is OK. It's obvious he's snapped or something."

Chris opened his mouth to tell Ladson about the events at his brother's house, but a small cautionary inner voice halted him. With all that had gone on, he was not quite ready to give anything away just yet. Ladson abruptly turned the car into a small dirt road crowded with underbrush. "Used to hunt down here," he explained. "The trail doubles back not far from the church." Satisfied that he'd pulled the car out of view, Ladson killed the engine. He reached past Chris to the glove compartment, pulled out two pistols and handed one to Chris.

"We're going to have a quiet look-see now. No cavalry charges. The police can do that when they get here. These are just for protection while we scout out the lay of the land.

Chris felt a surge of guilt as he thought of the now- empty pistol he'd carried into Ladson's office ready to do battle. Now here was, Ladson, handing him a pistol. Chris tucked the pistol into his belt. They moved carefully in the dark up the rutted path. Before long, lights could be seen coming from where the church should be. Several cars had pulled into the parking lot, and the church lights cast a cozy glow from the hilltop at odds with the malign project about to unfold. Chris and Ladson approached from the darkened back of the building working themselves slowly through the brush and up to the window.

On the top of the hill, the windows were accessible to the ground and Chris and Ladson carefully peered in the window nearest the altar. Inside, several men were working on various projects. Several were desecrating the church with spray paint, making huge point-down stars on the walls of the nave and the numbers 666. Several swastikas competed with pornographic renditions of the devil. A large cauldron was set up on an iron tripod in front of the line of pews. As Chris looked on, a large bowl of what appeared to be blood was poured into the cauldron. This was followed by several large canisters of clear fluid; a lighted taper was held over the side. The mixture ignited with a whoosh that Chris could hear even outside the building. Shortly after the cauldron was set alight, Chris noticed with a jolt that Ladson was no longer with him.

"Ladson, he whispered frantically. "Ladson!"

There was no answer in the cold night air. Chris sat back on his heels for a moment. Had he been betrayed? If so, why the gun? Chris flipped the revolver open. Slugs ringed the chamber. He snapped it back. A commotion at the front of the church caught his attention. Shouts and cries for help arose in the dark. Chris jerked the pistol up and scanned the darkness. The shadows made it difficult to make much out. Then, through the window, Chris saw the church doors open as Reverend Mosley was pushed inside and flung to the floor. Behind him, directing the captors, was Dr. Orr.

Chris was still staring at this latest turn of events when Ladson jumped down the hill to land silently beside him. Chris stifled a shriek of surprise, but just barely. Ladson shushed him frantically.

"Damn," Ladson hissed. "They caught Reverend Mosley. I saw someone creeping through the woods as we did, only closer to the front of the church.

I thought it was the police, but it was Mosley. He insisted on going down there. Said it was important to confront evil when it's found. I mean he just walked down there and started yelling at them, telling them off." At that moment, Dr. Orr came back into view.

Chris pointed an accusing finger quietly toward Dr. Orr. "He looks okay me," he hissed. Ladson looked at him and groaned with dismay. That Dr. Orr was in charge and directing the work could not be disputed. Chris recognized with a start that he knew more than a few of those working below.

Finally, the preparations seemed to be winding down. The conspirators uprooted the pews and pushed them along the sides of the church. One by one, the men left the church to congregate in the parking lot and talk.

Reverend Mosley was abandoned, gagged, and tied up in a corner. Ladson became agitated. "Damn it," he hissed, "Junior's men should be here by now! Where can they be? We've got to stop this before anyone else gets hurt or killed." The two debated about trying to rescue the pastor and even got as far as to consider sneaking further down the hillside. One of the cars started up and circled round the parking lot. To avoid being seen, Chris and Ladson dove under the edge of the church behind one of the brick piers at the front. Headlights washed over the side of the church and then faded up the dirt drive.

From their position, they could see several of the men talking, but could not decipher the words out of the low murmur of voices. Finally, Ladson nudged Chris.

"I think that idiot dispatcher at the sheriff's office must have thought I was a crank call. I'm going to call Junior at home and get his ass out here now! You keep an eye out until I get back. For God's sake, don't get caught." With that, Ladson crouched and scurried up the muddy hillside under the church until there was no room left to crawl. As Chris watched him silhouetted against the starlit sky, Ladson scuttled to the edge of the church and slipped into the underbrush and was gone.

Chris settled onto the cold hard ground. As his eyes adjusted, he looked around. There was the usual detritus found under a building: bits of wire, broken glass, occasional bricks, and some rotten boards. Nothing that looked helpful. Chris heard a loud thumping noise above him and for the second time that night, he almost gave himself away. After a moment, one of the few

remaining men burst out of the building. His speech was loud enough to for Chris to hear as he shouted to the others clustered in the parking lot.

"Hey, this pastor guy is getting kind of hard to hang on to., tied up or no, he's a big fella. Can we do something to him to restrain him more effectively?" There was a brief huddled conference. Dr. Orr's baritone voice boomed across the parking lot with chilling finality.

"I think I can solve that problem. We'll just let him hang around for a while."

"What?"

"Crucify him!"

"What?"

The little group followed the tall doctor across the parking lot. The baritone continued, "Come, I'll show you." The voices modulated to a murmur as the group passed inside the door. Chris followed Ladson's path up the hill under the building, slipping twice in the semi-frozen mud as he hurried away. Emerging near the window, Chris cautiously levered himself up and peered in. At first, all he could see was Reverend Mosley trussed up in the corner. Even through the window, gagged, Chris could hear him angrily denouncing the desecration of his church. Chris followed his gaze to the front of the church.

Shifting his gaze to the other side of the window, Chris looked in horror as the group worked the pulleys to lower the life-sized cross to the ground. The others stood back as one man used a broken board and his boots to smash apart the plaster representation of Jesus. Several more men walked towards the backside of the church. Chris shifted sides of the window. Two men picked up the struggling minister. Chris recognized one of the two as Charlie Davenport, the manager of a local feed and seed store, where he'd done business for years. As they dragged the minister to his feet, the gag came out and he spit in their faces. Reaction was swift as Charlie whipped out a pistol and clubbed the minister into unconsciousness with three hard strikes of the gun's butt. Two of the men dragged Mosley's limp form up to the front of the church and arranged him on the cross. Two others had passed through

the doors and into the night. One now returned with a wooden container which Chris quickly identified as the pastor's tool chest. Charlie bent over the toolbox and pulled out two large nails and retrieved the hammer.

Chris decided he could wait no longer. He couldn't let them crucify the pastor. He pulled Ladson's pistol out of his belt and stood. Carefully, he backed out of the view of the window. With a sudden cold chill, the business end of a pistol pushed smoothly against Chris's neck from behind. A familiar baritone voice whispered in his ear. "Good evening, Dr. Wilder. Didn't I say you should stay at the hospital?" Charles Orr slid the pistol back along Chris's neck in what could only be taken as a caress. "Turn around. I want to see your face," he crowed.

Chris turned slowly, hoping the shadows hid the pistol in his hand long enough. As he finished the turn Charles glanced down. As he did, Chris mentally apologized to Ladson and pulled the trigger.

Chapter 30

There was a disappointing click. Braced for the report that never came, Chris looked down at the gun in shock and jerked the trigger, again...nothing. Charles looked down too.

He seemed unsurprised to see Ladson's pistol in Chris's hand. "I see Ladson never got around to repairing the broken firing pin in that old pistol. The white handles are quite distinctive," he observed. "This one, however, works just fine." As he spoke, he brought the barrel of his pistol to bear on a point between Chris's eyes. Chris closed his eyes and swallowed, his mind raced, trying to find a way out.

There was no place to run, no place to go. He had lost. He felt a moment of almost preternatural silence in which he could distinctly hear the frenzied beating of his heart. Then, an explosion. He felt his left ear blasted off his head. His first thought registered the incredible pain that began as a howling roar as the explosion faded. Even as he reflexively grabbed at the remains of his bloody ear, his second thought was to marvel that he was still alive.

Charles Orr's composure never varied, "Like I said, my gun still works fine." Chris looked up from the spot where he had fallen. His probing fingers revealed a tattered gap in his ear. Aside from the fierce clanging buzz in his ear and the pain of what was left, he was otherwise unhurt. He pulled his hand away. Blood dripped from his fingers.

"No, Chris, you don't get off that easily," Charles Orr snarled over the persistent roar in Chris's ear. "Tonight, you're the main attraction for our special send-off service. Now, hands up. Let's get going. I've got other business to attend to." He gestured down the hill with the still-smoking pistol. Chris pulled himself to his feet, raised his hands, and began to stumble down the dark muddy hillside. Charles stayed behind and out of reach. A loud racket arose inside the church as the sounds of hammering began, followed by shouts, and then screams of anguish.

Despite the sound of gunfire, there was minimal interruption in the preparations. Only two men came out of the church at the sound of the shots. They peered up the hill past the church lights at Dr. Orr who waved back to show himself unharmed. When the two men approached, Orr turned Chris over to them, one of whom Chris recognized by his voice as Blueshirt.

Pausing briefly to rope Chris's hands together with a grimy rag, Blueshirt led the way to the pastor's office.

Under careful guard, they set Chris into the ancient desk chair on wheels. Removing the rag binding his wrists, they methodically roped Chris to the chair. When Dr. Orr was satisfied with the knots, he waved the two out. He closed the door and set down the pistol on the bookshelf well away from Chris. He pulled out a large, battered cardboard box from the corner and began to sort through the contents. He seemed completely indifferent to the plight of his colleague and supposed friend. Finally, as he began to find the items he was looking for, he turned a curious eye toward the chair and its prisoner.

The tone of voice he used was chilling for its lack of concern. "Tell me, Chris," he began conversationally, "What put you on to me?"

Chris glared mutely up at him.

"Oh, come now, what are you going to do? Hold out for name, rank and serial number? The war is over. You lost. You don't want to go to your grave, without knowing what's happening here, don't you? You answer my questions, and I'll answer yours. But you'll have to hurry. It's almost showtime."

Orr's voice was calm, flat, and dead sounding. Chris shivered. 'Showtime' did not have a comforting implication. The exchange had an air of unreality as Chris cleared his throat. "It was the AIDS and blood borne pathogens testing, " he answered hoarsely and somewhat loudly to compensate for the intense ringing in his left ear. "I was able to find a link between a patient who had one of your panel of tests and was later murdered." His voice was a little steadier now. "I also found out Elizabeth MacPherson did not commit suicide but was murdered, by a left-handed man. I notice you're left-handed." Dr Orr paused with a shaggy garment held in his left hand.

"So, I am." His face creased with a rueful smile; the first display of feeling shown so far. "Poor Betty. I don't think she ever knew what it was she told you under hypnosis. I just about had a stroke when Ladson told me of your account." He shrugged. "How did you find a copy of Dr. Sayaad's report? I thought I managed to get all the copies, plus those disks."

Chris hesitated.

"Come on, Chris. I don't mind if people find out she's murdered. It fits my plans quite well actually. I wasn't ready for you to know the truth just yet."

"Where's Dr. Sayaad?"

Orr looked nonchalant. He flipped the end of the costume over his head. His first word was muffled as he poked his head through it.

"Dead," he said. "Dead and filed away where he should be."

"Where is that? "

"Where did you find the report?"

"It was on the hard drive of his computer."

"Ah yes, computers. Such interesting devices. Your office staff has been teaching me all about them. I must get one for my office." Orr shrugged the hide-like costume shirt down on his torso. "I must be almost the last doctor in town not to have a computer. I thought it was just a billing tool, but your nurse Mary Ann helped me do a quick literature search and showed me how to access the poison control line for some kid that drank pesticide. Until your staff showed me what a computer can do, I really had no idea how these things are changing modern medicine. Alas, I am so behind that I couldn't even figure how to make Betty's damned printer turn on to make a printed copy. I was so afraid there'd be a power failure before anyone could read Betty's suicide note. Was that what made you suspicious of her death?"

Chris nodded, "That and the lack of fingerprints on the keyboard. Plus, she never called herself Betty to me but rather Elizabeth. I figured someone who was more intimate with her than I must have written the note." Charles grunted noncommittally.

"What does the star tattoo mean? Intimacy with the devil?"

Dr. Orr sat heavily in the pastor's guest chair. Chris had a momentary surge of hope that it might break under the load, but it merely creaked, to Dr. Orr's momentary disconcertion. He now wore a thick overshirt of deer hide. He labored to pull on a matching pair of shaggy trousers decorated with an anatomically improbable phallus.

"I see you've been talking with the good reverend. Here he jerked his head towards the church. In the pause that followed, Chris noticed the hammering and screaming had stopped. "Yes, that's what it means," he continued. "Kind of like a trophy, the star is." Orr favored him with an ironic smile. "You know, this conversation is sort of therapeutic. This is not the kind of discussion you can share with just anyone. Any other questions?"

Chris recoiled a moment, paused, pain on his face. "Why? Yes, why all this to begin with? You're a doctor, for God's sake! We save lives, not take lives." Charles pulled on boots meant to represent goat's hooves and increased his already tall stature. Then he paused, settled back in the chair, and looked thoughtful for a moment.

"Funny you put it that way. Because that's what started it, a medical problem. After his wife divorced him, the Merry/Orr family curse it seems, Ladson found he was impotent. He looked everywhere for a cure. Of course, he came to his big brother, the doctor, for advice. He saw me, then urologists, internists, psychiatrists, you name it. They all agreed, nothing, no physiologic basis. Everything checked out okay; he just had this tremendous psychological block. Hell, he even tried hypnosis."

"About two years ago, he went to a Halloween party in Charlotte. He told me he got hooked up with some girl dressed as a devil. After a while at the party, they left and went to her place. One thing led to another, and it was getting hot and heavy, even though he knew he couldn't deliver. As he was laying there on the couch wondering how he was going to confess his failings, she interrupted him. 'Honey,' she says, 'We can't go all the way. Wrong time of the month,' she says. And then to prove it, she pulls her panties down to show her pad. Can you believe it? Anyway, Ladson said he was about to open his mouth to say that was the most disgusting thing he'd ever seen when he says he realizes he's hard as a rock! First time in years. Just like someone pulled the cork out of some psychic barrel. Pun intended."

Chris tried hard to school the revulsion from his face. He had heard of worse things in the daily papers at the supermarket but there was something different however in a colleague explaining his personal reasons for mass murder. Chris tried to break in, to reassert some sanity.

Charles Orr, however, was warming to his topic. He silenced Chris with a glare and proceeded. "Ladson told me all of this the day after he was with her. Said he just about raped her. He ended up promising to buy her another couch to replace the one that got stained from his newly revived passions. He didn't care about the cost of the couch; he thought he was cured. He kept going back to her. Then after a few more times over the next couple weeks, his ability to perform started to wane. Having her put the devil costume on helped initially, but in a couple of months he was back to square one."

"Just about then,'" Orr continued, "the bimbo's dog got hit by a car. Came yelping back to the house, and of course, she let it in. Bled all over the house while they tried to capture it and take it to the vet. The dog died in her arms. Ladson came back to life, so to speak."

Chris listened, despite himself. He had a sick feeling he knew where this was headed.

Orr was caught up in his story. His face was red, and a faint sheen of perspiration damped his high forehead. "Shortly after that, he asked for my help to start this Satan's coven. The whole enterprise centered on blood sacrifice followed by an orgy afterwards. The blood seemed to be the key to his arousal. Initially it was a rabbit or later a goat, occasionally someone's dog. Trouble was that Ladson's rush from each kill diminished. The kill had to be increasingly spectacular to keep him going."

Chris interrupted, "I see, eventually he needed bigger game: people."

Orr shook his head. "No, I don't think he would have murdered at that point. I think his whole obsession would have soon died out. He wanted to steal farm implements to try slaughtering a bull. He was thinking bigger, not smarter. I think that once size lost its appeal, he would have nowhere else to go. My brother was not a killer."

"But he killed three people." Chris snapped

"I don't think murder would have crossed his mind had he not been interrupted in mid-robbery. Then, once the deed was done," Charles shrugged. "I don't know why he didn't just buy the damn tools, but he said it was important they be stolen. The police almost caught him that night. Instead, he killed the two of them, because Jake recognized him and put up his gun." "It developed into sort of an improvisation then. He figured if bull blood would be good, human blood would be better. He'd borrowed my truck to carry the implements in, though I didn't know why he wanted it then. He used the winch to hoist the bodies up to bleed them. The first I knew of it was when he called me after the fact. Well, what could I do then? The courts would have given him life in prison or even the death penalty, not to mention what the publicity would do to Merry Mills Inc. And he is my brother. Besides, the dead ones were just mill people."

"Meanwhile, human blood became a central part of the ritual. I made Ladson start testing it for AIDS and other illnesses such as hepatitis, so we don't start a local epidemic of something in our supporters. Now, we use a mixture of de-clotted blood and wine as the celebration libation. Top it off with some grain alcohol to keep the fire going. It's really quite impressive, isn't it?"

"Anyway, I kept quiet for a while. I tried to figure a way out of this disaster. By then, the mill villages went up for sale almost en masse. It is hard to see this downward spiral when the rest of the area's growing. Land everywhere else is going up in value and here, only here, the price of houses and land is going through the floor: Atlanta, Charlotte, Columbia, Spartanburg, the whole upstate area and adjoining areas are growing by leaps and bounds. Look at all the industries that have moved in like BMW and Mack Truck! Look at the companies arriving almost daily across the upstate. Only here has real estate not risen. Now the murders are driving down land prices. Although totally unplanned, Ladson's kinky doings are going to make us rich. With one or two more deaths, we'll be able to buy the mill villages for practically nothing. We've been buying up farmland under dummy companies out near the interstate. When we announce we've caught the killer, we'll both be heroes and clean up nicely." Charles finished dressing and slipped on an antlered deer mask. His voice was slightly muffled. "How do I look? The horned god rides one last time."

"You're doing all this for money?" Chris whispered.

Dr. Orr pulled off the mask and looked at Chris, his face set in an implacable glare. "I'm doing it for my family. The Merry Mills Company is ours and ours alone. At one time we pretty much ran this part of the state. These dealings will get us the money to buy back the rest of the company. My granddaddy always taught me running this company and town was our destiny. My mother's brothers were idiots who almost destroyed that vision. Those uncles were fools who gave away everything sacred to our family. They deserved to die! They sold my birthright. Now we'll reassert our rights to run the company and then the county the way they ought to be properly run and set our family back on top again at last!" Charles made a visible effort to rein himself in.

Chris gestured with his head to the church behind him. "So, what do those people get out of all this?"

Charles smiled. The same thing little people with insignificant lives everywhere get. The chance to be special, secret, important, plus, the sex." He gave Chris a crooked smile. "Ladson was right, the sex is pretty great too." Charles Orr gestured to the mask and costume, "usually, Ladson plays the high priest role. But we're the same height, and he's let me fill in just for fun once or twice. The hood keeps up the anonymity. When this is all over, there won't be any evidence to tie us to it."

Chris felt even worse. In a crazy way the plan all made sense. He had a gnawing suspicion. "Who turns out to be the villain?" he asked with rising trepidation.

"Oh, you are," came the expected answer. "It will be a terrible fight, but as you can probably guess, you get it in the end. Your body will be found in the ashes along with the good reverend, your last victim. What irony, everyone will say, the man who was doing the investigating was also doing the killing."

"What about Ashley?" asked Chris. "Don't you think she'll try to clear me?" As the words left his lips, he regretted them.

Charles Orr went over to a large jerry can by the door. Opening it, he then pulled several small disposable paint buckets out of the box. He set them on the floor and began to pour gasoline in each. "I'm sorry about Ashley," he began. "She really was the pawn. When I realized you were beginning to get a handle on the killings, I began to look for a safety valve. Ashley happened

in about then. It was perfect. I pumped her so full of tranquilizers so that if needed, I could distract you by pushing her into a relapse. I'm glad now I did. Otherwise, you might have finished calling the police. As it is, you've made it easier, even killing a man at my house. I am sorry about Ashley, though. The voice carried a leaden tone that made Chris realize there was more to learn about Ashley."

"What have you done to her?"

"Oh nothing, yet, but her next IV bottle is loaded with about 100 milli equivalents of potassium chloride. She should die of cardiac arrhythmias brought on by potassium poisoning within the next several hours." Charles looked Chris in the eye. His voice had a 'can't you be reasonable tone.' "I said I was sorry, but I just can't leave any loose ends, you see. As her doctor, I'll be able to declare her death related to her medical condition and no one the wiser"

Chris's world abruptly shifted on its axis. Nausea competed with vertigo as his stomach tied the mother of all Gordian knots. The impending loss of Ashley superseded his own concerns for survival. It also served to snap the spell of unreality that had enveloped Chris. He wanted to live. He wanted Ashley to live. All the frustration about her relapse -the pain only a loved one of an alcoholic can feel-was abruptly flushed away by the realization that she'd been set up. White hot anger flowed through him. He wanted the man towering over him dead, and he wanted to do it with his bare hands.

"You bastard! You let her go! She doesn't know anything. I never even confided in her, she has no idea what is going on. If you heard anything during all those counseling sessions, you know that." He struggled furiously against ropes restraining him and succeeded in scooting the wheeled chair a few feet closer to kick at the hide-bedecked figure. Orr merely shoved him back.

"I am sorry about all this, Chris." He shrugged. "Everyone who knows anything about it has got to go. That's why I had to do in my pilot too."

Chris stopped in surprise. "But how did you do it?"

Orr smiled at his own ingenuity. "That one I did myself. Who at the airport is going to question the company's board chairman when he comes out to look for a briefcase in his company plane?" Orr favored Chris with a sly smile. "I bet you didn't know that LSD can be easily absorbed through the skin. I confiscated some of the solution from one of the patients I am supposed to be counseling at the County Drug and Alcohol Commission. A few strokes of an LSD laced paint brush on the plane's steering yoke, and presto, nature and sweaty palms do the rest. I never liked that artist. He was threatening to sue over some previous work. Getting rid of him killed two birds with one stone. Making sure the artist was on the plane was Ladson's idea. We were just aiming for a simple crash. Plowing the company jet into a commercial jetliner must have been part of the hallucinations."

While they spoke, Chris was aware of many more cars pulling into the parking lot. Now a muffled tap came at the door. "Almost time," Dr Orr got up and hefted two of the gasoline paint buckets. "If it makes you feel any better, Chris, tonight is the end. I haven't told Ladson yet, but I'm going to disperse the group to 'evangelize' elsewhere. We both got what we wanted. His manhood is functioning, and I'm about to make another fortune in real estate and get our company back. Ladson's going to have to get his kicks elsewhere in the future. A pity though. I think he's become a true believer in all this crap." Charles reached for the door, opened it, and beckoned to the four men awaiting them. "It's time," he said.

He handed the collection of buckets of gasoline to the men. Two other men grabbed Chris's chair, picked it up with Chris in it and lugged him into the cold night air and across the parking lot into the waiting church. No one noticed the figure sneaking off on the dark side of the building as the small procession headed into the church.

Chapter 31

The double doors of the church stood wide open as the group headed up the stairs. A dim yellow-red glow shone from the doorway. A small crowd inside waited eagerly. Some of them peered out the door. Orr's face and silver hair was concealed by his mask and horns as they climbed the steps.

When they reached the top step, Chris kicked futilely at the men flanking him. Better to break my neck now than have them slit it later, he thought. He succeeded only in spilling gasoline on the wooden steps. It drizzled down step by step. The man carrying the buckets set one down and casually backhanded Chris. "Naughty, naughty," murmured Dr. Orr under the mask "Those buckets are to burn the church down after you finish off the Reverend." Ignoring the weal of pain on his cheek, Chris looked with a jerk to the far end of the church. There the black minister hung from the crucifix hoisted over the altar, still struggling.

His feet flailed wildly, but a gag prevented any noise. Charles Orr looked at the feet and shrugged apologetically, "What can I say? We ran out of nails."

They set the buckets of gasoline near the door and then pushed Chris to the back, away from the pails. The last few people came in. The only illumination came from candles scattered across the front of the church and the flames from the cauldron that waited in front of the altar. The antlered figure of Charles Orr took the massive bar and locked the door. He slammed the bar into place with a door-rattling boom. The room became silent, every eye fixed on the massive figure that waited for silence, arms raised.

"My people! Children of Shadow! The time has come. The winter solstice is upon us. Light is at its ebb. Darkness rules the land this eve, and the circle of shade completes tonight! The circle is completed tonight! Darkness is upon the land."

A hushed sigh ran through the crowd. This was followed by a murmuring repetition of the phrase thrown back in louder and louder cadences. "The circle is completed tonight! Darkness is upon the land." It developed into a rhythmic chant that reminded Chris of a cross between Gregorian chants and a homecoming cheer. The chant inflamed the coven. Chris caught several worshippers looking at him with less than covert anticipation. One woman even smiled openly at Chris and then slowly licked her lips and rubbed her stomach. As Chris watched in stupefaction, the woman's hand crept lower and she began to writhe quietly on the pew in exaggerated, sensual anticipation. Chris redoubled the frantic, but quiet squirming of his bound hands. With a shift in cadence, the chant shifted to a processional hymn.

A person who would have been the crucifer in a church bore the traditional processional pole with a cross on the end. However, the cross was covered over with black cardboard on which an upside-down pentacle was outlined in gold glitter. He stamped his way down the aisle in time to the chanting. The chanting grew louder and louder as the horned beast and attendants started up a snaking path through the center of the church towards the cauldron and the crucified minister. The chanting reached a fevered pitch when the procession reached the steps behind the cauldron. It stopped with an abruptness that left Chris' s battered ears ringing.

"Blessed be Satan, devil, demon and evil spirit."

Charles Orr was borrowing from the Episcopal liturgy of Father Bob's church. Readings from evil texts proceeded to supplant biblical verses. Tonight's first reading was from Hitler's <u>Mein Kampf</u>. Chris remembered that Mosley had said evil could only overlay and pervert what good had begun. The readings were brief, as were other activities on the coven's mind tonight.

The service continued into what would, at St Andrews, be the passing of the peace: a time in the service when church members take a moment to shake hands and express their affection for other members. However, tonight's congregation took the simple gesture much further with all of them disrobing except Orr, the antlered figure in front. Kisses quickly gave way to more vigorous fondling.

Chris took advantage of the commotion to slowly work his wheeled chair closer to the door. If he ever did succeed in removing his bonds, he knew he would have to be ready to run for it. Before he could quite reach the door however, Dr. Orr called an end to the budding orgy.

The antlered figure grasped the hammer back from the box on the floor where it had been left after pounding in the nails that crucified Reverend Mosley. A sharply struck hammer tap to the cauldron lip made a muted basso bong and brought instant silence to the panting crowd.

The barbaric figure stepped into the pulpit and began to preach. From behind, Reverend Mosley ceased to struggle. Instead, he hung gasping as he fixed Charles Orr with a look of unmasked malevolence. The gag worked spasmodically in his mouth. Orr talked about the rise of evil from Genesis forward. To Chris, it was like hearing the Bible from the other side of the mirror. It didn't sound good.

As Charles Orr followed the progression of evil in the world, he made it sound as if was a celebration of a story gone wrong: babies slaughtered, women raped, the prophets persecuted. The litany of evil proceeded through the Inquisition, the Salem witch trials and the Holocaust. Each was told as a perversion that had gone well, with more and more pain cast, like bread, upon the waters. On the rare occasion when Orr mentioned appeared, God, he made him the enemy who occasionally made well-laid plans go awry. The audience listened raptly. Orr's message was clear: murder, deceit and chaos were to be celebrated.

Dr. Orr appeared to be winding down with no concluding point when he reached back into Jewish history to the great Diaspora that cast the Jews throughout the world. His eloquence surpassed anything Chris had ever thought him capable of delivering, and as he spoke, he came down into the congregation sharing the story more intimately. Even Chris slowed his frantic twisting at the ropes to listen to the spell being spun.

"And now the time has come, "Charles intoned to the entranced audience. "The time has come for our own Diaspora. The time has come for us to spread across the land. Our people have become lax and comfortable. They lie at home watching TV, in lives of luxury while the Master's cause waits unfinished. Peace and prosperity are undoing our cause, but the other side has gotten lax too." He drew himself up to full antlered height. "In the name of our Master, I commission each and every one of you to go out of this place and town and settle elsewhere and begin to spread our message to all those who swelter and suffer in light hoping for the dusk."

Here he gestured to several coolers stacked by the side of the altar. The antlered figure threw them open to the light showing the blood Chris had seen stored in the Orr family basement. "I send you out with the sanctified blood of our beginnings until the harvest can begin anew."

"So, it shall be done," called a voice near Chris. The crowd, mesmerized, joined the first voice and soon the whole congregation joined in chanting their pledge. For Chris, the sight of the stored blood broke the spell of Dr. Orr's sermon-induced trance. Each of those coolers represented several lives wasted to the Orr's madness. On the side of each, a crudely marked label indicated its destination. Like a single bacterium expanding into an epidemic, Chris envisioned the exploding web of pain and slaughter each of these boxes could induce. For each town whose name was scrawled on a cooler's side, an outbreak of horror and death awaited.

Charles Orr stood, masked, basking as the crowd chanted his will. At last, he held up his hands for silence. The joined voices slowly dwindled. "Let us consecrate our congregation on its unholy task. With this, he stepped toward the cauldron and produced a huge iron cup for a chalice. "Let this be our last celebration together before the final sacrifice." Here he looked meaningfully at the still struggling Chris.

The antlered figure turned towards the cauldron, while the shadows of he and his congregants danced on the walls repeating the terrible figure. From a darkened wall near a tangle of discarded pews, a lone voice called out, "Stop!"

A hushed murmur worked through the crowd as Charles straightened up in surprise from the cauldron's spigot. Chris looked up from his knots as a naked Ladson Orr pushed his way up the aisle. Confusion warred with relief and anger as Chris stared at the return of Charles Orr's younger brother.

The antlered figure stood in riveted attention as Ladson approached him. Chris would have given much to know what was going through Charles Orr's mind right now. Oblivious to his nakedness, Ladson marched up to his costumed brother. Reaching out abruptly, Ladson jerked off the antlered mask, revealing his brother's face.

A gasp went through the group. Ladson's voice was hoarse with rage, "I overheard you. I listened outside the office as you monologued to Dr. Wilder. "For money? You helped this satanic coven along for money! To buy what? A broken-down mill firm that no one has cared about for years!"

Ladson turned to the congregation, "He's afraid of you," he shouted. "All this blood has spilled, and now he's trying to get you out of town so he can clean up! I am the true leader of the coven. My brother only wants to send you away, to make money from the work we've done here! He's buying up your land and houses on the cheap while people run away in fear! "An angry mutter went through the group. Ladson continued to shout his accusations as Charles made a clumsy grab at Ladson. Not surprisingly, his suit and boots weighed him down.

Ladson easily evaded him. He spoke again. "How could you do this?" he screamed at his brother. "You tried to steal my people!"

The coven was on its feet and crowded around the two. Chris shifted in the chair, trying to see over the collection of heads and backs turned towards him. The two scuffled a moment, then fell behind the crowded mass of onlookers. The momentary distraction brought his attention to the problem at hand. The knots would not give, and Chris felt a miasma of depression settle over him.

He thought of the recently departed Dr. Johnson, and wondered what he would say,

I'm in for it now, he thought I've used my eyes, my ears and my hands, and I'm in as deep a trouble as I'm ever gonna be. I'm all tied up and it doesn't look like I'm going to have a chance to use my brain. But it is all I've got left. Think!

As Chris felt the end drawing near, he felt a moment's grief for those who had believed in him. Horace was dead, Dr. Sayaad was dead. Now it looked like Ashley and Chris and many more would join him.

He looked around desperately. If only he could get out of this church somehow. Inspiration struck. The idea blossomed, but he'd need a diversion. He renewed his struggles with his bonds, but this time concentrated on his feet. He almost wiggled them free. He tried harder as he bit his lip to stifle a scream, and he forced his knee to contort in a direction never planned for by any creator. A knot slipped over his heel and gave slack to his other foot and at last his chair moved.

Ladson was still trying to dodge away from Charles in the tightening circle when he abruptly caught sight of someone he recognized and stopped short. "You!" shouted Ladson, pointing at someone in the crowd. "How can you be here?"

Charles took advantage of his brother's startled pause to grab him and deliver a stunning blow. Ladson clutched his brother for balance and together they staggered sideways into the flaming cauldron, spilling it over.

In the first moment, nothing happened as the two stood drenched in blood and alcohol. The flames guttered on the floor. Then suddenly with a will of their own, the flames crawled up the legs of the two brothers. Ladson flung himself on the floor and rolled frantically. The crowd pressed forward. At first, Chris thought they meant to help but they simply crowded around to watch in anticipation, and then Ladson vanished behind the crowd.

The shaggy suit Charles wore provided him a few seconds more of insulation. It also provided a better wick for the fuel. Flames sprouted brightly up the costume. Smoke and flame illuminated where Ladson still rolled in flames. Charles, ever a rational thinker under pressure, decided to try his luck in the mud outside. He was using his size to advantage as he shoved through the crowded aisle toward the same barred doors Chris had scooted towards on the wheeled chair. It was the diversion he needed. Brilliance born of desperation linked the charging flaming figure with the pail of gasoline now near Chris Wilder's foot.

The shaggy burning man drew up to the door. He fumbled desperately with the heavy board barring the door.

Like lightning, Chris's mind raced, connecting the dots, greased by white hot anger from mind to toe. If I've got to go, at least I'll take this bastard with me. Chris let fly a mighty kick. The world shifted to slow motion. As his right foot lashed out at the gasoline, his left delivered a mighty shove backwards, towards at best escape if not respite from the coming explosion of flames.

The ancient wheels of the pastor's abused desk chair screeched in protest as it rolled toward the nearest corner of the church. (At the same time, Chris felt the slosh of cold as his shoe connected with the bucket of frigid gasoline.) Propelled by his kick, the bucket jerked away from Chris and arched toward Charles Orr, a spray of gasoline following the bucket. Chris's action was fueled by a knowledge of chemistry and ignition temperatures of various liquids.

Despite the brilliant flame burning alcohol produces, alcohol burns at a remarkably low temperature. Charles had a reasonable chance of reaching the smothering the flames in cold mud outside the steps. Gasoline, however, burns much, much hotter than alcohol. Charles's last chance for life was extinguished when the bucket, still half full of gasoline, connected with his flaming figure. With a skin-searing whoosh, Charles blossomed again with brighter and hotter flames. Fire welled up from the figure of Charles Orr as he staggered across the back of the church.

An old farmer's adage ran disjointedly through Chris's mind: Never kick a bucket of crap, unless you like to wear the color. In contrast to the heat that seared his face, Chris was suddenly aware of the chill that enveloped his right pants cuff. Gasoline dribbled an inviting trail that connected the holocaust that now consumed Charles Orr at the far side of the church to Chris. Flames leaped fitfully from drip to drop, a snake of flame coiling for a strike. Chris could only pray that his idea worked in time. The rotten church corner Reverend Moseley had pulled him back from was almost within the chair's reach. His gasoline-soaked trousers hung above the faltering trail of flame like a meaty bone above a hungry dog. He gave another desperate kick to shove the chair along. It worked. Chris had one last view of his nemesis, wrapped in his own private inferno, stumbling into the other buckets of gasoline as the floor under the office chair collapsed and the room flipped upwards and out of sight.

One second Chris was in the flaming church. In the next, he was on the ground below with a spine-jarring thud. The ancient chair splintered to pieces around him. For a moment, he was stunned by the fall and how closely he'd approached a fiery death; Reverend Mosley was right: the termite-riddled floor would not hold his weight.

Chapter 32

He moved his arms and legs experimentally and found that, despite pain in his back, he could stand. Freed of the chair's encumbrance, he snatched a shard of glass and sawed through the remains of the ropes. He then hastily cut off the gasoline sodden cuff. He then ran out from under the side of the burning church as a pew came flying out a window landing near him. Unfortunately, this attempt by those trapped inside to escape; their breaking the window served only to provide fresh oxygen for the fire that raged inside. Still, a few victims tumbled out before flames reared up in the window. It was horrifying to listen to the screams of the burning and dying.

Chris had treated several victims of house fires. He knew that regardless of what one sees in movies, the occupants of the church had only but a few minutes to escape or die. The screams of the fifty-plus people with no way out rang in his ears, along with the popping and roaring of the burning church. Despite their willingness to kill him just a few minutes ago, as a doctor trained to save lives, he couldn't simply walk away from them. Chris sprinted to the doors at the front of the church. Despite the flames, and the massive bar, one man had managed to get the door cracked open. His charred body now lay half in, half out the doorway. The doorway which opened to the gasoline-soaked stairs was now engulfed in a curtain of flame blocking seemed the only way out.

But wait, there was another way! Frantically, Chris scrambled up the hill opposite the side where he and Ladson had watched the evening's preparations just a short while--and years--ago.

The tunnel the old minister had demonstrated had not been on that side, but it must be here somewhere. Chris frantically searched in the thick brush at the back end of the church. Abruptly, the light improved as the fire broke through the roof at the entry to the church. He could see a shallow, narrow ditch that led across the hill and under the church. Chris cast an appraising eye at the flames and thought he might have a minute or so. Throwing himself down in the cold mud of the ditch, he crawled along desperately. Firelight gave way to pitch-black, as he passed under the church. He was beginning to wonder how he would know when he'd reached the end of the tunnel when he abruptly collided face first with an earthen wall. He reached above himself in the narrow space. His hand traced a wooden square against the roof of the low tunnel. Rising on all fours, with the strength of the desperate, he shoved mightily against the altar floor that served as the tunnel hatch. The tunnel's low ceiling gave way and fell back as the altar tumbled over. Air whistled past him as the flames pulled more air through the tunnel to feed the conflagration inside.

Chris rose to his feet next to the toppled altar. The church looked like Hell on Earth. Only a few people remained standing. A pile of burning smoking bodies near the windows and doors testified to their failed efforts to escape. Chris stared in shock for a moment and then shouted over the flames to the few people who were still alive and huddling together away from the flames. He gestured frantically to the hole in the floor. They stared back in surprise and alarm and then, realizing a last-minute potential salvation, they fought and clawed to dive down the hole to safety.

Chris turned to join the small stream of survivors, when a foot waggled in front of him. He looked up. Mosley, eyes open, his body bathed in blood and sweat some parts of his skin blistered, hung over him, eyes silently pleading behind the gag. Quickly, Chris ran to the ropes and tried to lower the cross.

The preacher far outweighed Chris, and so the rope which was attached to the cross bearing the big man dragged Chris flailing into the air as Mosley slammed into the floor. Over the roar of the flames, Chris heard crucified Mosley's gagged scream of pain as he lost consciousness.

Chris desperately cast around for some way to free him. He knew the cross was too big and bulky to drag out through the tunnel. Even on the floor, the smoke was making him cough and gasp. Panic clawed at reason when, at last, his gaze lit on the tool chest left carelessly behind the now toppled altar. The heat of the flames blistered against his skin as he grabbed a crowbar from the box and began to pry.

Mosley groaned as the first eight-inch nail slid out of his wrist. He screamed and sat up as Chris pried out the second nail. Mosley's hands dangled limply at the end of his bleeding arms, but he took only a moment to survey the carnage before he succumbed to Chris's frantic urging and crawled painfully on his elbows into the tunnel. With Chris breathing on his heels, the preacher inched slowly under the burning church.

Mosley's pierced and bleeding arms made for excruciatingly slow going. He moaned with each painful shove forward. The church, engulfed in flames, roared, and crackled ominously above them. Chris ventured a probing touch of the church floor inches over his head. He yanked his hand back from wood only seconds from ignition. Finally, the end of the tunnel came into view. A gust of blistering hot air shot from behind them as they reached the opening to the ditch outside. Chris turned just in time to see the roof and walls of the flaming church collapse inward on what remained of the Merry family ambitions. With a tornado-like chuff of wind, the end of the church blew out, spitting bodies and rubble into the woods.

Mosley's gaze locked on his flaming church; bleeding wrists cradled in his arms. The big black man sank to the ground sobbing. Chris wanted to join him, but thoughts of Ashley's impending demise spurred him on. He quickly pulled off his coat and shirt, tore his shirt into irregular strips and wrapped them tightly around the minister's wrists to staunch the flow of blood. Next, he dragged the sobbing, aged minister down the hill. They looked in half a dozen cars before finding one with the key still in the ignition. Chris pushed Mosley in and started the engine. With a plume of gravel, they left the remains of the burning church and began the race to town.

It was a slow night in the Intensive Care Unit at Merry Hopes Memorial. Such nights were quite unusual. Most times, the three nurses were kept frantically busy caring for the desperately ill patients in the six beds of the little unit. Tonight, only two patients were so unlucky as to be denizens of the so-called expensive-care unit. One was Johnny Hawking, an 80-year-old man recovering from his second heart attack. Three days after the crushing pain that brought him in, he was feeling much better. Now, he was campaigning hard to be moved to a regular room where he might sneak the longed-for cigarette the unit nurses refused to give him.

"Some patients never learn," Helen Carnes, the head nurse, muttered as she walked out of Johnny's room. The other patient was, of course, Ashley Wilder.

Ashley's evening had been quiet. Billy Wilkes, a very bored deputy, sat in a folding chair outside her room leafing through a dog-eared magazine of ancient vintage. Ashley's sedation continued to be tapered down. Dr. MacAbee, who thought Dr. Orr was a little too free with sedation, had sharply cut the dose as soon as the nurses called him with an unrelated issue. Helen went into Ashley's room and checked the IV fluids. The IV pump was just beginning to chime the low bottle warning. Helen picked the next bottle off the shelf, flipped open the pump, expertly changed the tubing and the bottle, and started the pump again. According to Dr. Orr's orders, the drip rate for this bottle was to run in faster. She nudged the controls on the IV pump to the higher speed   Task completed, she walked briskly out the glass door, nodding to the deputy as she went.

The other evening nurse had some hot gossip on one of the new and very married pulmonary doctors that had been seen in a singles bar with a woman clearly not his wife. Helen didn't want to miss any of the titillating news. In her lightening doze, Ashley moaned a little as if in pain or she was having a bad dream. As the nurses discussed the sexual proclivities of the pulmonary doctor, the talk eventually turned to great affairs of doctors past. With only occasional glances at the monitor, neither Helen nor the other two nurses noted the increasingly pointed T waves on the rolling EKG that herald the onset of hyperkalemia, the tale-tell sign of potassium poisoning.

Chris flogged the aging Ford through the cold night as fast as he dared. He wished he had hunted a little longer for another car with keys in the ignition. He could see now why the owner of this car had not feared its theft. The car wheezed and shimmied as it chugged towards town. Exhaust fumes smelled plainly in the car. Wind blew through the open windows; Chris was afraid to roll them up for fear of carbon monoxide poisoning

Reverend Mosley huddled in the seat opposite Chris and whimpered softly. Chris worried that the elderly man was going into shock. He nudged the accelerator a little harder.

As he rose over the crest of the next hill, Chris could see a small gas station. The lights were still on in front of its two archaic pumps and a battered sign heralded a public phone of the Independent Merryville Phone Company. Jesus, they really did own everything, thought a detached part of Chris's mind as he pulled the battered Ford up to the pumps.

It had been a slow night at the Crossroads 66. Usually, a few of the old timers dropped by to sit in the station and drink beer and discuss the county's business. If anyone had asked Luther Ross, the station attendant, how he felt about his cheering section, he probably would have remarked on the time and trouble the geezers cost him.

Tonight, however, the cold was keeping them all away. Without admitting it to anyone, least of all himself, Luther missed them. Luther watched the as sweep second hand on a clock advertising Grape Nehi swept the minutes away until closing time. A rattling bump followed by the wheeze of a never tuned engine announced to Luther he had one last customer. He was not ready for the frantic ragged man who leaped out of the car and grabbed him.

"This is an emergency! Where's the phone?" Chris demanded.

Luther recovered and flipped a dismissive hand. "Pay phone's out of order. The only one we got is the station phone. I gotta keep that one open case a customer calls." Luther doubted that anyone was going to call, but the boss man didn't want no freeloaders gabbing on the phone. Sides, this guy didn't look too reputable, even out here in the dark. Chris dodged around Luther and sprinted inside. Luther uttered a squawk of protest and followed. Chris saw the phone on a battered desk by a Coke machine. He hastily dialed the hospital.

The rings seemed to take an agonizingly long time. On about the fifth ring the hospital operator answered, drawling:

 "MerryHopesMemoriaHospitaHowMayI . . ."

"This is Dr. Wilder, and this is an Emergency!" Chris cut in. "Ring ICU stat!" he shouted. The drawl paused and was replaced by the ringing of the ICU extension.

Helen answered the phone on the third ring with mild annoyance. One of the other nurses was telling the venerable and oft-repeated story of a surgeon of years back who broke a leg chasing a pretty nurse around an operating room table after completing a surgical case. was finished. A much better story, one she would tell for years to come was just beginning.

 "ICU," she snapped.

"This is Dr. Wilder. Is my wife, Okay?" Helen glanced at the monitor in annoyance. In her haste, she again missed the subtle peaking of the T wave.

As she turned back to the phone, she missed the skipped beat of the catastrophe to come. "Yes sir, they got the tube out and she's fine and coming round some." Helen answered in clipped tones even more annoyed now.

"Listen carefully," Dr. Wilder went on, his voice tight with anxiety, "Dr. Orr poisoned Ashley's IV bottle. If it is hanging, I want you to take it down immediately. Change her IV to a heparin lock, and under no circumstances are you to give Ashley any further IV fluids until I get there. Do you have that?"

Helen stared at the phone in astonishment. Covering the phone with her hand, she motioned to the other nurses.

Rolling her eyes, she commented, "He's flipped. Dr. Wilder finally lost it." Helen however, tried to put all possible reason and compassion into her voice. "Dr. Wilder, I'm sorry," she said soothingly, "Dr. Orr specifically told us if you tried to change his orders, we were to tell you we couldn't and that you should talk to him.

Now it was Chris's turn to be astonished. In his surprise, he blurted out the worst possible answer. "Damn it Helen, I can't talk to Dr. Orr! He's dead!" This remark didn't help matters. Helen's jaw dropped. Her gaze swept the room as she tried to think of a reply. Her gaze fell on the bank of monitors. Something else was wrong. She saw an irregular jump on Ashley Wilder's monitor screen, a picket fence of repeated PVCs. As Helen looked on, the line of beats jumped into the chaotic rhythm of ventricular fibrillation.

"Dr. Wilder, Dr. Wilder!" she shouted into the phone. There was no answer. She dropped the receiver on the desk and hastily punched a large red "PANIC!" button over the monitors. The other two nurses were already running.

Luther Ross's night continued downhill. Only two customers all evening and then this a-hole barged in and took his phone. He obviously didn't plan to buy nothing. And besides, he looked like he'd been drunk and beat up or something. He was covered in dirt, pants ripped, and it looked like someone bit his ear off. Now he was spouting crazy stuff into the phone about doctors and poison and somebody else being dead. Bad news for sure.

Luther had learned a few things about survival, being out here alone nights and weekends on this lonely road. He had been the recipient of several robbery attempts. After the first, he got himself some protection. He eased past the frantic and distracted Chris to the far side of the Coke machine where he kept a sawed-off shotgun. The handle was also chopped off and wrapped with tape to improve the grip.

Luther had learned that most petty thieves would first rob him of his money and then demand that he open the cash box on the drink cooler. Keeping the gun by the cooler gave him the advantage of surprise. The last thief had been really surprised, yes siree, right up until he died.

Luther's hand slid on to the grip of the shotgun. He jerked the weapon out and brought it to bear. At first, Chris didn't even notice, so intent was he on the urgent conversation with the nurse. Luther didn't shout or threaten. He tended to stutter under stress. The gun could talk for him. Marching across the floor with the assurance of a gambler holding four aces, he paused to rest the twin barrels on the bridge of Chris's nose. "AH… ah… out" was all he said.

Chris stared in astonishment at the two large black barrels confronting him. He carefully raised his empty hand and slowly set the receiver down on the desk. "Dr. Wilder, Dr. Wilder?" the phone called faintly from the desk. Luther shoved Chris across the room. Neither of them paid attention to the receiver anymore as Luther marched Chris out the door, the twin barrels of the shotgun resting on the back of his neck. Unheard by either of them, the faint voice of the hospital paging system called: "Code 99 ICU, Code 99 ICU, stat." Death from the Merry family madness had one final trick for Dr. Wilder.

Luther brought the shotgun to port arms position as he watched Chris throw himself back in the stolen ancient Ford. The engine still idled fitfully. wheezing and chugging even worse from idling outside Luther's station. Chris didn't care about the car anymore just so long as it would get him to town. Slumped on the far side of the car, Mosley nodded tightly to Chris.

"Any luck?" he whispered, even now more concerned with Chris's problems than his own.

Chris grimly shook his head. He pushed the car to speeds it hadn't seen since Jimmy Carter had been president. In his head, the little voice screamed faster, faster and Chris gave the voice its lead. Less than three minutes later, the car swung into the Merry Hopes Memorial drive. Skipping the doctors' parking lot, Chris drove straight across the lawn and slid to a stop in the muddy grass behind the back entrance to the intensive care unit. Leaving his passenger in the car, he sprinted up the steps and in the back door. "I'll send help, " he called over his shoulder."

Dr. Steve Garnes was a second-year psychiatry resident from the teaching program at Charlotte Methodist Hospital. He had enjoyed coming to Merry Hopes Memorial to moonlight in the ER. He liked the country doctoring atmosphere and the money, which was close to twice what he was paid in the residency program. While he enjoyed the esoteric ramblings of psychiatry, he also enjoyed what he called the "blood and guts" of ER work. He was a bit of a pedant who thought of himself as God's gift to medicine. This was only his third visit to the Merry Hopes Memorial ER.

He was still early enough along in his psychiatric training that he persisted in naming all the behaviors he saw- as if naming them would solve the problems. Thus, wife beating came to be labeled; a domestic violence/codependency interaction. Suicidal overdoses attempts were a temporary adjustment reaction. Just now, Dr. Garnes was sewing up a laceration on Artie Syke's forehead. A blue paper drape covered half of Artie's face except for a small cut-out circle framing the half-sutured slash. Artie acquired this damage in yet another drunken bar fight. Artie lay stuporous on the table, the end of the drape covering his mouth, rising and falling in time to his breathing to show he was alive.

Fran, the ER nurse, watched as Dr. Garnes studiously lectured Artie on his chemical dependency and substance abuse disorder, and she ruefully shook her head. Just then, Artie snorted and roused.

"Yeah, yeah doc, I hear you," he mumbled. Artie's eyes scanned the ceiling a moment and then focused on Garnes, eyes behind the clear plastic shield designed to keep infectious blood out Artie's voice sharpened a touch. "Doc," he lectured, "You're worse than Doc Wilder. Call a spade a spade. I'm a drunk. Ockham's razor, the simple or obvious answer is often the correct one."

"Okay, Ockham's what??" Garnes began.

Over the loudspeaker came the call, "Code 99 ICU, Code 99 ICU, stat!" Steve Games paused, torn a moment between the job at hand almost finished and the one that called. He stood and laid the needle carrier down carefully. Artie waved languidly towards the door.

"It's' a cardiac arrest Doc, ya gotta go." Garnes turned to the door.

"You're supposed to run," said Fran sarcastically. Garnes began to sprint. As she watched his backside disappear down the hall at a gallop, Fran asked aloud out loud, "I wonder what he calls a code? Attempted death response?" Garnes sprinted down the hall feeling a little foolish as he flashed by startled nurses and staff. He was also desperately hoping that another older doctor got there before him. Probably another fossilized chronic lunger on the way out he guessed. This mill town seemed to specialize in those. Garnes cheered himself by figuring he could at least practice some new procedures in the code. The double doors of the ICU loomed ahead. Might as well go for the grand entrance he thought, as he plowed into the doors at full speed.

No aging lunger this time. Instead, he found himself confronted by the frantic nurses furiously pumping on a youngish looking woman's chest. Another nurse held a bag and mask and was busily breathing for her. "What's going on here?" Garnes called. Helen rapidly briefed him on the patient, a forty-two-year-old female recovering from withdrawal seizures Garnes' mental picture shifted from an aging lunger to end-stage wino. In his clinical schema, he'd not yet had nice people die on him. He pulled himself back to the nurse's comments.

"She'd been fine until this abrupt arrest," Helen was saying. She didn't mention the conversation with Dr. Wilder and the possibility of poison. She was still under the impression that Wilder was crazy.

Dr. Garnes glanced at the monitor that showed the crazy gyrating rhythms of V-fib. "Have you shocked her yet?"

Helen shook her head. "Not yet. We were just setting up to do that.

Garnes grabbed the paddles off the defibrillator and squirted voltage conducting jelly on them.

Helen punched the charge button, and a high-pitched whine followed the rise of the needle on the charging gauge. The needle reached the midpoint of the gauge. The machine was primed for the first jolt.

Garnes leaned over the patient and rammed the paddles home to their assigned places on the chest. He felt fully charged himself. This kind of excitement was why he entered medicine. "Clear!" he called.

Everyone stepped back. He depressed the firing button. There was a pop from the machine, and the body below his paddles jerked up then flopped back down again. He looked at the monitor. Abnormal lines still churned across the screen.

"Dammit," he exclaimed. "Gimme full power."

The process was repeated. This time the pop was louder. Ashley's body arched off the bed like a bow pulled tight and then again flopped back. All eyes turned to the monitor screen. The voltage blanked on the line right off the screen for a few seconds. There was a pause; then the green line climbed from the bottom of the screen and began to move again. A normal rhythm danced across the screen.

Steve Garnes exhaled a breath he didn't know he was holding. His shoulder ached from the tight hunch he held them in. Tension response, he thought, maybe performance anxiety. "Okay, let's check a pulse and tube her."
Helen grimaced. It hadn't been that long since they'd gotten the tube out.

An endotracheal tube and someone slipped a long-bladed laryngoscope into his hands. Quickly he adjusted the patient's head and neck, inserted the blade of the scope in her mouth and lifted the pharynx. The patient's vocal cords popped into view, and he slid the tube home. Got it first try this time, he thought, I'm getting better. On the screen a PVC appeared, followed shortly by another. They administered more medications, but the problem got worse. The PVCs appeared more frequently. At any moment ventricular fibrillation might return! The room was a beehive of activity when Chris Wilder burst through the door.

Helen saw Dr. Wilder wrench open the door and thrust his way in. Deputy Billy Wilkes recognized him and stepped out of the way. Pointing to the IV stand, Chris shouted at Helen, "Is that the IV bottle I called about?!" Shocked, Helen nodded. "Take it down. . . now!" Helen just stared at him. Dr. Garnes turned around. He'd never seen Dr. Wilder, and what he saw now was a sweaty, scorched, ratty, bleeding, muddy, crazy man shouting at the nurses. This guy was certainly not invited company.

"Who the hell are you?" he demanded.

Chris, intent on Helen, ignored him.

"Get out of here…now!" Dr. Garnes yelled. "Guard, get this guy out of here NOW! Billy stepped forward, uncertain of himself. Chris was fixated on Helen across the bed.

"Take the bottle down now, Helen," he repeated even more loudly. Steve Garnes had all of this he could take. With a lurch, he shoved Chris back into the arms of the astonished deputy and hollered. "I said get this asshole out of here!"

The deputy caught Chris and held him up. A familiar lump under his battered sport coat nudged at Chris's back. The gun was empty, but of course they didn't know that. The deputy turned Chris around to speak to him and came up facing the barrel of the .45 Chris felt a momentary twinge of sympathy in his frenzy. He'd just been down this road himself.

The room became suddenly quiet as everyone saw the shove and then the gun. "Jesus!" Dr. Garnes breathed, "paranoid schizophrenia with homicidal ideation."

"Helen," Chris's voice was deadly calm, "Take down the IV bottle now." Helen leaped to comply. He motioned with the pistol to one of the other nurses. She came to abrupt attention. Chris's mind raced searching for the treatment algorithm for hyperkalemia. "You. Get a bottle of D-10 and some insulin". This would cause a chemical reaction to force some of the deadly potassium out of the blood stream. "Don't think about calling for help right now. Pointing to the last nurse, he motioned to the crash cart. "Give an amp of calcium IV stat." This too would help lower the potassium level.

Steve Carnes stared in astonishment. "Who are you and what the hell are you doing?" he asked.

"I'm Dr. Wilder. This is my wife."

Steve glanced at Helen as she nodded.

Chris continued, "Her doctor told me he loaded this IV bottle with enough potassium to kill a horse. I'm trying to lower her potassium and stave off further arrhythmias."

Garnes pondered for a moment. A line from his training floated to mind. Never challenge a hostile schizophrenic's delusion. Work with it to effect change. Professional demeanor reasserted itself. "I see," he said in his most professional and soothing tones. "And what makes you think that your wife's doctor would be trying to kill her? "

The nurses looked questioningly from doctor to doctor, medications in hand. Both nodded, Chris with a measure of urgency. Garnes nodded absently and thought to himself-best to go along for now. The meds he ordered won't cause immediate harm.

The nurses began to administer the requested solutions.

The look on Dr. Wilder's face was one of recognition of both the tone and face of Dr. Carnes. "You're the psychiatry resident that works down here on weekends?".

Dr Garnes nodded.

"You're probably wondering how to get past me to lay hands on some antipsychotic medications too, aren't you?"

Garnes nodded again, even as he kicked himself for being transparent. Chris Wilder paused to look at the monitor.

The PVCs had begun to fade to a completely normal rhythm.

His shoulders relaxed a little. He turned back to Garnes with a both quizzical and irritated look. "Tell you what, are you up to working with me to make a therapeutic contract with me and test my delusion against reality?"

Dr. Carnes blinked to hear his own jargon thrown back at him. He made an effort to appear casual. "Sure, what do you have in mind?" The nurses interrupted with a wave of their hands to gesture to the ventilator. Dr Carnes motioned for them to transfer the hand-assisted bagging of the patient over to the machine.

Chris still guarded the door. "There' s more at stake here than meets the eye." Dr. Chris Wilder continued. "I have an injured man in the car outside. It's Reverend Mosley. His church was on fire, with possibly many more people in the woods hurt. This standoff can't go on." Chris turned to Billy Wilkes in the comer. He sought to make eye contact with the deputy who waited arms still raised in the comer."

"Billy, you know me." Billy nodded. "Do you trust me?" Billy nodded but did not yet lower his hands.

"Billy, I want to trust you, but I also don't want to get shot. Here's the deal, Billy gives me his gun and then goes outside to the car. Reverend Mosely is in there, and he'll confirm my story and take him to the ER. In the meantime, the lab takes a specimen from the IV bottle and runs a potassium on it. It shouldn't take but a couple minutes. My 'delusion' checks out, and we get on with our business of saving lives. If it doesn't, I'll give both guns back and you strap me into a straitjacket and send me to the state psych hospital on Bull Street. Also, the Living Tree African Presbyterian church is on fire, lots of people injured or dead; call dispatch to send firetrucks and ambulances-ASAP.!

Dr. Garnes sensed the first glimmer of doubt in his diagnosis. Doctor Wilder had presented a well-reasoned set of conditions. He raised an inquiring eyebrow to the waiting deputy. "Sounds okay to me, doc." Billy agreed. His hands came down and he unbuckled the gun belt and handed it over to Chris. The deputy sprinted towards the door, already calling dispatch on his radio for help at the fire.

"All of you watch Helen as she draws fluid from the IV bottle. That bottle is evidence for attempted murder." Wilder said, "I don't want it said that it was tampered with." Helen drew off fluid from the bottle. Chris took the bottle from her and waved her out the door to the lab. Then he put the bottle into the arms of a startled nurse. "Hold this until the deputy comes back. It may keep me out of jail."

The wait was longer than Chris had anticipated. No one talked as the nurses cared for Ashley. The only sound was the wheeze of the ventilator. Chris sat in exhaustion in a chair by the door. His mind ran over the night's events. He looked again down the hall for any sign of return of the deputy or of the lab report. His exhausted gaze fell on the file cabinets in the nurses' station. What was it Charles Orr said about Dr. Sayaad? Dead and filed away? Where? "Perverse and twisted," Mosley had said. Chris looked at the filing cabinets again; inspiration flared in his mind.

The sound of running feet interrupted his thinking. Billy and the lab tech sprinted down the hall toward them.

"You were right!" they called in tandem.

"What took you so long?" asked Chris with a sigh of relief.

"Well," Billy answered, "once I saw the Rev was hurt, I took him over to the ER and it took a long time to get him there. We had to roll a stretcher across the lawn to get him in. Then Sheriff Charles called me to ask what in Sam Hill was happening?" To punctuate the point, sirens wailed in the distance.

The lab girl held out a slip. "The machine refused to believe the result. I had to tinker with it to get it to print the result. "The slip showed a graph labeled "Potassium" A dark area on the line indicated the normal range. At the far end of the paper, Dr. Wilder saw a red computer warning 'HHH, too high to read, grave danger to the patient.'

"No kidding," he grumbled to himself and passed the slip to Dr. Garnes in vindication. Garnes nodded knowingly and gestured to a new bottle of IV fluid hanging by the bed. "Ockham's razor, the obvious solution." Wilder looked questioningly at him.

"Say, Doc," Billy Wilkes interrupted shyly, "can I have my gun back now?"

Chapter 33

Chris handed Billy Wilkes his gun belt with a wan smile. Then he handed the bottle of IV fluids and his own pistol to the surprised deputy. "Here, put these someplace safe. I don't think I'll be needing them anymore."

Billy turned to comply when Chris's gaze swept the nursing station. His face hardened. "Billy let's lock these in the hospital safe. We have some more work to do."

After all that had happened, Chris needed large doses of will power, mixed with a bit of guilt in order to leave Ashley. As they walked down the hall, Chris told the deputy about the missing Dr. Sayaad and Dr. Orr's comment. "At the time, it didn't make any sense." explained Chris. "The only filing of people I could think of was in a filing cabinet or plots in a cemetery. Then when I looked at the ICU filing cabinets, I wondered if they were big enough to hold a dead body. I realized I'd seen such a thing right here.

Chris and Billy summoned the Henry the hospital security guard on the way down the hall as they headed into the Gerald Merry Memorial Wing. At Dr. Wilder's direction, the guard unlocked the morgue. He flicked on the lights in the cool room. A grid of four drawers, each man-sized, occupied the end of the room beyond the dissecting table. Dr. Wilder pulled open two empties before finding the correct drawer, then Dr. Sayaad slid out, headfirst. His face, for once, held an expression, one of marked surprise.

After pausing in a moment of silent prayer for his dead friend, Chris left it to the deputy and hospital security guard to notify Sheriff Charles. He returned to check on Ashley.

The respirator wheezed along comfortingly in the darkened and calm room. Chris pulled up a chair to keep watch. Crescendo/ decrescendo wails signaled multiple ambulances arriving at the hospital. A few moments later, Helen bustled in from a quick check on the other patient. Her face still bore some of her shocked expression as the ambulance wails that confirmed the terrible truth of Dr. Wilder's story. First, she checked on Ashley, and then she turned back to Chris.

"Dr. Wilder," she said quietly, "I'll watch her carefully. You must go to the

ER and have someone look at those cuts and that ear."

At first, Chris just shook his head. "I will later. I want to sit and be with my wife for a while."

Helen already had enough remaining guilt from not believing Chris the first time. She was determined that she would see he got the care he needed. With a little apologetic but persistent cajoling, after a while she finally persuaded him to limp off down the hall to the ER.

Chris could hear the shouts and screams that emanated from the ER long before reaching the double doors marking the entry. He first heard the voice of Sheriff Junior Charles, "Damn it, can't you see he's in pain? Give him something."

A placating mumble from Dr. Garnes was barely audible as he hustled from one stretcher to the next.

"What the hell is going on here?" continued Junior. "One of my deputies is missing on duty, a church gets burned down and another deputy tells me one of the doctors started a fire to save us all from the devil! Now you're telling me that two of the doctors are dead, and one of them is in his own morgue! Jesus! What the hell is going on here?"

In the background, a man moaned and fitfully screamed. The ER smelled like burned meat and hair.

The moans muffled slightly as Chris entered the doors. Junior Charles stood at one end of a patient's stretcher while Dr. Garnes pushed the rest of a vial of medication into an IV. A figure lay on the bed grossly disfigured by burns. Massive blisters and a few areas of charred skin rendered the naked body unrecognizable. Several areas of the body bore deep gashes. Dr. Garnes caught Chris's questioning glance.

"A John Doe, so far" Dr. Garnes in a voice near breaking with stress and fatigue. "They found him near the wreckage of the church. He's one of the few they've found alive, and he's in so much pain that we haven't been able to even get him to tell us his name.

Dr. Wilder, forgetting his own injuries, looked around to see who he could help.

Dr Garnes shook his head and gestured down the hallway to a collection of covered gurneys. "Several people they brought in were dead on arrival, two more died shortly thereafter. This one and Reverend Mosley are the only two still with a chance. I hope this last dose of morphine will relieve this one enough to either talk or at least sleep. I've already called for a chopper from Charlotte to carry him to a bum center."

The body on the bed thrashed a little more and lay still. The sounds of stertorous breathing filled the room.

Junior Charles fixed Chris Wilder with a malignant gaze. "Doctor," he said with his anger suppressed into a deadly calm tone, "I hear you're involved in all this. I'd ask you to explain all this now, but not a word yet. I want your lawyer present, so if any charges follow, I can prosecute."

Chris decided this was not the perfect moment to divulge where he thought his lawyer was. Instead, he shook his head. Exhaustion and pain hung like a shroud over his head. Chris sat on a nearby stool and gestured for Junior to do the same. "I waive my right to an attorney. I just want to make sense of what has transpired."

Junior Charles reached over to the desk and pulled out a chair. He turned it around and straddled it, arms folded across the back expectantly. "Okay, talk," he said. "Now!"

Chris began the story with the visit earlier that day-- My god, was that today? --to Charles Orr's house with Ladson. Junior listened to his account of the shooting, of finding Ladson and of the trip to the church. He asked for a point or two of clarification about Ladson's insistence that the Sheriff's office had been called. Junior vehemently denied it.

Chris sighed, "I'm not surprised, in view of what happened next." Then he resumed his narrative of the conversation in the pastor's shed and the burning of the church.

Dr. Garnes puttered around trying to be inconspicuous. He listened in obvious fascination to the tale as he made a show of caring for the patient nearby.

Junior listened in stony silence to the recitation that ended with the events at the hospital and the finding of Dr. Sayaad's body.

"So that's it," Chris concluded. "The whole blood cult began as Ladson's perversion. It grew and grew until it enfolded his brother and all these deaths."

Sheriff Junior Charles sat still for a moment, regarding the battered man across from him, weighing the evidence. Keys jiggled a nervous beat in his hands. "An interesting tale, doctor, but I think maybe we ought to keep you at the jail for safekeeping the next day or so." Like magic, handcuffs appeared in his hands.

A soft voice behind them interrupted, "No."

Junior Charles turned in annoyance to Steve Garnes. "Damn it" he began angrily, and then stopped. Steve Games looked as surprised as Chris did. The three of them looked down at the figure who lay on the gurney near the curtain, eyes open, watching them. The soft voice was a cross between a wheeze and a whisper. "It's true, or rather some of it is. I never killed anyone, and I've never been impotent." Ladson Orr coughed and lay back on the stretcher exhausted.

"Jesus Christ!" Junior exclaimed. "Ladson, is that you?"

Ladson nodded weakly. "When the church collapsed, I was blown clear. Everyone who got out thought I was dead until the ambulances came. He coughed and wheezed, then resumed with greater strength. Nodding to Junior Charles, he continued. "I did call the Sheriff's office. Unfortunately, the deputy I talked to was one of them. He showed up at the church. I recognized him." Ladson's gaze caught Chris's. "I'm sorry about the gun, Chris. I really didn't realize the danger. I just didn't want you to hurt my brother. Then he added with some bitterness, "Now I wish to God, you had shot him."

Ladson moved slightly in front of his spell-bound audience. He gasped as a new freshet of pain spilled over the dam of numbness the morphine had built.

Garnes abandoned any attempt to appear the disinterested physician and sat in rapt attendance on the stretcher adjacent to Ladson's. "I heard the shot from Charles," Ladson hissed through clenched teeth. "I came back just in time to see Charles forcing you into the shed. I hid outside and heard all that stuff he told you" Ladson's words faded into a whispery mumble. Junior and the two doctors leaned forward to hear better.

"…and then hid in the church. When the service started, I tried to blend in with the crowd. I guess I was hoping to rescue both of you." He shook his head ruefully, a blister on his cheek popped; it shed a monstrous tear. "When the crowd started to take off their clothes, I realized I was running out of time, and I had to strip too. I heard Charles say no one had seen his face. I figured I'd try to brazen it out, buy some time by claiming that he'd stolen my leadership."

The wheezing grew a little louder, the voice a little softer.

Ladson struggled to make himself heard. "I knew if I popped up and politely asked all those people to simply go home, they'd never buy it, and Junior would have found one more body in the ruins. As their leader, I tried to command them to leave." Ladson lay back wheezing ever louder.

"I get it," Dr. Garnes said with enthusiasm, "this is great psychiatry. He tried to buy into the coven's delusion to effect action. And his brother! What a classic case of projection."

Junior interrupted him, "What the hell are you talking about?"

Dr. Garnes was almost beside himself with glee. "Projection. A classic psychiatric coping mechanism. The patient cannot accept his thoughts or actions, so he projects them on to someone else thereby freeing himself of blame or guilt. Don't you see? The doctor couldn't deal with all the blame, so he gives it to his brother and makes all this his fault." He was interrupted by a strangled gasp behind him.

Ladson grasped at his neck and flailed about trying frantically to breathe.

"Oh, crap!" exclaimed Dr. Garnes as he ran to the bedside. "He must have a burn injury to his larynx. It's swelling shut!" He crossed to the crash cart in three strides. He yanked out a laryngoscope and tube. Ladson bucked even more furiously, trying to force air down his inflamed windpipe into his scorched lungs. Garnes tried to advance the scope down into the throat but could see nothing. He tried again. But Ladson's struggles began to slacken as life began to leave his tortured body.

The night was too long and traumatic for the aggrieved resident. Tears streamed down his face. "I can't get it," he sobbed. He turned to Chris. "Do something. Save him."

Chris shouldered him out of the way. He pried open the now slack jaws. The throat was sooty and markedly swollen. Chris shook his head. He didn't see how Ladson had been able to say as much as he did. There was no place to put a tube. No place for air to go. The jaws snapped back together as he let them go and stepped back. He paused for the split second required for a hard decision.

Chris grabbed the body and lifted it by the shoulders, "Gimme a scalpel. I'm going to try a tracheostomy," he said as he slid a pillow under Ladson's shoulders.

"I didn't know family docs knew how to do tracheostomies" said a wondering Garnes. Fran slapped a knife into Dr. Wilder's hand. He paused with the blade over the blistered throat.

He looked at Steve with a grin made crooked by desperation. "I don't, but I've read the book; this is a good time to learn." The blisters and swelling on Ladson's neck made the landmarks hard to find. Only desperation forced Dr. Wilder's hand.

The knife bit into the swollen flesh of the throat and then sank deeper under the Adam's apple. Blisters popped, and dark blood oozed out. Chris sawed another stroke. Abruptly, air whooshed out in a sooty, bloody froth. Turning the knife handle sideways, Dr. Wilder hastily enlarged the small slit in the windpipe to let in more air. Then he threaded a small endotracheal tube Fran had waiting into the incision. Quickly, he blew two strong breaths into the pipe. He paused.

The room held its collective breath for a moment. Ladson's chest heaved mightily and fell, and then he began to breathe on his own. After a few seconds, Ladson's eyes fluttered open again. His gaze was unfocused for a moment and then sharpened. "Thank you," he mouthed.

Above the ceiling, a rhythmic, pounding roar crescendoed as the emergency transport helicopter set down on the landing pad beside the hospital. Within a few minutes, the chopper crew rushed inside. Fran was slathering Ladson with a white burn cream that looked like vanilla frosting as she wrapped bandages around him. The air ambulance crew moved him from the hospital stretcher to a collapsible gurney and wheeled him into the night air. Dr. Wilder, Junior and Fran followed them out.

The helicopter sat in front of the hospital on a small patch of dirt squared off with flashing landing lights. The rotors churned a lazy circle above the crew as they loaded Ladson aboard. The final view of Ladson was a gauze wrapped hand waving feebly. The chopper door slid shut and the spin of the rotor increased to a roar as the craft lifted off and into the darkened sky.

"Will he live?" Junior asked Chris.

Dr. Wilder shrugged and then nodded. "Possibly. Most of his burns were mostly second degree with only about twenty-five percent third degree. The question will be how damaged his trachea and lungs are. Those doctors have done a lot more with less than that to work with." They turned back to the hospital.

"I wonder if we'll ever find out who was telling the truth in this whole story," Chris wondered aloud.

Junior took a few more steps and then answered. "Doctor, his story exonerates you. How can you question his version?"

"I don't know, said Chris. "He just seemed so, so righteously angry, back at the church, for it all to have been an act."

Junior stopped. Harsh breathing made his words steam in the cold night air. "Doctor, I was with Ladson the night Jake and Sudie were murdered. We were at the state meeting of sheriffs and county attorneys that night in

Columbia. We shared a hotel room trying to save the county money. I was with Ladson the whole time. Remember, that was why I wasn't there that night? When you question his integrity, you're questioning mine too."

Chris relaxed and smiled. He held his hands palm out in surrender. "Thank you, thank you," he said. "Now there's someone outside this whole mess to corroborate some aspect of my story. Until now, the crux of blame has revolved around the two of them. I liked and trusted both at one time or another. What I've needed is someone to verify something, somewhere!"

Junior grunted, "I 've got a hell of a lot of catching up to do. In view of how everything turned out, I don't think the solicitor will be bringing any charges. Good night." Junior turned back to the parking lot where his car waited, lights still flashing in the dark. Chris took his leave of Fran and headed across the lawn to the ICU.

Ashley was awake, eyes open and waiting, when he entered the room. Dr. Garnes stood by the machine watching her breathe. He smiled. "Good news, I think we can probably get her off the machine in a few more hours. Also, Reverend Mosley has been treated and sent on to Columbia for surgery."

Chris nodded. He had eyes only for Ashley.

"Well, I'll leave you two alone." Garnes mumbled, and he left.

Ashley tried to smile around the tube as Chris sat. Her smile turned to alarm as his face came into the light above the bed. She tried to reach for his ear. Two restraints caught her arms. Chris untied first one, then the other. "What happened?" she mouthed. Tears began to flow. She mouthed something else. Chris leaned forward and watched her lips three more times. Finally, he got it. "I'm sorry," she was saying. She waggled her arms in fashion to indicate for the hundredth time that he should learn to speak sign language.

Chris slowly, lovingly told her how she'd been set up and why. Ashley's eyes followed him as he spoke. Finally, he finished with an apology of his own. "I'm sorry I doubted your drinking. I should have known there was a reason. And I'm sorry I've been a lousy husband these last few months. I've learned that even death is preferable to losing you."

Tears brightened in Ashley's eyes. A hand rose from the bed. A finger touched her left breast, her wrists crossed weakly, then her finger rose unsteadily to his nose. "I love you too," he signed back, softly saying the words as he did.

Ashley finally returned to sleep, and at Helen's prodding, Chris once again sought the emergency room to get his own wounds looked after. Dr. Games had gone to the call room to nap. Only Fran was there. She offered to call him back, but Chris waved her off.

"Just needs cleaning and bandaging," he said. "Let the kid sleep, he's had a busy night." Fran got out the materials and began to carefully clean the wounds and dress them. Except for an occasional expletive from Chris when Fran cleaned too hard, there was a leaden silence punctuated by an occasional sniffle from Fran. They both were lost in their own thoughts about the evening for a while.

Fran finally broke the silence. "You know," she mused. "It's funny how history repeats itself."

"What do you mean?" Chris mumbled.

"Oh, about Junior vouching for Ladson. Back when they were in high school together, Ladson was accused of being in with a group of teenagers playing in an abandoned farmhouse when it caught fire. It looked for a while like there were going to be charges brought against him. Then Junior came forward and said he and Ladson had been together in Columbia watching a game. Despite Junior being from the mills and Ladson being a Merry grandson, it kept the Merry family out of the press, but Junior caught hell for being out when he was supposed to be home. Junior's family was religious and strict about no games on Sunday. Ladson never forgot Junior after that, even though most kids separate at the end of high school. When Junior wanted to go to college, Ladson helped him get a Merry Mills Corporate Scholarship. So, you see what goes around comes around. Here's Junior vouching for Ladson again." Fra sighed and dabbed at another bruise.

Chris ignored her. The room shifted a little as Chris felt a cold chill in the pit of his stomach. He shivered.

Fran noted the shiver. "Someone walking on your grave?"

Chris forced a smile at Fran. "Yeah, guess so."

END

Dedications

For Family Doctors: First: this book is a love letter to the rural family physicians of America who live and work with the disproportionately older, poorer, and most medically needy patients in America. They are an endangered species and I'm privileged to be one and work with them. This book depicts (other than the murders!) what rural family medicine was like when I worked and trained family doctors in the 1980s and 90's and into the 2000's. The work can be incredibly rewarding and at the same time heartbreaking. For a feel for a contemporary rural family doctor's literal heart break see the New York Times article: *A Rural Doctor Gave Her All. Then Her Heart Broke.* Sept 19, 2022. Rural medical care is getting worse. Poor and complex reimbursement along with government payment policies have closed and threatened many rural hospitals and are reducing care for our rural communities. In my state of Tennessee, ten rural hospitals have closed in the last decade and another fifteen are threatened.

Family Medicine physicians deal with the single biggest medical challenge: the undifferentiated patient who walks in and says: "'I feel bad." The possibilities are endless and can involve the whole bio/psycho/social and even spiritual dimensions. These patients call for the whole of family doctors and requires them to be present in a way not seen in many other parts of medicine where I like to joke 'there is a part for every doctor and a doctor for every part.' So, for all my fellow family docs. Thank you and hang in there!

Next: Gwendolyn Faith Hunter: author extraordinaire! When I first met her as a lab tech in the evening weekend shifts at our rural hospital, we would spend late night times (no ER doctor after midnight!!) waiting for tests or X-rays talking about books and other topics. One night she told me her first book a murder mystery called: *Death Warrant,* had been accepted for publication. (Her publications in both Mystery and Fantasy now number well over 30 books!) Although I had published several book chapters and articles, I told her I could never write fiction. "You should try," she urged me. It must have been a strong 'Stephen King like' mental shove! Two nights later I woke up with a gasp and hastily wrote out the first few pages of what would eventually become this book. She reviewed the first pages and encouraged me to keep going. She also gave permission to name a character after one she used in a different setting

Next is Robin Howe: my editor who read and repeatedly edited this book and harassed me to finish it saying it was too good not to finish. Any remaining mistakes are mine. Thanks Robin!

Likewise, my publisher David Tullock: at Parson's Porch Books who likewise persisted in asking when I would get this book to him.

Katie Baker who again has done an awesome job on the cover of this book as well as *Education of a Hospice Doctor.*

Finally, my wife of 44+ years and counting, Gayle Phelps RN mother of three, grandmother of four and small breed rescuer who puts up with my work, writing, constant forays into new educational programs and many other activities.

www.ingramcontent.com/pod-product-compliance
Lightning Source LLC
Chambersburg PA
CBHW061241210726
48293CB00003B/854